Praise for Irenosen Okojie

"*Butterfly Fish* is a novel of epic proportions… From sentence to sentence, Okojie conjures up acutely observed, beautifully-worded metaphors that resonate and delight… I fully expect to see *Butterfly Fish* on many an award nomination list. It is a fascinating read, and one I highly recommend." Yvette Edwards (author of *A Cupboard Full of Coats, longlisted for the Man Booker Prize*), *Words of Colour*

"Her West African heritage is richly spun into her novel *Butterfly Fish*… The tale is peppered with moments of magical surrealism: a glass bottle shattering on a South London street to release two tiny scurrying figures into the night; a butterfly fish bursts into a local pool and belches a portentous brass key… The lyrical prose brings poignancy to the familiar London landscape." Samuel Fishwick, *Evening Standard*

"Vital, vivid, witty, truthful…" Maggie Gee, *The Observer*

"A gripping tale that takes us on a journey… Okojie's story unearths a complicated past filled with family secrets, political upheaval, love and hope." *African Arguments*

"… a very impressive and beautifully written novel. It's especially impressive considering that this is the author's first. Irenosen Okojie is certainly a writer to watch." Kate Lunn, *For Book's Sake*

"Enchanting readers with the eloquence of a griot, Irenosen Okojie's début novel *Butterfly Fish* brings to life the magic of storytelling. In a spellbinding saga of ⁓ it tells of

the scourge of the sins of the ancestors upon the coming generation... The author's voice relates the ensuing drama with a gracious absence, bestowing to her characters self independence and authenticity. With a daring and distinctive tone, Irenosen is without a doubt a fresh addition to contemporary African fiction. *Butterfly Fish* is a dark and mesmerizing adventure packed with bitter sweet delights. This is one of my personal favourites this summer. I highly recommend it." *Afrikult.com*

"This is a very accomplished and colourful debut novel by a Nigerian-born English writer... Okojie tells not only a superbly well-written complex story of intertwining lives but uses a wonderfully colourful language and brings in Nigerian story-telling, myths and strange creatures, all of which make her English-based story more other-worldly. Okojie is clearly going to be an author to watch." John Alvey, *The Modern Blog*

"Split between contemporary London and 19th-century West Africa, *Butterfly Fish* is a debut novel with an epic scope... The novel's strength is its ability to make the abstract concrete. " Oliver Zarandi, *East End Review*

Butterfly Fish is a powerful novel of love, hope and loss written in Irenosen's unique and compelling style." *Greenacre Writers*

"A very able writer who has the gift of being able to paint the very picture that she is speaking of. Her writing has energy and her descriptions are full of flavour." Ashley Rose Scantlebury, *True Africa*

"One of the most original and innovative writers to emerge in many a year." Alex Wheatle, MBE

"Seriously unique and imaginative." Diana Evans, author of *26a* and winner of the Orange Prize

Butterfly Fish

By

Irenosen Okojie

JACARANDA

First published in Great Britain 2015 by
Jacaranda Books Art Music Ltd
Unit 304 Metal Box Factory
30 Great Guildford Street
London SE1 0HS

www.jacarandabooksartmusic.co.uk

A CIP catalogue record for this book is available from the British Library

Hardback ISBN: 978 1 909762 06 0
Trade paperback ISBN: 978 1 909762 26 8
Mass market paperback ISBN: 978 1 909762 31 2
eISBN: 978 1 909762 14 5

Typeset in the UK in Adobe Caslon by Regent Typesetting

Printed and bound in Great Britain by
CPI Group (UK) Ltd, Croydon, CR0 4YY

To my favourite usual suspects;
mum, dad, Amen, Ota and Iredia,
thank you so much for everything.
Big love, always.

Part 1

Modern London,
London 1970s
&
19th Century Benin

The Yeah Yeah Yeah Blueprint

View

A green palm wine bottle rolled on the wet London Street. Its movements were audible gasps made of glass. It didn't matter how the bottle had arrived at its location under the curious yellow gaze of the lamppost or whether the messenger had been a postman delivering for both God and the dancing devil. The image unfurling inside the bottle shimmering like moonlight trapped in glass mattered. Lick the edges of the picture presented and you could taste the sour, sweet traces of palm wine and trap your tongue in a different time; 19th century Benin, Nigeria.

A court was on display. An emerald-eyed man and a young woman attired in traditional Nigerian cloth were before a more ostentatiously dressed committee who bore glum expressions. The woman's head was bowed and she clutched a pink beaded bracelet, rubbing it repeatedly between thumb and forefinger. The man spoke in a calm, measured tone, his fate already hardened inside the Adams' apples in the room. An arm was raised, heads snapped up. Then the image in the bottle spun like a revolving door. Dust swirled, and a bushy path emerged. The man and woman were being led by soldiers who could perform the nifty trick of building distances between bodies in close proximity. The heat was thick and intense. Fallen branches lining the twisting path cracked loudly. Buzzing mosquitoes were winged witnesses. Reluctant to draw blood they formed a black net above the bobbing heads.

Out of the dark London night a teenager being chased by two raucous friends, leaning for breath under the lamppost noticed the green glass glinting in the grey light. Slightly unsteady on his feet the boy swiped the bottle up and threw it against the wall, watching it smash. He yelped as the contents spilled out, an amorphous mass, images flickering like ancient film reel. The boy's pupils were swimming in beer and he was uncertain of the picture before him as the scene dragged itself up the pavement, with bits of glass embedded in its outline. The bottom half of the bottle lay shattered on the ground. The scene continued to evolve, fragments of moonshine gleamed between puffs of red dust. Small movements fractured then reassembled as it hauled onwards stopping outside the chipped, wooden door of a quietly dark flat where only the sound of the trembling shrubbery flanking the recycle bin passed through the keyhole. It spun slowly on the thick, straw-coloured welcome mat. Inside the flat the young woman tossing in her sleep remained unaware of her breath clouding the surroundings, of turning her head towards two paths lined with coloured, broken glass, of the tiny people from the palm wine bottle pleading against her thumping heartbeat.

In The Beginning

The first time I met Mrs Harris, she'd told me she was certain that Buddy, her garden statue Buddha, had been eating her roses. Although, she'd added, there may have been a slim chance the fat, sepia-coloured cat of a neighbour was the one skulking around fighting her roses, who in turn offered only their blooms in scented, decorative peace offerings. Mrs Harris was my new next-door neighbour. A slight woman who chatted enthusiastically about all kinds of subjects, she lived alone and dressed like a hippy. Snow white hair hung past her shoulders in an unruly mess, shrouding her heavily lined face. A chicken pox mark on her left cheek looked like a teardrop. Her green eyes rippled with laughter and mischief.

That morning, she stood at my doorstep, hair slightly damp, clutching a small dark blue container with the word "tea" peeling off at the corners. She smelled of an odd combination of cigarettes and baked bread. "It's Buddy," she said. "He's gone missing." The sky swirled a moody grey. Along the street, the sound of doors shutting heralded the morning rush hour.

"Again?" I asked.

Her eyes narrowed into slits. "Can I come in?

I nodded reluctantly, stepping aside to allow entry. We moved down the wood floor hallway, the smell of damp clothes heavy in the air, past my messy sitting room with the previous evening's Chinese takeaway containers stacked on the floor, a large black and white picture of Jimi Hendrix blowing smoke into the lens commanding one wall. My mother's bright throw was slung deliberately over the blue sofa smothering past indiscretions. We entered the kitchen.

"Isn't this the fifth time?" I asked. I wasn't in the mood for visitors.

I watched her make herself comfortable at the worn wooden table an old traveller man with blackened teeth had sold me. I felt sluggish and depressed but I took the blue container from her and added bags of tea before handing it back. Three knives drying in the sink gleamed invitingly, old watermarks arched on their silver blades. Buddy had gone missing for days on several occasions. Each time, he was returned safely to a different spot in Mrs Harris's garden.

I wasn't certain if Buddy really did go off wandering -maybe it was a cruel trick played by bored kids on the street- or if Mrs Harris, a lonely, eccentric elderly woman engineered the whole thing just for some attention. There was genuine anger in her voice as she remarked, "I'm fed up of this happening! If I catch the little worm responsible God help them."

"Hey, you didn't see anything did you?"

I was slow to respond, putting the shiny kettle on and setting aside two cups with teabags, strings dangling down the side. " Can't say I've been following Buddy's movements." I answered in an effort to make light of the situation.

She laughed then, full bodied and warm. "I suppose I sound a little crazy to you. But you know, from where he was Buddy could see clear across several gardens. He was probably exposed to things he shouldn't have been seeing." This was said with such sincerity, my gaze lingered on her face but it was met with what appeared to be genuine candour. The pipes began to interrupt. *Thwack. Thwack. Thwack.*, as though someone was throwing stones against them.

"Oh God! You too! "Mrs Harris announced, groaning. "My pipes have been noisy all morning and now Buddy's vanished. Not a good start to the day!"

Sudden concern clouded her features. "Are you okay?" Your energy seems a little off." The kettle blew warm breaths at the ceiling. It hissed and the red light at the bottom flicked off. I filled both cups, handed one over. "Oh you know, okay. Getting on with things, actually you caught me in the middle of something. I was running a bath." The sweet scent of blackcurrant filled the air. Both teas were a rich plum hue that darkened our tongues as if with our individual anxieties.

"You should have said dear, I don't want to impose. I'll finish my tea and be off, just thought you might have seen something, kids climbing the fence maybe." She took another gulp, closed her eyes. "Oh that's good, tea's nice dear."

"Yes it is." I answered. "Maybe Buddy's gone off on a tea tasting tour of all the exotic flavours he can get his hands on."

"Maybe," she said wryly.

"Lucky Buddy." I took a sip, felt a strong undercurrent of something dark that made my limbs become heavy. I longed to be left on my own. The knives and sink had blended into one silvery entity, dripping small figures with expressions of distress and bladed mouths. Each drop reverberated in my head. I imagined Buddy in the garden commanded by something unknown, leading other garden statues astray up the highway, wearing a blushing pink azalea as an eye patch.

Mrs Harris gulped some more tea, interrupting my reverie. "You don't like to spend much time in your garden?" she asked.

"Never really gave it much thought." My dressing gown knot began to uncurl. I tied it back tightly.

"Ahh, I thought so. I can tell by the state it's in. Gardening's good for the soul." She motioned at her head. "It's a great stress reliever connecting with the soil like that. I can teach you sometime if you like? It's simple enough." She offered with an easy smile.

"Thank you, that's kind."

"I'll tell you a secret." She leaned in conspiratorially, "sometimes, I play classical music to my fruit and vegetable plants in the garden. It helps them grow you see!"

I smiled at the notion, the element of surprise, saw her apples ripening, patches of red spreading around the sweetness of fruit skin to the swelling strains of Samuel Coleridge-Taylor's violins and Chopin's piano.

"That's genius," I remarked appreciatively. "I'll remember that."

She tossed back the remnants of her tea and stood. "I'll leave you to it. Oh! Before I forget, I brought these for you." From her pocket she dug out a small bag of nuts, tied at the neck with a red ribbon. "They're Brazilian," she continued. "Lovely robust spicy flavour; let me know what you think!"

"Will do." I waved her goodbye at the door as she breezed out.

After she left I began washing up and as I opened the cupboard, slowly stacking the clean cups there it was, my mother's favourite mug, its handle jutting out, a hand-painted mint leaf curved across its white body. I hadn't been able to bring myself to get rid of it. Seeing it brought back images of mum swept in by the wind, a winter chill behind her, reaching for that mug, filling it with tea and regaling me with stories of her day. It's funny how the very things that once irritated you about a person were the things you missed most when they were gone. Like phone calls held together by an invisible current, or rummaging through markets because we were two creased people who needed steam ironing. Lately I tried to fill the silences with... anything.

Abruptly, a wave of fatigue swept over me. The thought of facing the day stripped any strength I had left. The stack of unopened letters I'd let build up on top of the DVD cabinet, upstairs the pile of dirty clothes overflowing from the laundry basket, the new battery I still needed to buy for the car, the call to the electricity company to stop them cutting me off. All the mundane dots we connect to keep going.

When I stood it was in slow motion. I was weightless; I didn't feel my feet touch the first step or know when I had made it to the top. I remember opening the bathroom cabinet and inside seeing the razor that had called me by my name.

I ran myself a bath longing for the peace the water held out for me. Lying there I watched an insect circle the light bulb on the ceiling and envied its frenetic flight. For years I'd been fed on incongruous things; smudges on windows washed away by rain, static from the TV, white lines just before traffic lights, wilting in shaky, packed train carriages. On the need to hold my loneliness, watch it change shape yet essentially stay the same. I felt woozy, faint. In the tepid water my grip on things slipped. The small, silvery, distressed figures I'd seen earlier in the kitchen offered their limbs to the dropped, bloody razor as the frantic black eyes of the dice spun.

At the hospital, I drifted in and out of consciousness a lot. One time, I caught sight of my blood eating into the bandages tightly wrapped around my wrists. When awake, I felt drowsy and dazed, unhinged. I saw myself at the end of a distant tunnel, vaguely aware of the things floating inside it. Of the glare of sunlight filtering through oppressively small windows, the blandness of the ward's cream walls, the chattering between patients and visitors, terrible food distributed on wooden trays and the squeaky wheeled contraptions delivering them crying against a resigned floor.

Other things lost their definition. I barely recalled swallowing tablets for the white, fabricated river lining my stomach. Nurses blended into one in those first few days. Strangely, I fixated on the staff with watches clipped onto the breast of their uniforms. Those compact keepers of time made me appreciate the beauty of small things and sometimes if I looked closely enough, the hands stopped or the Roman numerals disappeared. This gave the impression that somewhere a slate was being wiped clean.

One evening Mrs Harris came to see me, She sat at the foot of my bed concern inhabiting her face. She was clad in a red tartan coat, black corduroy trousers and a thick, woolly blue jumper. Her white hair was pale moonlight in the room. She picked at a thread on her jumper. "Will you be alright?" she asked in a paper-thin voice.

Her green eyes were kind, non-judgmental. I was grateful for this. I cleared my throat, suddenly parched. "I don't know." I answered, words slow in my mouth, tongue half asleep, heavy with the realization I'd ended up in hospital.

She leaned forward in the chair, clasped her hands together. "Is there anything you'd like me to do?" There was an odd tone in her voice. Not impatience or reproach but curiosity. Her pink lips were slightly upturned as though about to smile. I was drugged up and a little confused. Somebody dancing a life affirming ritual in the ward aisle could have appeared sinister to me. Hot shame burned into my bones. "… I don't think so". What should I have said? That I just wanted the horrible feeling to end. That I'd been walking around with this weird sense of doom for a while, having heart palpitations, anxiety attacks, not sleeping very well?

She nodded gravely, stood and edged closer to the bed. I looked at the lines in her face wondering about the secrets they held.

"Things happen dear, don't feel embarrassed. Sometimes, all it takes is that extra thing for life to unravel, a small push on top of everything else." She responded candidly, peered at me as though seeing me through a foggy window.

"Thank you for what you did." I held her gaze. "If you hadn't had come back…"

"It's alright, my ring had dropped off somewhere." She raised her finger in support. When you didn't answer the door, I got worried."

We sat awkwardly in the moment, waiting for the noise of my crash landing to fill the silence.

Mrs Harris made several visits. She was light and colour from the world outside. She entertained me with interesting news stories, gesturing dramatically as she talked. She brought vanilla cheesecake, avocadoes "to fatten you up!" A 1970s copy of Time magazine with a feature on Ella Fitzgerald, old magazines from The Petrie Museum on Egyptology, a packet of bright, lusciously rendered Iranian play-

ing cards bought from a car boot sale and swathed in plastic bags
several slim bottles of green ginger wine.

One evening, as syringes fed silences into waiting veins Mrs
Harris sat by my bed casually flicking my old Nigerian, copper kobo
coin. To my horror, I saw myself emerge from it, near the wheel
of the bed being spun by a cold, unidentifiable hand. Shock ran
through my body. I looked to see if Mrs Harris had noticed the fear
on my face rendering me mute but she was counting the coloured
buttons she'd bought, holding them up to her eye one at a time and
looking through their holes as if collecting new perspectives.

After she left, I began thinking about the difference between
chance and luck. I wondered whether it was chance or bad luck that
had landed me in the hospital. I thought about a Harmattan wind
hurtling Mrs Harris into my life, and that same wind blowing my
mother's life out. My name is Joy. But my story doesn't start with
me, my mother, or even with the brass head my mother left me in
her will. It really begins a long time ago, in a place where centuries
after they were gone you could still hear the wishes and whispers of
warriors, queens and kings.

Fish Out Of Water

19th century Benin

At dawn on the day the news of the competition reached the Omoregbe family, Adesua, with a bitter taste in her mouth, had risen to the gentle sound of her mother's footsteps. From her position on the floor, the unrelenting glare of the sun flooding the small but sturdy compound provided further an illuminating reminder of the tasks to be done for the day.

The news that the king was looking for a new bride had quickly spread all over Esan land and people had been buzzing for weeks about the competition. The special event was to be held at the palace, where all suitable young women were to bring a dish they had prepared, and the king would make his choice of a new bride from the maker of the best dish.

Mothers running around like headless chickens, each eager to outdo the other, constantly visited the market stalls keeping their ears open for any piece of information they could glean to give their daughter an advantage. Fathers resorted to bribery, bombarding the King with gifts. The palace was laden with necklaces, cloths, masks, sweet wine from the palm trees, goat, cow and bush meat. The rumour began that the palace stocked enough to feed all of Esan and the surrounding areas for two seasons, though this came from Ehimare, the land's most famous gossip, who was deaf in one ear and whose mouth appeared to be in perpetual motion.

Adesua was Mama Uwamusi's only child who arrived in the world kicking and screaming into broken rays of light. Uwamusi had almost died giving birth, and further attempts at having other children had resulted in five dead babies. This day as they swept their small compound in preparation for their guests she handed over the broom to her daughter, looking at her as if for the first time.

She must have known she had done well; Adesua was beautiful with a wide mouth and an angular face. She had the height of her father and his stubborn temperament but her heart was good and this pleased Uwamusi more than any physical attribute. Adesua was a young woman now, yet she wondered if the girl realised it, so quick was she to climb a tree or insist on going hunting with Papa Anahero at any opportunity

Later, they were expecting the company of Azemoya and Onohe, two of Papa's friends from a neighbouring village. She did not enjoy the extra work that came with attending to their every whim, for both men could each eat enough for two or three people and never failed to outstay their welcome. Azemoya had six wives and many children, and so was quick to invite himself to other people's homes to ensure a reasonably large meal every so often. Onohe was a very lazy man; it was a curse that had afflicted male members of his bloodline for generations. Instead of working hard to provide for his family, he was full of excuses. Either there was some bodily ailment (real or imagined) troubling him, or the weather was not agreeable or the Gods had not shown him favour no matter how many sacrifices he made to them. Onohe was at his happiest whenever his stomach was full, yet it was widely known that his wives and children could sometimes be seen begging neighbours for food.

Adesua shook her head at the thought of it, *so that is what it meant to be someone's wife?* Unable to understand how the men felt no shame at treating their women so badly, she set her mind to brighter things, longing for the day to be over, so she could have time to herself again and challenge some of the boys she knew to a hunting competition.

"You must send her to the ceremony, the King is looking for a new wife and Adesua has as good a chance as anybody else." Azemoya's loud voice could be heard over the crackling of wood in the fire.

"She is my only child, I think I will wait another season before I think of such matters", Anahero replied.

"She cannot belong to you forever, it is time to start planning for tomorrow", Onohe's tone was filled with amusement. "She is a woman now. I too will send my eldest daughter to the ceremony; if I have good fortune on my side she may be chosen."

"I have not seen such a smile on your wife's face for many seasons," Onohe added, biting heartily into a kola nut. "But I do not understand you Anahero. Why do you not have more wives? People have been laughing behind your back for a long time. You would have had many children by now. It is a foolish man that does not see what is right before his eyes."

"Let them laugh, Uwamusi has served me well."

"She did not bear you a son, and you know people talk, it is custom to have a son to carry your name", Azemoya said smiling, exposing various gaps in his brown teeth.

Anahero's voice rose defensively, "I have Adesua." He had always ached for more children and he knew his face revealed that need even when he attempted to persuade himself otherwise.

"My spirit troubles me about sending Adesua to the king's palace." Anahero spoke this concern lightly gauging the reactions, as his sense of foreboding for his only daughter was deeply troubling to him.

"You must consult with the oracle for guidance. It is time. She cannot continue hunting and climbing trees with village boys!" Onohe patted him reassuringly on the back with one hand while eagerly reaching for another piece of yam with the other.

After their guests left, Anehero and Uwamusi made sacrifices. They swam in the river with painted faces. And when the gods summoned those faces underwater, their heads broke through the rippling surface in acceptance.

Five days passed. On the sixth day an angry wind came from the north, hissing and spitting out defiant trees on arrival, whirling loudly and destroying whatever crossed its path.

Full Stops and Heartbeats

The human heart beats over 2.5 billion times during an average life-time. My mother's heart stopped beating on a warm Sunday evening in July. She was fifty-six years old. The other things I remember from that day are waking up with a craving for peanut butter and falling inside Jim Morrison's voice singing *Hello I love you*. I was probably watching taped reruns of *Only Fools and Horses* when it happened, gobbling down Wotsits that crackled in my mouth and melted on my tongue, staining it and my fingers orange.

I had called my mother earlier that day and there was no answer. I called her again and again and she still didn't pick up. By 11:30pm I was finally really worried. I grabbed the car keys, ran out of the house more irritated than concerned. In the car, I gunned the engine and reversed out of the yard, still wearing my white vest littered with florescent Wotsit crumbs and red checked pyjama bottoms with gaping holes at the crotch.

I sped down the A406, noticing only a few vehicles dotted here and there as houses, trees and bus stops flew past my window. Reaching the long stretch of Romford Road, I slowed down, ignoring the groan of my engine. I snatched my mobile from the front passenger seat and dialled again: still no answer. I steered the car to a halt as the traffic light turned red. The red light began to throb, like a pulse, and I thought *I should have gone round to see her earlier*.

I arrived to find the hall light was still on and laughter from the television was bleeding through the front door. The smell of cooking oil, heavy and thick, clung to the air. It was Sunday, that meant Tilapia stew for dinner.

I swung the door open saying, "A mobile phone isn't for decoration you know!"

She was lying on the sofa, dressing gown pooled around her, head angled inside the crook of her arm. She could have been asleep but she was so still… statue still. A cold, clammy caterpillar of fear slid down my spine propelling me forward apprehensively at first to touch her. She did not move, not even when I began shaking her body as hard as I could. I don't recall phoning the ambulance, but I must have done.

When they came, I was clinging to her, holding on so tightly, it took two of the crew to pry me away. Mentally, I recorded every detail. The slight dent on the bridge of her nose I used to rub the pad of my finger against as a little girl. The pointy chin that jutted out defiantly, the faint lines fanned out at the corner of her eyes and above her full top lip, a few stray hairs I'd never noticed before. Those and the beauty spot on her neck, right where her toffee coloured skin became a little lighter. Her perfume competed with the more insistent aroma of old, cold food nonetheless it reached me, the thin, sweet scent of peach she'd worn my whole life. In primary school, when she picked me up, I'd leap into her arms as she raggedly hoisted me up, resting my head on her sweet-scented shoulder. Then I'd tuck my hand under her jaw and try to carry her small oval face gently, as if it were an egg.

Inside the ambulance the crew stayed silent as they attempted to resuscitate her. *It was the law*. I wanted to touch her face again. They let me hold her hand. Her skin felt cool. Why hadn't they let me pack an overnight bag? She'd want to get out of those clothes in the morning. I made a note to myself to bring her some fresh underwear, her Shea butter cream, her comb and house slippers.

I said to her, "You know how much you hate hospitals." The silence seemed to concur.

"We'll be there soon," I murmured, watching for any sign of movement. "I'll make sure you're put in a nice ward, I'll speak to the doctor."

"Is there anybody you want to call?" the female crewmember asked. "It may make things a little easier for you. It's a lot to take in, finding her like that…"

"Why would I need to call anyone?" My voice rang out shrill in the small moving space.

Then the ambulance stopped and the back doors opened. A woman dressed in a nurse's uniform rushed to us at the ambulance bay area.

The female crewmember (Ann I think her name was) came over and touched me gently on the arm. "I'm sorry Miss but you have to let go now."

Sudden cardiac arrest. Gone. No explanations. There was nothing in her medical history to suggest that this could ever happen. The autopsy failed to reveal anything and I wondered angrily what the point of it was. All I knew was that when she really needed me, I wasn't there.

My last meeting with her was etched deep in my memory. I'd felt human again because of it. It had been a rare day off for us, both from our jobs and our roles even, as mother and daughter. We were barefoot on the park grass, she, casually sipping from a box of Mr Juicy orange juice, while I chased the ice cream van, my hat falling off in the process. Later we took turns to push each other on the swings, even though she didn't want to, kept on about being too grown for that and then once on the swing, she forcefully gripped the metal chain-link arms that anchored her to the weathered wooden seat and there had been something so childlike about the way she'd kicked her legs in the air as I pushed her as hard as I could so she could fly, her voice flailing high above, full of laughter and happy fear. Then, the rain came down like a curtain on a final act, and we walked arm in arm in quiet contentment while raindrops kissed our noses and the wet ground tickled our bare feet.

My hands are full and as I return to the hospital to be with her body, I hold this memory gingerly, frightened in case any part of it should fall and scatter over the ground. If it did, how could I rebuild the dripping ice cream, or her mouth widening in shock at the coolness of it against her teeth and us walking around with our shoes off as if we didn't have a care in the world.

The bus finally arrived in Whitechapel. I pressed the stop button and hopped off, relieved at making it through a plethora of sweaty bodies. The streets were bursting, people swarming this way and that. I wondered who of them had lost their mothers, who's chests were now holes filled with the fragments of memories. There are certain lies you tell yourself to stumble blindly through the bereavement. After the reality cracks you in two, you tell yourself that things will be okay. That time will erode the numbness away; you glue the split inside together by forcing yourself out of bed in the mornings, eating cereal with hot milk and leaving the radio on at every opportunity, scared of your own thoughts. And some nights when the loneliness is so bad and a frayed, rough desperation courses through your veins, you pick up your phone book and trace the cobwebs off names you suddenly want to leap over the margins to sit beside you.

Amidst the throng of people I watched couples. Some appeared anxious, some amorous. Most were oblivious to world beyond the other's gaze. Jagged pangs of longing unexpectedly hit me like mouths beneath the skin cutting across organs. I longed to be in love, to have a lover. I felt sad, inadequate and lonely. What must it be like to never feel the mumbled words of a lover become handwriting against your jaw?

As I hit the steps of The Royal London Hospital to pick up my mother's items, my thoughts flapped at crossed purposes sending me meandering down conflicting dead ends. *Might I die like that too...?* *Suddenly end up so still....* Weighing in, heavier than the rest is the last thought, the moment when I first arrived at the hospital when I was convinced mum would rouse, groggy but still fighting. I really did, right up to the point where she disappeared behind the large shrieking double doors with the NHS regulation blue and white paint peeling off. But she didn't. She became in that moment an imaginary being even, as evidenced by the thumping of my heart, she existed as still real through me. I saw myself clearly caught between life as I once knew it and life never being the same again.

I stood still on the hospital's grey steps, absorbing the nurses in their crisply ironed uniforms, the inaudible chatter of jaded ambulance men, people clutching official looking envelopes and folded letters, the tearing away of tires in the distance, all part of some strange, orchestral music the city produced. Everything stuck to the magnet of my pulse. I saw myself sitting on a crumbling rock, swatting cobwebs away from my privates frantically. When a tiny speck of rock was left, I fell to a bottom lined with broken eggshells.

Simultaneous Equations

If I'd been born a water baby, I'd liquefy into coffee-stained mugs so people could drink me and taste peach iced tea. On the London Underground during summer my clothes would become wet to cool me down and make a stunted river for the seven lives in my feet to float. I chewed on these thoughts as I watched Mrs Harris front crawl in our local pool, her movements slick in the water.

I was waist deep in the shallow end, walking on water trying to warm myself up. The pool was shrouded in a strange pulsing blue light. A young lifeguard in his high chair looked bored, stroked his whistle and the dormant sweet screams it carried, while the wet floor beneath him was slippery with invisible verrucas. I watched the kids at the opposite end fling themselves into the water in beautiful, awkward shapes that died on the surface. Their yells pierced the distance between us. My hair was wet, my skin tingled and a pair of white goggles felt tight on my head. I went under. I longed for Marpessa, my old SLR camera, to be waterproof so her greedy, rotating lens could capture the black lines that created lanes, the strokes that continued swimming after you exited the pool and the silver carpet of forks at the bottom nobody else saw. So I could tap people on their shoulders and say, "Excuse me, can I take pictures of your kick?" I named my camera after the actress Marpessa Dawn:

both were black, magical, and mysterious. Having her had taught me how to embrace inanimate objects.

By the time Mrs Harris made her way to me I'd had my fill of admiring other swimmers, wanting to steal their easy strokes as though they were costumes to be worn. She eased in front of me, white locks across her face fat with water.

We hadn't had a chance to really talk yet. I fiddled with my goggles trying to contain the anger rising. "I can't believe you fucked off and left me. You realise I have nobody right now."

A tiny bulb of water flattened on her neck. "What about the counselling sessions? I thought they would help." Her tone was patient.

"I'm not talking about a doctor that I'm just another case to," I spat. "I'm talking about you. He's a stranger paid to listen to me confess things they might use against me."

We went under, swimming towards the middle. I was aware of people kicking around me moving water through their fingers that would trickle down into the rest of their day. Behind my goggles I cried. It's possible to cry and hold your breath under water. We were at the bottom of the sea, not the crammed leisure centre pool in east London. She turned her head, grabbed my hand. We spoke silently knowing our words would not survive without air.

She just fucking died with no warning, I said. My words swallowed by splashes above us.

She always did things without preparing you.

What do I do now?

She squeezed my fingers. *You can't resent her for something she couldn't control. Shit happens. Some people go to sleep and don't wake up. Others cross a street without looking and get hit by a car. A man I once knew left an incense stick burning while he dozed off, the whole flat went up in smoke.* Then the water pulled her silent apology away.

We came up for air, holding onto the side, kicking gently. Mrs Harris squeezed water from her bun. "You want me to lie to you and tell you things will be better overnight? They won't be."

"No," I said, feeling the tug of my swimming costume strap on my shoulder, blinking at the strange blue light, at Mrs Harris as though she was a product of it. "I just feel... abandoned." A sour taste filled my tongue. I pulled my costume strap up before we went under again.

The bed of forks beneath us trembled; one came unstuck rising towards me. The water pulled Mrs Harris, lithe and free. She drew me along, anchoring me somehow through the dip of her shoulder, the flick of her feet, the curve of a turn. When we broke the shivering water, the remnants of our conversation sunk to the bottom to become tadpoles.

"Shit! There's a fish in the water." A kid squealed.

"Where?"

"Behind you, no don't move you'll scare it!"

Some teenagers scurried around trying to grab it.

"No! There, there-aw. Get it."

The noise level increased, the lifeguard blew his whistle.

"Who put the fish in the water?" he asked. "Where did it come from?"

Sure enough I could see the fish and I thought it could see me. It shimmered in my direction. Mrs Harris and I exchanged glances. It was silver with purple fins. Its fins were sewing needles stuck together.

Mrs Harris shook the water from her hair, "Quick, grab it before those crazy kids come down here." Heat spread on my throat as if someone blew hot breaths there. I followed the wriggling fish, tracing it this way and that. I lunged at it, fumbled, the tail tipping my fingers. I tried again to catch it with clutches that limped to the finish like the slowest swimmers in a class. The fish was roughly two feet long and so shiny I was sure its skin was made of light. I stopped then, momentarily, throwing it with my stillness. It swam back towards me and my hands were poised in the water. I grabbed it, feeling its rough, lukewarm slippery skin. I pulled up and out, careful not to let it slide back into the water.

"Got it," I murmured.

Mrs Harris smiled, she followed me up the steps and out onto the pale green floor. I heard the kids coming out of the pool, bits of their conversations trickled down.

"What? I don't know man, that lady's got it."

The patter of footsteps grew closer. Mrs Harris and I knelt on the floor. We held the fish, a heartbeat between us. The blue light travelled across the ceiling and the scars on my wrists hummed the hymn that fish like to sing when the tide comes in. The fish stared at me; inside its filmy eye shuttered a mini camera lens. A crowd gathered around us. The fish's mouth opened repeatedly. It trembled, then heaved and a worn, brass key slick with gut slime fell out of its mouth into my hand.

"No way!" a voice chimed. "Did you see that? It just threw up a key, man."

"How did a key get inside it?" another voice chirped.

I took my swimming hat off and put the key inside it. Heavy with the weight of water my released hair in two-strand twists slapped against my neck.

The lifeguard ambled over. "Fess up. Which one of you clowns put the fish in the pool?"

Voices became a chorus. "I didn't put no key there."

"Yo, the bogie man did it!"

"It was my Nan, boss; she came out of Holloway prison to do it."

Mrs Harris said awkwardly, "Can we get a container with some water for the fish?" She addressed the lifeguard. The fish trembled as if my hands gave electric shocks.

"It's dying!" I screamed. "It needs mouth to mouth resuscitation." I bent down and placed my mouth on its hard lips that felt like the opening to a defective bottle. I blew breaths into its clammy mouth. I felt Mrs Harris's entranced gaze.

"Nasty, she's kissing the fish man!"

"This woman's weird."

"What's wrong with her?" The voices hovered above me, tiny planes with broken wings crashing down. Then everything went quiet, slowed down as though I'd gone temporarily deaf. I was vaguely aware of Mrs Harris grabbing my shoulder while I took deep breaths for the fish, its filmy eye replaced by my brown one. By the time the lifeguard pulled me off the fish the kids were stuck to the ceiling, the bed of forks had risen to the surface of water and the key was still in my hand.

The fish didn't make it. Outside the sports centre Mrs Harris and I sat in my beaten up, blue Volkswagen Golf. I turned on the engine and the car spluttered to life. We sat quietly, processing what just happened. It settled in our mouths, rich and thick. In the back seats lay a bent copy of Trace Magazine and two dirty frying pans, a sheet of crinkled foil between them. Gold sweet wrappers were stray lights on the floor. To the far left corner, my silver spacesuit costume sat like our third passenger.

"What an incident!" she said finally.

I strapped my seatbelt in. "I know, the universe is speaking to me."

"The universe could indeed be communicating with you."

I swung my body to face her. "Seriously, that fish let me catch it. You saw what happened, it swam right to me."

"I saw you got lucky."

"What about the key?" I asked, pulling it out of my pocket, waving it at her.

"Maybe it's as random as a fish swallowing a key, magical."

I held up the brass object to the rear view mirror and reflected back at me wasn't a key but a finger, a slender, tapered brown feminine finger. I slipped it back inside my pocket.

"You think the pool has some sort of pipe in it?" I sunk back into the grey seat.

Mrs Harris popped a piece of gum in her mouth, "Can't say I've ever noticed. That was some sight, you giving a fish mouth to mouth!" Then she said, "You're grieving but be careful, behaviour like that can get you thrown in the funny farm."

"It was reactive!"

I looked out the window at the gaps between the leaves of the tree leaning to one side.

As if addressing the wing mirror I said, "Whatever we come back as in the next life, it's mandatory for you to be my swimming partner."

"Done deal", she laughed. "RIP, fish."

I hit the gas, turned the wheel and steered the car forward. I watched the right wing mirror on my side. People dripped out of it onto the pavements with bits of glass embedded in their bodies. I placed my left hand on the lump of key in my pocket, felt its finger guise against my thigh. The fish, the finger and the people were in my head. Swimming at the speed of a bullet from one end to the other, if my head got sliced open they would fall out, bucking with afterlife.

The Advantage of Nmebe Soup

Adesua recalled the advice Mama Uwamusi had given her earlier that morning. The secret of good Nmebe soup is balance and employing a light touch. All the flavours combined must play their part for the overall taste. The wild tomatoes should be ripe but not overly so, the onions sparsely added, a small portion of peppers for the required burst of heat, a sprinkling of bitter leaf. All cooked in the juices of a tender fowl. All around her, people were milling to and from the various stalls, their raised voices an ever-increasing hum. She often wondered whether people who came to the market thought they were in competition so keen was each person to out-shout and out-talk the other.

Apart from Adesua's duty of cooking the soup, today was a special day for the bridal choice ceremony was to begin at The Royal Palace after the setting of the sun and the market was rife with gossip and high energy. The scent of peppered meats lingered in the air and children with small sugar cane sticks in their mouths, were roaming freely, happy to escape their mother's heavy hands, their eager fingers quick to reach out and touch whatever caught their restless eyes.

At the furthest stretch of the market next to Ijoma's fish stand, Adesua saw a young boy eating watermelon who helped himself to another healthy sized piece whilst Ijoma's back was turned, and was soon chased. There was a juggler dressed in red with multi-coloured pieces of string tied across his head and two sets of white feathers tucked near each of his ears. In the middle of the market, as well as various fruit and farm produce stalls was Esemuede the palm wine seller who was always remarkably merry. Next to him sat Ahere, the one armed beggar accompanied by his dog who was quick to imitate his master and stick a needy paw out at passers by. On the opposite side across from them was Emeka the tailor who sold some of the finest cloths and materials, all laid out in an elaborate fashion to tempt the most disciplined of market visitors. Beside Emeka was the curious figure of Ehinome, the medicine man surrounded by bags of herbal remedies, each designed to resolve ailments such as back pain and bowel trouble.

This was what she loved about market day, the familiar comfort of mayhem that surrounded her. The women with their generous hips and ample bosoms, chopping fish and slaughtering chickens, ignoring the sweat that glistened on their furrowed brows and the sheen it left on their taut skin. The men wielding produce in their powerful arms, jokingly exchanging banter across the amused heads of customers who would at times pass judgement and salute their chosen winner; smoke rising to the sky and the distinctive aroma of goat roasting, your stomach growling, mouth watering and tongue snaking across your lips in approval.

It was during this moment of reverie that Adesua saw what she was destined to purchase on Emeka's stall. It lay right at the very bottom under a weighty pile of displayed attire and she'd never have even noticed it had it not been for the left corner folded up, like a crooked finger beckoning her towards it.

Emeka smiled knowingly when she reached him.

"Aha, I know what you want, it is the only one of its kind that I have," he said smoothly removing the desired garment from its position and spreading it on the top where it truly belonged in all its glory. "You will be a vision in this; I have been waiting to sell it to the right person, a person who truly deserves it."

Adesua resisted the urge to laugh in response, knowing full well that Emeka would have sold it to a giant grasshopper had it presented him with a half decent offer. "It is beautiful," she whispered, stroking the bold print of deep blue and orange angular lines that your eyes traced until you touched the outer edges kissed with gold.

"My father will give you a week's supply of farm produce in exchange for this cloth and the matching head dress," Adesua said careful to keep a pleading expression on her face.

"What? No, no, no," Emeka responded, shaking his large head from side to side adamantly. "You want people to laugh and say Emeka is a fool. No, you will pay me like everybody else."

"But I am not trying to get out of paying sir, I am simply giving you another choice of payment, please I am like your daughter. I have nothing to wear for the king's ceremony."

At last Emeka agreed, biting heavily into the chewing stick dangling from his mouth. He made a show of packing her item for her, folding and tying it so it rested neatly and addressing people walking past, "Let nobody say Emeka is not a kind man oh! Let nobody say Emeka does not have a heart that gives." He gestured pulling at his ear lobe urging people to listen, instead they were only fleetingly distracted.

"Thank you sir," Adesua responded. "You will be well rewarded."

"Yes, just make sure your father is ready to give me what I am owed, I will pass by in a few days to collect my payment."

"Yes Papa Emeka."

"Be sure to tell him I am coming, I do not want to be a bearer of bad news."

It was only after she picked up her cloth and walked away that Adesua saw the monkey approaching. Before she could react it had jumped on her back, desperately clinging on. She tried to ply its wily brown body off her but it would not relent. It brought its pinched face close to hers and bared its teeth, grabbing at her hair and pulling tufts out, noisily screeching while her hair fell to the ground. It scratched her face and neck drawing blood and she felt a stinging burn on her skin. She screamed at the top of her voice, furiously flailing her arms about and hopping up and down, yet the stubborn animal remained there, boring its black eyes into hers, hissing and spitting angrily. She raised her palm in defence but it shot its head forward and bit her finger. By the time Emeka and a few others reached her, she lay in a heap; there was no hair on the ground, no marks on her body, and no blood.

The monkey had vanished but momentarily Adesua had felt that there was nothing she could do to get that monkey off her back.

It was a sign of things to come.

Will

The cat's meow drew me outside. I recognised the neighbourhood rambler, black with a split white stripe down its back. It stood on a half smashed green bottle, back arched, body poised. Its amber gaze bore into mine and momentarily it looked like an artist's sculpture: *Cat on a Green Bottle*.

"Hey boy," I cooed gently, tightening my dressing gown. "Get off that." I bent down to shoo it off amazed it had at all managed to balance on the bottle. Smoke filled its eyes as it leapt off in a nifty trick. The bottle rolled towards my feet, and its jagged base stared down my fluffy slippers in an unequal stand off. The cat circled, tail upright like an antenna drawing an invisible line in the air before approaching the bottle again. It leaned low, stretched its neck, shot its tongue out and licked, deftly avoiding shards.

I slapped my hands together. "Stop that! You're a bad boy." I ran indoors, grabbed the plastic bag that was a green tongue poking out of the kitchen drawer. By the time I re-emerged, the trouble-maker had disappeared into the shrubbery separating my house from the neighbour's. The sky was shedding one darkening blue to reveal another. I scooped up the bottle by its neck, sniffed. It smelled like palm wine. Fermented wine was a sharp scent that lingered; I wondered if the smell would remain in my nostrils throughout the rest of the day.

The bottle slipped, nicked my finger. My blood became a small red tide that ebbed down settling on the jagged rim in a circular, bloody kiss. I dropped the broken bottle inside the green plastic bag and shoved it in my wheelie bin. I locked the door, checked the post hatch. It was empty. The cut throbbed and the blood drop began to grow into a red bulb. I looked at my finger, noticed the tiny piece of green glass grinning inside the wound.

I had a meeting planned with my mother's old friend and solicitor Mervyn for later in the day. Mervyn and his family collected strays. He was the centre, a warm, pulsing nucleus people surrounded. You never knew who you'd see at their house; maybe a Jamaican cabbie with gambling debts needing an unlikely haven to lie low, or broken prostitutes with heroin babies needing rescuing, or a friend whose hands were disappearing, who needed help before his whole body vanished, reduced to a heap of clothes on a side road.

I'd known him for as long as I could remember and it was hard to separate him from the things I associated with him. The smoothness of his bald head, like a crystal ball hiding the night, crumpled expensive suits, expressions of concern, large Cuban cigars dangling jauntily from the corner of his mouth. As a kid, I imagined he slept with one of those cigars firmly lodged between his lips, lit and burning with particles of the cases he'd taken home. I saw him tossing and turning without dropping that cigar, and winding curls of smoke twisting in the dark around him like flying white snakes.

I used to play hide and seek with his sons as a kid. I hid so well behind the line of cushions on the soft, plum sofa I slipped into a world beneath where coins and old conversations hummed their approval. Mervyn was a great dad. I watched the way he threw his sons in the air as if they were the only suns allowed to set and rise back up with each catch and fling. In Mervyn's home, the warmth and love was inescapable. Whenever I saw this, the well inside me deepened, lengthened. Only there was no water at the bottom, just stones thrown swallowed by silence. All this made me like Mervyn, even love him a little. I pictured my mother and me arriving in his life as two stray winds creating small havocs for Mervyn and his boy's but that story she'd never told me.

I caught the train from Elephant & Castle to Mervyn's in Harlesden. In a fairly empty carriage, heads unconsciously bobbed to its rhythm. I coughed and the coloured train lines flattened. The train paused for breath frequently at main station stops, and at pits in-between, the ones left off the map. It squeaked and sputtered, its sounds creating a low, dark horizon on tracks were mice flew. It shuddered along.

At Harlesden, I moved with the throng of people spilling out of the station like a language. I spotted a young woman stealing a bouquet of blue azaleas from a flower stall right behind the owner's back. Her arms were outstretched, mischievous grin in tow. Her body was arched and she was dressed in a yellowy brown African wrapper. Braided in multiple single plaits, her hair looked neat. She stood tall and the lines of her body seemed familiar. Then, she looked right at me, and as if it was a signal of sorts, turned to run. Instinctively I followed. I chased her and the distance between us shook like a rickety, wooden bridge. She flew, dipped, turned and twisted. Her movements were rugged musical notes. She had moonshine on her back. I removed my rucksack from my shoulder, rummaged for Marpessa, soon solid in my hands. I pressed the power switch, watched it light red. I snapped away. Marpessa's lens whirred the way cameras did when they spoke. Above us, pigeons flying drew another skyline with their beaks. They cooed at each other, grey wings spreading.

I followed the young woman's moving back. *Follow, follow, follow,* I muttered to myself, small beads of sweat springing up in my arm-pits like translucent crops. Marpessa's frayed strap bit into my neck. The summer streets were fully occupied by clusters of people, their perspiration dripping along the pavements. I shoved Marpessa back into the rucksack. Ahead, my pied piper of sorts waited outside the inviting, yellow sign of Honey's Caribbean takeaway.

She'd paused, as though giving me an opportunity to close the gap between us. She sat on the steps outside, hand on her jaw, flowers beside her, wrapper riding up smooth, brown legs. Something about her on that stairway made the hairs on my arms stand to attention. I spotted moss growing on the stairs, green dreams of concrete she'd somehow commanded. I fished Marpessa out once more, snapped away.

"Hey!" I said, "I'd like to photograph you some more."

She sprang up, shoved Marpessa away, grabbed her flowers and took off again. Past the laundrette with washing machines mid-cycle, the funeral home set in large green grounds, past rows of quaint shops sporting colourful window displays that shared one neon heartbeat they rotated during breaks.

At the compact, red-stoned building on a raised kerb with a roof that looked like a low brow, she dropped her flowers and disappeared around the corner. Slanted, elegant typography on the window read Williams & Co. Solicitors. Near my feet something rustled. I stared. The azaleas she'd dropped were no longer flowers but crushed blue butterflies near death. Some had wings shorn, some were partially squashed. A few attempting to unstick themselves, fluttered pathetically. I tasted their desperation for one last broken flight.

Inside the building, the secretary Pauline sat behind a black-flecked grey desk that might have been made of marble and fog. She wore a crisp white blouse and a brown woollen skirt. Red-framed glasses finished the look.

"Well, well, well," she said. "Wonders will never cease." A finger and its long nail curled away from the keyboard. "You allergic to this area or something?" she asked. I always enjoyed her warm, Bajan accent, even when it was biting.

I dropped the rucksack and helped myself to a cup of water. "Nice to see you too. He in?"

"Yeah, he's in," she said leaning back into her chair.

The hallway curved snakelike and was flanked by rooms on either side; there were cracks of light underneath the doors that were closed. On the left, I passed a grey-haired man standing behind a desk piled high with files, talking insistently into a mobile phone. Spotting me he smiled distantly and shut the door firmly. To my right a slender black woman in a charcoal grey trouser suit paced back and forth. I caught the wink of a slim gold watch from her wrist. At the end of the hall stood Mervyn's office. I knocked.

"Come in," his voice boomed.

I could smell and feel his presence even before seeing him. Paco Rabanne aftershave mingled with Cuban cigars. He sat in the sky-light window at an enormous sprawling oak desk that managed not to swallow the whole room. There was a chocolate leather chair at the back next to a compact library of Law and fishing books. On the walls were hung certificates, photos of him and his sons, his staff and a picture of him holding a kingfisher on a hook.

"The prodigal daughter returns," he said enveloping me in a hug. He had a habit of doing that, drawing me into things whether I had a say in it or not. It felt good. At 6 feet 2 inches he towered above me, a black skinned man with broad facial features and a Jamaican lilt, like molasses melting in his voice. When he became angry the molasses turned molten.

"Sorry," I said, dropping my rucksack at the foot of the chair opposite his desk. "I've been busy."

"Yes but this meeting was for your benefit." He walked back round, folded his considerable frame into the seat. At my mother's funeral, he had cried for her. I'd never seen a grown man cry other than on TV. His body had trembled in grief while my own wails stayed caught in my throat. I held his cries gently, as if they were the delicate rims of fragile cups.

He nudged the open file on his desk towards me before reclining back into his seat.

"This is it?" I asked studying it as though it was in a foreign language.

"Yes, your mother's will."

I pulled the file closer, felt a fresh film of tears I blinked away.

I shook my head. "I can't believe she was organised enough to arrange a will, she never said a word."

I could feel Mervyn's gaze on me, I snuck a look and the corners of his mouth were drawn making me wish I had a father to hold my hand. To tell me how to navigate emotional landmines that unexpectedly went off and rendered you crawling legless because the lines of someone's mouth triggered your memories.

"Well, she was your mother and maybe she didn't want to worry you," Mervyn said, yanking me out of my reverie. I felt a twinge of jealousy that he'd known this secret.

"She managed to tell you though." I didn't quite keep the resentment from my voice.

"I was her lawyer and friend, of course she told me. Your mother could be very secretive, in fact annoyingly so at times. This she was absolutely clear on."

A fat tear ran down my cheek.

Mervyn brought out a worn piece of paper from the file. I bent my head, drank the words in:

I, Queenie Lowon leave the sum of £80,000 to my only child Joy Omoregbe Lowon. As well as my house at 89 Windamere Avenue and all the contents within it, I bequeath a brass head artefact and her grandfather Peter Lowon's diary to her. She'll figure out what to do with them. I leave her everything I have. I ask my lawyer Mervyn Williams to advise her should it be necessary.

Below it was the date and my mother's signature which looked hurried and leaned to the right, slightly squiggly, as if it would morph into a mosquito and fly off the page, fat with her blood.

I leave her everything I have...

It was there in black and white, the proof my mother wouldn't suddenly re-appear and declare this a joke. The offending document was becoming a white room with words dripping black ink on the walls.

Mervyn loosened his tie and motioned at the wide, square windows behind him. "You mind if I open them, bit stuffy in here."

I shrugged, barely looking at him. "It's your office."

I glanced to my left and Mervyn's picture with the fish on his hook had changed. The fish's mouth had become a woman's jaw straining against the hook, threatening to leap out through the glass.

I was holding my breath and didn't even know it. Mervyn fished out from the bottom drawer of his desk a white plastic bag bulky with the shapes inside it. From the bag he pulled out a brown leather diary and the brass head. He laid them on his desk. "These are yours."

All the sketches of myself I'd drawn in my head with a finger dipped in saliva seemed to show up. Better versions of myself in a suit facing Piccadilly Circus tube, waiting to pick up another version of myself from a curved, red carriage. Another dumping an attempted suicide version in a grey bin bag, me walking a black tightrope in the sky, naked. In this life, my mother would never see those versions of me but maybe all they needed was her gaze from the next life, to stop them jumping into the orange sea at the horizon.

I picked up the brass head, weighed it. I ran a finger over the high, proud forehead, its broad nose, wondering how many lives it had seen with its defiant expression. I placed it back on the table.

I murmured, "I've never seen this."

Mervyn leaned forward, smiled reassuringly. "It's just an art piece, she probably kept it among her personal things."

A tiny drop of sweat ran down my back. "If you had something like this, you'd display it though wouldn't you?"

"Not necessarily, I have lots of things I've collected I haven't displayed."

"Hmmm, it's just odd I've never seen it. And £80,000? Where did she get that kind of money?" I felt flat, dispossessed, thinking of all the ways I'd wanted to get money and nice things, but never like this. Never without her here to help me squander some of my new found glory.

"She used to own a flat in Brixton, sold it a while back now."

"Oh my God! Something else I didn't know about. Was this woman even my mother?" My hands became wet cloths I wrung.

"I'm sure she had her reasons."

"Yup, and she's taken them to the grave. I have no idea what to do with her money."

"You know that youth project in that abandoned building I volunteer for? Why don't we run something there together?"

I shrugged, slightly surprised at the ease and speed with which he found something for me to do with the money. He continued, "There's lots of space and you could incorporate photography into it. Think about it," he advised.

I stood abruptly, slid the diary back over. "Will you hold onto that? Just for a little while," I instructed.

"Of course." He walked round the table, hands stuffed inside his pockets. I took off my cardigan and wrapped the brass head in it, placed it carefully inside my rucksack. Mervyn hugged me again and right then I wanted to tell him about the young woman I'd followed from the flower stall, who'd oddly enough led me to him as if I didn't already know where he was. But I thought better of it. He already seemed to think my behaviour was strange. I didn't want him worrying even more. I said goodbye, feeling the familiar tug of my strap on my shoulder. On my way out, I noticed a red ant crawling in a step I'd taken. I watched it drag my step to a corner and feed on its memories.

In my bag I felt Marpessa and the brass head in a loose embrace. I crossed the gauntlet the road threw at vehicles daily, passed through ghosts that signalled when traffic lights stopped working. Could you leap from all the tipping points in your life at once? In the distance, a breeze carried new beginnings in unsealed white envelopes that hovered just beyond my reach.

Monkey Dey Work
Bamboo Dey Chop

Blessings sometimes travelled in pairs. And when they did, especially during a rainy season, there was a unanimous decision by the Gods to give way to them through the traffic of the living. They floated above the still moist beds of earth where cassava plants slept, bounced off the hard backs of restless tortoises in humid unforgiving nights, joined the march of ants under remnants of partially eaten sweet wild berries and clung to the tiny wings of fireflies that appeared as small bursts of light in the belly of night air.

When they finally deposited themselves on Adesua's head on the morning of the ceremony at the palace, the only indication that they had arrived was an itch to the right side of her brow. This itch did not stop after the necessary scratch, no. Instead, it spread like fire all over her head and the only thing that cooled its ardour was the kiss of cold water. The blessings laughed because their seeds had been sown. They knew that later in the day when the family set out for the palace, the skies overhead would part and shed tears upon them all.

It did not stop Adesua from sweating while she laboured over the pot of nmebe soup she prepared under Mama's supervision. Nor did it stop Papa from killing their biggest goat that he said had tried to run when it saw the glint from the newly sharpened blade. It did not stop Adesua from having her thick hair plied into submission by nimble hands, her body oiled till it gleamed and the wrapper material she purchased from the market tied and fitted so perfectly around her tall frame it would have convinced anybody the material was made with only her figure in mind.

All over their village a variation of this occurred. Households in small and large compounds were busy preparing their suitable daughters as though the king had made a personal visit to request for their daughter's hand. Prayers were said, offerings made. It seemed there was nothing people wouldn't do to beat the competition, but nobody except Mama Adabra knew what the neighbouring villages were up to. There were whispers in the village that she had travelled as far as Shekoni to visit a medicine man who claimed he could insert himself into scenes of the future then come back to tell you about it. These whispers were soon slapped away by the hands of excitement and expectation.

For days before, the soil was fruitful; yielding cocoyam and plump melons that changed the colour of your tongue momentarily. Blades of grass shot out from hungry, dry patches, plants reached up high off the ground as if attempting to have conversations with the heavens. Purple and yellow petals scattered around like their hopes and dreams clinging to a foundation of dust. Even the air seemed filled with expectation. It touched the villagers or maybe they touched it, and it sighed in appreciation and carried them along in this period of madness and desire.

Adesua had asked about this king many times. But each person gave a different answer each time and she was convinced very few of the villagers had actually seen him.

"I heard he fed one of his wives to hyenas for disobeying him." Old man Ononkwe had said, "Wise man."

"You know he changes into a lion at night," Amassi offered another time.

"The King has dealings with pale men from lands far, far away,"

Obiriame, one of the village elders, had told her, conspiratorially. Of all three, Adesua was convinced Obiriame was the biggest liar. Imagine such a thing, pale men!

And so it went on and on, till Adesua became tired of all the talk and wonder at this King who did not even deign to visit his people and who seemed to have too many wives already by all accounts. Adesua could not wait for the day and the ceremony to be over so the village could stop humming with gossip, she could go back to swinging from trees and not worry about cuts on her skin or Papa's disapproving eyes. She could race some of the young men in the village near the riverbank and when she won join them on their jaunt to a hidden clearing where they said human bones lay in wait. She dreamed of following Papa on one of his hunting trips, watching from a secret place while he stalked and captured his prey.

By early afternoon many of the villagers started out for the palace ceremony. The beautiful young women in their colourful prints and intricately plaited hair, were led enthusiastically by their mothers each desperate to outdo the other while the fathers loitered behind slightly, chewing on sugar cane while they speculated on the day's events to come.

On they went, past riverbanks with edges like disfigured faces licked by keen waters. Through long, dusty paths that coughed up red dirt as determined feet trampled along their winded chests. Past the gaze of tall trees whose branches shook slightly in greeting. They paused for food and rest on the outskirts of the town of Ego. They marvelled at the hospitality of some of the townsfolk who although welcoming them with curiosity still offered cooked ripe bananas and palm wine.

It was here that the villagers met a man called Igwehi. His hair was completely white and he walked with a stooped back and propped himself up on a stick. Igwehi said that he had worked as a craftsman producing leather for the previous king, Oba Anuje, the father of the current king. He had witnessed many royal ceremonies and even been favoured by the king. He relayed that Oba Anuje ruled with a strong fist and on discovering a coup to overthrow him by one of his closest advisors in the royal court, had ordered his rival's head to be chopped off using a ritual sword. For ten days the advisor's head had been left for all to see on a specially made clay mantle within the palace walls. And even when high-ranking members in the palace had pleaded with Oba Anuje to have the head removed, he refused. He let it sit on the mantle till the blood dried into all the creases and crevasses in the clay created by the baking sun and the stench turned the stomachs of nervous courtiers.

Igwehi told this tale with relish, chewing over the words like the flesh of a tenderly cooked cow and rubbing his left thigh with one hand while gently banging his stick on the ground with the other. Then, he accidentally revealed that he having lost favour with the king had also been thrown out of the royal court. The revelation slipped from his mouth the way a breast spills out from a loosely tied wrapper. He attempted to contain it by covering his mouth as it had not been meant for the ears of strangers. When Adesua asked him why the king had banished him, his eyes began to roll in their sockets as though running to take cover in the far corners of his mind.

Benin was a city that had flourished over time under the rule of the different obas, and for the most part sat in quiet, satisfied contentment. You could see it in the number of undamaged gates there were throughout, many of them reaching eight or nine feet in height, with doors made from single pieces of ancient wood hinged on pegs, behind which smart and sometimes opulent homes had been built. You could see it in the Queens' court which stretched for over six miles and was protected by a wall ten feet tall, fashioned from enormous trees tied to one another by cross beams and in-filled with red clay. Even along the streets the houses sat in neat rows.

The palace of Benin was divided into several quarters, apartments for courtiers and houses in sprawling, endless dust-shrouded grounds. Beautiful square galleries kissed by the breath of the gods rested on wooden pillars covered in the finest cast copper. In the afternoon, the sun shone on the ornate copper engravings depicting war exploits; images of soldiers rushing into battle wielding finely crafted spears and carrying sunrays in their mouths. Each roof had a small turret with copper casted birds harbouring the sounds of battle, waiting to carry them into angles of light swirling in the blue sky.

When Adesua and her family finally arrived outside the king's court to be greeted by four appointed armed guards, they were ushered through a spotless square shaped courtyard, passing members of the palace dotted around in groups who turned to watch the new arrivals with a mixture of amusement and trepidation.

Adesua drank in the harried servants carrying bundles of wood and rushing into a side entrance where more shouting could be heard. A man ran out blowing through a copper instrument that alerted the palace a gathering before the king was occurring. Then came a procession of dancing men and women with their faces painted white wearing tight costumes made of luminous green cloth.

Eventually Adesua and her family were shown into the biggest room they had ever seen. On the walls were plaques carved from the finest brass commemorating more battles. The space was so wide and lengthy she was sure the inhabitants of six villages could fit into it. It was spilling over with people who tumbled around each other adept in the way they managed to avoid colliding. There was a specially allocated section for the royal advisors who talked among themselves, whispering behind cunning fingers and releasing eager laughs. To the right of them sat the king's wives, a brood of decorated hens, clucking niceties to each other while brimming with resentment. They cast roving eyes over the proceedings their faces drawn with sour expressions and intermittently adjusted their childbearing hips as though the servants had placed insects there. They ignored the performing acrobats who somersaulted to a sweaty drummer's beat for their pleasure. For centuries it was custom that some of the king's army and courtiers sat behind the wives of the palace. From them the acrobatic spectacle drew gasps and applause as well as from the happy crowd who had travelled from all corners of the Edo kingdom to be assailed with wonders they could never have imagined seeing.

In the gap running through the crowd, a long line of women stood on offer, one behind the other like sacrifices to a God. The king himself sat in an exquisitely crafted chair made from ancient teak wood, flanked by his royal priest on one side and a member of the court council on the other. You could not tell how old the Oba was from looking at him but his black skin shone and his head seemed too big for his body. The wrapper he wore was heavily embroidered with a frill overlaid by a waistband sash with tassels. He had royal *iwu* tattoos on both arms that Adesua was too far away to see in detail.

As the family tentatively moved to the front, the procession of dancers began to navigate through the room. People clapped along as they wiggled and shook body parts, drawing admirable glances and whoops of encouragement. By the time they had worked their way to the back, the councilman beside the king stood up and held his hand out for silence.

"You!" he said pointing to Adesua, "come forward and introduce yourself to the king."

Adesua walked towards them "I am Adesua sir."

"And where have you come from?" the councilman asked.

"Ishan."

"Tell us what you have brought as a gift for the king and why you would make a good wife."

"I brought a pot of nmebe soup and I would make a fine wife because one day I'm going to be the best hunter in all of Edo."

The crowd burst into laughter and the other wives giggled. Adesua turned to see that Papa had his hands on his head and Mama was trying not to smile. After the laughter died, the councilman looked to the king. He was sitting forward in his chair and studying Adesua as if she were a rainbow piercing through the heart of the sky.

Condition Make Crayfish Bend

If during his time as king Oba Anuje had been an unwavering rock that even tidal waves bowed to, his son Odion was not. Anuje had sowed the first seeds of inadequacy in Odion when on picking him up as a newborn he had wrinkled his nose as if the child smelled rotten. When the baby curled its lips and let out a wail as most babies do when born, Anuje seemed to take it as a personal affront and declared, "This child is useless," then handed the baby back to its perplexed mother.

Nobody in the palace knew why Anuje hated his son Odion. He had many children from various wives, some whom he loved, some he tolerated. But his reaction to his fourth son was as strange as an antelope mating with a hare. When Odion was a boy he did everything he could to gain his father's approval. He won wrestling matches, attempted to squash any signs of rebellion from villagers who didn't want to pay their annual tributes, he solved riddles Anuje liked to set to amuse himself. All to no avail, Odion was not even a crumb on his father's plate. Through the years, he longed for his father's approval.

Sometimes when Odion dozed at night, he imagined that a Mammy Water with her big tail wriggled into his head through his ear and like a broom sweeps dirt, swept away the faults his father saw, leaving behind multi-coloured scales that glittered like rare gems. Despite this, Odion continued to suffer under his father's hand haunted by one dream; a human heart swelling, then shrinking on a copper plate engraved in a foreign language and his father eating the heart with his bare hands before releasing his bloody mouth to the kingdom's sky. He never asked Anuje to whom that heart belonged.

Years later Odion, now a young man, stumbled on Anuje in one of his rooms, clutching at his throat and gesturing wildly for help. Aware in that moment of being the only person his father needed and the only one who could help him Odion stood rooted to the spot, basking in his father's weakness. Something exchanged between father and son that was worse than death tapping you on the shoulder. Anuje had been poisoned. Fully aware his son had no intention to help; with his last breath he cursed him.

After Anuje returned to the ground, flesh to dust, Odion was left still chasing a ghost. And even as king he heard the mocking laughter of his father's ghost sneaking through the gaps in the palace gates and laying claim to the Oba's chair.

And so against the advice of the head councilman and private berating of his priest, Odion insisted on marrying Adesua. "Such insolence Oba! She is not fit for marriage and will embarrass the palace. Think of your reputation!" Odion could no more explain his choice of a new bride as he could the desire that drove him to be king. Seeing her for the first time reminded him of a stalk that refused to be bent by the wind and for reasons unknown to him he equated such strength of character to mean loyalty. Adesua bid goodbye to everything she knew. To days spent exploring and wondering where her adventurous feet would take her, to nights around a fire listening to her father's stories while Mama threw in a word here and there. Goodbye to old friendships and maybe blossoming new ones.

Her village rejoiced, their daughter had been chosen. If Adesua, a beautiful young woman, but one who walked purposefully rather than swung her hips to catch a young man's eye and preferred playing with animals to learning recipes, could become queen, then there was hope for all their daughters! But there was a muted uproar, too. Within the palace walls vicious whispers circulated amongst courtiers, noblemen and women like a plague amidst its victims. Preparations were made to celebrate the king's new bride under what struck Adesua as false jollity. Some people smiled but were not really happy. Others seemed to welcome her with open arms but their embraces left her cold.

In the days before the wedding Adesua paced the palace floors with a lump in her throat no amount of spit swallowing would push down. She wished her Papa and Mama had never brought her to the ceremony but wishing could not erase what had already come to pass. In the palace walls something dark hatched in the stomachs of hungry creatures growing small, ambitious tentacles, whispering to body organs at night. Adesua prayed and pleaded with the Gods, feeling like a small stone catapulted into a dense forest.

During the night before the wedding, after pre-celebrations had slowed to a close and the trees sunburnt leaves still trembled with the last notes of music, Oba Odion wound his way through the back routes of the palace. Benin was beautifully shrouded in a feverish orange glow, as if the lines of the buildings would shift beneath his touch and the copper birds on the turreted roofs had returned from secret journeys, pressing their newly inherited irises against a darkening skyline and lining the rooftops with small spoils visible only in a certain light.

Clutching an empty green bottle of palm wine, Oba Odion stumbled along, an almost comical figure. His large belly stuck out, he followed its rumblings, occasionally looking down, patting it affectionately. He could smell the palm wine on his own breath, could feel the looseness and lightness of his tongue, as though it would shoot out and keep the rooftop birds company, or trace a coming dawn with saliva before being swallowed by its pale mist.

Oba Odion raised the bottle to his lips, thinking of the new road to Benin he'd instructed his workers to start building. Not only would it lead to more trade for Benin but it meant labour for some of the people of the kingdom, who repeatedly came to the palace begging for scraps. Who knew what that road would bring to Benin's gates? Arching his neck, he spoke to the bottle. "Go and tell the world about Oba Odion! Tell them the wonders I can do!" He flung the bottle. It landed in a gnarly patch of shrubbery, neck jutting out, and ready to catch tiny silvery cracks winding their way towards it.

When the Oba arrived at Omotole's quarters she was naked, and voluptuous. He knelt before her in the warm dark room, reached for her waiting body. He traced the line of sweat snaking between her breasts greedily with the remnants of the wine from the mouth of the green bottle. He did not tell her about seeing her spread-eagled on that new road and that the copper palace rooftop birds had passed through her womb in a blurry blue light that rendered a person temporarily blind. Instead he stuck his face deep into the folds of Omotole's bountiful breasts and told his mind to quiet down. Meanwhile Adesua the new bride paced her quarters, unaware of the slow erosion eating through the virgin movements her silhouette shared or that bits of the red trail had found its way into the Oba's thrown bottle.

On her wedding day Adesua was struck by two things: that life would never be the same again and secondly, it would always be divided into sections: life before and life after the wedding. The day itself rolled in as if reluctant and with the pace of a snail. The palace roused with a gentle hum that turned into a buzz of activity on discovering Oba Odion had gone missing. Adesua heard the news through her personal servant, a young woman with tribal markings on her arms who stammered slightly. She bore a cut above her left eye and her small frame belied a sturdy strength of character.

Her name was Etabi and it was she who burst through the wide door of Adesua's living quarters as if a flame had been set on her backside. "Mistress! Mistress! The Oba is nowhere to be seen," she said, out of breath having run all the way from the servants building. There she had heard it from one of the noblemen's servants, who in turn had eavesdropped on his master's conversation with one of the councilmen and took it as his duty to spread it to any equally lowly person within the palace grounds.

On hearing this good news Adesua had to stop herself from jumping up and down. She smiled and it was wrapped in sunshine and nearly threw her arms around the servant as they went through the motions of dressing her for the day. Throughout she hoped this meant her predicament would change. She fantasised that the reality of having her as a new wife had troubled Oba Odion so much it had given him stomach ache and he was crumpled in a heap somewhere. Or that he was in a secret meeting with one of his advisers who was doing such a good job of persuading him to send her back home, that by the following day, she would be back in her village trying to outrun her shadow and making stupid bets with some of the elders. By the time she was fully dressed, Etabi fuelled by both instinct and excitement said "Mistress, this is the happiest I've seen you in days."

This happiness was fleeting because a few hours later, the king finally arrived for his wedding. Caught up in the excitement that ensued as for the whole palace, the moment they had all so long anticipated was finally here, they prepared to produce the most impressive wedding any of them had ever witnessed, for their Oba Odion. Adesua waited anxiously as Odion approached her. He was unsteady on his feet and rocked slightly from side to side and for the entire ceremony appeared as if impatient for it to be finished. His breath was wine-soaked and intoxicated words tripped off his tongue. Adesua felt her nails digging into her palms; it reminded her she was alive because throughout the wedding, it was as though she was not there but rather in the crowd of guests somewhere, watching a frightened young woman being dragged into what looked like a steep grave. She watched the unfamiliar faces surrounding them. She resented the pitiful glances that came so frequently. It was hard to miss Papa's nervous shuffle and Mama's wringing hands.

The celebrations went on for a while, till the sun and moon swapped greetings as the moon took charge of overseeing the proceedings. It shone over the courtiers who speculated on the Oba's whereabouts earlier in the day, and the tailors and craftsmen who marvelled at the coolness of the new bride whom they had all hoped would crumble a little to make the spectacle even more amusing.

Darkness wasn't just outside, it waited for Adesua in the king's chamber.

Under the force of his clammy body and his insistent tongue in her mouth, Adesua's innocence was taken.

She'd finally become a wife in the truest sense of the word.

After the deed was done the Oba relaxed on Adesua's chest, his own rising and falling in the satisfying comfort of a deep slumber while his snores slid off her cold shoulders and escaped through the ceiling into the night. With all her might Adesua shoved him off her grateful body and listened as he rolled over and fell to the floor. He did not get up and the only move she made was to turn her long frame to the opposite side. Meanwhile a tiny spider crawled onto her heart. It sat comfortably and arranged its slightly crooked legs. It sipped a little blood.

The next morning Adesua woke to an empty bedchamber. To the smell of stale sweat clinging to the air as if they were lovers too. The sound of unfamiliar voices loitering in the palace grounds gave her no comfort, instead it was a reminder that today was the beginning of a new life. She longed for her Mama and Papa and for the yesterday she once knew that was now napping in her village. She felt a throbbing at the juncture of her thighs and an ache that ran through to her stomach before pausing in her chest. She touched the inside of her left thigh and felt dried blood. She rubbed it hard, then harder, as if to wipe away the night before.

Oba Odion's face swam in the waters of her head, his full bottom lip dropped down and arms stretched out of his mouth like branches with open palms. She sat up and shook the vision away with the vigour of an angry father shaking a stubborn child. She counted her toes as if she didn't know how many she had. She stroked her smallest toe; it leaned against the other toe like an anxious sibling vying for support. She studied her feet, soft front hard back. Soft front hard back, she spoke the word out like a chant. These were the feet that had carried her through the yolk of childhood and into the bowels of adulthood, along a road that appeared to have no ending. And into a clearing of thorns disguised as eager smiles and forced jubilation. It had brought her here; where betrayal slapped you awake and waited patiently while you dressed. The voices outside grew louder. But outside could have been inside and inside outside because she was thinking of her feet, soft front hard back. She wanted to cut them off.

Once again Oba Odion went to his hiding place, between the soft folds of flesh of his Omotole. Whenever he laid his head to rest on her generous breasts, the howl of wild beasts could not drag him away. He forgot about rebellious villagers who needed to be made examples of and the nagging doubts of members of his council with selfish interests. He forgot about the invisible rope that hung around his neck daily.

Omotole was the daughter of a nobleman who had travelled to Benin in search of fortune and prosperity. He did not find prosperity but found fortune in the form of a bow-legged, light skinned beauty who thought after she spoke and was never really made for motherhood. She bore him five children and each time she gave birth a little part of her seemed to die. Omotole was her last born and the Oba believed she schemed her way out of her mother's womb. What she lacked in looks she more than made up for with her wily ways.

It was Omotole who had devised the plan to snare more villages outside Benin to increase the kingdom and Omotole who whispered the idea of a fresh bride to confuse the greedy noblemen who resided in the royal court. If Oba Odion had his wish, he would have dismissed some of the council and appointed Omotole as one of his official advisers. But a woman could not be given such a coveted position and a king could not be openly seen to do such things. Omotole was dutifully rewarded for her contribution; the Oba was affectionate and of all the eight brides, she resided in the most comfortable quarters in the Queens' palace, but to her, there was still more to be done and she knew that for her the Oba possessed an easily bent ear.

"Ah, tongues will be wagging that you have wickedly abandoned your new bride." She said, tucking her legs between the Oba's. They lay on a large leather mat that cushioned their bodies and their plans.

"Then let them wag, the girl should be grateful. Does she know how many young women would like to be the wife of a king?"

Omotole laughed coldly. "You should at least wait a few days before leaving her like that Odion, it is cruel and believe it or not, I sympathise a little."

"Silence!" Oba Odion stood abruptly and tightened the dropping cloth around his waist.

"I thought this was what you wanted?" He reminded her.

"Yes but you must at least play the dutiful husband for sometime, let things settle eh?"

"Who is the king of Benin, you or me?"

She moved towards him and wrapped her arms around his waist. "You are king, Oba of Benin and strong in your ways and will."

As she settled her ample frame into his, Oba Odion parsed a single thought and it was this: that he envied simple men, with their simple ways and trivial problems. Yet again that night he abandoned his new wife and stayed in Omotole's quarters. While they slept, the spirit of his father, Oba Anuje chuckled outside Omotole's door. And knocked. Twice.

Wahala Don Wear Shoe

The fall of a great kingdom did not always start with war. Sometimes, it took a vicious wish shrouded by the hot breath of a bitter woman, or rebellious words broken out of the mouths of ambitious councillors desirous to form their own army, perhaps even the good intentions of a craftsman, locked in an arm wrestle with the voice of a king's slain rival.

Ere was such a craftsman who had toiled in the service of Oba Odion for many years. He worked leather, clay, wood and brass. There was nothing his touch could not mould or caress into life and there was no royal emblem that Ere had not had a hand in since Oba Odion fought his way to rule over Benin. These included the crown, ritual swords, the throne, showpieces and art brass pieces he had created, to celebrate Benin and the power the Oba possessed. Oba Odion also had a wealth of weavers, carvers and potters who threw their backs into his biddings without the slightest hesitation. Ere did as he was told, how could he not? But despite being hailed as one of the finest craftsmen in the land, he was just a fleck of spit in the Oba's river until surprising circumstances delivered a new assignment.

Two weeks after the Oba married Adesua a golden nugget dropped into his lap and propped his back straighter. Some of his soldiers had captured Ogiso, a rival of Oba Odion who had been plotting the end of the Oba's reign and steadily gathering supporters in villages like Ego and others dotting the back end of Benin. Once upon a time Oba Odion and Ogiso had been boyhood friends. They had chased the same girls, run through the dirt tracks of unidentifiable animals and collapsed against each other many times under the influence of much food and drink at Igewhi festivals, the memories of which, as they grew older, weakened in their grips like a slippery rope. It pulled and they let go.

Eventually it became who could outperform the other and this created a litany of rivalries like tiny stones in Odion's eye. Ogiso did not know his place. One day they argued, worse than ever before. But this argument did not come from thin air. It had been sniffing at them for years, waiting for the scent of distrust and resentment to line their dealings the way soft silk lined the inside of a decadent outfit. Fuelled by anger and full of simmering resentments Ogiso left the kingdom but vowed to return one day to reclaim what he insisted was also rightfully his. He was warned to never return again.

Ogiso was found in the town of Epoma, amongst a plethora of like-minded bandits, caught in his bed, in that sweet induced state between being half asleep, half awake. They brought him to the palace in heavy, hard chains that cut into his wrist. Oba Odion fought with the burden that landed his way. He sought out his council for advice and they insisted Ogiso be tried; if found guilty, nothing less than death should be his punishment or the Oba would look like a weak king. Strangely, Ogiso did not plead for Oba Odion's mercy. He accepted his fate, switching between whistling merrily and laughing hysterically. Four days after he arrived at the palace he was tried, and found guilty of scheming to overthrow the king by every single member of the council. All fourteen of them.

Ogiso's last words were to insist Oba Odion have the courage to personally tell his mother what he had done to her son. Oba Odion did show a mercy of sorts; instead of being beheaded, Ogiso was hung. He was taken to a spot deep within the heart of a near forest.

When his neck snapped and his feet spasmed next to the trunk of a bewildered ebony tree, a crushing pain exploded in Ogiso's mother's head and shot all the way down to her toes at the same moment. After she was told the news of her son's death, she was unable to move the right side of her body. It was paralysed by despair and loss. From that day onwards until she passed, Ogiso's mother would slur from the far left corner of her mouth every morning the mantra that Oba Odion should receive a fate worse than his father before him. Her daily ritual was done, without fail.

Craftsman Ere was called to one of the king's chambers on an afternoon when the sun was intent on punishing the inhabitants of Benin. It was so hot that a person could be tempted to walk around naked had it not been for social etiquette. People were gulping pails of water as if Benin had turned into a desert overnight. Little children waded into the shallow ends of rivers to cool down and older ones splashed their faces enthusiastically. Ere met the Oba standing next to the wide square window that overlooked the main courtyard in the palace. There were intricately designed, plump, dark brown cushions on the floor. Throws in hues of amber, gold and maroon covered the circular, tall chairs made from the finest teak wood. A large, straw coloured mat trimmed with red beads lay on the ground. The high ceiling was golden and copper plaques showing old battles decorated the walls. The room had a subdued glow, as if it was waiting for a soldier from a plaque to come to life, pull the ceiling off and let it combust with light.

"Oba, you called for me?" Craftsman Ere said, bowing his head. Oba Odion faced him squarely, unlocking his hands from behind his upright back.

"I want you to make a brass head in Ogiso's likeness for my collection."

Craftsman Ere sprang back, startled. "Surely you cannot be serious Oba?"

The Oba's face crumpled, "Do I look like a jester? Explain yourself!"

"Oba, I know it is tradition to often make pieces in honour of your conquests but I think in this case you should make an exception."

The Oba stroked his chin as though it had suddenly grown a beard. "Why make an exception this time? Ogiso was an enemy, who showed no regret for his actions."

"Oba, he was your friend, and like a brother to you before."

Oba Odion raised his hand abruptly. "Have you forgotten who stands before you?"

"No Oba, I feel this is not right, my concern is for you. It is asking for trouble."

"Ere, I will be the judge of what or who is trouble. Never question my authority again, or you and your family will find yourselves thrown out of the palace. It is only because of the great work you've done that I am sparing you."

Craftsman Ere, being a man who knew when he was beaten, gave up and held his tongue from arguing any further.

"I expect this to be a wonderful example of your skill, Ere and remember as much in Ogiso's likeness as possible."

Craftsman Ere nodded and only the pulse in the side of his neck fluttered. It was his final sentence of protest.

The next day Craftsman Ere began to work on producing the brass head. He recalled every feature of Ogiso's. He set about sharpening his tools and choosing the best brass the palace stocked. First Ere made a wax model of Ogiso which was framed over a clay core. When he finished the model, he painstakingly applied the clay over the wax, almost tenderly, pausing now and again to admire the lines of the figure. Ere started to detail the dead warrior: the flared nose, wide forehead and tribal markings. He was so saddened by the death of this man, he barely realised he'd made a small tear of betrayal at the corner of the model's eye.

That night, the tear fell then evaporated into the air. The next day, the children of the kingdom began to change. Filled with an overwhelming sadness, they ran to the rivers' edges crying quietly into the waters. They gathered around trees holding long, dark cloths, circling the trunks and communicating in a silent language only they understood. They clustered at the palace windows grabbing and squeezing their throats violently, feet jerking uncontrollably while they tried to be still. For four nights, the children did not sleep. They wandered the kingdom with bloodshot eyes cloaked in a heavy, melancholy silence. At night they sat in the king's garden, crying into the soil. When their mothers found them, they removed tiny brass tears from the corners of their eyes. They held their children's brass tears over fires, watching them melt into the lines of their palms.

For the next stage, Ere proceeded to heat, then melt Ogiso's model, pouring it into a mould. Later, after the clay hardened, he began to chip and cast the image. When the brass head was finished, the children became themselves again, though there was no ceremony to honour the completion, no celebration of the return of the children's laughter, no music that ignited the switch of hips no thunderous applause. Instead it was presented on an evening when a hushed silence fell on Benin. And the clouds coughed raindrops that dampened not just the land but the spirit of people.

Once the rain passed Benin looked like a kingdom that had risen from under water and was drying itself off. Craftsman Ere had worked long hours to ensure the head was finished on time. He had joked with his wife that you could fill a large metal bowl with the amount of sweat he had produced over this task. Ere was convinced he had been watched. There was no proof of this except there was occasionally a whoosh of air that threw dust in the doorway of his workroom followed by the sound of rapid steps in the distance. When he had relayed these fears to his wife, she promptly squashed them with a lashing from her mouth, and warned him not to embarrass their family with tales based on hot air.

When Oba Odion finally first saw the brass head, he studied it hard for so long without a word that Craftsman Ere was forced to ask, "Oba is it to your satisfaction?" The Oba touched it tentatively, as if afraid his hand would be snapped off.

"It is too much like Ogiso, as if he is standing here before me!"

Craftsman Ere shifted his weight from one leg to the other along with his patience. "But Oba, that is what you asked me to do. I did as you instructed."

"I did as you instructed," Oba mimicked him. "Don't you have a mind of your own? 'In his likeness' does not mean I want it in his exact image."

Craftsman Ere gritted his teeth; a braver man would have slapped the Oba. He saw himself doing so in his head, a slap for every day he had spent producing this artefact now met with scorn. Instead he said, "Oba what would you have me do? Surely you cannot expect me to make another one?"

"No, you will not have to make another head," Oba Odion said, but it sounded hollow, as if the words were coming from far away and not him.

"Besides," he added, "I am now sick of the sight of you Ere."

"I only did my best Oba, after all, this was what you asked for," Craftsman Ere grumbled, feeling deeply insulted that the Oba had not complimented his skill and hard work. Stupid king! Just then a fly swept in encouraged by the heat and noise. It buzzed around perusing the Oba's chamber as if deciding if it was good enough to languish in. It finally settled on a tiny crack in the wall that looked like it was a scar healing.

"Will it be displayed with the other pieces Oba?" He watched as Oba Odion tried to kill the fly and failed. It laughed at him before rising to the ceiling for a celebratory jig.

"I have not decided where it will go yet, when I have Ere you will know."

"Thank you Oba."

"You can go."

"Yes Oba," he said, bowing again on his way out.

Oba Odion thought long and hard about what to do with the brass head. He admitted the truth to himself only, which was that Craftsman Ere had been right, the brass head had an unsettling power about it. It was a little disturbing to see it finished, as if it would come to life the minute he turned his back. At night, he began to sweat thinking of the head. His heart rate increased whenever he passed it, a feeling of suffocation overtook his body. He couldn't breathe looking at it. Oba Odion gave the brass head to Adesua and lied to her that it was in honour of their marriage, although this had never been the case by an Oba. She accepted it gratefully and when he handed it to her, it was the first time he had seen her smile in days, as if it had slipped from someone's face and fallen onto hers. Word spread around the palace that the Oba was showing favour to his new young bride and upon hearing this the other wives seethed like boiling pots.

Deep in a forest another body dangled from a tired tree. Dead for months, it too had sweltered in the heat. Oozing a rotten stench that stirred sated barks and crinkled the faces of leaves, stinging bush wilted and poisonous nettle shuddered, as the toes of the hanging frame trembled one last time, Ogiso left his body at last to find a new home.

Vicarious through Fuchsia

I threw on clothes and hopped on a few trains to Harlesden, to Williams and Co. Solicitors. The scent of curry goat and hot rotis wafting from the Caribbean takeaway meant I didn't have to glance at the clock to know it was nearly lunchtime. Inside the building, Pauline the gatekeeper was typing swiftly on her PC and barking orders into a telephone handset. She winked before waving me through with a wiggle of her multi-tasking fingers. Mervyn was at the fax machine yanking documents out and scrunching them into paper missiles before flinging them into a wastebasket.

"Hey," I mumbled in greeting.

He turned to face me. "Go inside nuh."

On his desk, a mug of steaming coffee rested dangerously near the edge. An atlas sat right next to a new photograph of Mervyn and his two sons in a boat in Jamaica. They were holding large crabs that looked as though they'd crawl over their heads and eat their expressions. Big smiles were plastered on their faces. Behind them the water was like a big, rippling blue sky.

I studied his extensive library; *Fly Fishing for Beginners* and *How Not to Kill Your Wife on Holiday* held my attention among the heavy bound volumes of Law. He walked in whistling, more papers tucked under his left arm and clutching a bag of sweets in his right hand. He dumped them unceremoniously on the desk.

"So wha'appen, answering machine brok' up again?" He pointed to the bag and I popped a chewy cola bottle in my mouth.

"Naw, I hardly check it."

"You've come for the diary," he said.

"How did you know that?"

"Because I know you." He stroked a finger over his lip and took a quick sip of coffee.

"You haven't read it have you?" I leaned forward in the chair watching for any deceptive body language.

"Nope, I'll admit I'm curious though."

"I don't know why my mother didn't give it to me years ago."

"Me neither but about three months before she died she came to see me."

"So?"

"Well she was behaving odd like, agitated."

"Did she say why?"

"Nah man, I told her to chill out, she was still young with plenty of time but she was insistent about the will, so I obliged."

He jangled some keys in his trousers before using it to unlock the bottom drawer. Took out the worn, black leather bound book and handed it over.

"Thanks." It felt warm against my hand and I bent to rest my ear on the cover as if it would speak. I plunged my finger in, flicked to a random page.

I said, "I wonder what a handwriting expert could tell me about him from this?"

"Somehow I don't think you'll need that," he replied, stuffing three cola bottles in his mouth.

Throughout most of the train journey back I clutched the journal tightly. It looked remarkably ordinary and was light to carry with a slightly stale smell. Besides some thumb indentations it was still in good condition. At some point I noticed the name Peter Lowon scrawled haphazardly inside the cover and the date beside the name read 1950. A black and white photograph slipped out. In it three black men wearing army uniforms sat around a tiny wooden table filled with beer bottles. A curvy woman sat in the lap of one man who appeared to be laughing at something the man opposite him was doing. It was the third gentleman who caught my attention. He was sat slightly apart from the others. There was a handkerchief tucked in his breast pocket. He watched the other two with an expression that can only be described as disdainful. I flipped the photograph over and printed on the back was Ijoma's bar, Lagos. I thought about starting to read the journal on the District line from Mile End but when an arguing couple stepped inside my carriage, it was a reminder to save my reading for another time. I played with the idea of who these men were. How they were linked to my mother, if at all. When I got to my final stop, I let out a sigh of relief and felt deflated as if my body was a deployed airbag.

Chewing Sticks

A near-sated Benin now gorged on fat sunrays producing warm belches of air-spun dust that tethered to the tips of body hairs and coated the fingernails of its inhabitants. Adesua stood on the brink of being a little pleased. A sweeter alternative place to the misery she had experienced, not full happiness but a small portion she could be persuaded to dive into. This was because the Oba had handed over a peace offering that chipped somewhat at her newly erected barricade of a hard heart.

Adesua had never seen anything like the brass head. It was so beautiful and so well polished that had it been possible to see her reflection in it, she would have found that an interference and attempted to wipe her image away just to continue admiring it. The proud expression captured on its face was disturbingly life-like and inspired the viewer to want to stand to attention. Adesua felt the sculpted face was the face of a true king, but of course did not say this to the Oba. Instead, she genuflected gracefully and thanked him for his consideration.

Oba Odion in return forgetting his motivation for disposing of the object preened at her obvious pleasure. She was certain if he could have patted himself on the back he would have. He made a show of slapping his chest and announcing to her, let nobody say the Oba neglected his wives. He was so loud she was sure even the servants who kept their ears hovering near the ground at all times had already heard and digested the news and by the next day, would have repeated it to each other amidst their morning tasks while swapping complaints and gnawing on chewing sticks. Adesua did not complain when the Oba insisted he had court matters to see to, she caught the look of relief on his face, although, even that did not detract from the new prize in her possession.

Oba Odion had eight wives. Eight wives who lined their chambers every morning like the curious bottles of perfume a Portuguese ally had brought for him several seasons ago. Eight lives he attempted to delicately shelter depending on his mood. His platoon of women were there to bear his children and prop up his pride even when their hands were bruised and left wanting. Of course the Oba did not love all of his wives. This was a task he was convinced most men would fail at even if they tried, so he did not pretend to try. Sometimes he imagined himself cut into eight slices served on a different platter for each wife to swallow. They were an unlikely bunch, each one different to the next, like colourful seashells thrown into a sandpit of the palace rather than coughed up freely on the banks of the sea.

Omotole was his third and favourite wife and the smartest of all, with dark beady eyes that pulled you into their depths. His fourth wife Ekere was always sickly and each season the palace fretted whether she would see the beginning of the next. She had an angular jutting face and looked like thin brown skin poured over walking bones. At night she clutched her youngest child to her side as if she would draw strength from his soft smooth fleshed youth. Filo the fifth wife wore her sadness on her wrists like haphazard bracelets that wounded her skin. Her womb had apologetically born three dead babies, and on days when the air was thick with disdain for all who resided in the royal enclave, she could be found wandering the grounds harassing whoever she encountered to return her children. When the Oba had important guests visiting, she was kept hidden as if she were dirt sullying the Oba's name.

The sixth wife Remitan was known to stretch the truth as though it was a large ball of string. Most people in the palace believed every other word she uttered was a lie. Her hair was the envy of many. Full and long, it was the colour of a raven's wing; it spiralled down her back in a tumbling curly mass. Sometimes she would be spotted leaning against the palace walls and joked that it was the weight of carrying so much good hair that caused her to pause for breath. The seventh wife Ono was feisty and held the moral heart of the group. The first two wives Kemi and Ore were busy bodies. They were opposite in every way except for their love of rumours and gossiping with each other.

Then there was Adesua.

The Oba's marital life ran as well as it could, most of the time. But now that a new bride had arrived a sense of unease among the women crept in and widened the holes that were already becoming apparent. The Oba had added further insult by giving the brass head to Adesua, a bush village girl who did not appear to recognise her luck. Wonders would never cease! The other wives knew the palace was privately laughing at them, sneering as their stupid loyalty had only turned around to hold a dagger to their backs. Tempers and resentment bloomed like water lilies stuck in the slopy underside of their breasts.

It was the seventh wife Ono who first openly voiced her dis-approval of the Oba's actions with Adesua to Omotole. They two banded together, not out of genuine friendship and loyalty, but rather a tarnished, copper-tinged 'safety in numbers.' They watched each other through heavy-lidded pretend collusion, putting on their masks of camaraderie and mutual interests, only to rip them off as soon as the other walked away. That day Ono and Omotole strolled together through one of the palace hallways, a lengthy teak-hued seemingly never-ending stretch, with decadent rooms curving off into lofty spaces. As they talked their breaths were laced with sour spirits and jealousy.

"Oba is making us look foolish, giving Adesua such a gift! A brass head! Does she even know what it is?" And when was the last time any of us received such a thing? Nonsense," Ono whined, refusing to leave anger behind. Omotole scratched the stems of connecting green veins that rose to the surface of her skin as if Ono's voice had irked them into motion. The scratch reassured them and they flattened down slowly.

"Be calm Ono, remember she is fresh to the palace and the Oba is only doing his duty by welcoming her. Still, I was not given such a welcome."

"You see!" Ono screeched smacking her thigh for effect. "Even you, and we all know the Oba thinks highly of you." A smattering of light gathered at their feet before breaking up to plunder more interesting things.

"All I'm saying is she has to learn her place, not cheat and jump to the front of the line. She is a lot cleverer than we gave her credit for. Before you know it Oba will be giving her even more consideration than the rest of us." A pair of panicked wings fluttered. Omotole stroked the tender lobe of her ear and the snakeskin amulet just beneath.

If the truth was told, and the palace crier told it with slight reservations to his wife, all was not well in the palace. On appearances, things ran well but underneath, tiny cracks were beginning to appear. Oba Odion had debts, owed to white men from foreign lands and they did not loiter when it came to collecting what was due to them. Hearsay circulated that the Oba may have to sell some of his land or indeed some of his people. Even if they were just prisoners whose captured lives had been reduced to the worth of animals, the rumours both terrified and soothed the courtiers. Councilmen were seen coming out of meetings with the Oba wearing worried expressions. Palace officials hung around their superiors subtly to catch coded sentences. And the cooks were ordered to watch rations carefully, though all meals for the Oba were still to be of the highest standard.

In the north of Benin there was spreading unrest; increasingly dissatisfied with the Oba's rule, people were claiming that the palace got richer while some of the Oba's people starved, yet fees for inhabiting land were still being collected. Oba Odion was robbing broken people. These people wanted to put their cases forward, take their legs, hollow with disappointment, all the way to the palace gates to complain. But they knew what awaited them was a punishment more severe than they already suffered. Some of the Oba's army were dispatched on palace grounds poised to attack at the first sign of trouble. They were strong and lean and wore hammered shields that hugged their upper bodies so closely the men appeared to be made of metal. They carried long, well-sculpted wooden staffs with angular tips. Their eyes roamed not just about the palace and its flock of odd people but over it, as though they were waiting for something way beyond the palace and its high gates.

It was inevitable that Filo, the Oba's fifth wife would develop an unusual interest in Adesua. The novelty of becoming the king's fifth wife had long gone; the shine dulled by the harsh reality of life as just another piece in the Oba's collection of wives. Filo liked new things; when things were new for a brief moment in time they possessed an air of invincibility, of endless possibilities. This was how she saw Adesua, like soft new skin before it started to leather and toughen. Filo studied her discreetly, as though she were a rare butterfly and saw the way Adesua hummed to herself with innocent abandon. How she practiced unusual hunter-like stances she must have imitated from her father or the other men from her village, crouching down low on her haunches as if ready to pounce on any living, breathing thing should there be a need to.

She watched Adesua walking through the palace with an expression of barely concealed boredom. It was clear that becoming a king's wife was not the exciting life this unusual young woman had envisioned for herself. Filo admired her for her gumption, which she allowed to bubble through to the surface. She knew how it was to feel out of place. She understood. She too was walking around with a big hole inside her. She knew the others could see it because they winced when she stood before them, as if it wasn't only her words that caused offence but her very presence. The other wives were uncomfortable near her, their silences told her this loudly.

These were the thoughts swimming in her mind when Filo sneaked into Adesua's chamber, drawn mainly by the sweet energy of the king's new wife and the fact that she seemed as out of place as Filo herself felt. She had not really intended to take anything, but once inside her eyes alighted on the brass head and it seemed to call to her. Once she had seen it, she could not un-see it. She picked it up and touched it tentatively at first before boldly rubbing her hands on it. It seemed to know her sorrow, to offer itself as her saviour. It was difficult to keep thinking of ways to fill a hole that was too big for your chest. She decided then that if she were caught she would tell the truth.

In another corner of the palace, a gift lay in wait for Oba Odion. He had discovered white oval seeds with cracked edges and a soft centre that throbbed strewn over the floor of his private room. People were questioned but the Oba never found the guilty party. He did not throw the seeds away either, instead, he called for some of the most experienced farmers in Benin to study them. Nobody knew what sort of seeds they were, where they had come from or what they would grow into. Intrigued, the Oba offered a reasonable reward to the farmer who was willing to grow them. Several accepted but nothing happened. It was as though the seeds they buried were dead. Finally Oba Odion instructed that they be planted in the palace garden. Soon, the soil began to rumble. Small blue bulbs popped their eager heads out, simmering while they gulped on leftover dew and tiny embers of dissent.

Queenie, London 1970

At Victoria station the train screeched to a halt, jerking Queenie back in her seat. She paused momentarily to catch her breath, then stood, wide-eyed and excited. She'd just turned twenty and had promised herself on her eighteenth birthday that by the age of twenty she'd be in London. She wanted to reach back in time and pinch her eighteen-year-old self. Instead, she pressed her face closer to the slightly dusty, finger-printed window on her right, swallowing the sights of people milling about. *Aah ah!*

She'd never seen so many white people. They dispersed like rats into every direction wearing long winter coats, dark colours and guarded expressions. Their eyes looked like pieces of pale sky and their even paler skin seemed thin and fragile. Of course she'd seen white people back home in Lagos. There were the white business-men her father had entertained in their beautiful, old house. And most of the nuns at Our Lady of Lourdes secondary school were white. Sister Wilhelmina who had a perpetually grey tinge to her skin had a fondness for telling her, "Queenie, you have the disposition of a cockroach! Why are you always where you're not supposed to be?" And she'd smile back as though she'd been paid a compliment. "Thank you Sister, cockroaches are great survivors." And Sister Wilhelmina would reply, "Not if you have the correct insecticide." But secretly, despite her severe nun's outfit, she was charmed. She'd shake her head at Queenie and smile.

Queenie grabbed her medium-sized black suitcase and two out-sized red checked bags, and waited behind a small group of people. She followed them out of the carriage, marvelling at the smoothness and ease of her journey so far. Even eating on the train had been an experience. They didn't have transport like this back home. Uniformed stewards pushing trolleys containing sandwiches, chocolates, bottled water and doughnuts amongst other things approached and asked if you wanted a drink. Queenie had longed to try the Queen of England's tea! She'd ordered a cup and drank it daintily, imagining her girlfriends from home gathered around her, *ooohing* and *aaahing* at the sophisticated way she sipped, saying very loudly, "Nah wah oh! You have truly come a looong way!"

Queenie dragged her bags along, imagining British angels filling her pockets with pound sterling! She was so lost in her reverie she nearly bumped into another one of those uniformed station guards. This one had a whistle in his mouth and held his hand up to signal her to stop.

"Watch your step dear," he said, eyeing her as though she was an imbecile. "The way out is through the barriers and then down to your right."

"Thank you," she said, intrigued by the man's accent, which wasn't like the Queen of England accents she'd heard on TV. It was rougher. She grabbed her bags tighter, encouraged by the mass of people heading every which way. There was no ambling along or lazy steps, the cold didn't allow for it. Instead she noticed they all moved with a sense of urgency. People weren't talking in a leisurely manner either; she caught bits of conversations that were functional, efficient.

"Zip that coat Tommy, I won't tell you again!" a woman ordered.

"Mum!"

"I mean it, if you get ill; don't expect me to waste my time sitting at the GP."

The mother tugged at the lapels of her woolly, black coat where a red, lizard-shaped brooch was pinned and marched ahead, her son, a boy of about seven in an ill-fitting navy jacket running fast to catch her.

Queenie's stomach rumbled. She noticed a few shops lined the edges around the station. They had brightly coloured signs that read Manny's Pie & Mash Shop, Beggar's Feast and Longjohn's Café where thick-crusted sandwiches heavy with slices of cold meats were arranged in small pyramids in the window. A smoky, meaty smell clung to the air. What she wouldn't do for some rice and stew with fried plantain!

It could have been the thought of eating such comfort food alone but suddenly she felt fear inside her. She knew nobody in England. She didn't even know where she would stay. What she'd done was either very stupid or very brave. She'd followed the lure of a man's laughter that every time she attempted to turn back had reclaimed her heart and mind. The sound of rushing traffic ricocheted around her. The air was crisp and when people spoke their breaths turned white as though they were blowing smoke out of their mouths. Queenie trembled, struggling to adapt to the cold. In the distance a siren wailed as though it was giving birth. She was fascinated by the enormous, red double decker buses rumbling through the streets bearing oddly named destinations; Oxford Circus! Peckham Rye! Southwark! They were completely unlike the yellow, dust-covered buses back home where the jumbled in bodies were sweaty coins in heat.

Her destination, St Michael's hostel in Borough, was a squat, nondescript building tucked beneath a short flight of concrete steps covered sparingly with moss. If you blinked you'd miss it. The door had a large, black lion knocker and a dirty white buzzer was positioned roughly at eye level to the left of the entrance. Queenie had circled the same street at least four times before finding it. She'd asked the Indian shopkeeper who ran the corner shop with a fading green sign that read *Ali's Market Place* and at the hairdresser's where a white woman blankly looked her up and down. *This London nah wah oh!*

She hadn't known what to expect but Queenie found the houses disappointing. They weren't like the sprawling, brightly coloured houses back home in places like Festac, Ikeja or Victoria Island where grasshoppers fed on invisible lines of heat and sweat formed on tall iron gates and the foreheads of lazy mayguards dressed in white vests with chewing sticks dangling from the corners of their mouths. Here, the houses all seemed to share the same glum expression, all squashed together and small. She wondered what the people did when they threw parties. Maybe they just had them spilling out into the streets, threading between lampposts and captured on car windscreens.

When Queenie pressed the dirty buzzer, the male voice that said, "Come in," was distorted by static. He spoke again but she couldn't make out the words since it broke up and only a hissing sound filtered through. Instinctively she pushed at the wooden door. It opened. By now her earlier excitement had worn thin and tiredness had set in. She patted her right linen trouser pocket for the reassuring feel of her newly exchanged pound notes then began walking down another flight of stairs, admonishing the tiredness in her limbs. The building was an extension to St Michael's church, more modern than its Gothic host, but hints of likeness could be found in the high ceilings and the large stained glass windows.

Queenie arrived in an orange coloured hallway where a large grandfather clock stood and a water fountain littered with coins glistened. *In Nigeria that money would have been gone!* A vase filled with blue flowers sat on top of a dark wooden display cabinet filled with china. A large notice board on the wall had sheets of different coloured leaflets pinned on it. Dragging her bags she veered to the right where she met another flight of stairs at the bottom of which was a painting of a woman planting in her garden. The burnished orange light within it with hints of red permeating its glow reminded her of the late afternoon sunlight back home and seemed to set her mind at ease.

Behind the reception desk, the guy wore a bored expression. His lank, greasy brown hair pulled into a ponytail. A scar marred his left brow and his black t-shirt was decorated with skulls. A tattoo on his neck looked like the roots of a tree. She regarded him curiously, imagining him watering those roots with beer. He was definitely not like the white businessmen she'd seen at home, in their pristine shirts with their sleeves rolled up. She paid for two nights up front, exactly £25. The crisp notes felt alien in her hands.

"So where are you from?" he asked in an attempt to make conversation. "You've come to find your fortune? An age old tale."

She rubbed the copper room key. "I don't know about fortune mister but to come to England is a big thing."

He laughed, threw a couple of peanuts from a bowl on the desk into his mouth. "Good luck, prepare yourself for miserable weather and a frosty welcome but you should know in advance not everybody will be like that."

She shrugged, mind and body already in the bed that awaited her. "Thank you for the advice, oracle."

His mouth twitched at her humour. "Hey, it's free. Come to Oracle Jay any time, always happy to lend a helping hand and other parts of my body to very attractive damsels in distress. Let me know if you have any problems with the room."

Queenie nodded, lugged her bags ahead. Her mother's voice rang in her head.

I hope you know what you're doing; a pipe dream can be just that under the right angle of light.

Random

Over the next few days, I thought about my mother dying suddenly in her living room, the TV blaring, the open basement door revealing its stale breath: no history of pre-existing medical conditions. Leaving behind on an island, one daughter who flaps her right arm like a broken wing. It had rained heavily, the echoes of something drowning bounced off the windowpanes. Spiders made of water crawled on my skin. I kept the key that became a finger in my bottom bedroom drawer, next to a copy of Yan Martel's *The Life of Pi*. I was worried it would morph into a whole body if it somehow accidentally caught its own reflection. I left the diary on top of the chest of drawers and the brass head in my rucksack, not quite comfortable with displaying it yet. I was superstitious about things you brought home and what they carried with them. I had no idea why my mother had left me these gifts. A brass head I'd never seen, the diary of a grandfather I'd never met. I didn't even know if he was alive or dead. Did she want me to find him? To give the diary back? Then there were the properties I never knew she'd owned. It was odd she didn't mention any of this to her only child. There had been her phone calls back home, muted conversations with my grandmother, her mouth curling anxiously. Maybe dead people left behind puzzles for their loved ones all the time.

During the next few days I began a project for Void magazine on street style. The premise was simple, trudging around London I'd shoot people whose striking style caught my eye and ask where they drew inspiration from. Fashion as an extension of creative expression; that kind of angle. I walked around the streets of Dalston with newly migrated hipsters. I liked the art venues showcasing unknown artists whose work was sometimes terrifying, and sometimes made me gasp and I loved the big old art deco façade of the Rio cinema. I shot dandies in skintight trousers, brightly patterned shirts and fedora hats. In Camden, I captured punk chicks wearing ripped denim, orange hair, studded leather jackets and chokers. The goths came out to play, dressed in faux misery and doom. Goth girls boasted slashes of black lipstick and shredded, rebellious expressions.

Brick Lane was full of the annoyingly, arty, cool young crowd. Too many students with overly contrived senses of style ran the gauntlet of the curry houses, where exotic looking men badgered and smouldered, begging you to eat at whichever outlet they happened to represent that day. I snapped pretty, thin girls in vintage dresses, girls in men's blazers, quirky t-shirts and penny loafer shoes sporting wispy hair styles; girls who teamed boyfriend jeans with loud, 80s tops. I shot tattoo addicts brandishing intricate designs that shimmered and became multi-limbed black creatures on pavements. I took a picture of a handsome red-headed guy who carried his guitar like a lover and a broad faced gypsy woman with flat features. She had a multi-coloured shawl draped over her shoulders, sold tiny, dead flowers and didn't seem to care. She shoved them in your face as if they were good interruptions.

Over two days I developed the photos and noticed a strange infiltration. The young woman I'd chased in Harlesden appeared in the background of some shots. I recognised the flurry of her long limbs, her rich dark skin and angular face. She was flicking a coin up behind a picture of a bald woman with a stud in her tongue like a small, silver nipple. Next to the dread-headed African man who sat by his stall in Dalston wearing an orange Fela Kuti shirt, she was naked but adorned in heavy, pink traditional jewellery. There were white markings on her face, a blackboard on which past and present were rewritten. Behind the blank-faced gypsy woman selling dead flowers in Brick Lane, she held the flowers and they were alive, becoming purple flames in her grasp. She looked directly at the camera, at me, as somebody on the fringes getting closer.

On Friday night I broke my sometime habit of watching film noir while slowly sipping Irish cream absorbed in the moody world of dark vices, intrigue and tortured loves. In one of my favourites Bogart and Bacall's razor-sharp dialogue exchange and electric chemistry entirely transported me. I missed my days as a student, smoking weed, sitting cross-legged writing song lyrics and strumming my guitar, singing folk songs and stealing looks at inanimate objects as if they'd give feedback.

I'd checked TV listings earlier and Spike Lee's *She's Gotta Have It* would be coming on Channel 4 at 1am. It annoyed me that channels usually showed black interest films late into the night when nobody could watch them. I fought sleep, entering the hazy space between sleep and wakefulness. I spotted a stray feather from my pillow, grabbed it. I heard the hum of traffic from outside and cars running over conversations that limped into the night. By this time of night the foxes would be rummaging, the glow from their eyes rivalling the street lamps while they sent ahead prowls to cover more ground. I saw the woman walking through the photos, swapping backgrounds and settings as if it were a game, armed with the wits she'd honed in travel and the wet second tongue she used to pick locks and change the lines of things. I saw her reduced to a small, jagged entity in the corners of pictures, and the early arrival of wear and tear lines creating a white silence over her mouth.

At 1am I was still up and headed to my room. The "blue den" I called it. My crappy, old Alba TV had no antenna so I fashioned one using a hanger. It still produced semi-decent pictures. I'd left the window open earlier and the scent of smoke teased my nostrils. I went to close it and looked into my garden and those of some neighbours. In her garden, Mrs Harris stood over a short mountain of fire, a cigarette wedged in the corner of her mouth. Some of her hair was upright in white tufts. She was having a clear out, burning what looked like documents. Smoke twisted into the sky. I retreated back to avoid being spotted. For a few minutes, I watched flames lick and curl piles of paper in illicit, final kisses.

Cunning Man Die,
Cunning Man Bury Am

Half a season passed. The Festival of Yam came and the Oba was bombarded with the best the farmers of Benin had produced that year. The unusual seeds they had planted in the palace garden bloomed into flowers with blue stained petals that covered the ground. The wives continued to bicker amongst themselves. And whenever Oba Odion came to visit Adesua in her chamber he remained uncomfortable, shooting ill-at-ease glances at the brass head as if it would attack like an enemy. The brass head however had seen the slow blossoming of Adesua. It had noticed her desires seeping through her skin, her need for adventure, her longing to hunt. Sometimes in the evening when the hum of Benin settled to a gentle murmur Adesua liked to wander, beginning at the forest, behind the blue garden and onto the weathered pathway that led to the Queens' palace.

Then a worrying thing began to happen; Adesua would wake in the mornings to find the brass head rattling on the mantle. The first time it occurred she dismissed it, walked to its place and steadied it. But it continued like that over a few mornings as though shaking with anger. She reported it to the Oba who in turn told her she had an overactive imagination and wasn't it time she adjusted properly?

Instead of creating tales about a gift he was kind enough to give her, he warned her to learn from the other wives or she would lose his favour. It was not long before the Oba began to avoid coming to her quarters. She would see him walking out of Esezele's door, rushing to Omotole or Ono's chambers. Adesua struggled to know how to feel about the Oba's rejection of her but there was small comfort in one thing. Filo was ignored too, and Adesua did not believe it was only because Filo had been unlucky during childbirth. There was a strange quality to Filo, pain so strong a pungent aroma emanated off her skin. You looked into her eyes and saw the shadow of things you couldn't put a name to as she flitted about the kingdom injured but still breathing. In a way, this made Adesua warm to her.

It was a funny thing when a powerful man had more than one wife because the posturing never stopped. It increased even more when an opportunity for one to outshine the other arrived. Such a chance presented itself when the Oba suddenly became sick. His body burned with fever and he couldn't hold food or water down. His stomach shrunk and his eyes sunk deeper into his head. He became bed-ridden and his medicine man was called upon to provide a concoction of healing herbs. The wives pounced, fussing over the Oba as if the illness was chronic. His fourth wife Ekere refused to leave his bedside for the first two nights till his sixth wife Remitan came and pushed her out, saying that the last thing a sick king needed was to be cared for by a wife struggling for good health who would only infect him with her feeble disposition. Ekere said that the last thing the Oba needed was a lying wife who would reassure him he would survive even if he were drawing his last breath. They bustled in and out, and continued to swap turns keeping vigils by his side. Remitan left and was replaced by Yewande who was shoved aside by Esezele, the oldest and first wife.

Omotole did not hurry to him immediately. She waited for him to improve, letting news of his progress filter through to her from the others before she deemed it safe enough to see him. After all, what use was a sick husband to her? And even the Oba noticed this

despite his sorry state. Weak and scared he reached out a hand to her
in relief as she had finally arrived to his aid, wiping his mouth and
posturing the movements of a dutiful wife.

"What is the meaning of you only coming to see me now?" he
asked.

"Oba, you know I'm not the first wife, so I have to give her respect
as the eldest and wait till she saw you before coming. How would
it look if I had openly ignored her position? I know you care about
appearances." She grabbed his hand and he said, "Omotole you are
right, you are always right my dear." She stayed there mopping his
brow and cooing over his feverish body while confirming in her
mind she was still at the forefront of his heart and desires.

Gifts

Gifts began to appear in my flat. I found a broken, pink beaded bracelet under my pillow. I kept it in my bedroom top drawer. On the kitchen counter an overly ripe plantain lay blackening, an audience of flies buzzing erratically about it. The bedroom mirror showed long, tapered handprints I didn't recognise. A green fluffy towel in my bathroom was wet from having been handled. In the toilet, tiny drops of blood ran down the white bowl. I felt uneasy seeing these things, anxious. I ran to the bedroom to check my belongings and there was blood inside my trainers, in the heel area. I inspected my feet for cuts and bites I may have missed but there was nothing.

I padded back to the bathroom, flushed the blood down the toilet, and brushed my teeth. I glared at my reflection in the mirror in case she may have seen something but she only looked back at me wearing a perplexed expression. I pressed play on my answering machine and listened to messages reel off. There was one from Mervyn asking me to call back to check in. His deep voice filled the room, even from a machine. Another message came from Robinson Way debt collectors about an HSBC loan I'd been dodging paying back for years. A feeling of sickness crept up my throat.

In the kitchen I stuck my face under the tap, ran cold water to cool down. On the fridge a couple of holiday snaps from a trip to Greece tucked between stuck bottle tops blinked at me. I noticed that I was missing from some of my pictures: the shot of me in a seafood restaurant next to large tanks of lobsters that threatened to smash through the glass and perch on tables. Another in the city square surrounded by brightly coloured sugar cube shaped houses with a large, grey fountain and birds swooping down to feed on light. On the boat after a day of island hopping, being helped off by a man holding a bottle of water, one by the old town wall where I'd popped my head through an opening. Only my head had disappeared and the opening was filled with a blurred, bright light.

I hadn't been sleeping very well for a while, staying up late and I didn't even know why. My nerves were frayed and my body clock had washed down the bath plughole; upright with its eyes open. My Doctor prescribed anti-depressants and anti-anxiety medication but I wasn't sure they were doing much. I always swallowed the white tablets with trepidation. Looking like pit stops on my tongue, I sometimes saw tiny versions of myself resting on them to catch their breath. When I couldn't sleep I watched films late into the night, surfed the net or cut out pictures from magazines to create odd random images on my collage board. A man entering a shark's mouth, a baby's head growing on a cactus, a dirty angel flying out of a fan.

The notion of an uninvited guest lingered. In my mind's eye I saw her at the flower stall, in the photographs I'd taken. She appeared to be doing her long-limbed dance from a distance but each time she and the dance drew closer.

Queenie London 1970:
London Nah Wah

After two months in England Queenie still hadn't fully adapted. She missed her mother's marauding smile. She caught it circling the sink taps in her room or hovering near cracks on the white ceiling. Sometimes it was the last thing she saw before falling asleep. She missed the sight of lone street vendors on hot tarmac roads, selling spicy rice and stew on broad, green leaves and warm balls of greasy *akara*. She longed for raucous house parties where there was always somebody new to meet. And the pleasure of bodies dancing so close you could smell intentions mingled with sweat.

She missed the markets. She often recalled the endless chatter and the lingering rich scents of fresh fish, sweet ripening fruits, people's strong, healthy bodies. Markets in London were not the haggling, bustling markets of back home. Lagos markets fed off the heat. They were animals in their own right, with the heads being the upper halves of traders mid-custom and the tail-ends the backs of customers walking to stalls. Queenie now carried the unfamiliar sensation of the cold in her bones. It even changed her walk, instead of the practiced sashay she'd unleashed in Nigeria drawing admiring glances; she now walked hurriedly, body tucked in and braced with the cruel cold climate perpetually at her heels.

At times at night her room got damp, making her fear of catching flu very real. Mice had gnawed their way through floorboards making holes in her underwear the weight of a yawn. They screeched at each other in an abrasive language and repeatedly flew across the table as if they planned to topple it. In retaliation, Queenie threw anything she could grab quickly at the moving targets of sound. Usually weapons that had no impact: books, shoes, a purple hot water bottle. Sometimes, she saw herself caught in a mousetrap, giant mice hurling objects at her.

One evening she took a walk up Lavender Hill, an undulating stretch of road peppered with shops. She liked the odd, interesting stores; the retro sweets haven selling multi-coloured sins that became small planets on your tongue, the pink and white umbrella shaped treats in tall glass jars that made her think of sugar cane sticks. There was a typewriter shop with rare models in the display window, neatly arranged in rows of five on each side. She imagined the ribbons coming undone at night, pressed against the glass imprinting half formed sentences.

At Sal's Café, an armpit of a place sporting chipped wooden tables, maroon walls were decorated with old film noir posters and the smell of coffee and hot chocolate intertwined. She saw men who worked construction slouched in their seats, dried bits of cement splattered on their jeans, faces bearing an unhealthy pallor. Broken shadows inched forward and sipped from their cups. Sal himself was a stocky Italian with thinning black hair and a tic in his face travelled through his features. He always wore a stained white apron over his clothes. She liked Sal's because it was warm and cosy, and because occasionally the same drunken tramp would come in spouting poetry. He'd tell her she was beautiful, and eventually stumble out with a piece of cake in his hands. Sal's became one of her havens; she often rushed in counting coins from fingers made crooked by the cold unintentionally blowing cloudy breaths in the paths of those she crossed.

She was on her way to Sal's that day, when she caught the white handwritten sign in the Gift! charity shop window: **Store Assistant Wanted. Stop by for details**. She peered in, noticed racks of used clothing, stacks of crossword puzzles next to old videos, scuffed shoes dented from rough travels. Beautiful abstract paintings were propped up against mauve walls. Bookshelves teemed with paperbacks. Records, lampshades and china tableware all shared an area. A jewellery display cabinet was positioned beneath the cash register and in the window display sat a family of puppets.

Slouched and wide-eyed, the puppets looked as if they spoke to each other between the ringing of the cash register making up stories about the customers, where they'd come from and who they were buying gifts for. A slender, pink haired woman wearing blue-framed glasses emerged from a set of double doors with a poster of a naked woman entering a lamp. Next to the doors a white arrow read **Staff Only** underneath. The woman also carried a basket of scarves. Queenie pushed the shop door open gently and was greeted by an upbeat song on the radio about rockets. She smiled at the sole staff member who darted a quick, curious glance her way. She walked leisurely through, studying items that grabbed her attention picking up a few here and there.

"Looking for anything in particular?" the lady asked a warm, open expression on her face. She'd set the basket at her feet next to a rack of empty hangers and was efficiently slotting scarves into them. Queenie edged closer. "Actually, I'm here about the sign."

The woman's face crinkled in confusion. "The sign, what sign?"

"The position," Queenie said, her accent suddenly sounding thicker to her own ears.

"Oh the job!" Realization dawned with a half laugh on the woman.

Sighing audibly, Queenie internally admonished herself for not stopping by after having prepared. "You are a charity?" she said with a tone of uncertainty that Ella the store manager found charming. As if she'd come in on a hunch and Ella liked the idea of Gift! delivering the unexpected.

"Yes, we're a homeless charity. Do you like the shop?"

Queenie's lips curved. "A lot, it's like a contained mad market indoors."

"I never thought of it that way but you're right. That's a good way of putting it!" Ella replied, already half way through emptying her basket. They were still the only two people in the shop and the song on the radio changed. A man was now singing about living in a missing train carriage with a bright-eyed girl in rough, urgent tones over heavy guitar riffs.

British people nah wah! Queenie thought, *even their songs were strange.*

"Sorry about earlier, sometimes there's just too much going on in my head. Have you had any experience working in a shop?" Ella asked, glancing at her over a shoulder and admiring Queenie's striking features.

"A little, back home I worked in our local tailor's shop. I learn fast and I like people."

"Well, liking people certainly helps in this job, in fact a lot of jobs I suspect!" Ella was intrigued by this warm young woman who seemed very present. Queenie walked towards the display window. "I love the family of puppets. You sold one?"

Ella followed suit, they stood together behind the items. The puppets leaned into each other.

Bending forward, Ella touched one. "They came in last week. Great aren't they? No we sell them as a complete set."

Tugging at her coat, Queenie decided that she'd get a warmer jacket as soon as she had more money. "One's missing."

"Shit!" Ella darted forward for a closer inspection. "How did you know that?"

Queenie shrugged as though it was nothing. "It's a family and there's only a little boy, usually there would be a girl too. And… they look as if they're missing something."

Brow furrowed, Ella touched the boy puppet in case he disappeared before her eyes. "God well spotted! Somebody must have pinched it."

"Pinched? Who goes around pinching objects?"

"Sorry, pinched means stolen, some little thief helped themselves. We've had trouble with thieves for a while, another reason it would be good to have an extra pair of hands and eyes."

Digesting this information, she held Ella's gaze. "So how many people work here?"

"At the moment, there's just me and Simon. They locked eyes briefly. Queenie saw that she was being sized up. Then Ella finally said, "You know the WAC Arts centre down the road?"

Queenie nodded.

"Well," Ella continued, "Every six months we convert their basement hall into a restaurant for the homeless, serve them three course sit-down meals so they can eat and have some dignity. We've served up to a hundred people in one day and the atmosphere's great. We get lots of volunteers come down to help."

"Really?" Queenie asked surprised. "Back home beggars and homeless people are considered pests."

"Oh, there are plenty of people who think that way here believe me! Can you come on Thursday around 3pm for an interview? I'm Ella by the way."

"Yes. Queenie. Nice to meet you."

"You too, see you soon."

"Thank you."

"No problem." Ella said, watching Queenie's back disappear through the front door.

At the hostel, Queenie stuffed a pile of dirty laundry into a wheelie bag with a faulty squeaky left wheel. She dragged the bag to the local laundrette and the wheel talked all the way. She flung her clothes into the large, circular mouth of a big, dark yellow washing machine that shook after she slotted coins in. Silently she cried watching her reflection in the machine's glass door. The water rose steadily over her face. She was running out of money, lonely and cold, constantly cold. She had no idea where to start looking for him. She'd come all the way to England riding the split tails of a feeling, on the words of a broken man. Her gut instinct's slippery outline lay on the ground. She left the laundrette with washing machine cycles whirring inside her and mumbled a short prayer soon caught in the flimsy Ferris wheel of a cobweb clinging to the wet sheen of a lamppost.

Ogoro Must Jump

In the end, it was neither the wives sweeping in like the changing seasons nor the heady, bitter herbal concoctions that fuelled Oba Odion's recovery. It was a childhood memory, a lie that had lined the mouth of a child and rolled out slowly. This lie had fed on Oba Odion's guilt as a boy, till he was certain it stood small shoulder to small shoulder with him. At naming ceremonies, it tripped him up even when he was perfectly steady and rested in the black crescent-shaped shadows under his father's eyes. So the boy Odion wrestled with it and won temporarily.

On the day he left his bedchamber, it was to an air of disappointment from the servants. As if they had hoped death would squeeze him in its grip till he succumbed, limp and placid, while death escaped with another life pocketed. But the servants at the bottom of the palace hierarchy reserved their true irritation for their private quarters. There, they would serve up their disdain for the Oba along with the latest mishaps that had befallen palace residents. The Oba sought out his councilmen who on seeing him pretended to be relieved as well. In their array of bright native outfits, they appeared a council worthy of any good king. They welcomed the renewed health of the Oba with outstretched arms and tense laughter but an outside eye would have noted that just before the Oba appeared they, an assortment of plotters, angled their necks into unspoken questions, traces of a possible coup evaporating behind false smiles. When the Oba finally sat down after all the back slapping and hailing, he did not stop to ask why none of them had bothered to visit when the fever sat inside him like a stubborn tenant refusing to leave the owner's land.

Stranger things may have happened in Benin but Adesua was convinced the brass head was stealing her dreams. That it waited for her body to be loosened by slumber before it helped itself to a large selection of past and present dreams. Stripping her till she woke up empty-headed and feeling bereft. She wanted dreams that tasted like pink watermelon juice, sunshine in her mouth. But these she believed were being snapped up by cold, hard brass. Even though a short arrow of fear hovered at her chest, she did not want to give the brass head back to the Oba. She knew it had raised her status amongst the other wives, a sword against their lofty sense of import-ance. She knew it had stolen the words of her dreams, which meant she could not express those lost dreams to anybody. As if the head had sewn invisible stitching in areas of her tongue.

When Kalu the medicine man lay cocooned in his mother's belly, many, many years ago, his preferred view of her womb was from the side. This inclination had not changed; it was the way he liked to look at the world. When giving readings, he would stare dramatic-ally from the side, intensely scrutinizing the pile of useless bones, nuts, leaves and haphazardly gathered debris that meant absolutely nothing before declaring, "This is serious!" to his latest victim. He would pause, let his remark sink into their chest like a tingly oint-ment, all the while inwardly contemplating the delicious meals he would eat from the plump fowl and fat lambs that they were to bring him in payment. He would allow his bottom lip to tremble, and even managed to break into sweat now and again, before whispering in an otherworldly voice, "to resolve this, we will have to do another reading, this is what you must bring..." Then he would proceed to chant loudly in a made up tongue, widening his eyes till they appeared to pop out of his head and frighten any doubts out of his customer's mind. Finally, he would throw spiritual liquid (water) sparingly over the stash of nothingness that separated him and his visitor, to slow down whatever doom was cutting a path towards them.

Kalu did not see himself as a trickster; he was a counsellor, a sage. As a boy, he had realised quickly that he did not want to toil the land as a farmer, nor learn a craft. It was too much hard work. His true calling revealed itself to him when he happened upon a travelling medicine man with a tongue easily loosened by wine. The man had revealed that his gift was an act, a deception that had served him well for many years. Kalu, ever the inquisitive child, asked him about guilt. But the man shrugged it off. Most people, he said, just needed you to confirm what they wanted to hear. They agreed of course that there were real, truly blessed medicine men. Men who could read the heart of another man from looking at his face and could sniff out the intentions of a customer hearing a single word. Kalu and this medicine man were not naturally gifted in that way. Kalu had lived in the same place all his adult life. He liked his familiar mottled terracotta hut with its sloping, patchy roof top of long palm leaves and the eroding, not quite square make- shift window, where he could keep an eye out for arrivals. Kalu preferred living reclusively and of course, it added to his aura of mystery. This hut he'd built with his own hands, was hidden inside the forest away from the gaze of outsiders. At night, he usually lit a fire and it would guide his visitors to him, the gangly brown man with the head full of lengthy locks like twisted grey snakes fighting to flee his scalp.

Very early in his career, a prediction he had plucked out of thin air came true and shook the eerily calm Kalu to the core. A boy had come to see him, moody and with determination etched in his face. He had looked Kalu in the eye and said, "I want my father dead, what can you do to make this happen?" Kalu had unfolded his feet from their position resting against the firm, rounded walls of his backside and cracked his dry lips open. "Are you mad? Have your friends dared you to come and say such a thing? Go away and don't waste my time again. I can turn you into a snail if I like." The boy grabbed Kalu's wrist firmly and dug his fingers in, "I'm not joking, if you don't help me, I will go to someone else." Then he added slyly, "or are you not powerful enough?

"Why would you want to kill your father?" Only stoic silence met him. So Kalu entertained the boy, instructing him but expecting it to amount to nothing. But the boy took Kalu's advice and turned his wish into a song. That evening, Kalu the fake medicine man became the keeper of a terrible secret and won himself his most powerful and loyal customer

Omotole decided that smashing stones never hurt anyone. Not like the desire to break the bones of someone you once loved, to quench the thirst of hot, dry earth with their blood. She sat at the mouth of the Ijoye River, watching the water lap at her scarred feet, only temporarily cooling the ardour of the other thing inside her, this thing she tried to contain each day that wanted to jump out of her and wreak havoc on Benin, the kingdom that had taken away so much from her.

During times like this when she had risen bathed in an unrepentant, molten rage that led her by the hand to the water's edge, she could not ignore it. The rage gathering within her heated her blood and shot through her veins, wailing inside her mind as though it were being whipped. It had not always been like that. Once upon a time she had been a wide-eyed girl and Benin the bountiful land of prosperity, where the impossible happened and the possible watched from the outskirts gulping its envy.

She stood, straightened her shoulders and cackled, convinced her laughter flirted with the rushing, rippling river. She stretched her arms behind her and rocked on the balls of her feet as if she would shoot off the ground. But she was dancing, and spinning, tamping the dry ground till the disturbed dust settled onto her body and lay there protectively, a third, fickle skin that she would sweat off in the hours to come. She reached her arms up to the sky and cried out, pleading to the Gods in anguish, the way a desperate woman with two faces would.

It was forbidden to enter the old, abandoned Ikere wing in the palace. It stood west of the building, like a forgotten thought. This rule had been in place since the days of Oba Anuje's reign and for the most part, the inhabitants obeyed it. But on rare occasions, encouraged by a mixture of curiosity and boldness, someone would cross the empty entranceway with its intricately woven spiders' webs listing in crooks and corners, like small, translucent nets bobbing in an airy sea.

Adesua was there because of a story with no ending. As she wandered through a broad, dry communal room, past another room with old garments gathering films of dirt and resentment, into a circular chamber with steep steps leading in, she remembered the beginning of the tale. According to the gossipers and story spinners, during Oba Anuje's time, a woman had stayed there for a short period. She was not a potential wife or relative of the Oba's so nobody knew why she was residing in the palace. But one day she disappeared, in the same way she had arrived, without announcement. Only the blood- soaked wrapper that she wore on her last sighting remained and was buried immediately upon instruction. As Adesua traced with her eyes the bed mat and sombre throw cloth covering a high, imposing chair, she realised that one visit to this wing would never solve the mystery of the missing woman. She watched as a yellow ladybird with its dotted, bulbous back scurried across the floor, stopping now and again to flex its tiny black legs. She wondered if Oba Odion knew anything about this woman's disappearance. And would he tell her if he did. There were so many things she did not know. Among them she did not know that death tasted like sweet, sugarcane kisses. She returned to the main palace to discover more news. Omotole, the Oba's favourite wife was pregnant and Filo, the wife convinced her dead babies wandered the palace grounds, had lost her voice.

Drawing Tables

In the days to come my intruder like a defiant squatter made more appearances in my house. I was secretly impressed; I'd never have the balls to do it. Only I wasn't resigning myself to being ambushed, despite feeling as though we knew each other. Maybe this woman, this mysterious entity that stole flowers and slipped into background scenes of photographs used to be a nurse. Maybe she had held my mother's hand while she gave birth to me. Maybe hers was one of the first faces I'd seen when I squealed into this world covered in gunk. And like a thumbprint on the brain her face had imprinted itself into my memory. Perhaps she'd fallen through a wormhole from the past. Maybe she'd come to collect something that would reveal itself on the expanses of my skin. Maybe, maybe, maybe...

One night she appeared on my bedroom ceiling, sleeping with her back against it as if it had sprung from her spine. She sat curled in the chair next to my TV with a forlorn expression on her face. She planted herself in the big copper pot growing my cactus, sitting in the soil and openly absorbing its sustenance as if for a resurrection. Plucking the plant's bristles, she waited to throw them in my path. She surfaced in miniature form in Marpessa's lens. Coming up for air with blue hands and things she'd fished from Marpessa: a damaged, old crown, a thick masculine neck with markings, torn bits of traditional cloth, a worn copper key. She pressed her eyes to the lens when it hardened into glass again, pressed her tinted gaze against mine.

On Tuesday, I bought a six-piece chalk set from the pound shop down the road. They also sold egg timers with hands and feet and colourful imitation Arabian carpets. I hunted for other random things since I didn't have a photo shoot until evening; a musician called La La Love wanted photos taken on the gleaming, split Tate Modern Bridge for an album cover. Strangely, I'd found a blackboard at The Salvation Army store, perched next to an oval magic distortion mirror that scrunched your face up when you looked into it.

At home I leaned the blackboard against a wall in the kitchen beside my radiator that was covered in splatters of purple paint. Occasionally, it made a knocking sound from a metal heart that beat inside it. I decided it was fate since I'd spotted chalk and a blackboard on the same day. With assured fingers, chalk in hand I drew a table documenting recent sightings of my intruder on the board.

Date	When	Where
10th April	8pm	In the car left side mirror walking forward.
10th April	1am	Hanging from the bedroom ceiling and swallowing the light bulb.
12th April	6am	On top of the TV set cross-legged, playing with static.
16th April	11pm	In Marpessa's lens becoming a flash
16th April	2am	In the bedroom placing her pink bracelet back in the bottom drawer.

In my head I marked the areas she'd appeared with white chalk, they blended into the whites of my eyes. I began to set traps around the flat. I couldn't decide whether they were for her or me. I left the bath full hoping she'd fall in, and that I'd find her submerged under water, unplug the plughole's mouth of dead skin and watch her get sucked under. I opened the loft entrance, wishing she'd rummage through the old clothes, photos, paintings, roller skates, and maybe slip. I doodled on sketchpads, drawing trap doors and a slim woman falling through. I breathed over these drawings willing them to come to life.

On Sunday I resorted to attending an the evangelical church I used to visit in New Cross. I hadn't set foot in Guiding Light for years. I sat through extortionate requests for tithes, the week's miracles, people being filled with the Holy Spirit convulsing at the touch of the pastor and a story of a jealous colleague becoming a one-eyed goat. Throughout proceedings, the smell of meat pies filled the room from a small kitchen at the back. Pastor Matthew wore snakeskin shoes, a crisp black suit and punctuated each anecdote with, "If you need a revelation say Amen!" I left the service with some holy water in an Evian bottle.

At home I kicked off my suede shoes and began. I sprinkled holy water on the sofa, in the kitchen, at my bedroom ceiling and wherever else I'd spotted her. I felt like a hypocrite since I wasn't even particularly religious. But I was ready to clutch at any potential solution. Any life raft I could heave myself on to. All the while I was aware of the medication in my bathroom cabinet, suffocating inside the sickly brown glaze of its round-headed container. I was like a musical conductor; flinging holy water everywhere at a one-woman orchestra who'd brought her strange music into my home. I waited to see if it worked, convincing myself I could go back to the church and tell them about my miracle. So the congregation could chorus, "God doesn't work on miracles part time! He delivers, Amen!" followed by drumming of feet and deafening handclaps.

I believed it would work, the Holy water, that it covered cracks on the walls, protected the depths of wardrobes, the small holes in the circular hobs on the cooker, pores on my skin. Gaps I'd left around shaped like me. Any holes an unexpected guest could slither through, gently tugging the lines of your body till she held them in one hand.

For two days it was bliss, I felt some semblance of normality. I printed pictures from the La La Love shoot, tried a yoga class before a swimming hangout with Mrs Harris and realised how stiff my body was, visited the Tate on a research trip about art installations without enough context. I helped Mrs Harris repaint her bathroom while we listened to the soundtrack of *The Harder They Come*.

The following night I woke up to feel someone's breath on my neck. I padded into the kitchen, the metal heart inside the radiator throbbed. I drained half a glass of exotic fruit juice. In my sleep-coated blur of movements the blackboard caught my eye. Written at the bottom in an unsteady scrawl was the line **why don't you remember?**

Holy water evaporated in my chest. It hadn't done shit.

I walked back but couldn't feel my steps. In the bedroom my guest sat on the pile of books laying on the dresser. She was covered in chalky white ash, thumbing through a book with blank pages.

Queenie London 1970: Gift Mouth

Queenie got the job at Gift! During the interview, she had the impression Ella would have given her the position even if she'd had no experience and could only speak pigeon English. For whatever reason, Ella had taken to her and the interview seemed to be a formality. She worked Mondays to Wednesdays so she could shadow Ella who was warm, pragmatic and efficient. Queenie began her training in the stock room, sorting piles of items into baskets.

After her first week she could identify the different areas and items from the clothes racks to the bookshelves to the clusters of china with her eyes closed. The new display window had two female mannequins at opposite ends dressed in Forties fashion. Sometimes, Queenie thought she saw the footsteps of passers-by rotate in the mannequins' plastic eyes. Sometimes she envied their stillness and wanted to join them in that window, complete with braided hair and flared black trousers. She would be on display just in case he ever wandered by and discovered his little girl all grown up in a shop window.

One evening after a tiring shift, she came home to her lonely hostel room and the echoes of other people's lives in the building. They had become familiar to her; the skinny Pakistani student whose room smelled of cardamom spice, the white lady with rhinestones for eyes who always snuck her scruffy, gap-toothed junkie boyfriend in and the strange girl blessed with fine features and close cropped hair that reminded Queenie of a helmet. The girl claimed she'd escaped from a cult and that mice in the building had stolen her voice. The receptionist called her "Jeanie the habitual liar." They were all misfits in one place with lives intertwining in tiny steps. It wasn't like back home where people living in such close quarters would know much more about each other.

On her bed, Queenie heard doors shutting, the wide yawning of windows opening. And broken conversations gathering like the breeze between fan blades. She rummaged through one big travel bag she kept under the bed, fished out a brass head and some pictures, things she'd borrowed from her mother without asking. The brass artefact, a warrior's head, stared back at her with an intensely calm expression. In one photo, her parents posed next to a white Volkswagen car, filled with youth and laughter. Her father wore a green army uniform; her mother was dressed in a pretty dress the colour of a purple seashell. She was laughing at something in the distance; he was looking at her mid-chuckle, as though seeing her for the first time again. A memory fell through the ceiling and her parents were there in the middle of her room, dancing to Fela Kuti. Their bodies threw robust moves and they were staying in love. They danced in an invisible, movable frame. Queenie silently asked the memory to stay the night. The weight of the brass head sank into her left hand.

After two weeks, Ella moved her on to the till and she learned quickly. She became used to the curious gazes of customers and their questions. *Where are you from? Is it just you or did you bring a family along? Oh Africa sounds fascinating but… is it safe? Did you fly here?* Some of the questions were asked in a friendly manner and she was fine with that. *Simple curiosity never killed anybody*. But there were a handful of people who asked those questions in an accusatory tone. When she picked up on this, she answered mischievously. *No, she hadn't come alone, she'd brought eleven members of her family with her and they lived a cramp, gleeful existence in a one bedroom flat. Oh Africa definitely wasn't safe! In fact, when you arrived at Lagos Airport there were taxi cab drivers in horn helmets that lured stupid foreigners into their cars. They butchered them and used their flesh to make money, bought land and dined on suya for days. And no, she hadn't flown to England but she'd ensured all eleven members of her family had been illegally smuggled into the country. Ah Ah! She herself had arrived on a boat so weighed down by bananas; it had nearly sunk en route.* When she made these comments, chuckling within at some of the ignorant questions thrown her way, a small red sea frothed in the corner of the shop floor, then flooded the faces of guilty parties. Glints of embarrassment turned into cataracts in their eyes. Their lips pursed tightly, curved upwards reluctantly as though the wanted to rip their smiles off and use them to strangle her. "Oh Ella! Delightful girl! Interesting humour…" One customer said. And Queenie smiled too, hiding the daggers beneath her teeth.

On the morning of her first experience of a Gift! Banquet for the homeless, all signs pointed to a good day. Sunlight streamed through the cream curtains of her bedroom, filling her rat-infested palace with a special kind of hope. She had a clean pair of odd socks to wear, something she considered good luck, one blue, one red. She'd also managed to save a bit of money for a shopping trip to Petticoat Lane market on the weekend. She'd try to decode some of the cockney lingo falling from the mouths of traders. If that failed, she'd simply ask what the hell they were talking about. Queenie was pleased she managed to send some money to her mother, having queued behind all the other foreigners at the bank watching them hand over their hard-earned cash many with relief showing on their faces. The same feeling swelled in her chest. That exchange indicated their sacrifices meant something, deep in the cold, loneliness and unfamiliarity of an alien country. Then they left with all the expectations of home on their shoulders, stalking through the streets like rooted up trees.

At around 9.30am Queenie arrived at the WAC Arts Centre to assist Ella along with all the other volunteers. The old basement hall where lunch and dinner would be served from 1pm was a large space with the capacity to hold two hundred people. The stage area had blood red, pleated velvet curtains, with the smell of old performances trapped inside them. There was a tall, standing lamp covered by a colourful chintzy lampshade. A black leather chair faced the audience and in case the chair wanted to talk into it a microphone stood directly in front. Big square windows with glass panes were slightly were open. The polished dark oak floor gave the room warmth. Golden, ornate candlestick holders were mounted on the walls.

Ella had rounded up all volunteers in the kitchen area, tucked away through an archway on the right. They gathered like troops; social workers, teachers, nurses and all sorts. Queenie was repeatedly surprised by how many people Ella seemed to know. How was a woman who managed a charity shop so well connected? She noticed a tall, broad shouldered, bald-headed black man amidst the group. When he laughed the whole room filled with it. For some reason they gravitated towards each other. Maybe it was because they were the only two black people amongst the volunteers. He walked right up to her, swallowed her hand in his. "I'm Mervyn, willing victim and volunteer. Who are you and how did Ella bribe you? Come nuh, don't be shy." The musical lilt of his Jamaican accent was attractive. A good tool to disarm people with Queenie thought but she smiled and held his gaze. "Queen, I work in the Gift! Shop."

He chuckled then as if an anecdote he'd heard was coming to life. "Oh! So you're the African lady. I've heard a lot about you."

She felt self-conscious then, a little annoyed at him for having a hand he'd been waiting to play all along.

"What have you heard?" she asked, unable to keep a slight bite from her tone. For some reason, she found herself standing a bit straighter, lifting her chin; a compass that pointed north. He bit back another smile. "Well for one, I've never met an African. You know? A Motherland princess."

She nodded her understanding. "Ah, I know what you mean Methalyn."

"Mervyn," he corrected.

"Ok Melvyn, we Africans even walk and talk at the same time!"

They both burst into laughter, the ice had melted.

"Sorry," Queenie mumbled, shoulders still shaking with mirth. "It's just sometimes people say really stupid things to me!"

"I know me too!" Mervyn said and they both collapsed into a heap of laughter.

She discovered from him that Ella's family was rich, her estranged father was an earl and the charity was her passion. Mervyn was studying to be a lawyer. He told her that one day he'd own his own practice. He had a fiancé who was a nurse. She couldn't come since she worked nights and needed daytimes to sleep. Queenie saw her then, hovering above their heads deep in sleep; a curvy, Jamaican woman in a blue nurse's outfit stretched taut against her dark brown skin, a thermometer tucked in the corner of her mouth.

They filled the hall with circular, wooden tables decorated in red and blue checked tablecloths. Rings of wine-red fake flowers and upwards facing playing cards lay on top. There were small, glass bowls bearing pick "n" mix sweets. One chair on each table had loose Christmas-style lights draped around it. Printed cream coloured menus with gold lettering rested on tables in square, wooden holders. On offer was a traditional hotpot with a twist and a prize for whoever guessed what the secret ingredient was. Prawn cocktail, Spaghetti Bolognese, chilli con carne, beef risotto and Chicken Kiev were options. Pork pies, sausage rolls, cheese and pineapple on small sticks were also on the menu. For dessert; butterscotch angel delight, arctic roll, black forest gateau and lemon meringue pie.

By 12:30pm people started filing in. As meals were served and Queenie interacted with the homeless men and women, she discovered there were people from all kinds of backgrounds. One teenage girl had run away from home due to her mother's violent, alcoholic boyfriend. Another man had been a civil servant. When his wife left and took the children, things spiralled out of control. One woman had been sharing a house with squatters but the property was torn down and she found herself on the streets again. Queenie enjoyed talking to the people. They were underdogs down on their luck. She knew what that felt like, maybe not to the same extent but she understood.

In admiration she watched Ella steering the whole operation with ease. With her slender frame, you could spot her easily. Pink hair now gone, she sported a sharply cut black bob and her features while delicate were reminiscent of Popeye's Olive Oyl, only much prettier. She wore a red jumper and red floral-patterned trousers, as if she'd arranged her outfit to coordinate with the décor. She ran the whole operation effortlessly, gliding from table to table, chatting with people warmly. She'd organised the team of volunteers commandingly, thanking them now for their efforts and seemed to be everywhere at once, cooking, serving, taking orders and liaising with the arts centre staff. She'd hired an artist for a few hours, a scrawny guy with long brown hair, holes in his green jumper and a thick moustache. Queenie got the impression this guy lived on other people's sofas. He spent his time drawing amusing caricatures of people who captured his imagination and worked on a piece depicting the joyous, chaotic scenes there that he called "*The Banquet.*" At one point, holding a stack of plates, sweating profusely and balancing three orders on her tongue, Queenie passed Ella by the kitchen. "Oh God! How can you look so calm, it's chaos out there!"

"It's great isn't it?" Ella replied. "From my count we've had an even bigger turn out than last year. Inside, I'm not calm, just resigned to the fact that no matter how precisely I plan, something always goes wrong!"

Sure enough it did. The house band Ella booked as part of the evening programme had been double-booked. Mervyn pulled a favour from a ska band he knew called The Pipers. By 6pm the evening programme kicked off; a mix of writers, open mic poets and the band. There was some good poetry and some terrible poetry. The band held it all together nicely, playing infectious, melodious songs to an audience who'd really only turned up for some free food but were happy enough to be entertained. Behind the scenes Queenie and Mervyn exchanged anecdotes.

"Come nuh, did you see that drunken guy reciting the poem about catching his girlfriend in bed with someone else?"

"Oh God! Yes, now I wan you ru die a thousan' deaths a thousan' different ways!" Queenie mimicked the poet's slurred delivery. "I didn't see the whole thing but I thought he was going to fall off the stage."

"He did," Mervyn said, cracking up.

"Are there a thousand ways to die?" Queenie asked.

"Probably." Mervyn answered and they convulsed with laughter.

At the end of the evening Queenie was exhausted. After the room had been cleared, rubbish tied, leftover food distributed in Tupperware, and volunteers filed out of the back entrance, swathed in her new £15 grey tweed coat from Petticoat Lane Market, Queenie waved an animated wave goodnight to Ella and Mervyn. She walked through the hallway where the large notice board hoarded leaflets that flapped like pinned paper wings whenever the door opened. She felt someone grab her elbow from behind, turned to find Mervyn, one hand buried in his pocket. Cool and casual. "Hey Africa, you escaping already nuh? The night is young. Come for a drink, The Pipers and I are heading to this blues bar. We can give you a lift in the van."

She noticed specks of food stains on his rolled up blue sleeves, fine hairs on his arm. Her pulse slipped into the face of his gold watch. "I don't think so, you have a girlfriend remember?" She said, tugging self-consciously at her jacket lapels.

"Oh come on man! Just as a friend. I'd like to hear about Africa, I'm curious. Besides, if I was trying to get you into bed you'd know it, trust me. And…"

"And?"

"You're interesting but you're not my type, so rest assured girl, I won't be pouncing on you any time soon."

Queenie didn't know why but a small part of her felt disappointed. Did he really have to tell her that last bit of information? Typical.

Sheepishly she said, "Okay, why not."

The Blue Havana in Oxford Circus was a cosy, smoky bar with low lighting perfect for shape shifters. Alcohol-lined voices in intimate conversations rose and dipped in cycles. Plush leather chairs and tall, black stools were dotted around a marble bar area. The barman's weathered face and rough voice gave the impression he'd probably sampled every drink they served. On the tiny stage, a black woman wearing a slinky, long purple dress cried into the microphone under a blue spotlight. A white flower grew out of her head. She sang as though she lived on disappointment, cigarettes and whisky. In that light, Queenie worried Mervyn would see under her skin and realise half of her was mangled. Since she arrived, she'd been walking on a rolling tide throughout the city but something about him steadied her. He was a man who took things at his own pace, even in England. They talked, laughed and talked some more. He watched her knock back shots of rum in amusement, often adding, "Gwaan girl!" and "Is that you?"

He told her about his love of magic, he carried an ace of spades playing card in his pocket wherever he went for good luck. He performed the trick of pulling a perfectly tied red ribbon from behind her ear.

As the night progressed Queenie became drunk. She decided then she'd tell him at least some of her story. She didn't know why. Maybe it was the loneliness, or the intimate setting, cigarette smoke curling through the room like mist gathering and ash from the embers of stories dying quick deaths in body temperature ashtrays.

Maybe it was the howl of the woman's piercing voice. Something came undone, floated inside her. She saw her own tongue on stage, wagging underneath the blue spotlight.

"What's your favourite magic trick?" she asked

Mervyn drained the last bit of cream liqueur in his glass, looked her dead in the eye. "That's easy, the disappearing act. Vanishing without a trace, it's the greatest trick of all."

Fist Of Drum

It was the cool north breeze that swept Sully Morier to the palace gates on the night that was to change his life. They found him, the guards, at the foot of the gates, beaten and bruised with his face buried in a puddle of dirt and rain. They patted his roughened, battered body down gently. He responded by cracking open a blackened eye, mumbling something unintelligible, and then slumping his slightly raised head back to the ground. His long body was strong and firm and as the guards lifted him they *humphed* under their breath as he began to kick at them in short bursts that were surprisingly well landed. He seemed to be trapped in another moment that refused to let him go. "Hold him!" one guard said.

"I'm trying," the other guard paused his hand hovering over Sully's one dropped ankle as though it were a slippery fish he was attempting to outwit. Then a decision was made for him as Sully landed a sly kick that caught the bridge of the guard's nose. "Fool, the sooner we take this white man inside the sooner we can visit the servant women's quarters," guard number one hissed, while the other guard clutched his injured nose, tilted his head back and drew some night air into his nostrils slowly to ease the spreading pain. Then, Sully's body relaxed, punctuated by a deep grunt. The guard rubbed the knuckles on the hand he had used to quieten Sully, albeit temporarily.

As the guards carried him through to the holding section, lazy moonlight spilled over his body revealing brown khaki trousers and a torn loose cream shirt. There was a thin grape-coloured leather strap wrapped around his waist with two small shallow pockets that had been emptied by roving hands. A bag fashioned out of what looked like an old sack was strapped to his back. His chest bore nicks and cuts crusted with blood. Once in the holding pen, a plain room with shabby straw mats, Sully was left to rest. Half-starved and weak, he spluttered and coughed through the following days that ran into each other, only roused awake by the shuffle of footsteps to look through the blurry recurring crimson mist that clouded his vision when food was brought to him. He ate and found himself clutching his stomach at night despite food like roasted yams and hot vegetable soup sating his hunger. But just as night was showing its hand, a hot spurt of fire would run burning through his stomach. He tried to comfort himself by rocking his body back and forth, ignoring the sting of salty sweat that trickled into his eyes, dousing his lips with a feverish tongue.

News of the handsome foreign stranger spread through the palace like a whirlwind. Did he have any identifying tribal marks? No, but his arms were solid, his face rugged and his eyes greener than the densest forests in Benin. Had he said anything about where he came from? No, only incoherent mutterings that fell flat on the ears of the uninterested guards. Was he recovering well? Yes, but slowly, and there were shadows lingering in the corner of his eyes. Overgrown black hair grazed his neck, days old beard covered his jaw and a tear shaped birthmark nestled high up his inner left muscled thigh. To catch a glimpse of him female servants armed with wet cloths and herbal brews offered the excuse of nursing him while their eyes struggled to absorb every small detail of the new stranger who now languished in the dark. Surely the arrival of this pale stranger meant something? Nobody knew. Unaware of the hum and flutter he'd caused in the palace, Sully was waging his own battle, a battle that rushed through his veins and boiled his blood. He shook fervently and violently. He wrestled as the naked taunts of the old whispers choked his throat, twisted his heart with long, brutal fingers and echoed his cries off the hollow, bruised walls.

Oba Odion was still celebrating the news of Omotole's pregnancy when a councilman came to him brimming with excitement at the news of a stranger in the palace. He thought his tongue would leap out and of it's own accord tell Oba Odion about this new development. Instead, it resigned itself to darting out sporadically, pink and shining.

There were times when the Oba saw his council as resentful, hungry shadows that loomed over him and were barely tethered to the line he drew for them. He imagined them picking at the same white line with their greasy hands till it became faint from each mauling. So when councilman Ewe came to him, green beads jangling against his hairy chest, Oba Odion's reaction wrong-footed him. "But we should use this opportunity to make the stranger talk while he is weak, a little pressure and he will surely crumble before our eyes!" Ewe said. Oba Odion rocked back patiently in his, sturdy chair "Leave the man alone for now; I have other things troubling me. When he recovers, bring him to me."

"Ah, Oba you are becoming soft, I know you are still celebrating your good news but do you not find it troubling that this pale man comes from nowhere to find himself clinging to the palace gates? This is no accident." The Oba shook his head in annoyance, "When I speak to him, I will decide what happens to him. He may be somebody who came to the palace for help. Did you not say he was beaten?"

"Yes Oba, but let us ask why he was beaten, this is a prosperous land, and there are enemies out there willing to try anything to destroy us."

"Ewe, I will think over what you have said."

"Most of the other councilmen agree with me Oba."

Oba Odion sighed wearily, "Must I have my own council's approval on every decision? Get out."

"Yes Oba" Ewe replied, turning on his heel, his anger smarting two steps behind him.

At that moment, Adesua was biting back her fury after discovering the brass head vanished from its home on her mantle. She could still feel its imposing presence in her chamber, shifting the air till there was a powerful undercurrent of expectation, as though something chameleon-like was coming, and menacingly entwining itself with her hot breath. So she swallowed a dose of it daily. She searched every inch of her chamber till having had enough of that point-less exercise; she hit the palace grounds barefoot. She screamed at the servants to find the thief among them who'd taken her prized piece. Gone was the uncertain young woman who had arrived at the palace, wary of the strangers surrounding her. The woman in her place had roaring flames in her eyes and barked orders as though she was born to do so.

The servants pushed by her slicing ire scoured their quarters keen to escape whatever terrible punishment awaited them if they failed to find it and kept the fact that the brass head was missing to them-selves so desperate were they to make sure word did not reach the Oba. Adesua continued to search the grounds her veins swelling in anticipation. She dug her nails into her palms. Fresh sweat popped on her brow and down her back. She tried to dampen the panic that was eating its way into her heart.

In the end, it was a raven-winged bird that led her to the brass head. She watched it from the main palace flapping repeatedly above the roof of Filo's quarters as if was alarmed, before running. She ran through the glare of disapproving councilmen, past the open mouths of servants and the glee of two other wives. She met Filo's door open and the sound of sniffing drew her in. Filo was gripping the brass head as if she would never let it go. Tears trickled onto her raised knuckles and onto the head. Filo only looked up at Adesua briefly and then turned away, as if she had been expecting her for some time. She continued to sob, gut wrenching cries that wandered all the way back to the entrance of a palace darker than the first scowl of night. She heaved, as if emptying her insides out.

The murmurings over Sully's presence were such that after a few days, even some of the lazy guards were bitten by curiosity. As his body slowly recovered, something else happened. The guards became less suspicious. He told them that he had travelled from the north where the golden-hued land was dry and stretched wide in endless waves lit with sunshine. Land that could break you if you did not use a gentle hand on her. He spoke of the women, dark, dusky loose- limbed nubile beauties who walked the land as though wading through water, bearing miniature reflections of themselves tied onto their backs or at their breasts. At night he said, when the brazen glow of the moon courted the pliant land, you thought you could sometimes see the fragments of light falling down from the sky.

The guards were spellbound, why would he leave such a place? He told them he was a restless soul, an explorer and that Benin had been hailed as the land of possibilities. He wanted to travel and see as much as possible. He had been coping with an unusual affliction for as far back as he could remember. His feet could not stay still in one place long enough to grow roots, as if as a child an itchy curse had been cast on them. What of his family? Surely they disapproved of his running from place to place. He told them he had no real family. Sully answered their questions, throwing a patient smile here and there, a nonchalant shrug if they attempted to pull his tales apart. He informed them that he had just crossed into Benin when bandits attacked and stole some of his belongings. Joking and laughing with all of them, he found himself telling the story several times to different guards. In each instance, he told it as though it were the first time.

On the day Sully was to be taken before the Oba, he awoke craving ripe mangoes. His limbs were still sore and thin, black scabs had formed over wounds only the eyes could see. He was quiet too, only nodding his thanks to the slight servant girl who brought him a small pail of water to wash himself. He sniffed his armpits; an, eye-watering smell emanated from them. Disgusted, he picked up the cloth left beside the sleeping mat, dampened it in the water and gently began to wash his body, careful not to wet his wounds. He waited for his body to dry before slowly slipping on the loose fitting shirt that had also been washed and dried.

Outside, the two guards sent to take him to the main palace, jokingly shoved each other pretending to play fight. He whistled his readiness and sniggering over something both men came to him, one on each side, lightly holding his arms. As they took the walk up through to the palace, he eyed the bustling, sprawling courtyards, the neat apartments for those of royal lineage and finally the high, imposing terracotta palace building, its conquests depicted in brass plaques embedded on the front view of the roof. He swallowed a bitter smile at the cruelty of the gods.

Inside, he was made to stand in a room before the Oba and his councilmen. A small river of accusatory stares followed. Oba Odion's voice boomed "Tell me what has brought you to Benin." Sully did so, calmly, with the right intonations of humbleness and disbelief at his misfortune. Inside, he locked away twinges of pleasure as he held his audience rapt, watching their doubts fall to the ground like fish scales. He told himself that sometimes you had to take the beginning you deserved. This was his.

Say Anon

I began calling my uninvited guest Anon. Somehow, weirdly, I'd adjusted to having another presence in the house. The blackboard in the kitchen was full of sightings; the wooden floor had small areas cordoned off with white chalk. My bedroom ceiling bore splatters of purple paint from attempting to capture her body using colour. Traps I'd set failed. Buckets of water placed in corners of my living room so she could fall inside her own image and drown. Instead, the water rippled from her breath and sometimes her wet mirror images left the buckets so there were four of her wandering through the flat. Water versions of Anon eventually collapsed into puddles I mopped dry with shaky hands. Sometimes when I turned the radio on and listened to LBC she swallowed the frequency using silence the weight of a room. And I found myself beneath it, arms and legs flailing to survive.

The days became darker.

I played drunken bingo with Mrs Harris, mulled over what to do with my inheritance money and ignored Mervyn's phone messages. Anon persisted, she dangled off cobwebs in my throat with one finger and inserted her gap-toothed smile in the mouths of people I shot. I functioned, the way a person carrying broken things inside them does, until they start bleeding from a big wound on their face that has seemingly arrived overnight.

One evening I lay on my blue sofa, my mother's throw covering my feet, watching a rerun of Deal or No Deal on More4, playing with the key from the fish. I rubbed it as though it could grant wishes, Anon sat in a single wooden chair on the side. Noel Edmonds wore a ridiculously loud shirt, the clothing equivalent of a box of Smarties. In between the boxes opening on screen, with revelations of blue or red cash values inside, I listened for heartbeats Anon may have borrowed from someone else. I was resigned to us living an unsettling co-existence.

The heating was on full blast; subconsciously I thought I could make her sweat until she evaporated. The smell of weed lingered, what was left of the slim roll burned in a glass ashtray on the floor, its tiny specks of orange light with smoke curling into the amber iris of a third eye. I drained half a glass of Baileys and set it on the floor, next to it I laid two flattened cereal boxes, Cornflakes and Rice Krispies. I'd planned to use them to make robots but got distracted by my vices of weed, alcohol and television. From the kitchen, the bottle tops stuck to my notice board of weird collages rattled, releasing whispers.

Anon unfolded her limbs and walked to the kitchen. I slipped the key into my trouser pocket. In my mental fog I could straddle two planes. I was aware of her movements, a series of scratches wearing skin, rummaging through the cutlery drawer. She appeared by my side wielding my sharpest knife, the one I used for cutting stubborn pieces of meat. I saw a green vein reflected through the blade, from tip to handle. It throbbed; I couldn't tell if it was hers or mine. A purple haze floated into a parachute, hovered above us. I felt a slick of sweat on my neck, heard the scurry of unidentifiable things in holes. Anon held me and it was like holding myself, the gleam of a blade sat between us. She pressed the knife to the left side of my head, made an incision just above my ear. She placed her mouth on it and spoke into the cut.

I found myself on a dusty, lengthy road, warm against my bare feet. Broken stones dug into them. The dark fell in swoops then broke off into marauding limbs. My blue living room curtains billowed against an anaemic moon, swirling dust tainted part of it red. Static from the TV ceased, swallowed by my eardrums and Noel Edmonds voice waned in the distance. The silence around me spun like a colourless kaleidoscope. A river situated to my right rippled gently washing over rocks that could have been heads barely bobbing above water. I saw a cluster of large terracotta buildings situated in sprawling grounds surrounded by tall black gates. The gates were flanked by guards in traditional clothing, their eye-catching material of a golden leafed design and the leaves curled up as if they intended to crackle into life. I heard a faint murmur of chatter between the guards. Angular pieces of stained glass window fell from my mouth onto a path of coloured glass. I walked tentatively on the glass path, even though I had a feeling that if I ran it wouldn't have broken.

The guards held wooden spears with sharp, brass tips. As I drew closer, one signalled to the others. They'd been sucking on oranges, sharing anecdotes and swatting fat, hungry flies. Another guard spat orange pips into his hand. I stared, expecting an orange tree to bloom from his palm. My throat constricted, a nervous habit. I stopped myself from chanting aloud, just. For one, I didn't want to appear crazy and two; it wasn't a good idea to jar men holding weapons. I drew my shoulders up, prepared to spin a lie from the small bank of wool that resided in the scars on my wrists. Wearing respectful expressions, the guards opened the gates.

"Good evening," they each said in turn.

I nodded, walked through. My pulse hummed, I stayed quiet. I didn't want to talk and give myself away. But these men seemed to have mistaken me for someone else. One foot stepped in front of the other, guided by an invisible hand. Voices filtered from the surrounding smaller apartments. Noise slipped out as if the rooftops were lids that weren't closed properly. I wandered into a square courtyard where footsteps were still visible. Vines crawled up tall pillars and whispered to the drawings of battles won, etched in a golden undulating ceiling. I wanted to go down and talk to the footsteps, to see if they'd move. For some reason, I felt I knew who they belonged to, that the lines were telling me. I grabbed a handful of earth and it ran through my fingers, warm and real. Sweat coated my body. I knew this place. I sensed the new and familiar all at once.

I knew that the short copper-toned flight of steps outside the main building led to a room I'd visited before. Brass artefacts were mounted on walls near the stairwell; they shifted under the sly night light. I'd been thrown into something incongruous, like a piece of time landing in a glass bowl. I walked up the steps to the first floor. A guard sat snoozing outside a room tucked behind a golden arched doorway. One eye flew open as my gentle steps approached. He stood groggily to attention. Tightened the knot of the green cloth he wore at the waist and wiped some crusted drool off his chin.

"When I last checked, he was still awake." He edged the door open slowly.

I entered the large bedroom, closed the door. A dishevelled, raised wooden bed dominated the room. Two brown mats lay on either side. Carved wooden masks hung on the walls, watching with the expressions of Gods. In the thick of the heat I gathered my breaths and smelled palm wine in the air. On a dark stool with a low gaze, a kerosene lamp rested. Its flame flickered, bending in a glass bubble. I heard a rapping noise, a fist knocking inside my head. A small river in my left foot threatened to leak out. The tingly sensation of pins and needles pricked my skin.

In the corner, a man's shadow rose above him while he hunched low. He washed his hands in a metallic bowl, feverishly muttering to himself. This continued for a few moments as he muttered "Iz not clean, never clean again."

I walked into his shadow, touched his shoulder gently, driven by instinct and adrenalin. He uncurled slowly, his native wear covered in sweat marks. His protruding gut revealed a man with a very healthy appetite, wild eyes blinked at me.

My voice seemed to come from somewhere else. "What happened?" I asked

The whites of his eyes grew bigger. A red ant clung to a hair on my arm. An army of ants scurried into cracks on the floor and in our speech. He curled his hands into fists, knuckles straining.

"Nothing can be done." He held up his palms, red from vigorous washing. "My enemies are no longer of this world. Are you one of them?" He pointed a finger accusingly. There was madness in his eyes.

"Nnnno, of course not!" I stammered.

"Why are you dressed in those clothes? Are you trying to mock me?" His voice bellowed.

"I found them in my room; I don't know where they came from." I managed a sincere expression, tugged at my baggy boyfriend jeans and loose Ren and Stimpy t-shirt.

"I will have whoever is responsible for this flogged! They may lose three fingers."

"No need, it's just a bad joke done in poor taste; I put them on out of curiosity." I placed both hands on his rising shoulders to steady them. The sound of something dripping caught my attention. He drew me closer, wrapped one trembling arm around me and pointed to the ceiling. A ring of red appeared in the centre. The ceiling talked in a language of blood. It dripped onto our heads. Fat drops fell into my right eye as I looked up. I rubbed urgently, alarmed by the sight.

"What have you done?" I asked.

He threw his back and laughed dementedly, crawled into the unmade bed and assumed the foetal position.

I left the palace with my vision partially blurred. The guards lay slumped back into sleep. At the palace gates I remembered the key in my pocket, an invisible hand guided me again. Relief surged in my chest as I inserted it into the lock and turned. It opened. I thanked the dead fish that brought it to me and shrouded it in luck. Now the road felt cooler on my bare feet. The singing crickets had half whistles inside them; their sound grazed the night. An even paler moon morphed into a broken plate and its red dust disappeared back into the ground. Hovering in the air behind me was the sprawling red palace, somehow uprooted by my visit. Beside me the riverbanks arched, water rippled.

In the distance the sound of static beckoned me. I walked till my feet ached and the sound became a wall close enough to touch, twitching like the instances we change our minds. I couldn't tell when I was swallowed into the other side.

In the morning, I rolled off the sofa and landed with a thump on the floor. Red ants crawled out of my pockets and made a trail. Anon sat opposite me laughing, more ants spilled from her mouth. I traced the cut on the side of my head, a morning alarm. I stood still for minutes, covered in a cold blanket, rubbing an optical illusion that had landed in my hands. Turn it one way and you had a lady with a cut on her head that would change location. Turn it the opposite way and a woman with blood becoming a small, red country in her eye appeared.

Part 2

Modern London,
Lagos 1950s
&
19th Century Benin

Tales of Kin

Tandem

Three months after I picked up the diary from Mervyn, I woke up one morning needing to know more. I fished the leather bound journal from my handbag. Inside the front cover the name Peter Lowon was scrawled on the page. The diary was teeming with paragraphs. A grey margin line became a needle sowing a stitch into my side. I saw ink arrows morphing into real arrows, hurling themselves at words, the wounded words would escape with letters lost from injuries, limping off the papers, leaving a trail of blue black ink to drip onto my palms. I could hear the chants of kids playing easing through my letterbox and the screech of impatient car tires. My phone began to ring, but I licked my finger and turned the first page of the journal into another life. I glimpsed a sketch on the back cover. It was a drawing of the brass head with words orbiting around it. I didn't run my finger over it, in case it came to life.

Crying Fins

Adesua did not report Filo to the Oba. Instead the wall of anger she'd erected against her, crumbled on seeing the lost, vulnerable woman clinging to the brass head as though it held the answer to her problems. Adesua grabbed her arms and gently shook her. "Filo, *ah ah*, what has happened? Tell me, has somebody done something?" She'd pried Filo's fingers off the warm brass.

But Filo would not speak. Adesua crouched down further till there was only the space between teeth separating them. She snaked an arm around Filo's back in support, held Filo's body while she slowly stopped shaking and the sniffling subsided. Outside in the distance the laughter of the palace inhabitants was heard. Adesua didn't know it but the birds that had been repeatedly circling above Filo's chamber, listened too. They heard Adesua's anger, noted the confusion in her voice and still they did not move.

Finally when her concern burst through the roof and touched their heavy wings, they huddled their heads together, and waited. One bird fluttering down to the doorway would have seen the two women sitting with their knees raised to their chins, holding hands as if they were little girls on a farm rather than young women in a palace, their bottoms against the soft, weather-beaten earth, providing a temporary ceiling for the bugs and worms that scurried and slid layers beneath.

Meanwhile Adesua and Filo clung together listening to the sounds of the palace, bearing the weight of a silent thing, cloaked in a comfortable peace. Somehow within that chaos the two women had found a temporary relief. The silence crooned its intent, and unspoken words were exchanged through the small space between their raised knees and entangled fingers. They ignored the comings and goings outside the fragile bubble they were in, the noise from the rest of the palace that at times threatened to burst it. Adesua listening to Filo's breathing even out again continued to hold her hand and waited. Not because she thought Filo would confide in her, but because she knew she wouldn't.

Eventually, Adesua dragged her feet up to leave. By then Filo was staring blankly at her walls, but the corners of her lips were no longer pulled down and by the time Adesua walked away with the brass head tucked under her arm, Filo's shoulders had ceased to hunch up. For the first time Adesua felt as if it wasn't just a piece of art that belonged to her, but it was a real, live human trophy.

She left Filo's quarters with a new, slick, uncomfortable knowledge. Of the darkness of Filo's bedchamber, from the brown cloth she'd hung over the window to stop light flooding through. The wooden platter of days old half-eaten cassava and stew rotting in the far corner and the pungent, rotten smell that filled the room loitering just beneath their nostrils. Of the garments strewn across the floor, leaving a rainbow- coloured mess of materials you navigated your feet through to find a space. Next to the window, a once beautiful, wooden chair sat, chipped and worn. Bits of its top layer had been scraped off, leaving an awkward, bruised thing. It looked lonely, in a jumbled room where the mouth of the green bed mat grazed the terracotta walls.

Beside the bed area was a small, rectangular brass box on a wooden mantle, its one drawer half open, like a jaw dropping in shock. Inside it, you could see Filo's jewellery. Glinting silver bangles, winking gold necklaces, dark maroon rings peeping coyly from the edges, a fountain of lime-coloured beads dripping out and down the side of the box. Beneath your feet, the hardened floor felt hot and unsettling. As if you were subject to its moods.

Unaware that the brass head had been found, the servants gave up looking for it. In fact, they secretly wished it were never found. Of course the Oba would rant at them and they would soak it up, as they always did. But that artefact seemed to brew nothing but jealousy and resentment.

It was sweltering as Adesua trudged back to the main palace, suspiciously so. She knew something was amiss. The air was thick with promise. Even the flies seemed skittish. Sun-stroked, burnished green leaves from the Iroko tree had abandoned their branches to scatter and rustle against the scorched ground. There were shouting, agitated voices mingling into a chorus of noise you couldn't clearly decipher ricocheting through the air. Above the clouds seemed to frown before shifting, one moment a face, the next a half-bitten guava.

Adesua decided that night she must see the Oba. Her husband. A man she knew less well than her personal servant. Gone were the days when she felt like a young girl, and all she worried about was falling from tall trees or the scorn of her Papa's tongue whipping at her when she was caught attempting to wrangle her way into wrestling matches with boys from the village. Now a new, sneaky awareness had arisen, simmering to the surface, a slow burn. There was no going back; she was the young wife of Oba Odion. A king's bride, a coveted and envied position, but this did not give her comfort, it never had. And as she followed the winding path back under the half-watchful gaze of the guards who held their spears too loosely and their slack mouths even looser, suddenly a rock of fear lodged in her throat. She tried to imagine what this thing she felt was coming could possibly be. Moments later the tantalising smell of roasted fowl infused the air and filled her nostrils. She imagined the palace cooks with their sweaty brows and teeth-dented bottom lips flapping around each other to prepare the meal on time, while her visit to Filo still weighed heavily on her mind.

Oba Odion did not delude himself into thinking he was a particularly wise man. In fact, as a boy he had been laughed out of several challenges set by his father Oba Anuje. Oba Anuje would create a riddle for him to solve and then summon him back later in the day when the hum of the palace had died down to a buzz trapped in his ear. The boy Odion would watch as Oba Anuje gleefully rubbed his large, dark brown, calloused hands together as he stood before his father trembling, pressing his thumbs against the other forlorn fingers desperately trying to settle himself. Telling bulbs of sweat would pop out of his armpits before sliding down his sides to languish in the flesh above his hips. Inevitably, when he failed, Oba Anuje would stroke his strong, jutting jaw and nod his head as if confirming what he already knew.

Several times when this ritual humiliation occurred, a boiling, yellow thought would conjure a heat so strong, it spread from Oba Odion's head to every part of his body. It lit him up, and he was shrouded by this gleaming yellow aura before his father. Even then his father knew. Oba Odion could see it in the narrowing of his father's eyes till they became black slits and the curling of his top lip. Finally, Oba Anuje would roar, "Get out of my sight." And Odion would jump out of the protective gold light, which then shrank, to a dot in the air.

He remembered his father's room as it was then. The circular shape of it, with its fading sickly plum-coloured walls. Sometimes he thought he heard the walls laughing at him and whispering to the bronze masks that decorated them, to the sturdy, shining brass chair with its crisscrossing pattern that left holes just big enough to stick fingers through. To the long, polished wooden stick that often lay by his father's feet. It had smelled like new sweat and something else. A sickly sweet scent that cocooned something rotten which subtly oozed through the walls. Many times Oba Odion had tried in vain to figure out what that rotten smell was. He never did.

As if by doing so he would kill a memory possessing too many lives, the first task Odion completed when he became Oba was to have that room knocked out and rebuilt. On several occasions Oba Odion found himself making decisions based on avoiding his father's haunting disapproval, although this revelation did not show its face at first. It was only when it began to eat up the ingredients that made up his judgement that the Oba ceased denying this truth. When he caught himself gauging how Oba Anuje would have reacted in a given circumstance and then vehemently deciding to do the opposite, it became even clearer.

So when Sully stood before him and the council, Oba Odion found himself clinging to the young man's words, plucking them from his mouth as though they were fruits. And what words! It struck him that this stranger had what could only be described as a gift. With spit and perfect intonations he weaved his tale, rocking on the balls of his feet, talking not just with his lips but his hands, shoulders and it seemed every part of his body. Shrugging dramatically, angling his head at all sides of the room, and pointing to his bruises he informed them that he was an explorer from England who had travelled to India and around Europe, the Americas and the far corners of the East along his adventures. That he had heard so many tales of the great Benin kingdom from the Portuguese he had decided to come see for himself, bringing copper, brass bracelets and other items to trade.

Oba Odion had judged him before he even opened his mouth to speak, in the moment when their gazes held and Sully did not blink, his eye not automatically dropping down in false humility, nor cowering to their corners. The councilmen shifted in their seats, as though somebody had rubbed nettle leaves there to itch their backsides. They drew long, slow breaths that puffed out their cheeks and short, shallow ones through dry, pursed lips. They drummed their fingers and tapped their feet, throwing cynical glances for each other to catch. They shot Sully clever threats posing as questions which curled above their heads in circular patterns before wilting on contact with his skin. When a tiny, fleeting smile cracked across the Oba's face, the councilmen noted it. Clasped hands unclasped and their coughs fell at Sully's feet.

Talking before the Oba and his council, Sully felt the heat of their gazes. He was pleased. He did not crumble nor lose his will. At that moment, he thought of purpose and how it could con you into a different direction, lull you into a trap. He could hear the comings and goings of the palace above a bubble of gas, which roiled and gurgled in his stomach.

Booming laughter, strangled shouts, what sounded like the blade of a cutlass slicing into a coconut shell. He imagined juice spitting as it split into two. He curled his fingers into his palms to stop himself from running to the large window overlooking the grounds and sating his curiosity.

"And you say you have no family?" The question from a councilman stilled him. He turned to face the culprit.

"No sir, I have moved from place to place since coming to Africa." This was met with a rigid "*humph*."

Beneath his chest Sully's heart quickened and the cut on his lip began to burn as he forced a bright, deceptive smile. He wondered how long this ordeal of questioning would last, not that it worried him because challenging trials were part of life, just as long as they came to an end before you did. The Gods would see to that, but he knew that sometimes the Gods displayed a vicious humour.

The ground began to swim a little and he rubbed his right hand over both eyes to wipe the fatigue away. He felt as if his body was about to cave in on itself. So he chided himself, *not here, not now.* In his head, a whistling sound began to grow louder and take shape, slowly, till it became bigger swirls of white noise that blew out of his ears. He waited for Oba Odion's ruling, as all the men did. And when it came it was this, "Welcome to Benin."

Journal Entry December 12th 1955
Peter Lowon

I am not a sentimental man, but on this day, the eve of my 26th birthday, I Peter Lowon have joined the ranks of the Nigerian army as a second lieutenant. So, I am tasting a kind of happiness that is hard to reign in. A few of us are in Lagos staying in the house of General Akhatar. Earlier this evening, my fellow officers and I celebrated in style, having been invited to another higher-ranking officer's house party. There, we drank Guinness and watched the women shaking their waists in that effortless way that African women do. A few of my fellow officers mocked me, joked about the way I speak and my education at the hands of British missionaries. "Ah Ah Peter! Sometimes you sound just like a white man from the BBC," one said chuckling into the mouth of his beer bottle.

Predictably, some of the men there were also high-ranking officers and generals. You could spot who they were even out of uniform. It was there in the respectful way others hailed them, and how they carried themselves tall, crooking their fingers at the houseboys and girls in someone else's home to demand "come come, more beer for my friend." As though it was their right. Watching them chuckling mid conversation and absentmindedly patting the fat wads of Nigerian British pound notes in their pockets. I can tell you that power is an aphrodisiac. It is an infection difficult to describe but you know you want to catch it, you like the reception it com-

mands. I am a man of potential. I like to keep my eyes open because you learn so much from doing so.

At the party, I exchanged jokes with my group, hemmed into a darker corner of the room as more people arrived and the noise reached the ceiling. High Life music was keeping people shimmying, and one or two had conked out indiscreetly on the floor and on chairs. Something else was playing on my mind. I was on the periphery of the exclusive club of big players! So I was looking to see whose ear to bend. The British colonial influence is still visible in Nigeria but grumblings have continued. Things are changing here, and change means opportunities. Oil production is increasing, an exodus of people are leaving the villages to rush to the cities. In Lagos you see rusty Volkswagen cars defiantly pushing along the roads, their bonnets almost bursting open with engine noise. On some streets there are children and adults with their heads tossed back gulping Coca Cola from long, elegant looking bottles.

I am sharing this room with Obi and Emanuel, also new to the army and both of whom snore so loudly, it is a wonder this room is not vibrating. Lazy boys! They still have their party clothes on, Obi on his back with his arm carelessly flung over his forehead and Emmanuel nearly off his creaking mattress face down into the floor.

Right now the kerosene lamp is burning a steady, low flame of light as the night sounds of the city become fainter. I am leaning this journal against a short stool that wobbles initially before stabilising. It is only a stool but I like this flaw in it, so applicable to human beings and the new situations we often find ourselves in. There is something about being here and seeing how the rich live that makes you yearn for more. Here, everybody "wan chop", so I want my piece as well! I cannot sleep; it is my excitement over what is to come that has me reaching for this journal, a parting gift from my father along with his letters. And his neat handwriting seeming to say: "Be careful! Say your prayers, God is watching."

This writing and reflection is giving me an appetite, I wish I could go down into the kitchen to help myself but since I am only a guest, I will have to bear the stomach rumblings till morning. To the left of our room is a stiff wooden door and hanging on a nail is my uniform, a dark green tunic with patrol collar, light coloured khaki-style trousers and a peaked, jaunty cap with gold braid. Something strange happens every time someone comes through that door. As logic would have it, I don't expect it to make my uniform fall in a heap on the floor. Instead, I see the yanked door handle lift my uniform off the nail so it stands to attention before me. One sleeve of the green tunic raises to the cap in a salute. I actually want to try my uniform again right now, it fits very well, but if Obi and Emmanuel wake up and find me dressed in it at this time, I will be the butt of their jokes for days.

Somebody else is awake; I can hear their feet shuffling downstairs, the creak of a window sliding open. By the time that sound ceases, it has become a different window from the past. My mother is leaning out, reliable shoulders hunched up, bits of springy hair sticking to her sweaty forehead, screaming for me to come in from the streets. Usually, I would be loitering on a corner somewhere when I heard it, swapping marbles with boys who bore neighbourhood war wounds of freshly scraped knees and healed cuts. Or I'd be testing catapults from a safe enough distance on strangers who crossed my eagle-eyed view.

Whoever was moving downstairs must be trying to get back to sleep. I am admiring the round buttons on my tunic. They are spotless and a coppery colour, I polished them yesterday. They could be coins, like the ones my father used to give me to buy white Tom Tom American candy from the sweet seller that were so sweet your teeth hurt and gave your mouth a zingy coolness. Inside the copper buttons another memory is moulding itself to them. This time I am twelve or thirteen, my head is buried in a book as my father points out the inconsistencies in my arithmetic, teaching me the way good missionaries do. This lesson would then be followed by English. Then later on, sitting in a church pew wriggling my bottom in anticipation of the ending, of the clapping and singing out of tune. Obi has now turned onto his front, dishevelled, doing a very good impression of a tortoise. He sleeps too deeply; this is a weakness for an officer. I will make a good officer; I am controlled and swift to react in most situations.

There is no way I could have failed the recruitment process. Tests, endurance exercises but more importantly, who is open to bribes.

I watch people because human beings are fascinating. A person's body language can tell you what you need to know, even shows when they are weaker than you. Look at an unsteady arm and you will see a lie reflected there, a sweaty upper lip in a tight situation and sooner or later that person will crack from fried nerves. My most useful skill is my ability to adapt, something I learned early having been the child of Christian missionaries, a child with no real interest in faith whatsoever. Since it was clear that you couldn't escape God because he was either watching you, having plans for you, or making a way (God will always make a way!), I decided to have a talk with him. When I was nine, I took him aside right by the guava tree that dipped its branches into our small compound. I warned him, don't give me any wahala and you and me will be okay. Of course, I did not tell my father this. I believed he would have had a heart attack, his thin-rimmed, round spectacles steaming up, his body keeling over right there on our black and white squared linoleum floor.

I have made friends with Obi and Emmanuel, not because they are my sort of people but because you have to have team spirit in the army. You cannot be seen to be a loner or an outsider looking in. In fact I am not a team player, never have been and never will be.

Recently, I have taken to smoking cigarettes. I think too much as some form of a release. I like taking long, slow puffs of sin. I see myself at the army barracks in Epoma. The wide grounds with dark, unevenly, shaped buildings popping out of it like teeth. The identical hard beds set in rows and dressed in flat green sheets with thinly stuffed pillowcases. The thud of feet pounding in unison on the concrete during training exercises. The officers with bags containing stuffed, squashed versions of their lives spilling onto their beds and the floors. The black truncheons flashing in warning, tucked under the stiff arms of officers who look as if they've been swabbed in liquid discipline. The high wire fence surrounding the building that surely had the scrutiny of superior officers welded into it, and the taut, shrill, piercing sound of whistles that sent your socks rolling down

*your legs. The green and white Nigerian flag raised on a high, white pole
flailing like a ship's mast as if the grounds could set sail at any moment.*

*I am going back to all of that in a few days, to this new life I find hard
to switch off from. But even within the confines of the barracks, there
are signs of something wrong. The caretaker whose name nobody knows,
his hair is grey with secrets. Every day he marches around the grounds
dressed in full regalia making sure the buildings are as they should be.
Yet he appears to be searching for something, bending to study the dirty
bottoms of walls where there is nothing to see, sliding his hands under
filthy, corroding pipes and boring his eyes into the front of the building.
And when I greet him, "Mr Caretaker man, what are you looking for?" he
responds in kind, "Just making sure everything is in order sir."*

*There is the officer three rooms away from mine, who writes letters
to himself every week before ripping them to shreds. People have been
known to walk in on him attempting to stick those torn shreds of paper
together with shaky hands. Besides, I am convinced worms are trying to
take over the barracks. It began with seeing one some weeks ago crawling
in a leisurely fashion on a windowpane, its pink body wriggling a slimy
path. Since then I have seen more, crawling up the table leg in our eating
area, slipping between the laces of an officer's heavy black boot, curling
and uncurling itself near a small puddle on the training base.*

*There is a small prayer room tucked away in the gut of the main
barracks. It is sparsely decorated with thin, pristine white curtains and
worn Bibles gathering dust on the wooden table. The few greying chairs
croak when we sit down and the walls are a muted cream colour. Next to
a high, square, stand, three fat white candles sit in silver holders. At the
front of the chapel a robed, blue-eyed Jesus, arms outstretched, counts your
guilty steps as you walk on. The officers, crass, loud, young men unaware
of their ignorance, go in there, kiss the crosses dangling from their chains
and feverishly voice their longings.*

*So far every officer I have met has a story to tell. This is to be expected;
we are young, keen and hungry. There is something about putting young
men in an enclosed, restricted environment that produces unexpected
results. Not only the predictable strutting and competitiveness; it's also*

how territorial some people have already become. Even over small, insignificant things like who misplaced so and so's razor and who borrowed someone's pen and forgot to return it. As if ownership of things keeps them sane.

It is nearly 3 am and I should really try to sleep. The ticking has stopped in my temples and the sounds of Lagos have dwindled to virtually nothing now.

Another thing; I have never set foot in England, but my fellow officers laugh, and tell me I have funny ways. And they call me the British gentleman despite my being a black African man.

Able Bodied Thirsts

Beyond the Benin palace gates, was a long, dusty, sweaty stretch of road that led to a vast clearing. One night, Adesua dreamt she was in the clearing trapped inside a twisted vine growing there. And at first, her voice was bold and loud. It shook the vine and its scraggly branches. But each day as the vine grew bigger her voice became smaller. She called out to passersby but they continued on their journeys towards the palace as though they could not hear her. The palm wine maker? Merely gave a shrug of his slack shoulders, relaxed from consuming too much of his own product. The court jester? Let go an audible cough midway through her cry as if to cover her voice with his. The tailor? Only paused to bite a chunk out of juicy, ripe pear, the aroma reaching her like a sweet, cruel taunt. She continued to cry, her voice like the murmur of a shrivelled thirsty leaf, inside the vine. But it only soaked up her tears. "Look what you have done!" she accused.

"No," the vine replied "it is what you have done, have you forgotten? Each day you remember less and less."

"Tell me why I am here," she pleaded. The vine stayed silent, then said, "If you can remember why you are here you will be free." So Adesua tried and tried... She prodded her thoughts till they formed a line, one behind the other, each peeping curiously over the shoulder of the thought in front. But the thoughts were all immediate, there must be another way to escape and her tongue felt irritatingly heavy. She was certain the vine was somehow tricking her. Then the vine said, "Since you have come, I no longer feel lonely."

"Aha! I knew it," she croaked, knocking her thoughts into a messy chaos just above the roots of the vine, and they clung to wherever the landed, jarred and frightened of being sucked under. "You caused this to happen. Don't you know I am the bride of Oba Odion? I will have you pulled out and destroyed." The vine laughed and rocked her sideways. She felt tiny and insignificant. Inside, the vine felt moist and warm. She stood and began attempting to tear bits off. "You can go when you accept what you have done; attacking me will not help you."

When Adesua woke up she rushed around her chamber feeling her walls. There were cuts on her toes and she found herself craving the taste of sweet pears.

It is in the nature of beings to sometimes wield brutality with a gentle hand. A vicious blow can come from the most placid of characters, or a damaging whisper from the mouth of dear friend. Some motions once set loose outside of ourselves cannot be undone. It was with this thought in mind that Oba Odion made the decision to allow Sully to not only remain in the palace but appointed him his personal guard. The council fumed while the Oba appeared increasingly erratic, rebelling against their advice and making questionable decisions at which even a monkey would scratch its head.

A plan of action was required; the council members circled the palace grounds in fragmented groups, listening to everything that was said and endorsing it with silent approval. They scratched each other's backs with ways to foil any more ridiculous decisions from the Oba. The plan was, they agreed, to present any decisions as though they were the Oba's in the first instance. Wasn't that what every good king sought from his council? They agreed to keep a watchful eye on Sully. It was no coincidence surely, they thought, that this stranger should find himself in the Benin palace. No, they could smell something was amiss, a subtle, sickly scent that wrinkled their noses and furrowed their brows. Meanwhile, the strange seeds the Oba discovered in his bedchamber continued to flourish in the place garden. They were above knee length now, and still shedding their leaves, their round, bulbous bluish heads still rotating watchfully over the palace. Their long green stems were a little bent, as though they leaned into each other to exchange conversations. But the plants were still bleeding; the soil beneath them tinged bluish green. They were moaning, low-pained groans that you could only hear if you bent your ear to the ground. But the Oba did not notice any of this. Nobody had.

Adesua waited till evening, when shadows fell across the sky. She wandered the palace grounds as she often did, just as the fireflies became restless, decorating the air with dots of green light that guided her to a sturdy, mango tree weighed down with fruit. In the palace garden, she sat at the base of the tree and listened to the sharp, shrill chirp of grasshoppers as they called to each other, jumping across the grass as though the waning heat still scorched their long hind legs. She followed their sound, crawling towards the bed of strange looking plants hemmed in by the sparse trees and high earth-coloured walls. On her knees, with her nose to the ground the waft of something rotten filtered through. As though the offending patch of earth had released a smelly belch and all it needed was the rain to come down to wash it away.

Omotole knew about the wish that had impregnated her, the desire for a son had danced its way into her womb. The Oba had done his share of work too but it was the sweet desire she'd kindled on their nights together that finally came to fruition. A son would firmly seal her position in the Oba's life and the palace. Omotole had no real proof the child she was carrying was a boy, except that innate feeling in her bones, a deep tingling that began way down inside her stomach and spread right through her body. She could have consulted an oracle but there was no need. The stewing scowls she caught on some of the other wives faces before they vanished confirmed this. Only Adesua truly seemed unaffected either way and had congratulated her with an empty hug and a distracted smile. That one was an odd young woman, Omotole thought, recalling the way she bounded about the palace grounds, hiking her wrapper up to her knees. At times muttering to herself, a slip of uncontained energy.

Oba Odion was happy on hearing the news of her expectancy but these days he was not himself. Omotole like everyone else discovered he was regularly in disagreements with his council and becoming slimmer around his waist as if something was eating it away. Some nights he spent in her company would see him tossing and turning, at the mercy of some invisible hand flipping him from side to side, breath infused with the scent of worry. She asked him what was troubling him and unusually, he did not tell her. Instead, he lamented on how useless the palace cooks had become, that the spoils were making people lazy. A tiny gap opened between them, the Oba was now keeping secrets and Omotole's mouth formed a grim, suspicious line at the thought. But she did not push; a man would reveal his secrets in his own time. Instead she would knead the worry out of his shoulders and use his back to plan her next steps. And she did not tell the Oba that on discovering she was carrying a child, small oval shaped blue petals had began to appear inside the moist pocket under her tongue.

Trouble was coming. So when Sully heard the whimpering of snapped branches behind his quarters, he sat up in attention. If it had just been the scurry of a monkey or some other animal, he would have ignored it, allowing the thought to melt away like a drop of water into a river. These movements were tentative, deliberate in their attempt to attract as little attention as possible. He had always had an ear for picking up even the most secretive of sounds; he had even heard the tiny wings of baby's heartbeats fluttering in their chests. He crept out of the back window silently, landing in an unkempt yard flanked on either side by thick shrubbery and scattered sticks. He crouched low on the ground, spotting a woman's back arched down way ahead. Her head was bent, fingers rummaging through dirt, so intent on what she was doing that only his hand grabbing her shoulder broke the spell and she gasped.

"Are you stupid?" Sully asked, thinking he had happened upon one of the servant girls. "Running around at this time?"

She jerked her body back alarmed. "I lost my beaded bracelet!" Then, "How dare you open your mouth to speak to me like that?"

Sully took in the thick, full hair jutting out of her head in tight springs. The long ripe body with her breasts looking like globes of fruit pressed against her wrapper while her black eyes spat embers.

"Do you know who I am?" she asked slowly, as though speaking to a child.

"No."

"I am Oba Odion's wife."

"Hmm," he said. "Which one are you?"

"My friend, do not ask me questions as if your father owns this land! Who are you?"

"You will find out soon enough." He looked at her knowingly and said, "You will never make a good queen."

"Insult upon insult!" she fumed "I will shame you and report you to the Oba first thing, you will be thrown out."

He nodded then, almost amused. "Before you tell him, I will escort you back." He took her arm gently and knew then that she would never sit still. He knew without understanding how he did, that she was a curious woman and recognised an adventurous spirit when he saw one. The scratches on her neck, the restless eyes all spoke of this.

On the walk back they both ignored the thing between them that had come alive and breathing, through the long, winding curves of the servants area, past the compact, terracotta apartment blocks where some councilmen resided and the empty, gutted courtyards and settled deep within them. Later, Sully would remember details;

the glimpse of her naked ankles, the sound of laughter carried in the air, beads of sweat on her long neck that sat like jewels waiting to be plucked. At the entrance to her quarters she still glowered. Even if she had bathed then, she would not have been able to wash away the imprint of his hand on her arm. She did not thank him and he had expected nothing less but her haughty back disappearing into her haven.

Out of her sight he ran, thought it funny how you travelled to a place to find one thing only to discover something else, because it had truly begun now. He ran till his knees ached and he felt his feet take off the ground, careening forward till he couldn't separate the expanse between the sky and the solid earth. And he thought he could grab stars out of the firmament, shards of silver light glittering in his palms.

Pupa: Stage 2

As a child butterflies fascinated me. One of my earliest memories is of catching one, placing it in a tall, empty hot dog jar and watching its purple wings skim the glass. And scraping my knee in our garden from a fall aged twelve, only for a blue butterfly to land on the bleeding wound that momentarily became its respite. Since then, I've never forgotten how a butterfly could flutter down and change the shape of a moment or the line of a body.

As Mrs Harris and I trudged up the steep London Road in Forest Hill, I thought I heard the butterflies in the museum breathing, waiting. Rain had washed our earlier expressions away. A bitter wind argued with clothes that flapped back and umbrellas were led astray from firm grips.

"Did you bring it along?" Mrs Harris asked, referring to the brass head tucked out of sight in my rucksack. She stopped, stuck her tongue out to catch drops of water. Her grey raincoat was soaked, beneath the hood at the front exposed shocks of white hair were damp.

"Yes I did." I tugged her forward. "What are you doing?"

"I used to do that sometimes as a kid. Rainwater makes me see possibilities!" She answered, picking up the pace. Her eyes were alert and there was a spring in her step. I began to think maybe it wasn't such a good idea to have asked her along. You never knew what she was going to say or do.

"I hope this is productive and creepy." She said, wiping her brow.

I moved a fat, wet twist of hair from my cheek. "Why creepy?"

"Every now and then it's good to experience uncomfortable things."

From the corner of my eye, I spotted the green man leave a set of traffic lights to rescue a broken beam of light landed outside a betting shop. A frail woman stood beside the cinema handing leaflets to people. I tried to recall the last time someone disguised as somebody ordinary handed me a leaflet.

Finally we entered the large grounds of the Horniman Museum. A concrete path snaked its way through the middle, separating spotless areas of grass that bore a wet sheen. Wooden benches were sparsely dotted around. The gardens had been sectioned off due to renovations. Threading our way through mothers pushing prams, lovers casually meandering and the odd group of school children bunking off, we eyed the distant, sprawling green longingly. The air was cool and crisp. A white Victorian cast iron conservatory perched resplendently, accustomed to the gasps of appreciation coating its windows. Magical, it looked, as if a breath over the blueprint had instantly brought it to life. At the main entrance a rush of heat hit us, sweeping our grateful bodies. A flash of white wall greeted us inside as other bodies dripped back and forth to the reception area, where a woman in her late twenties took enquiries. The wooden floors gleamed so brilliantly you could pet reflections in them. In my mind's eye I saw a scrawny immigrant woman flitting about efficiently at the crack of dawn, only to be rendered invisible by the time the harsh glare of the morning light had arrived.

Mrs Harris unzipped her raincoat, slung it over her left arm and blew a breath out slowly. "Do you want to ask for your acquaintance now?"

"Naw," I answered, rocking restlessly from one foot to the other and swallowing a feeling of anxiety, a stone in my throat. "Let's take a look around first."

I'd been carrying the brass head around a lot, torn between wanting the option of getting rid of it at a moment's notice and a fear that doing so would mean some terrible thing would happen.

We headed downstairs and wandered through rooms with subdued lighting housing different exhibitions. One held odd, foreign instruments made out of things like a can, strings and part of a saddle, as well as ancient harps, flutes, and guitars. Another was a photographic exhibition on birth and death. Images of new born babies held up to the camera's eye and those of the sick who were fading, the tired lines on their faces plotting to sink into the taut skin of other bodies. In one I saw my own mother holding me up as a baby in one frame. Her Afro hair dented unevenly from leaning back against a pillow. I had barely any hair and my eyes were unfocused as though trying to adapt to seeing.

I edged forward hypnotised, tugged Mrs Harris along.

"Did you see that?" I asked, pointing at the black-framed picture on the wall.

"No. What am I supposed to have seen?" She answered, curiosity etched on her features.

Up close, the picture had changed. Another mother and daughter were now depicted holding each other with their faces pressed together laughing. They looked so happy, so assured of their time together. I felt foolish, cheated and sad all at once. A pain tore through my chest, a sneaky stroke from someone using a heated, metal spoke to poke from the inside.

"Nothing." I muttered, silently admonishing myself. "I thought I saw my mother and I keep seeing things…"

Tears sprang. I blinked them away. I envisioned the exhibitions in their well-kept prisons breaking free one day, wandering the floors uninhibited, marching to a melancholy tune the instruments played that nobody knew the lyrics to. Mrs Harris ushered me away, threw an arm around my back offhandedly in a way that gave the impression she'd been doing it for years. "Don't worry." She said reassuringly. "I think this is part of the process, being confronted by memories when you least expect it."

"It's impossible for anybody to remember that far back."

She shrugged. "Maybe you're a rare case. It could be an old photo your mum had resurfacing. The mind can distort things when we experience extremes of emotion."

"Could be," I replied, mulling over the idea. "Only I don't remember seeing a picture like that." As we moved away, I peered back suspiciously at the framed offender taunting me. Now my mother had a large opening in her chest. In the top right corner of the frame, a bloody heart floated down slowly until it obscured most of my baby face.

Beneath the painted deception were lights acting as third eyes. Behind panels of glass tall, dark wooden cabinets housed all sorts of oddities: a large jar of tightly packed moles, feet curled against each other and eyes squeezed shut. Then an ostrich's heart that was formed like a white baby octopus, glimmered, catching fractions of light. Varying sizes of monkey brains floated ominously in off-yellow liquid, threatening to enter our heads. In one corner on its own, was an elephant's heart, bulbous and thick, bearing veins that shot around stunted rivers of dismay. A skeleton of a flying bat was still in its stripped beauty. A copper toned infant aardvark lay curled in its glass womb. Mrs Harris splayed her hand emanating warmth against the glass, leaving a wet impression from her blue sweatshirt sleeve. I thought I saw the baby aardvark uncurl and suckle on the watermark as we passed.

We roamed, blowing onto glass surfaces grey tunnels of breath that quickly evaporated. We stitched a strange tapestry of fingerprints, *ums* and *ahs*, hurried, excited sentences that ran into each other until one started and another finished the observation. We spotted the butterflies just as broken laughter filtered through, an indoor sun in disguise. There were thousands displayed in glass cabinets.

Tiny slithers given fallen bits of rainbows as wings. Their names made me think of exotic places; Sapho Longwing, Banded Peacock, Orchard Swallowtail, Banded Orange Heliconia, Question Mark, Juonia Coenia, Spicebush Swallowtail, Battis Polydamas Antiqus, White Admiral and Silver Washed Fritillary amongst many others. I couldn't decide which one I was but they made me think of things in flight and how devastating it was to fly with one broken wing. I sensed Mrs Harris at my shoulder. "Ahh," she said with a smile in her voice. "You're a butterfly, I thought so."

I bent down for a closer view. "Magical things aren't they?"

"That they are, creatures of wonder. Do you know about the cycles of a butterfly?" She asked, wiping away the damp map that was receding into her raincoat.

"No." I answered, feeling slightly ignorant. The butterflies, swirls of colour, began to flutter their wings in the whites of my eyes.

"There are four stages." Mrs Harris continued. "The egg, caterpillar, pupa or chrysalis and finally the adult stage. You my dear are in the pupa stage."

"What happens in that stage?" I enquired.

"This is the thing!" She waved her finger animatedly as her voice rose. "It feels as though nothing's taking place because you feel suspended, but major things are happening internally and externally. Things buried inside you forming eyes and wings."

I nodded, drawn in by the sudden intensity emanating from her spritely, small body.

"It's a shame though," I retorted. "They have such a short life span."

She pulled me closer secretively. White tendrils of hair had escaped the loose bun she'd curbed her mane into. There was a hole at the front of her sweatshirt you could poke a finger in. "Flawed, mad butterflies grow extra wings," she said. "Even after they die, they come back reborn." A weird expression clouded her face and there was a wild gleam in her eyes as she straightened her body. For a moment she appeared wizard-like, dancing on some detached edge, dressed in pauper clothing to accompany a friend on a museum trip.

By the time we'd gone round twice I was still paranoid. I stood in a corner next to a baby Quagg skeleton I knew was breathing echoes down into my eardrums. I flickered like a light bulb low on wattage, suspicious of more sinister hallucinations winging their way towards me, flanked by bits of night in jarring shapes. A film of sweat lined my upper lip. I eyed things warily; a trouser pocket of a passerby, a museum brochure in the large hands of an imposing security guard, dusty windowpanes, velvet curtains hiding shadows, a woman's exposed collarbone. Mrs Harris appeared oblivious to this, steering a running commentary on everything. In a way it helped.

"Ants, bloody resourceful things!" she commented at one point, followed by a short monologue on their habits.

"Aren't they something?" This in reference to several stuffed owls starring moodily at a distance neither of us was privy to. Eventually she pulled me aside. "Don't you think we should see that curator contact about the brass object?" she asked, reminding me of the very reason we'd come to the museum in the first place.

"Sorry for dragging you along, I'm not feeling so well. I don't think this is the right place for it anyway." I answered, turning to walk away quickly, leaving Mrs Harris trailing in my wake. She threw her hands up at our corpse audience in their glasshouses before following me. I was embarrassed and sad. Tears blinded my vision. Angles of light in alliance with the picture frames lodged in the corners of my mind. A hard bottom swallowing the sound of rolling bottles pulled me under. Damp trails on my cheeks wet the feet of people on stairs and escalators all over the city.

Outside I took deep breaths as if oxygen was running low. The rain had stopped but the world was shrouded in a dim, muggy air-lessness and you wish you'd stayed indoors. Mrs Harris placed a steady hand on my back. She seemed to understand that moments of grief could loiter around corners.

She smiled patiently. "I know just the thing to make you feel better," she said pushing back some hair from her face. I thought of the butterflies, of their beauty silenced behind a manmade prison and cried even more. A crack emerged in my mind's eye, shimmery from salt water and blinking. Mrs Harris's teeth flashed white. Then, I saw butterflies being fed on my tears, growing taller, wider, like plants until in the thousands they smashed through their glass cabinets destroying them entirely.

Peter Lowon Journal Entry
February 14th 1956

Ultimately, people will let you down, the reverence you once gave them shrinking to the last drop of tea in a cup. I know this from experience. I have settled into army life. I am now used to the routine of being told when to wake up, eat, train. The comfort of rubbing your finger over a willing rifle, the daily exchanges between the feuding door locks and their keys. We are ticking clocks simply waiting to stop. There is beauty to the unexpected when it happens, whether good or bad, because it doesn't take your feelings into account.

Consider this: a proposition from a General, a soldier dead forever, and a brass head. If I offered these bare bones to a thousand people, there would be a thousand different stories and a thousand different attempts to make skin cover these bones. Two days ago Mr Caretaker man finally found something worth discovering. A soldier named Mohamed Fahim's dead body was found in the small, cramped outhouse toilet with his hands behind his back and his head crushed in the throat of the toilet. As deaths go, it was an undignified one, since when the traces of life left him, his last breaths must have smelt of a shit and piss. I can say this. I can also say that there will be no real investigation; his death will be ruled as an accident. Although how a man can accidentally kill himself in a toilet is highly suspicious. This is what the army do, they protect themselves and ironically there is no sense of injustice.

I do not know about Emmanuel and Obi but I have been stashing the guilt I feel in my uniform pockets, inside the soles of my boots and under my bed in my squashed green bag with its sturdy, reliable strap. We are good actors and didn't even know it; we were appropriately shocked like every one else, enquiring if anybody had seen anything or how come no-one had come upon his body for most of the day. This act in itself is normal; people ask questions they know the answers to all the time, like you are eating egussi soup and pretending not to know that in fact what it tastes like is what lies taste of. Mr Caretaker man looks sad but unruffled. He has been reeling off questions to soldiers left, right and centre. Somebody should remind him he is only a caretaker!

Three nights ago, on a calm, balmy evening at the barracks when most of the officers were wandering about, and anybody could have been anywhere, I, Obi and Emmanuel were playing cards in the common room and drinking beer and stout, poisons that were good for us. Looking back, I think I must have been drunk, I did not feel like myself and I was laughing a lot even when something wasn't funny. I was choking a little on my laughter when General Akhatar walked in. Initially it surprised me that he was unaccompanied. He was out of uniform and is a big, imposing man with neatly cut hair and cold black eyes. The left side of his face sinks in on itself, as though someone had repeatedly punched him there. It is a hazy picture but a picture still. He was jovial, he laughed with us, cracked a couple of jokes, even stopped to sip from a can of beer. Then came his request, although it seemed more like an order because of his no nonsense tone. Would we be willing to kill a fellow officer who had not only disgraced himself and the army by propositioning the General in a shameful way but had also put the General's life in danger? He would pay us of course, he said. Plenty money! Easy money. Obi, Emmanuel and I looked at each other, at the General's smiling face and easy manner. We communicated in the short silence that followed. I squeezed the glass bottom of my Guinness, Obi tapped his knee, Emmanuel leaned forward. Say yes or no to the promise of rewards and advancement through the army. In time, I cannot say if I had been sober whether I would have walked away. I would like to think so. In the few nights since, when I lie with the little conscience I have, I tell myself this. But that night when we walked away from that room we were high and ambitious.

Mohamed Fahim was alone in the quarters he shared with other officers. He was in the hard, familiar bed when we got there, not quite asleep but his chest was rising and falling. I wished I had thought to ask him what he knew that was worth killing for but I could barely breathe, my hands shook. My heart raced. The fear in Mohamed's eyes made me panic, made me feel sick. I could sense his confusion, his shock but we had come too far. There are witnesses who saw what we did, but they are things and not people. They cannot speak. If it could, the doorframe of the dormitory would say that we plied his fingers off when he held it, desperately. The dark, long corridor just outside it would state that Emmanuel covered his mouth as we dragged him through and that he kicked and fought all the way. Emmanuel had one red eye from drinking earlier and sweat covered his forehead. The toilet bowl with its shaky black seat would say that Obi held his head down and that he turned his face away as if he couldn't bear looking. That he slumped to the ground and held his head just after Mohamed took his last breath. I vomited a little on myself, I am ashamed to say this but I remember thinking, even after what had happened, that I hoped I could get the stains out of my uniform. It is a miracle nobody saw us, we disappeared out of there like magic, the tensions between us pulling our bodies along. Immediately afterwards, I felt disconnected, like there had been two of me, one fleeing the scene and one watching as I did so. Following a heated exchange, Obi and Emmanuel went off to be seen, to blend in. They seemed surprisingly more sober, but I suppose murder can do that people. For sure I was a sinner now, and no amount of praying about the blood of Jesus would wash this sin away. I saw the blue-eyed Jesus falling to his knees in the prayer room, floored by the weight of what we had done. In the corridor I walked over my last steps, wishing someone could pull my elbow and yank me out of the night, the scenes beforehand, the meeting with the General. My mouth became dry like sandpaper, I found myself in the bunkroom I shared with eight other officers including

Obi and Emmanuel. Suddenly, each identically made bed became a pit you fell into, no matter how cautiously you climbed. I sat at the end of my bed and began to take my uniform off. I washed my shirt at the sink round the back. My fingers trembled. As I undid the buttons, my right leg seemed to spasm uncontrollably. I will never forget the sound of a man pleading for his life, begging us to stop. And how his voice sounded thin and shriller the more he must have realised that there would be no return for him that night. Inside my bed, in my white singlet and shorts, my body felt hot as if I would burn through the sheets. A couple of soldiers began to drip in. "British gentleman, you dey sleep already? He's a funny one that guy, my friend get up. Should we leave him?" I recognised the voice and didn't move a muscle. I closed my eyes and longed for the chaos of the following day to come.

The next morning, things were fairly normal, because surprisingly, no-one had discovered him yet. I arose to the familiar, musty smell of sleep sweat-coated male bodies. When the whistle, the usual morning wake up call, tore through our eardrums for a moment I felt that the night before hadn't happened. But I was born too knowing and the sand dry mouth, the humming in my temples told me otherwise. Soldiers padded about barefoot, nicking their rough feet on stories from the previous night. My uniform shirt had dried and there were no incriminating stains on the brown khaki. I did my best to avoid Emmanuel and Obi, despite us sharing sleeping quarters. We did not look at each other, as if we knew the thing we did would be mirrored in our faces.

I went to breakfast. The cook was in his usual dirty green vest serving hot akamoo, stale bread and butter.

"Oya, oya, don't waste time," he said shoving our plates into our hands as we formed winding queues.

By afternoon, it felt like only a matter of time, and so it was. I had already picked up on officers querying soldier Mohamed's absence. I noticed the buttons on my uniform jacket looked red, or maybe they were always red and somehow I had missed it. My uniform felt too tight. During our training drill, the sergeant had to shout an order to me four times because I didn't hear the first three despite standing nose to nose.

A confusion settled in my brain. And then late afternoon, the news of a dead soldier came from a sergeant and with it, the order of the day scattered. A hum rippled through the barracks, and the soldiers separated into packs, only to be assembled before higher-ranking sergeants who poked and prodded us for more information. We were told in a wide, dark room, our bodies crammed in like sardines in a can, that we were our brothers' keeper. To have our eyes and ears open, report anything unusual. Standing there, in the room, the continuous drone of a large grey portable fan was the backing track to the senior officer's voice. He stood lecturing us at the front with his dirty collar and rumpled uniform. How he expected anybody to take him seriously looking that shabby is a miracle. The men were coiled strings attempting to stand still, but shifting from one foot to another, their unease obvious in their tight shoulders, low grumblings and weary looks. I caught the tail end of rushed conversations. How could this happen right under everybody's noses? One of us? Was he made an example of? How was it nobody had seen anything? Or did somebody just look away? We were warned that whoever was responsible would be caught and punished severely. A shudder ran through me. I spotted Obi and Emmanuel near the front row, their backs straight. If backs could be read, you would never be able to tell what they were guilty of. In that moment, I felt reassured; maybe they knew something I didn't. By this point, most of the soldiers began to get even more restless; you could see it in their glances towards the doorway. Eventually we were dismissed with the reassurance anybody holding information could go and see a higher-ranking officer privately.

It is such a terrible thing, the death of the young.

Today I received a gift from General Akhatar, wrapped in old, yellowed newspaper. I sat on my bed looking at it for several minutes before opening it, somehow daunted by what would lay within. I removed the layers of newspaper to find a brass head in perfect condition. It is a beautiful piece, life-like with its proud, defiant expression. I am guessing that it is quite ancient, a collector's prize. In his brief note that came with it, which amounts to two lines, the General writes that it is his favourite piece. I have no idea why he has chosen to give it to me in addition to what will be done. I know a good man would not accept this gift, but life is not so simple and I am not necessarily a bad man for taking it. I will keep this brass head because I am selfish. I want it. I will not mention it to Emmanuel and Obi. I can write a version of the truth, so I will say that for a long time I will not have to worry about money and that the terrible night binds all four of us together; me, Obi, Emmanuel and the General. I will live with myself because I can and because I have to. I cannot undo what has already been done. Still, information I would rather not know has begun to circulate through the barracks. People say that Mohamed was a good soldier, a quiet man who mostly kept to himself, that he had a pregnant girlfriend waiting for him back home. And that his mother had been reluctant for him to join the army. Things that paint a picture you try to look away from. Now more than ever I avoid going to our prayer room, though I should. I am frightened that the blue-eyed Jesus's head will snap and roll on the floor before my feet, that I will have to be carried out of there. I will send some of my tainted money to my father. It will make him happy, the irony being if he found out where it came from, he would be disgusted. This is why I want to share some of it with him, so he can unwittingly spend my burden. People will let you down; I have been feeding on this slab of truth since childhood. As I grew, it grew. It is still excreting its blood stained bits under my fingernails.

Throw For Loop

Filo was gradually turning to stone before the dismissive eyes of the palace, after their words that had been knives to her skin, driving her to check her body for cuts, had finished their assault. Her skin began to thicken into impenetrable layers of shame and loss. Now the laughter behind her back bounced off and the pitiful glances slipped through her fingers like tiny grains of sand. She still mourned the loss of her children, child after child and suffered all the heartbreak that came with it. She resented the role she occupied in the palace of the damaged, troubled wife. Even the Oba had completely lost interest. Then Omotole had become pregnant, and she could not find it within herself to pretend to be happy. Her blood ran cold in the punishing heat for no reason, and the other wives looked at her as if questioning why she could not pull happiness from inside herself and dangle it before them. It was selfish of her not to share in their joy. But when she thought of this all she saw was her gunk-filled hand, drenched in slime clutching the remains of her battered womb. So her heart had hardened, lodged within her chest, a fortress trapped within a fortress.

Meanwhile Oba Odion refused to step in. He did nothing to help his forgotten wife. He caught distorted, miniature reflections of himself in her black pupils and believed it to be an attempt to suck him in. So he would skulk away, his face in a scowl, mouth disapprovingly grim. Filo's anger grew. It was then that Filo realised waiting for one person to breathe life into you with guilt-soaked breath could break you, just a little, each day.

So when the brass head called her, she was unable to resist its slow, rolling whisper. Soft yet insistent, it had fondled her lobes before slipping inside her eardrums, saying her name softly, repeatedly. She carried it as though it had always belonged to her. The weight of it had rested comfortably between her thin arms, and she had hopped daintily to her quarters, ignoring the sandstorm brewing between her toes.

Inside the disarray of her chamber, the heat emanating from the brass head singed her rough fingers. She accidentally dropped it on her foot. That act jarred her into thinking; *now I am even stealing*. It was only when Adesua came to see her that the humming inside stopped. She thought she would resent Adesua for coming to take back what belonged to her but she didn't. She could not have imagined she would welcome the company of another wife, but Adesua's presence had calmed her. Somehow, silently a common ground was discovered. Yet behind her raised knees, something inside her locked. The birds could have told her when it had happened because they were waiting, hoping their soft-feathered breasts would muffle the sound when it surely came. When it did, the birds had flown away, and Filo decided to stop crumbling beneath her desperation.

Nestled within a room in the shoulder of the palace, Sully stood behind Oba Odion who was slumped in his chair. You could almost taste the Oba's sweat in the room and the terracotta walls, punished long enough, could have been shrinking within themselves. Since the Oba had appointed Sully as his personal guard a funny, unexpected thing happened. Oba Odion began to confide in him, his tongue loosened by a well of stories and incidents. Sully was an attentive listener, and he *ahhed* and *tutted* when required to do so.

If his face began to crumple, he would stop himself and smooth his expression down.

When the Oba started talking of his wives, he found himself genuinely riveted by the Oba's tales and how different each wife sounded. And eventually, when the Oba mentioned Adesua's name, Sully felt his face flush, his pulse dance against his temple. He lifted the Oba gingerly and rested his back against the seat properly. The Oba let slip that he did not trust his council, and that they in return simply tolerated him. Sully glanced through the window; the afternoon light was now dimming slowly, changing into the more seductive, burnished glow of evening. He could hear the chatter of hens and imagined them pecking at each other, charging around in delicious freedom sniffing each other's backsides. There was an orangey tint to the sky. Oba Odion's mumbling in his stupor drew Sully's gaze back. There was a crack in the ground in the back corner of the room, and he wondered what secrets of the palace had slid inside it. Voices travelled through the apartment blocks and the surrounding area, Oba Odion spluttered, the coughing racked his body. Sully patted the Oba's back and offered him his hand; Oba Odion stuck his hand out limply in response. The Oba's hand turned into a piece of thread, and all Sully had to do was hold on to the tip while it continued to unravel.

Soon after that, while attempting to deposit the Oba in his quarters as discreetly as possible, he saw Adesua. Ironically Sully was steadily carrying the Oba, an arm thrown behind his neck and across his shoulder, when he caught the flash of a green, patterned cloth. She was standing beside the tall, sturdy worn pillar watching her husband as though he was a stranger. And she did not rush forward to flounder after him. She rubbed her neck, sighing and throwing an irritated look, as if she wanted them to disappear from view. A little servant girl approached Adesua and genuflected. The girl smiled as Adesua picked her up. Keen to get the Oba to his quarters, Sully continued to lead him gingerly through small clusters of people who wore embarrassed expressions and chuckled under their breaths.

Sully dumped the Oba unceremoniously in his chamber, barely flinching as he hit his mat with a thud. The Oba giggled and pointed, "I like you, good man," before slouching back onto the floor. Sully fumed, the Oba's indignity taunted him. Is this what you came here for? It said. He could only crouch down and watch, in response, patience simmering under his skin. He contemplated throwing water over him but this was the king, an Oba who was trying to dilute the fervour of something nipping away at him. He could feel dust and grainy bits between his toes. There were grainy bits inside him; they needed to be smoothed away. Deep down he knew only one thing could do it. His face twisted at himself and his surroundings. A guava sat on the mantle beside him, plump and beckoning. He reached for it, took a chunk out, but he couldn't taste it.

Braid in The Hat

It happened accidentally. Not that you could follow somebody by accident but Sully had not planned it. He had been scouting for trails out of the kingdom; one because he enjoyed it and two, it was always better to be prepared. He was mentally mapping his latest route which began from the back of the soldiers' quarters, then wound behind the long, dusty new road which had delivered him to the palace gates that fateful day. He was chewing kola nuts, savouring their slightly bitter taste when he spotted a familiar looking, slender young woman darting past, wrapper hiked up and what looked like a broken wooden spear in her hand.

Quick on her feet, she turned occasionally to look around. He paused behind an Iroko tree, recognising the king's youngest wife. *Good grief*, he thought. *What on earth is that creature up to? How had she managed to slip out of the palace unnoticed and more importantly, how did she do so with that spear in her possession?* He chuckled at the thought, waiting for some distance between them before emerging to pursue her discreetly. She headed in the direction of the river, humming to herself, elated at the feeling of freedom. Dust tongues of quiet Gods stilled. Footsteps of hidden creatures with stones in their mouths rustled crinkled leaves. The heat was punishing. Sully's skin had browned somewhat since arriving in Benin but it still burned now and again.

As he watched Adesua weaving between trees, he spotted the tell tale signs on his chest, a patch that looked like a small red sky crawling up his skin. *Damned heat*, he murmured. Thank goodness he had worn his large brimmed brown hat. The mosquitoes liked to feed on him too but he had managed to resolve that problem somewhat in his living quarters, having put up grey netting all around to keep the little buggers out. He had adapted to his surroundings. The way he always did. He could never really blend in but he had picked up some of the customs and habits of the kingdom that endeared him a little to some people.

In the mornings, he walked around with a chewing stick dangling from the corner of his mouth, he had fashioned a piece of orange traditional cloth the king's tailor had given him into a handkerchief which he tucked into his shirt pocket. He ate their delicious food with gusto and quietly observed the kingdom with a keen eye as people continued to gossip about the white man who had charmed his way into the palace. He had found himself coming to this particular river several times because it was out of the way. Hidden behind a wall of forest, an untrained eye could easily pass it without realising what was there. *So she liked it there too*, he thought, warmed by the idea.

At the river, he loitered behind a stack of rocks. She was knee deep in the water, spear in hand, head bent in concentration before lunging at movements below the surface. He watched a few more of her spirited, unsuccessful attempts. Charmed, he uncurled his lean body. Slowly approaching, he whistled. "Why that's the best fishing technique I've seen in Africa."

Adesua dropped the spear. She had been concentrating so deeply, she barely heard him coming. Either that or he was good at catching people off guard.

"Oh. It is you. Should you not be following my husband around?" she spat.

"Shouldn't you?" he asked, giving her an amused look. "You must be the least enamoured bride I have come across."

To her horror, he took off his boots and began to roll his trousers up, exposing tanned well-defined bow legs lightly covered with fine brown hairs.

"No, what are you doing?" She held the spear up, aiming it at his moving chest.

"Easy," he chuckled, barely breaking stride. "You're not going to use that thing on me are you?" The water felt cool on his limbs. If she had not been there, he would have stripped and taken a dip naked. The devilish part of him almost suggested it. Barely a hair's breadth away, he wrapped his hand around hers, gently prying the spear out of it. "I'm your husband's guest. Do you not think you could bring yourself to be more hospitable than aiming a weapon at me?"

He thought he saw a flicker of shame in her expression but it vanished quickly. The water rippled, mouths of fish glimmered seductively below and the afternoon light threatened to bend things to its will. The air between them crackled. He could almost hear the flutter in her long, elegant neck. He knew that flutter could catch things; a bright neon fish scale, the frayed thread on the inside of his trousers, the cut on his jaw he had given himself shaving with his pocket knife three days earlier. He knew if he ran his finger over that flutter the skin would be soft, the shape unpredictable, that he would remember the contours days later.

The catapult in his left pocket was firing a series of jagged objects at an entrance Adesua did not know she had.

"Why do you wear that annoying hat?" She asked suddenly, breaking the tension.

"Oh, this offensive thing?" He answered, giving a half smile and pointing at it. "To protect me from the kingdom's curses."

"You are mocking me!" she exclaimed, wiping a trickle of water from her forehead.

"Come here." He instructed. "I want to show you something." He grabbed hold of her hand. She jerked it back, a scowl on her face. "How dare you? I am one of the Oba's brides. You show no respect.

I could report you to the Oba for that, have you flogged, made an example of."

A tight expression appeared on his face, as if he was considering throttling her. He laughed instead, taking her hand again. "Come and I'll help you catch a fish," he said softly.

He led her to the bank where the water gently lapped at scattered stones. They sat down. He took the hat off, turning it in his hands. "You see this hat? I negotiated with a Chinaman on a ship for it, gave him my pipe in return. Was compelled to at the time, couldn't understand why."

He placed the hat on her head, tugging it down firmly. "There. You look like a modern young woman. What a picture."

She put her hand on her head uncertainly and her lips curved realising it provided shade.

"See?" Sully continued. "Not so bad after all."

She touched a braid poking out, rubbing the kinky hair that had somehow partially unravelled. "Why are you in Benin?" she asked, slapping away the fly she had one eye on, listening to the soft trickle of water, the gentle crackling of the surrounding bush. He turned foreign, cool green eyes at her. "Why is anybody in Benin? I'm a man of adventure. My travels led me here. I have to tell you, that hat looks much better on you than it did on the Chinaman, beautifully turned out fellow that he was. He looked like an Emperor, gave me opium too. I never did ask him how he got the hat."

Adesua did not know who a "Chinaman" was or what "turned out" meant or what "opium" was. Some kind of seasoning for food maybe? She did not ask for fear of appearing ignorant. She knew this shifty stranger would add it to his arsenal of weapons, using it against her when she least expected. She took those funny sayings to be yet more unusual things from this strange man with the crooked smile and unsettling ways.

Later when they caught the silvery fish, Adesua was struck by how quick Sully was, striking with the spear while she was still trying to follow its movements. He made her hold it down on the riverbank.

It felt cool and smooth, a watery distance shrunk in its gaze. He tied it with some string. "For the palace cook! When you eat this tonight, you'll remember our time here," he said, holding it up.

On the way back, she kept the hat on to stay cool, following his lead, his easy manner. He whistled, occasionally peppering their silence with bits of information about the forest's inhabitants; lady-birds, lizards, snakes, throwing curious, loaded looks her way. A molten heat began to spread through her body. She could hear each sound fully, intensely; his long strides eating through the ground, her damp wrapper dripping into the earth, watering the heads of creatures underneath, her breath lined with unspoken things. She watched the curve of the fish's mouth, remembered it bucking against the stones, struggling to breathe and at that moment, imag-ining it turning blind in one eye from the brightness of the light. She returned his hat just before they snuck back into the palace separately, their chests expanding with the weight of new secrets.

And all the way back to her quarters, she thought about her treacherous braid coming undone in the wide-brimmed brown hat.

Adesua responded to the call at night. It winged its way across the palace grounds and she sat up restless. Listening, she succumbed to it. It rumbled its intentions and she only paused to gather frag-ments of her resolve with a scented cloth laced with coconut oil. She followed the call. She counted out her steps to the rhythm of it, as it skirted along the empty trail that led to the main palace. She was so light; if someone laughed it would surely carry her away. She went on past the high iron gates abandoned by distracted guards and rounded the backside of the servant quarters brimming with people. Past the servant quarters, the call tested her, she came to a threshold, a low wall, and beyond it in the near distance was a small, familiar building surrounded by shrubbery. She could make out the outline of a man, and the building behind him was glowing amber approval. She could hear her breaths and the faint thrum of hundreds of caterpillars hatching out of their cocoons and she was crushing them with each step towards Sully's quarters, leaving a trail of squashed, meshed, butterflies spilling colours.

Sully was waiting for her. The sky seemed wider, open with longing, the stars twitching in their ceiling. In that sweet darkness, with only the elegy of the grasshoppers nudging them on, in the clammy anticipation of the night air, she wilted as Sully's face close to hers, naked with intent, seemed to block all that surrounded her. Somewhere on the palace roof her caution plunged down. She ran her fingers through his thick, dark hair, holding his head to the rise and fall of her chest. In the dark, his green eyes seemed bewitching, calming. His beard was rough on her skin. He kissed a trail down her firm stomach, then further down still, till his head was buried between her legs. His tongue softened the bud there. Then he caressed her belly button, running his tongue back up, murmuring her name in slow seductive chants. He held both breasts, chuckling; he named them.

Behind the curtain of a mist that made the palace dewy, as though it were floating in a giant watermark freshly wet, two ghosts peered through. The blurry figures of Oba Odion's father Oba Anuje and his hanged childhood friend Ogiso were keeping busy, spinning a curse so potent, it whipped through the grounds gathering momentum and snatching solace from its unwitting bearers.

Made up of bitter punishments, things left unsaid and repercussions that couldn't be undone, it continued to spin an invisible web over the walls. Between pillars and under the noses of the palace inhabitants, this was a curse that would travel on the back of time, out-shadow shadows and lie in wait at corners where really good fortunes rounded.

The two ghosts stilled their fading fingers and admired their handiwork. Now, there was a fine colourless film sticking to the palace that only they could see. Sometimes, they forgot what they were; there were holes where their hearts used to be. If you looked through them it would turn your eyes bloodshot with scraggly thin lines darting across it. Red lightening in eyeballs, they began to whistle, a charming melody sounding both familiar and new. When dawn came, some people would wake up whistling it too, not knowing why. When the palace was like that, in that silence, it was beautiful. And there were things you could see in that light; like the servant girl who wouldn't live past twenty seasons, the small boy who couldn't stop chewing his thumb, he didn't know it but one day it would just fall off. And the dwarf court entertainer who couldn't stop dreaming of a certain councilman's wife. The ghosts stopped their whistling and paused, after they had cast words that would rain down woes, they savoured the moment because it was a joyous thing! The mist was starting to disappear. They listened to the snoring of the sleeping palace, yet to yawn out its share of crusty, smelly morning breath. And strangely, there was a comfort in that.

Footnote Parables

In Harlesden people milled about. It was a spring day and cocoa buttered brown skinned beauties were out in all their bare-limbed glory, ready to lure willing victims with the promise of their sweetness. I felt under dressed in my scuffed Converse trainers, ripped faded jeans and Betty Boo t-shirt. My head was full with revelations, family secrets that were severed fingers lying on my carpet crooking their way towards me.

Mervyn lived a walking distance away from his practice. On his road in full Technicolor, men sported versions of green, gold and white string vests, standing in groups outside gates catching blaring music beats. I was amazed; here were neighbours in London who spoke to each other. Mervyn's house had cobblestone-like walls. Stunted sprigs of grass with no ambition grew in the small, concrete jungle of his front yard and the oval black gate creaked. He answered on the third knock.

"Hey princess! I'm glad you made it man." I was swallowed into his hug and immediately picked up the smell of grilled meats.

"Can't miss a good barbecue."

I handed over a bottle of white wine that had been sweating in my cupboard for weeks. In the hallway, I stepped over children with missing teeth and mouths full of sweets. Armed with crayons, they huddled over drawing books. A Lover's Rock tune was playing on the stereo. "Wha gwaan sis?" A man with a long beard dressed in an African print shirt said. He was holding a plate of curry goat and rice as if it was his last supper. I was impressed that he managed to peel his eyes off it to say hello.

"Leon, Joy," Mervyn said by way of introduction. In the living room, more bodies were gathered on Mervyn's cream leather sofa. People were leaning on walls chatting between bites of crisp salad and patty. There were some elders sitting at a table talking about cricket and sipping rum. I nodded respectfully as Mervyn went to the kitchen to get me a drink, rum and coke for starters. You could smell the barbecue in the garden from the living room. I knew I only had to walk out through the kitchen door and into the neat, well-kept back garden to find succulent pieces of chicken browning on the barbecue flavoured with spices. Mervyn loved his food.

I sipped the drink Mervyn gave me casually but underneath, thoughts of Peter Lowon were cooking in my brain, sizzling and spitting. I couldn't quite get my head around the fact that my grand-father had participated in a murder, drunk or not. Maybe my family were cursed and it was just a matter of time before I got dragged down with everybody else.

Mervyn had a brand new fitted kitchen that didn't so much wow as comfort. A warm, homely space kitted out in wooden cupboards and grey marble-like countertops. There were trays of food spread out like elaborate Japanese fans. I grabbed a plate. Jerk chicken with barbecue sauce beckoned, ackee and salt fish in a big glass bowl, steamed fish and vegetables, plain white rice, salad, rice and peas and fried plantain. I served a good portion on my plate and tucked in. It was a nice day for a gathering; Mervyn was the sort of man who never lacked company. If I stopped by at two am I could guar-antee there would be strays wandering in and out of the house. I parked myself on a stool at the counter; more rum and coke was needed.

In the garden, Mervyn stood at the barbecue comfortably flip-ping chicken sausages and lamb burgers, affably passing his laughter around as if it were napkins. I happened upon him from the back, my shadow following his baldhead.

"You alright princess?" he turned to face me, still poking a sausage.

"Yeah, this is a nice do, great food, thanks for inviting me." A few people bit into their hot dogs wholeheartedly.

"Hmm, but that's not why you came is it?" he smiled astutely. I made a show of feigning ignorance, wrinkling my nose and attempting the blank eyed look. "What? No."

"Yes, I know you, can't get you down these ends on most days."

"About my mother."

"Ahah! I knew it." He stepped away from the barbecue to give me his full attention. Now the Staple Singers were playing, waiting to do it again.

"Did she talk about her father much?" Internally I smoothed his puzzled expression as pieces slotted into place.

"Not really. You been reading that diary?" he said.

"I think I might need your help."

"Oh yeah? What for?"

"I don't know yet, I'm just warning you in advance."

"So you need my help but you don't know what for? You're a strange girl you know that."

"What does "not really" mean? Just now when I asked about her and my grandfather that was your answer."

He pinned me to the spot with a calm look, "Not really means not really." I didn't believe him.

After that, I got a condensed education on the merits of chess from a bunch of black nerds. Somebody caught me on the video camera and I pulled a face Freddie Krueger would have been proud of. Then, I slunk away to relieve myself.

Mervyn's house had three floors and I went straight to the top. You would think that his house would be full of facsimiles of him and all the people he entertained, plastered everywhere, but especially as I climbed up to the top floor toilet the walls grew emptier and the house took on the feel of somewhere much more functional and far less inviting than it had appeared down below. The walls were bare, painted a dull greyish white and the carpeted stairs held not so much as a stray hair, as if no-one really spent any time up here. In the bathroom I found myself wondering about Mervyn and his family and what made them tick.

I emerged from the toilet to the faint scent of perfume in the air. It was lightly exotic and sweet smelling. With each step I took, the smell grew stronger. It seemed to get stronger further along the hallway. I followed it to Mervyn's bedroom. The hairs on my arms stood up. The smell felt overwhelmingly familiar. The bedroom door was firmly shut. I opened it.

He'd had it redecorated after his wife died. It was a masculine room with dark oak panels and huge wooden bed made with a blue duvet. An un-emptied ashtray spilled old cigarette butts onto the dark nightstand while some big shoes frowned at their temporary neglect. I could have blinked and missed it. Peeking out from beneath the soft breast of Mervyn's pillow was a strip of light purple material. There was a searing, short sharp pain in my chest. I picked up the material. It was silky and light. It weighed nothing but felt heavy in my chest. I held it to my nose, inhaling the scent deeply. Now the smell was inescapable. White spots on the material polluted my memory. I recognised it instantly, my mother's Hermes scarf. She used to tie it into a bow at her throat. I pulled it out gently, touching it. It had the faded smell of Yves Saint Laurent *Opium*, her perfume. I was a low, grainy resolution of myself in that instant.

The thick, maroon carpeted stairs must have cushioned his footsteps because I didn't hear Mervyn come up. I only heard him at the door, shuffling from one leg to the other, his stance slumped and awkward, the expression of deep sadness on his face. He opened his mouth several times but no words came out. He looked smaller in the doorway. I asked myself how that could be possible. Fresh tears sprang in my eyes. We stood there just looking at each other. I took my time, putting my mother's scarf back under the pillow, as if he wasn't standing there watching me. By the time I left the party, Gregory Isaacs was crying for his night nurse.

Outside, the night had the illuminated intensity of an owl's gaze. I took off my Converse shoes and walked barefoot, carrying them gingerly. A white van tore down the street, its exhaust pipe panting magic smoke waiting to catch my sleepy eyes. Later, I knew I'd get home and think of my mother's scarf still faintly smelling of Opium, a red flag under a white pillow.

Peter Lowon Journal entry
March 20th 1956

I met my Felicia. I only met her two days ago but one day I will marry her. It was inside a small, thriving shop several miles from the barracks in Onisha. She was sitting behind the till, sipping from a Supermalt bottle. I have never envied an inanimate object before! She looks like a Fulani girl, with delicate features and her hair braided in an elegant style. She is beautiful. About five of us stopped off to buy some refreshments, maybe bread and tins of sardines to eat on the ride back. She barely glanced our way as we descended on a wave of noise.

I listened to one soldier call her "pretty girl" and wink at her after asking where the beer was kept. I had been pretending to check out maize flour while watching her discreetly. Her voice was calm. "Soldier man, is under the sign that says beer. You dey lose sight for army?" We laughed and she dismissed us, turning to concentrate on the magazine open in front of her on the till counter. She looked no older than twenty to me but her voice had an assurance to it. I watched her bend down in her little shoe-box of space, head disappearing under the counter only to come up again with a cigarette stuck between her lips. The slim cigarette glowed. I found myself starring at the white strap of her top on her shoulder. I picked up more than I needed, bottles of beer, Fanta, pounded yam flour, Bournvita, bread, a packet of Tom Tom sweets. The others were teasing each other at the back, grabbing products, putting them down again.

At the counter I laid everything out carefully. Smoke curled from her mouth. Stupidly, I told her smoking was for fast women! I don't know what made me say that, especially considering I smoke myself! She rang up the goods laughing, telling me if I wanted to ask her out that was not the comment to make! Throughout our brief conversation, she managed to watch what the boys were doing at the back. After she asked if my friends were in the shop to play. I whistled at the boys.

Inside the rusty, white Volkswagon on the way back to the barracks I couldn't stop thinking about her. Up close, she was slim and not too tall. Say 5ft 5in and had the kind of shifting face that looked subtly different each time you saw it. Felicia seemed capable of being a little cruel. For some reason, this made me more curious about her, intrigued. The boys teased me. "British gentleman nah wah oh! See how he just become smooth in front of woman!" They slapped me on the back as if they were proud. "She fine well well but she dey make yanga." I didn't care about their words. I knew they were jealous. I kept playing my conversation with her over and over again in my head, thinking about army life. I can no longer say whether I like it or not, the sound of soldiers boots is constantly in the background. But I like what the army can do for me. It is why I am still here, waiting to take opportunities when they come.

Obi, Emmanuel and I have not talked about the thing we did that night, but there is a coiled string attaching all three of us. These days, when we talk, our sentences have double meanings. I can see the truth, white words written in chalk on their foreheads. Obi is jovial as ever, you would think he has won the lottery. I wonder how long it will last, but the money is good, nawah! Emmanuel is surprisingly calmer than I've seen him in the past. For now this situation has been the making of him. These boys are confident nothing will happen. The General has paid us well, made good on his sugarcoated promises but we will see. I thought of sending the brass head home to my father, a gesture and gift he would love. This would *amuse me, the irony of it. But yet I want to keep it to myself, it is mine after all. It is safely tucked away amongst my possessions. Whispers of a military coup taking over the current government have begun slipping in and out through keyholes. Who knows if this will manifest, but if it does, the death must not be for nothing. Also the General will think of me for the bigger plan, if not I will remind him. I have not told Obi or Emmanuel about the brass head, it is better that way. At unexpected moments I catch myself wondering what I have become now that my heartbeat is no longer my own.*

Felicia. Unflappable Felicia was still on my mind the day after. But Caretaker man, the white-headed seer, a ruffled man in his rumpled uniform, still drifted around looking for clues and making strange proclamations. The mystery of Caretaker man's identity is something the soldiers like to get their teeth into during moments of boredom.

"He must be related to somebody high up, why else would they let a mere caretaker roam around in full military uniform? Ah ah, it is like something out of a comedy." Soldiers often say or, "Oya, something is not right with that man in the upstairs compartment. You know what I'm saying. How old is he?" This is another mystery to us. You cannot tell his age, his face is smooth and unlined, but his completely white hair tells a different story.

At times I imagine he must have received some terrible news in the past, that this news was too much to bear and the days which followed saw the changing of his hair, like a change of seasons, greying and whitening itself from the roots up. Unrealistic I know, though this has stuck in my brain. Other times, I imagine him rising and brushing cobwebs from his head. There is no mention of a wife, children, or family. Nobody knows. One evening, a few of us took it upon ourselves to spy on him. We crouched low under the window of his quarters, listening to high life music coming from his cheap radio. The light from several candles was flickering. He sat on his bed in his white vest and shorts staring into a distance. One soldier imitated a cock crowing and we ran, most of the group chuckling. I felt uncomfortable having seen him in that state. We had intruded on a private moment and whatever he was seeing had rendered him completely still. I remember his uniform hung neatly on a hanger on a nail. I liked him just a little bit more for that.

Earlier that same evening, Caretaker man was sniffing around looking for answers. Mustapha, the soldier who tore his letters to shreds, ran through the barracks naked, screaming at the top of his lungs. He interrupted groups huddled around playing cards, polishing their boots or arm wrestling. He spoke in a strangled, voice and ran frantically to people, shouting that there were demons in uniforms that made promises with smiling faces. That the dead soldier's crime was knowing too much and he was silenced. I did not witness this scene; this is what I was told.

Shortly after this display, three superior officers came out, one holding a syringe in a gloved hand. They held Mustapha down, right there on the common room floor in the presence of all those soldiers. He wriggled his body still screaming for all it was worth, as if something had possessed him. One officer punched him in the face. Blood spurted from his nose and dribbled into his mouth. Then he was smiling blood. The soldiers' voices filled the room, beseeching the officers to take it easy man sir! Feet shifted nervously around the suddenly hot floor. The silver needle, a slim spear in the big room, pierced the stuffy air before it did him. He was sedated, and then they carried him away like it was nothing. I am glad I did not see this; it would have ruined my day.

This weekend I will go back to the shop in Onisha where the beautiful girl Felicia sits on her shop counter throne as if she is in the wrong picture. The lines of her body will be as I remember. She will come to life when she sees me. I will buy gari, cola, and peanuts. The portable fan will blow air over her shifting face; other customers will shop themselves into the background. My hands will be steady. I will make useful and useless conversation with her. She will tell me more about herself. She will give me my change and in the process, something else will be exchanged.

Two-Legged Race, Three Legged Stool

One type of destruction has a way of serenading its victim. It led Oba Odion through the next few weeks with a sure steady lyrical hand. The Oba had a problem; it was not that he was forgetting things, but that he couldn't forget. He would rise late in the day craving the taste of days-old palm wine, sinking himself into the drinking of it till people could smell him long before he entered a room. He stumbled through the palace halls, arms outstretched, balancing himself with fingers splayed on the walls. In council meetings his mind abandoned his head, thoughts balking at the voices. He found himself mumbling agreement to the suggestions of the council members, while distracted by the most irrelevant details. Like how crooked Councilman Ewe's teeth were, and why it had only recently begun to bother him. With every other breath the room grew smaller, as if it were shrinking.

Seated at their table of crumbling self-importance, Oba Odion had also lost his ferocious appetite for the wiles of his wives. In the mornings, his flaccid penis would greet him, the small slit at the crown frustrated by its wasted pleadings, lost in the snarling thatch of curly hair that extended down the softening expanse of his brown thighs. He avoided the questioning eyes of the palace and took to using the long twisted parched path that led away from the gates. That way he could compose himself and talk down the speedy jolts slamming against his temples. He realised on a murky, tangled day that something you thought you wanted badly may turn out to be your undoing. And on that day, he began wearing an expression of deep sadness he knew he would never be able to take off. He would have to cry through it, talk through it and laugh through it, because something was happening. Inside him something was spreading from the pit of his stomach. It was unstoppable, but he tried to slow it down and dilute it with drink. It hit him then, this was what it must feel like if somebody took a heated bar of iron and scraped it along your bones.

Adesua and Sully found themselves staining patches of ground at night as their scents of coconut and a pleasing manly odour that permeated the air mingled and curled the branches of trees. They wallowed in each other whenever possible. Stole glances amidst busy throngs of people filtering in and out around the yards. Glances that burgeoned into the soft pad of a finger against parted lips and later into surrendered bodies. There was a delicious pleasure to it. Adesua struggled to keep this happiness from bubbling to the surface. She had to bite her lip to stop it spilling out. Their betrayal didn't thin their blood; it left only a slightly sour taste, which was washed away by the abandon of two people who couldn't help themselves. They were careful treading cracked lines across the palace with a rhythm of light steps. The possibility of being caught loomed before them, large and steadily arranging itself into caution. Bright-eyed, they attended to their duties with a muffled vigour.

Sully guarded the Oba with an expression of dutiful concern, but the veiled glee in his eyes told another story. By now Adesua had developed a healthy disdain for Oba Odion, insult upon insult! Had he no shame? Trembling and falling all over the place like a useless drunkard. What had gotten into him? But really, what had gotten into all of them? Under the punishing heat in the palace, people were falling apart. Only the day before, in the palace kitchen between piling the ingredients of cocoa yam, goat meat, cassava, wild mushrooms, bitter leaves, baby tomatoes and the bustling servants, the head chef Ahere had ground to a halt and screamed. He stood there screaming while his eyes bulged out of his head and piss trickled down his leg. Nobody knew what he had seen but he was inconsolable for the rest of the day, sent to lie down while the other servants squashed their alarm with tightly-spun snickers.

On the nights Adesua did not see Sully she would lay on her mat turning restlessly, wondering if his feet itched the way hers did, thinking how she never meant to start this unspeakable thing that belonged to them. But it would go on, because she felt alive while the spicy, addictive flavours of dissent swelled her taste buds.

Omotole's burgeoning stomach by now stretched out full and rounded and preceded her wherever she went. She waddled about the palace pleased with herself, a puffed up hen crowing above the others. She was beginning to tire even more easily, but she told herself that was what happened when you carried the Oba's heir, as she began the long, arduous walk to the river, on a dirty, loping path littered with stones and shrivelled leaves worn by the sun. It was not too far but far enough from prying eyes. She spat and gulped her irritation at seeing the blue, bubbling spittle on the ground. The petals were still appearing inside the wet fold under her tongue, and every morning she had to rinse her mouth out several times so it wouldn't stain her teeth. She knew she had to talk to the Oba and soon. The fool was spoiling everything, and did not seem the least bit concerned about becoming the laughing stock of his own kingdom.

As she neared the river, she could hear the chattering of birds and close by smoke from crackling firewood wandered up into the endless expanse of darkening sky. She thought she spotted the ears of a hare behind a clenched bush, foraging for what remnants of food it could find. At the edge of the rippling river she steadied her body for a moment to listen to the water gently caressing the banks. This was where she came, clutching at her throat on days when she felt possessed and was fleeing from discovery, to howl out the fire within her. There was nobody around and that was how she preferred it. She took off her wrapper and naked, she waded gingerly into the river. Her swollen breasts sank into the cool water and her dark brown nipples tingling a little hardened to nubs in relief. One day soon she thought, Benin's new heir would be born, suckling all the strength he would need at his mother's breast. His tiny fist curling and uncurling, she saw this vision so precisely, she almost sighed out loud in pleasure. She submerged her head under the clear water, as thin blue veined streams escaped from her nostrils merging with the ripples.

Years before, under the reproach of the shrieking sun and a sticky, suffocating heat that made you weary of your dry mouth, the boy Odion had stumbled upon a truth that was to become the making and the ending of him. It was a day before the Festival of Yam and the palace was humming with activities. People were carrying slaughtered meat, poultry, yams and such a dizzying assortment of ingredients he could barely count them. After slipping into the palace kitchen for a cool drink of water, bored, he kicked jagged stones as he walked round the back of the palace, eyeing its high familiar terracotta walls; daring it to become something else. His friend Ogiso was nowhere to be seen and he wondered why for the third day running he had not come upon him. Usually, they were together, rummaging through some unfamiliar room, following pretty servant girls with their eyes or play fighting.

But something had changed between them. Not just that recently they had become more competitive with each other; but they had argued. It had started off as an innocent comment, under the mango tree suckling the juicy flesh while they joked. When Odion had said that one day Benin would be his, instead of agreeing with him, a strange look passed over Ogiso's face while he said that no, Benin would rightfully belong to him. Suddenly, there was a tension between them as Odion asked his friend to explain. Ogiso chuckled but the expression is his eyes remained serious. Instantly, Odion was on him and the two boys were pummelling each other. Wrestling their bodies to the ground and trying to fight away the shift that was already changing everything. Then it ended almost as abruptly as it had begun and the boys went their separate ways, neither of them really spoiling for a fight.

The boy Odion continued along the back of the palace as it curved like a voluptuous woman. He heard raised voices coming from a wide window overlooking the gardens. He recognised Oba Anuje's voice and his own mother's. He crouched low under the window. The voices became louder, fraught with tension.

"Stupid woman! You think I don't know that Odion is not my son?" From the beginning I have known, do you know what I can have done to you?"

"Do your worst!" The voice he knew to be his mother's responded but there was a wildness to her tone that he did not recognise. He stayed still, completely rooted to the spot.

"I no longer care, as the Gods are my witness. I found comfort when it came and I will never regret it." Her tone was defiant and he imagined her pacing the room. "Your son will grow up and-"

"He is not my son!" Oba Anuje wailed, "You should be thankful that I have spared the lives of you and that useless child for this long. Come to me with this again and I will have both of you thrown out of Benin." His mother laughed hysterically. Then some unforgettable words came through the window so swiftly, they stung his heart. "And who is your son Anuje? Why not officially announce to the palace, to the whole Benin kingdom that Ogiso is your son. Everybody knows you have been lying with his mother, that good-for-nothing servant woman, all this time!"

Odion heard a *whap!* from Oba Anuje's hand as it crashed onto his mother's cheek, and the sound jarred him into movement. He straightened himself up and ran. It all made sense, Oba Anuje had never been able to stand the very sight of him. The humiliation he'd suffered, the coldness, this was the reason all along. The words reverberated in his head; hot tears trickled down his face and along with them went the essence of his childhood. He had thought the blood of kings flowed through his veins but instead it flowed through Ogiso's.

When he met the medicine man Kalu who had given him the ingredients for death, he knew his prayers were answered. It wasn't until he came upon Oba Anuje poisoned and broken, when in that searing moment their eyes bore into one another's, Anuje's hands desperately reaching out to him for help, that Odion finally felt vindicated. In those last moments before he slipped away, Anuje knew what Odion had done. Never had a moment been so sweet for Odion, the song of death had served a dish of revenge and served it well. Benin was his to take; he had earned it. Now even within the grip of self-pity Oba Odion knew that far from being rewarded, he was being punished. Walking aimlessly about the palace he admitted that he deserved it. His guilt was now fully mauling his conscience. But that was the price you paid and even in death, he knew Anuje and Ogiso would haunt him for the rest of his days.

The halls were swelling with people and they lowered their voices when they spotted him, bowing respectfully as he moved past them; regardless of the depths to which he had sunk, he was still Oba after all. But his dwindling condition was so apparent, they were touching him and wiping their hands afterwards. Oba Odion summoned Sully to meet him at the gates of the palace. No questions were asked as they fell comfortably into step. They trundled on through a rough, coiling road that would take them to a place Oba Odion remembered all too clearly. It was time to see an old friend, and even the worst weather would not have stopped him.

Eventually, they came to the opening of a dense, sprawling forest with twisted, gnarling trees and pathways weaving at you from every direction. At this point Sully walked in front leading the way while the Oba directed him. Finally they came to a small hut and Oba Odion ran to it, calling out a name only for it to be carried in the wind. He rushed inside the hut but it was empty. He shouted the name more frantically. Kalu! Kalu! As if it would conjure the man before him. But there was no one and Oba Odion imploded, because Kalu the medicine man was nowhere to be seen. The keeper of secrets had gone, and all that remained was the shell of his hut letting the breeze stroke its abandoned walls, and the tall grass stretch burnished blades towards it in sympathy and remembrance.

Pendulum

The local park was tucked away behind high, Gothic black iron gates that I suspected snagged things unexpectedly; a pair of hands gripping its bars in disappointment after closing time, a letter blown by a gust of wind, one dirty, sodden trainer caught on the angular tip of a bar at the top, laces dangling down like threads. It was fairly large and unfurled maze-like, intersected by paths heading in different directions. On entering, a lengthy walkway was lined by trees that shook. To the right, at the back a pond shimmered, and the benches before it understood the language of ducks.

As I headed there, the high street hummed. Early evening meant scrums of school children dipped into buses that seem to sag beneath their weight. Shop doors whooshed open and shut, lone customers hunched over menus in poorly lit takeaway restaurants. Handles of heavy shopping bags tugged at the hands of people rushing to get home. Cars nudged each other towards the end of the day and streetlamps yawned light. A chill lodged in my bones. The gentle wind blew my coat open, exposing its red lining to bulls that leapt from behind steering wheels, ran through traffic naked, searching for their horns. I sank my hands deep into my coat pockets, lamenting on how small things could turn sinister; lumps of brown sugar in my cereal becoming dusty red stones, double breathing in my room at night, the rhythm of my breath being copied.

At the park, I cut across the middle, avoiding the long way round. Sometimes, I liked to sit by the pond gathering my thoughts, catching bits of conversation as people meandered by; intrigued by contexts I'd never fully know. Approaching the pond, I spotted a familiar, slight figure sitting on one bench, swathed in a bright, kaftan, there was smoke curling above her white hair. Mrs Harris looked very much like what she was: an old hippy drawing from a shrinking cigarette. She leaned forward, staring at whatever caught her eye in the distance, cigarette tip glowing amber. She threw pieces of bread at some ducks, turned to her left. It was too late to pretend not to have seen her and she waved me over enthusiastically. "Hello there!" She greeted.

At the bench I smiled sheepishly. "Hey there yourself, you're in my spot." I teased.

"Plenty of room for two." She patted the space beside her but didn't bother to remove the gold box of Marlboro Lights that stored weightless nicotine lungs. The ducks argued amongst themselves. I sat down, undid a few buttons of my coat to allow myself to breathe. I took in her side profile and realised then Mrs Harris had once been a looker with her emerald eyes, charming gap-toothed, wonky smile and high cheekbones. With white hair that was reminiscent of snow, hers was a sly beauty, which made it even more attractive in my eyes.

"What are you doing?" I asked. "Taking a break from something?"

"Aren't we all usually trying to take a break in some way my dear? From routine, the cards we've been dealt. I was talking to the water." She took another draw from her cigarette, blew smoke that curled into a root before disappearing.

I laughed. "You're crazy."

"It's true," she exclaimed wisely. "The water never lies. How do you think I knew you were in trouble that day? It was the water that alerted me, not just dropping my ring. The pipes had been clanging and hissing in a really odd, persistent way. I stopped by to hear if you were having the same problem and of course Buddy going missing gave me the perfect excuse."

"That's unnerving," I said.

"Maybe, but it did happen that way. When you didn't answer that second time, I let myself in with your spare key. I found you and the bath water was still running."

I thought of her discovering me on the cold, chessboard linoleum floor. One Queen Piece in a limp heap, watering roots the eye couldn't see, staining her forever with my blood, strange how you could inexplicably bond with someone by trying to slip away.

She threw another piece of bread at the ducks. "How are you doing?"

I shook my head, wanting to cry on her shoulder. "Oh you know, trying to breathe. Do you think becoming increasingly isolated can make someone see things in a distorted way?" I turned to face her fully, edging my body closer. She pinned me with an intense, luminous gaze. As though she could see what I meant behind the question.

"You mean like some people who for whatever reason don't connect to others, lose their moral compass and become serial killers?"

"Well, not exactly, I'm not struggling with a lack of moral compass. I'm-"

"You meant losing touch with reality?" she interjected.

I blew out a tense breath. "Something's shifted; I can feel it in the air. I'm anxious about being alone in my own flat. Once or twice I've woken up in the middle of the night thinking I'm having a fucking heart attack."

"It's not the flat, wherever you were, you'd have this issue. You see the grooves in that?" She pointed at the nearest tree, hand trembling. "What do you see?"

I studied the fat trunk, already leaning against a harsh wind to come, the pattern of swirls. "I see a sad girl with legs that don't feel like her own."

"Really? I see a resurrection and it's not Jesus." She smiled thinly, laugh lines deepening. "So who do you think is right?" she asked.

"I don't know, both of us. Neither of us?"

She took my arm gently, held my gaze. "People like you and I sometimes find ourselves embracing different realities. There's a beauty in it. It's like having a key."

Her eyes glowed and I felt their pull. For a moment she wasn't a sweet, older woman. She looked feral and other worldly. Then the flames in her pupils shrank and she let go of my arm, flicking her cigarette butt away coolly. The noise of traffic grew louder, threatening to break into our green oasis.

"It doesn't seem fair; you know this big thing about me. I don't know enough about you. Pretend we're strangers, tell me something true." I instructed.

"I used to be an escape artist."

"Tell me a lie."

"I used to be an escape artist," she sputtered, biting her amusement down.

"Come on!" I whined. "Play along."

"Okay. My father was a Scotsman, tall and arrogant, a Doctor. My mother was Romany, a free spirit, what they call a gypsy. They were as different as two people could be but my father fell in love. His family were horrified; he married her anyway. He said it had been like something came over him."

"What happened?"

"It turns out she wasn't the marrying or motherly kind. Oh she was beautiful and had this mysterious quality that drew people. She could be kind but she was selfish, self-possessed. She took what she wanted from people without an afterthought. I'm not sure what world she was from."

"What did you want from her?" I asked.

"What any child would want I suppose. To know her more, be loved by her, it became increasingly difficult, my parents... they had terrible arguments. At times it felt like the whole house shook." She paused, reaching for things long buried then continued. "My mother liked the company of men very much you see and that caused even more quarrels. Over a certain period of time, she started coming home with strange cuts and bruises." Mrs Harris shook, touched by a memory. "There were woods near where we lived and sometimes she'd arrive home from there covered in bruises, chanting bizarre things nobody knew the meaning of. One night when I was twelve, she left while we were asleep. Not even a note, I never saw her again."

She ignored what must have been pity on my face, patted my thigh reassuringly. "In the years to come, I felt like I'd dreamt her. In a way you're luckier than me, you can make your mother indelible."

The silence shrouded us in a deepening vacuum. There was no more bread left; Mrs Harris crumpled a white plastic bag before shoving it in her pocket. The ducks had begun to gnaw at shadows of passers by and pond water lapped at the curved lines of their bodies. The trail of white crumbs scattered into nothing. Maybe my mother was indelible, in the crackle of coppery gold autumnal leaves, in the slipstream bearing the ripples of a familiar looking back, in my one winged arm as I held the edge of a dark sky by mouth.

"Also, I'm celebrating." Mrs Harris remarked, breaking the silence. "It's the anniversary."

"Congratulations. What's the anniversary?"

"It's the date I was discharged from Bedlam." This was revealed casually, in the same way a person would say, "Pass the salt."

"You mean Bedlam the psychiatric hospital?"

"The very same. I even wrote a poem on that day:
Once I had a spell in Bedlam,
Dancing beneath a hat,
They came for me goggle eyed,
Wearing the whites of angels.

This was followed by a bitter chuckle. I was stunned into silence. Mad butterflies, I thought. Now that the water knew secrets, it wore the glint of daggers. Bathed in another silence and connected by the mottled umbilical chord of lost mothers we stared at the water, lulled by its gentle, deceptive motion.

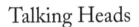

Talking Heads

Windswept and ashen, Mrs Harris stood on my doorstep flickering like the flame on the candle I held. Blanketed by night, her white hair shone even more ferociously. She'd thrown on a black hooded jacket over green pinstriped pyjamas. Glancing at windows of the other houses it was clear the power cut had affected the whole street, I saw the dim glow of candlelight silently breathing against glass in many of them.

"Are you okay?" I asked, ushering her in. "You look sick."

"It's these terrible headaches I get occasionally. God! They're worse than migraines, as though someone's sawing my head in two." She shrugged her jacket off, trailing behind me and slung it over the sofa. "I don't have any candles you see, it's horrible lying in the dark alone like that with an ice pack on your head." Her voice was croaky and sleep lined, as if she'd just woken up. It was after 11pm. I'd lit the sitting room using fat candles that burned the scent of orange blossoms into the air. Some of my mother's old photographs were strewn on the small, wooden side table in a weird time line. The TV sulked quietly and half a glass of green ginger wine promised warmth, sweetness and spice.

"It was so bad; I took some sleeping pills to knock myself out." She continued amiably. "When I came round, everywhere was dark. I had to feel my way slowly out of the house."

"You can sit with me for a while," I offered. "I know what you mean, I hate being ill if I'm on my own. I get this horrible feeling of dread worrying that the worse case scenario will happen. How long have you been suffering with these headaches?"

She sank into the edge of the sofa, right next to the photographs. "They come and go. They first started when I was a little girl. It was horrible; I used to cry from the pain. Anyway, it's dulling now somewhat. I feel like a stray! This is good of you, thanks." She chuckled nervously and raised a trembling hand to wipe her brow. I headed into the kitchen; put the kettle on for some peppermint tea. I moved the blackboard covered with Anon's comings and goings further back, glad I'd had the sense to wipe away some of the chalk markings from the sitting room. In the dark, things changed shape. I was used to it but I didn't want disgruntled, faded markings to accost Mrs Harris.

The kettle hissed its intent. I looked around warily, watching for Anon to make an unexpected entrance. It dawned on me that she usually liked to wrong foot me during quiet times. I filled a cup with the word *grubby* emblazoned on its ceramic, blue body. Since Mrs Harris had revealed she'd spent time in Bedlam Hospital, I felt even more of a kinship between us. I wondered why she didn't tell me all those times she came to visit me at the hospital. I was intrigued by the things that had been set in motion, which bound us together and were tracing our movements with their secretive tongues. I carried the steaming mugs back into the living room where Mrs Harris eyed the pictures curiously. The sound of an ambulance siren flooded the street. I handed a mug over.

"Do you need any painkillers?" I asked politely.

"No thanks, I took some already. I love old pictures," she mused. "They reveal something to you every time you look." She nodded at the display on the table and the short piles on the floor. From my vantage point, the pictures had chalk-drawn miniature nets etched over my mother's mouth. I shook the invasion away. "I'm looking for anything that seems unusual. It's hard to see her appearing so alive... But I need to do it."

"Is this in connection with the brass head?"

"I don't know, yes, maybe. It's to do with her in general. I'm not sure what I'm looking for but I'll know when I see it, if that makes sense. Will you help?" I asked.

"Sure, happy to be of use. I'll earn my drinks," she said.

As we rifled through the pictures, the rough, thick scab inside me began to peel. The wound beneath was red and angry, snarling against bones in my chest. And there was my mother, leaving footprints on my organs, removing the lines on her palms to make one long thread that dangled hauntingly. Each picture showed versions of her plotting to keep growing in the damp soil of memory. There she was, running on a bridge looking behind, cream coat tails flapping in the wind. Outside a café called Sal's, wearing tattered dungarees and a white vest, laughing and holding a paintbrush dripping globs of red paint. In another picture she was on a pier, sunlight streaming over her body, clad in a Fifties flowery, orange dress. There was a wine red butterfly brooch pinned at the right side of her bust that looked ready to flap its wings and fly into my mouth. Mrs Harris watched my expression.

In the pier shot my mother's gaze was direct and intense. The backdrop consisted of a candyfloss stall and a fairground ride of plastic horses, illuminated by smatterings of light on their false bodies. I felt the waves crashing beneath the pier, the pull of the tide. I saw sand-speckled memories washed up on the beach, until the water's unpredictable line dragged them in again. My mother's lips were pursed; I tasted the salty sentences that had loitered on her tongue. Mrs Harris had remained quiet for a bit, rubbing her temples, smiling sadly, and sipping tea. Suddenly she piped in. "Very striking woman, elusive somehow. There's something in her gaze…." She paused, and then continued. "Chameleon like, I bet she navigated social groups easily, whereas you're more of an odd character, in a good way," she added, touching my hand.

I wondered if through my touch on the photographs, my mother could feel my fingerprints on her back. Sending her limbs into movement, crawling through dead soil onto fractured planes only those left behind could breathe into existence.

As we rummaged through more snaps, Mrs Harris's face swam closer, then further back under the gaze of candlelight. The candle flames burned wax, flickered, threatening to lick the edges of the photos. She gingerly set her empty cup down next to my glass. "You can ask me you know, about how I ended up in Bethlehem Hospital. It's only natural to be curious."

"I guess I was surprised when you first told me but then it made sense, that's why you came to see me so much in the hospital, why you took an interest. I'm grateful for that. You don't have to tell me if you don't want to." I snuck a sideways glance at her; she seemed calm.

"No, its fine, I want to." She drew her shoulders back, as if steeling herself then continued. "I had a break down just after my marriage ended. Nicholas, my husband was a very creative man. He had this ethereal quality about him." She smiled wistfully. "He used to make the most beautiful scenes and figurines from wood. Oh, they were stunning! The level of detail... He'd lock himself away for hours carving those things."

"Did he ever make any money from it?" I asked.

"Well, there were small commissions from friends, people we knew but nothing steady," she answered. "He was your classic frustrated artist, delightful if you caught him on the right day. Struggled with terrible mood swings though. We fought a lot over money since I was covering most of the bills. He accused me of attempting to turn him into something soulless." I stood and opened the window slightly to counter a growing tension in the air. She tucked a wisp of hair behind her ear.

"One day, we had a terrible fight. He'd asked me for money, quite a large sum. I wanted to know what it was for. He claimed I was emasculating him. He was in a rage, he flew at me, grabbed me by the throat strangling me." She stopped again, stared at the memory head on. "At the time, I was battling one of my awful headaches. You have to understand that sometimes when they come, things take on a dream like quality; I can lose my sense of time. I picked up the metal poker we kept by the fireplace and hit him. I kept hitting him until I saw blood and he went limp. The headache was screaming."

"Jesus," I murmured sympathetically.

"I was stumbling around, my head felt like it was split open. I left him lying on the floor. I went calmly upstairs to find my medication. But he'd thrown them away you see. I blacked out on the bed the pain was so intense."

"Sorry to hear that," I responded, squeezing her arm. She laughed her eyes bright and leaned forward assessing my face. "You're shocked, you think I'm heartless. I have to admit at the time, I thought he was dead. When I came round, he'd disappeared, taken my bankcard and wiped out the account. Everything fell apart after that." The sadness in her eyes cloaked the whole space. I felt sorry for her, sorry for both of us, cardboard cut-outs of ourselves crashing into real life.

"What about those pictures?" She pointed to a stash in a grey envelope at the foot of the sofa.

"I've looked, didn't pick up on anything." I grabbed them, handed them over. "Feel free," I added. She leafed through, lips curving up and brow furrowed.

"That's interesting, " she said, spreading them on the table like a stack of trump cards.

"What?" I navigated myself round for an even closer view.

"Well… the lens on her. See the light in which she's been captured? It's beautiful, personal. Look at the way she's interacting with the camera. See the look in her eyes? It's quite intimate. It's like a lover's gaze."

I peered closer and she was right. In the photograph my mother wore a thinly-strapped white top teamed with a red velvet miniskirt that exposed her long, lean legs. One strap had slipped down teasingly against her arm. Her feet were encased in fire engine red, traffic-stopping heels. A purple Hermes scarf was tied jauntily around her neck and she leaned back against a beat up, blue Ford. Of course, I recognised the scarf. It was the one Mervyn kept beneath his pillow. She was laughing in some of the shots, head thrown back, light falling gently on her neck. In others, smiling coyly, a hand splayed invitingly on her chest, sweat beading on the rise of plump breasts. And others still, mouth twitching knowingly, staring at the camera head on. She penetrated it with a subtle defiance, communicating to the glass eye in a language imprinting itself on the roll of film. I animated her with the flicks of my finger.

Mrs Harris picked up the bottle of green ginger wine, unscrewed the cap. I moved to grab another glass but she motioned with her hand. "Don't worry; I'll use yours, no point sullying another glass. And you don't have anything I can catch?" she said in jest, filling the glass and moving to stand by the window. "Did you know any of your mother's boyfriends?"

"Not really, she was discreet about that sort of thing. An unmarried African woman with boyfriends having no intention of getting married would have been frowned upon back home." I ignored the ticking in my temple.

Mrs Harris rubbed her face, eyed the glass. "It's just a thought but maybe her last lover knew something, people tell each other all kinds of things in bed."

A sick feeling crept inside me. I watched her raise the glass to her lips, thought maybe I'd pushed glass rims towards her unwittingly all evening. We caught the arrival of car headlights engraving yellow travel journeys on the road. For a moment, watching her knock her drink back, it was as if her head had split in two, drowning her silhouette yet harbouring daylight in her eyes.

The Shape Of Traps

Rumours of a curse in the palace began to take on funny shapes. A servant fixing the hole on the roof could have sworn he saw a woman drumming her fingers on her jaw inside it. She looked lost and forlorn, but before he could reach out a hand to help her, he slipped and fell to his death. In the roughened, scab-ridden feet of the chief courtier that had ceased leaving footprints, making him marvel as to how he could both be and not be in a place all at once. In the ever-burgeoning belly of Omotole whose greedy baby was sapping all her strength. She found herself pausing to check he hadn't stolen her heartbeat too, placing her clammy fingers on her chest and at her wrists, anxious for the faint throb of her existence. And where was Oba Odion? Locked away in his chamber worshipping the darkness of his shadow, and the murky, distorted shapes that flittered from his lids and darted across the warm floor.

The council were now running the kingdom but their quiet triumph fell flat on its face, gashing its thin skin under the altered glow of a waning Benin. The people did not know why things were happening as they were, but it continued. One of the Oba's tailors became stuck in a moment of coming in and out of his door with a small pail of water. He kept repeating this action again and again, until he was dragged out of it, flailing his arms in resistance. The palace appeared unsettled, there was a hushed fear rubbing the walls and the teeth of the gates had a sinister gleam when the light caught. People wondered why their lives began to droop right in front of their eyes. Their sympathy shrank. Where was the king to rule over his kingdom? Where was he to stroke their questions with reassuring answers? A thick resentment began to build, passing between them like morning greetings, lagging at the entrance of the palace waiting for any opening. And when blood started leaking through the roof, nobody dared go up there to see why. Instead they scrambled to their knees, at once mopping the jewel-like droplets with a snatched cloth and the loosened shock from their jaws.

It was that time of day when Benin was caught between late afternoon and early evening. When the daylight dimmed to a duskier yellowy orange, and you could swear that someone was shrouding the sun. The smell of cocoa yams doused in flavours of wild peppers, onion and meat stock wandered from the main palace like a drifter requesting entry at the nostrils of irritable inhabitants. When the day stopped deceiving itself and it finally became evening, it was the perfect time for two lovers to meet because everybody was distracted. The palace servants had gathered wood for their small celebration of nothing and would soon form a ring of mouths around a ravenous fire. Most of the councilmen were in their various apartments, doing anything to stop their stomachs from somersaulting over the future prospects of Benin. The Oba's wives, disconnected pieces of a game, loitered in their compound. They were braiding their hair into submission, attempting to wash the stubborn odours of the palace from their clothes or tracking their restless children.

So two lovers met, on the wrong side of a stretching, split dirt road, on the right side of betrayal and all it entailed because it was with them now, a third, palpable thing, that was not just rearing its head, but its arms and legs too. It carried them and they in return stoked it, fanned it. On that dirt road Sully lifted Adesua onto his back, her legs wrapped around his middle, thighs rubbing against his bare skin. She was laughing, transformed by giggles, and then nipping at his neck with the certainty of a young woman in bloom.

She rested her face into the crook of his neck, mumbling into it. It didn't matter that he didn't know what she was saying right then, because something beyond his control lit inside him. He could have wept, just stood in that moment and wept; instead, as she slid down, he hefted her further up his back. Rushing into the waiting night, rushing into a cruel trick of life, the way the unfortunate ones do. The heavens watched Adesua and Sully in the distance; it was a matter of time before somebody spotted them. Benin's decline was imminent and they were a part of it.

The roof continued to leak blood. This baffled the palace. When a few servants began to see reflections of themselves swimming in that blood, they abandoned cleaning it, stilled by the fear dancing on their spines. Small puddles of blood formed on the floors within the main palace, as if the heavens had a wound that kept opening up to drip down upon them. It had an ancient, rotten stench that the servants cleaned but could never get rid of entirely. They took to opening the doors for long periods of time, and the air wrestled the smell out only for it to find its way back in again.

The council ordered a new roof be built but in their hearts they knew something serious was at work. Something that no amount of intricately entwined palm leaves woven into the skull of the palace could stop. So they did what they knew to be their only plan to combat their worries. They continued to rule and to live. While they rallied what was left of their army of men in preparation for an over-throw, the servants continued to maintain their beautiful palace, and the farmers fed and ploughed the land. Then worry began to strip some people of their sleep, hiding it under their mats or the folds of their lids. So they would not know the irony of it being close by. Tense bodies slick with moonlight glow you wanted to lose yourself in traipsed around the grounds. It was a funny sight from above, to watch the cornered. To see how they stayed and how sad it was when all you know is all you think there is. These people were hold-ing onto their beloved kingdom, keeping it alive with their breaths. But what would you have them do? If only the people in the palace knew what they were doing, baiting their own traps with the very things that could release them from it. And Sully, the stranger in their midst became increasingly comfortable, touching the cracks in the kingdom with dusty, pale hands.

When Omotole finally got to see her husband, Oba Odion was dipping into the shallow end of his pain. He sat on the shabby, wheat coloured mat on his floor, legs splayed. There were dried crusts of food on his chin and his eyes were red-rimmed and distant. He was dishevelled, his hair noticeably fuller than it had been, his clothes were so wrinkled and dirty they annoyed you to look at them. He was plumper than he had been, refusing visitors but clearly not refusing food. In the stale, trapped air, Omotole lowered herself beside him slowly, her protruding belly a visual reminder of the future. It was something to jar him out of the state he was in but he only continued to stare blankly ahead. She wrapped her hand around his wrist, yanking his arm towards her, then splaying his fingers on her stomach. "Oba, your son is coming." The smile he cracked was wobbly, unsteady on his face.

"What is the meaning of this Odion? Terrible things are happening, what have you done?" She turned to him, the urgency in her voice almost a third person in the room. "No, no, no!" Oba Odion answered, "It is what he has done. Can you not see he will not leave me in peace!" Omotole glanced around the room quickly to indulge him. "What are you saying Odion? Who will not leave you alone?"

"Anuje." The name was soaked in spit as bits of saliva slipped from the corners of his mouth.

"Anuje is dead Odion."

"No." Oba Odion shook his head so hard that it wouldn't have been a surprise had it begun to spin clean off his neck

"Yes!" She grabbed his shoulders digging her nails into him, "You killed him. Stop this nonsense and look after your kingdom. You think the council should be running it? This is an insult."

Oba Odion shoved her away with such force she slammed her head against the wall before sliding down to the floor. He could only mumble to himself as her whimpers rose towards him before dropping down again.

Occasionally, Councilman Ewe wandered over to the servant quarters to ask for one errand or another to be done. On this night, it was to put in a request for kola nuts for the next day's council meeting. In between bits of bitter, crunchy kola nuts, the men would lament over events in Benin; it was clear that something had to be done. After a slightly annoyed male servant stretched his sluggish frame through Ewe's instructions, Ewe began to head back. He was thinking of the odd occurrences that had been happening and whether they would get through it. Really Oba Odion's inability to oversee his kingdom was a gift as far as Ewe was concerned. Without a qualm he'd relinquished control to the council who were all too willing to take over.

As Ewe contemplated the fortunes of Benin he spotted Sully's quarters further down the trail of the worker's area. Later, he would not be able to say what exactly it was that drew him to it. Whether it was the way it had appeared in his vision suddenly. Or if it was the resurfacing of his annoyance at how quickly the Oba had taken to Sully, allowing him freedoms no white stranger should ever have been afforded.

Before he could change his mind, he found himself moving towards the terracotta hut Sully had taken as his home. It was a short walk and as he neared it was surprised that Sully, the man who always appeared so alert had not come out to greet him. At the door he was torn about announcing himself, but his voice tickling his throat made the decision for him. As he stepped round the back he jerked quickly from what he saw before him. Sully sitting on the ground with the Oba's youngest wife Adesua between his legs, her face resting sideways against his chest, eyes closed, both barely clothed and what clothes there were, arranged in complete disarray. Councilman Ewe took pains to leave as silently as he was able to, armed all the way back to the palace with the hard, disgruntled image of the two lovers embedded into his head.

Light Shade

There is a moment that trespasses sporadically inside my head. I don't know if this is an actual memory or something my brain cooked up, but in it I'm no older than five or six. My mother and I are inside a café; the sign outside it reads Denny's. At the counter, there is a portly white woman with brown hair and a foreign accent. She is wearing a blue apron with white stripes and indiscreetly biting her fingernails. I am wearing a white dress with a yellow sunflower pattern on the skirt. My mother has on a blue T-shirt and faded denim dungarees; there are lighter spots where the material is thinning. We are sitting by the window with a man who looks older than my mother. His hair is lightly peppered with grey but his brown face is smooth. The table hasn't been wiped down properly, there are crumbs on it and the plastic ketchup bottle has sauce running down its white mini cone lid. Underneath the table, the man is tapping his feet on the floor. I take a sip from the steaming hot chocolate before me and burn my tongue. Here's the weird thing, they open their mouths to speak but I can't hear a word. There is no sound coming from them but they are definitely talking. Though I can hear other things, the cash being rung up on the register, the door swinging open to allow hungry customers to make rushed orders of the lunch time special soup, chairs scraping back against the floor, Roy Orbison driving all night on the radio and the jingle of cutlery coming from the back kitchen. It is like a semi-silent movie where you can hear everything, but the main actors. Then my mother's facial expression turns, she looks furious and is pointing at the man with short, sharp movements. Her mouth is moving, doing that thing she did when angry; curling down, like it will drop to her chin. The man shakes his head, he looks beaten, and his twitching left leg has taken on a life of its own. He stretches his arms out to us pleadingly. My mother stands up jarring me, more words are exchanged and yet… more silence. She grabs my hand, pulling me away; the man cuts a lonely figure. It seems he is wearing a Sunday best grey suit on a bleak midweek day. I turn to wave at him; it feels as though my fingers are skimming something bigger than me. He waves back. A smile cracks his face. Outside, the door chimes shut behind my mother and me. Her chest is heaving. Each time this scene comes to me, I am desperate to hear what was said.

Peter Lowon, Journal entry
October 1956

Felicia and I are married! She is three months pregnant but not showing yet.

We said our vows inside a neat, packed church in Lagos. Our families came for the wedding. While the minister's voice was booming, I caught my father's movements using my side eye. He sat in the front pew with my mother who was dressed in a bright yellow wrapper and blouse, her hair braided and styled into a bun, her neck adorned with thick, heavy pink beads. At one point I was sure he took off his glasses to study the proceedings more intensely, something he does when he cannot believe his eyes. He wore his favourite black suit, he looked proud. To my surprise, a lot of my army boys came, teasing me in the annoying but familiar way I have become accustomed to. "Ah British gentleman don marry oh! Funny character, your wife fine well well"

"Nah wah oh, wonders will never cease, why the rush to marry now? You are making us look bad my friend, you are still so young."

"Leave British gentleman alone, he knows what he wants." This from Obi who had Emmanuel with him.

It is funny how I cannot separate the two of them now. I think of one and the image of the other attaches itself. It wasn't always that way. Despite everything, I was surprisingly happy to see them. It is as if I too in my own way wanted to say see? Life can carry on as normal! Let me confess that on the day I was also very nervous, not because I had any doubts about marrying Felicia, no, she was a vision in cream. But because I was frightened something would snatch away my good fortune. That Felicia may pull me aside and say I cannot go through this with you. That while blessing us I would suddenly be violently sick on the minister and he would proclaim that my soul was tarnished. And then the spirit of the dead soldier would appear, just as I was about to kiss Felicia and seal my vows. Thankfully none of this happened. By the time I was walking away from the minister with Felicia's hand in mine and the guests were whooping there was a stitch in my side.

General Akhatar came to our native ceremony with a big-bottomed fair skinned woman I did not recognise, his sunken, beaten side face floating amongst the sea of guests with full faces. I wondered why a man of the General's stature and success had not married. But then I was caught up in a dance with my wife, which swept the question away.

That night she held my fingers firmly. In our adequate apartment in Lagos, just big enough for us, I made love to my wife. I kissed the faded scar on her left knee, shaped like a caterpillar. I made a replica one on the opposite knee with a trace of my finger. In her belly button I whispered to my growing child. I drew her ankle down to my face, read her fortune from her beautifully arched feet. I predicted she would marry a foolish man because like attracts like, and listened as she laughed, falling against my chest.

Afterwards, we lay on our backs on the squeaky mattress coated in a lovers' sweat and I asked her why she'd agreed to marry me.

She said, "Because I love you. You are reliable, quietly strong. You are still getting to know yourself and I see your potential." Then she kissed my shoulder. I slid down and rested my head on her stomach. Silently, I told my child I would teach them to sit on top of their weaknesses. I warned them not to make my mistakes. All three of us were a triangle of flesh, nerves and electricity reflecting in the blades of the whirring ceiling fan overhead.

Several days later Felicia discovered the brass head in my bag whilst unpacking my things. "Peter, where did you get this?" She stood facing me in the doorway of our box kitchen holding it up, a curious look on her face. The bottle top I'd removed with my teeth from the cola grazed a lie a husband must tell his wife. I informed her it was an early wedding gift from General Akhatar, from his collection, one of his favourites.

I watched my wife run her fingers over it, as if she were blind and trying to memorise its image with her hands. Finally she said, "that's so generous of him, this is something special, and he must think a lot of you to give you this. You have to stay on his good side."

Felicia carried it away to display in our parlour. I bit down a sudden worry. That in my absences the brass head would be a mirror. It would show her she was more than just a shop girl, more than a wife and mother.

On our first date I brought Felicia a gift, a packet of cigarettes I laid in her palm gently. One eyebrow shot up and there was amusement in her eyes. We stood outside her miserable looking rickety grey house. She was beautiful in a white dress.

"I thought smoking is for fast, loose women" Was her comment.

"Maybe, maybe not" I steered her towards the black Volkswagen sitting there like a blown up bug.

I told her I wanted it to be our last packet of cigarettes.

I knew she was laughing inside at my hypocrisy. I stood there feeling exposed. If I looked down, there would be a trap around my foot, and she would pluck out a slim cigarette, light up, then offer "cigarette?" as I howled. Instead she dropped the packet inside her handbag. We sat inside the car watching the house for a moment.

"You're not like some of the other soldiers that come into the shop. You seem sad for someone so young."

I didn't answer but flicked the engine on. Heady, wild flower perfume filled the car, and I swear I wanted to tell her right then.

We went to the cinema and watched a horror film where the acting was so bad it should have been a comedy instead. We laughed and laughed. Afterwards, we took a walk by a bendy road. I asked her why she was not studying at the university for someone so bright. And she told me.

When Felicia was at secondary school, she had been an A student, always performing within the top of the class. At Our Ladies of Light School she was a popular girl but was always getting into fights defending one stray or another. This resulted in memorable run-ins with the head mistress. Either her skirts were too short, she couldn't mind her business or she had no respect for authority. But to the head mistress's annoyance she continued to excel. She spent every spare moment in the school library, tracing the spines of books and poring over their pages greedily. She read books on physics, biology, philosophy, history, law and economics. Her first love was the work of Soyinka but she cheated on it with the poetry of Keats. The school librarian was so enamoured with her, she began to keep books of interest aside for her. Though Felicia was an only child, even with their little shop, they were still poor, her father elderly and sickly, her mother changed by bitterness. They could not afford to send her to university but one day something wonderful happened.

Felicia was called into the principal's office and told she had been recommended for a university scholarship and she would have to apply to the Ministry of Education for it. The deadline loomed. That day, she ran home excited, foolishly showing the forms to her parents. Two days later, the forms disappeared. She searched everywhere but her search came to nothing. She never asked which one of her parents was responsible; it was too painful to know. Instead, she spent her nights re-reading old library books by candlelight on her bedroom floor. And the candles without fault were always apologetic, shedding their melting hot skin onto her resigned knuckles.

We followed our steps back the way we came, creating a map of the latter half of our date. The air hummed with night creatures and we held a comfortable silence heading back to the car. I wondered at such normality after that terrible night. The three of us, Obi, Emmanuel and I were walking around as if nothing happened. I asked myself how a beautiful, smart girl couldn't see me for what I am; a self-centred opportunist willing to do whatever it takes. Or maybe she could see it and just locked it away. I drove her back home and we sat again looking at her house for several moments. I didn't want to stop myself when the words came out.

She didn't say yes that time, she squeezed my hand and laughed. And when she shut the door behind her it felt like the beginning of something. I know it is funny and true; I proposed to my wife at the end of our first date.

Discombobulated Herd

First the wives went bald, their gleaming crowns like plump brown melons waiting to be pulped, left them clutching their thick, fluffy hair as if they were vanishing puffs of smoke. And by now the palace grounds were vomiting. Dead insects littered hidden cracks, red ants rolled on their backs in haste and confusion, mosquitoes buzzed about in panic swirled patterns and the strange bluish plants in the garden had wilted. As though the heat off a cutlass had crushed their hopes to death, and really, they couldn't blame the heat. Not when hundreds of fish lay on the red earth trail leading up to the gates, bucking against each other in those precious few moments before their stories of water escaped them forever. Not when it began to hurt to look around the palace, to see the tiny bits of crumbling walls that a virgin eye wouldn't pick up, the abandoned rooms unattended gathering only dust for comfort, the circular courtyards once bursting with congregated shades of brown bodies vacant and naked in their loneliness because people stopped lingering. Instead they rushed through, shutting themselves off from the miniature storms whipping through their heads.

And the days merged into one long passage of time that seemed to never end or repeatedly began depending on how you looked at it. The palace rumbled, grumbling low so gold-kissed leaves left their trees to drop down and listen, carrying what they knew to the feet of the inhabitants who couldn't understand the crackly language they spoke. Some people began to not know themselves, frightening their hearts out of their chests. So they sought the council, begging them to do something to stop this invisible hand that was twisting them all. Their worry was now distorting their voices, even to their own ears, changing their walks, splitting their lips. They were being smudged into their picture, blurred, till you wanted to check their bodies for thumbprints. The council members bit down on it all gently, apprehensively. Bloated with their cheapened version of power, they kept their stiff necks outstretched. This was bigger than them. All they could do was to show the people of the palace their palms, empty of answers.

Omotole and her baby survived the incident with Oba Odion. She was too strong to allow an inept king to finish her, husband or not. It was bottomless will that allowed her to crawl her way out of there; while he sat rocking himself into the bleak, dark enclave he had built for himself. She had not sighted him since, so when her water broke, the blue tinged liquid splashing between her feet in the yard outside her chamber, she did not ask for the Oba to be told. Instead, she grabbed the hand of a servant girl tightly and a wince flashed over the girl's face before she lifted her up, shouting out for more help.

One of the other wives came. Omotole recognised the eldest wife before they gripped her arms, one on each side as they moved her back inside her chamber. There, a musty scent was clinging to her clothes and her headdress. They laid her down on her newly made grape coloured mat with its thin, slightly rough edges. The pains of childbirth came thick and fast and her screams pierced through the rooftops. Later, other details would come back to her; taking short sharp breaths, the feel of a small wet cloth on her forehead, advice that rained, a jumble of words that fell all over her body and her legs propped up. And a hazy feeling of confusion that continued to grow throughout. Both the servant girl and the first wife were alarmed at what was happening, though they tried to keep it from their voices.

When the baby finally came some hours later, the servant girl was unable to stop shocked words flying through her lips. "Oh the Gods help us!"

"What is it?" Omotole said, limp and tired she struggled to raise her head up. They handed the baby over to her wrapped in a sucking, gloomy silence. The first thing she noticed was a soft looking, small exposed chest and it was a boy. He was wriggling in the way that newborns do, covered in an unusual blue gunk. As her eyes wandered up, a horror gripped her by the throat. He was alive, but her baby had no face.

Bad news like good news travels fast, and before they knew it, residents in the palace found themselves making excuses to visit Omotole, just to get a look at the baby. Some even made bets on how deformed the baby would be, but nothing prepared them for it. From the neck down, the baby was perfectly healthy. Its arms, legs and body were just as they expected. But it was his face... It was such a shame and they had never seen anything like it. It was completely flattened, as though what lay under the skin wasn't bones but mush. It looked as if he had been filed down; there were no angles or planes, just an insult of a face stuck there. An ugly, terrible face not even a mother could pretend to love.

Even with the eyes, tiny slits of flecked brown and the gash of a mouth, you couldn't tell anything about the child. Whether it was happy, sad, and hungry or tired because you just couldn't see it. It was all Omotole could do to interpret his thin, high cries as the instincts of motherhood abandoned her, frightened away by the sight before them. And she was inconsolable those first few days afterwards. Her eyes wet with tears, carrying him as if he were a mistake, labouring over why it had happened, how it had happened. Shame, heavy and scorching burned her, so much so that she felt hot even when it was cooler in the evenings, and you could smell the dry earth and relief of the suffocated air that darkness was coming.

She thought of the bluish excretions from her body that had suddenly stopped, and the petals under her tongue no longer appeared.

How deceptive it had been and she almost felt she had imagined it all, only she knew she hadn't. A hard blame began to form in her stomach, as she thought of Oba Odion up there sheltered away from it. No, this was not her doing, but the disgrace would never leave her. And she would sit there, on the cusp of night, staring at her son dumbfounded, beads of resentment popping on her brow, she and that wailing baby; attempting to talk expressions into his face.

While Omotole's baby sent tremors through the place, something else was bubbling beneath the surface like simmering soup. Councilman Ewe could never keep a secret, particularly if it was of no benefit to him to do so. If you knew you wanted to keep a secret protected, they should never pass your lips in his presence. That night after he had seen them, he was almost drunk with this knowledge, coming back to the apartment he shared with his wife. How those fools could be so brazen right under their noses! Oba Odion's appointed guard and his youngest bride laughing at them all. The council had warned the Oba about her, they had all seen that she would not make a good wife but bring shame on the palace. No amount of undoing could change what had happened.

He arrived home to see their small, apartment had been swept, and the terracotta walls darkened by night made his eyes swim a little. He was a success, a member of the Oba's council, residing in the palace with a wife and two children. He had truly arrived, and he imagined the tiny village he came from just shy of Onisha hailing him. The dancing and music leading a trail all the way back to his family's hut. So engrossed was he in that image he nearly tripped over a chipped dark wooden chair they usually left in the corner of the back room. The apartment smelled of the homely mixture of cooked goat meat and Ewe's ambition. As he stopped to listen to them he could hear the reassuring breathing of his children caught in sleep, their young chests rhythmically rising and falling. Finally, he took off his beaded adornment and crept in to sleep beside the broad, fleshy frame of his wife who murmured a little in response. He tried to sleep but found himself tossing and turning, till his wife frustrated by it said, "*Ah, ah* what is it?" So the secret entered her ears.

"Tell the council Ewe," she *humphed*.

"You know what the punishment is for such a thing?"

"Tell them."

And he ran his excited tongue over his dry mouth.

Amidst these events in the palace, Filo remained surprisingly calm. As if the shrieking Harmattan-like wind inside her that had pulled her furiously back and forth suddenly stopped. She thought it funny that the slow destruction happening around her created an opposite effect within her. And she began to run towards her thoughts instead of away from them. Just outside her narrow chamber doorway, if you stood on your toes you could see the Oba's back room window staring the horizon down. Every time she looked, somehow it seemed further and further away. She had allowed a thought so delicious to leave her head and sit in her mouth that she no longer felt guilty carrying it with her. And it was this: she was glad Oba Odion was suffering. Through her hair falling out, the blood from the main palace roof and the stream of bad luck that had plagued the palace it was clear that he knew. He knew why these terrible things were happening but couldn't show his face. The Gods would disapprove but she was happy the Oba was being handed the fate she believed he deserved.

It was a clear, slow-burning day when it happened. Filo's skin felt sticky and no amount of water wetting her dry throat was enough. She was tentatively tending to the group of fowl that hung outside their back yard, throwing grains of corn to them and watching them pick at it. At the same time thinking of the street vendors that lined the roads on market day, whistling through their teeth and shoving handfuls of material, native jewellery and spicy food wrapped in broad green leaves your way. But then a curious thing happened, a seminal occurrence. Filo softened, her body had stopped turning to stone. She dropped the corn, haphazard yellow mouthfuls scattered as if to be replanted.

The fowl, her only interested audience, sensing the importance of the moment began to cluck, as she started a sure, confident retreat. She took nothing; she turned to do the walk towards the main palace where the gates were waiting. People were milling about within pockets of the grounds and she passed some guards laughing at words hanging between them. They nodded at her and she did not stop. She walked out of the palace gates and didn't look back. She threw the spare gate key she had stolen from a guard into the river, imagining water creatures using it to unlock a town beneath their tremors. And she kept going because beyond her, that body and that life, the rivers and the land, another world beckoned. Winking just behind the edges of broken clouds, she imagined people filled with so much light, it would be blinding, and a place where the shame of this life was not smothering the next.

Applique for Beginners

Reading my grandfather's diary felt like I was on a canoe, in the sea. I didn't even know if I liked who I think he was, or if I knew enough about him to patchwork quilt his personality together. He was just fragments colouring white paper. When someone does a terrible thing, a thing that continues to have repercussions, it's hard not to judge. It is difficult not to stick a label on their box that says *damaged, carry this side up.* It is hard not to be reminded that you are alone and that maybe, a puppet master made these strings for you long before you were born.

Tomorrow, in households across the city, door hinges will creak emphatically as the air sweeps failures and successes of the day. Fathers will tuck their children into bed and smile knowing that one day this moment too will change, mutate into a different version because you can't protect your children forever. And somewhere, a moth begins its day by laughing at me.

Peter Lowon, Journal Entry May 1961

My daughter Queen is now five years old; she is like her mother in the sense that she is all-seeing. I have heard people say this and it is true for me too; the day she was born was the happiest day of my life. Everything else paled in comparison to her toothless grin, her pointed nose that is a replica of mine and her first attempts at walking. I named her Queen because the first time I held her perfect little body, she opened her bow shaped mouth and crooked her tiny finger at me as though she were a royal and smiled. So I call her Queenie and her mother calls her Queeeeeenie! Because most of the time she is shouting her name.

Queenie is a fearless child. She sticks her hands inside holes in the ground, touches everything, attempts to catch lizards with her bare hands and talks to the flea ridden stray dog down our street that begs for food. Sometimes, she angles her head to the side when you are talking to her, as if she's questioning the validity of what you're saying. On my trips home, after the gate has squeaked and announced my arrival, she runs as fast as her feet can carry her, clutching my uniform clad legs. "Daddy you're home! What did you bring for me?" Queenie does not stop asking questions, in fact Felicia has joked that she is considering taping Queenie's mouth for at least two hours a day. Daddy what is rainbow? Why do people call you Lieutenant Colonel? Is fried dodo banana? Why do they put pepper in suya? Doesn't the man selling corn on the road with no shoes have a daddy to buy him shoes? Daddy why? Daddy, daddy, daddy.

Yesterday she told me she drew an eye on a tree. When I asked her why she looked at me as if I was an imbecile and said "so the tree can see, shhh don't tell mummy!" Now the mango tree with one eye is our secret.

Life is good, the General kept his word and I have advanced to a higher rank. We moved to a bigger house in Lagos. It is white and Queenie thinks it is made of sugar cubes. We have a mayguard at the front named Nosa but Queenie calls him No sir No sah! When I carry her on my shoulders and she giggles, I forget who I am, what I've done.

Now, the brass head sits in a glass cabinet, right on the top shelf, looking down on everyone who enters the parlour. It is safe from Queenie's hands. It used to be on the first shelf, but once Queenie picked it up and played with it, tossing it around carelessly. Felicia was furious; she smacked Queenie's hand and warned her it wasn't a toy. I couldn't help thinking that it had began to weave its pattern of trouble. I wanted to get rid of it then. But if I disposed of it I knew I would have to tell Felicia the real reason why, and I couldn't do that, not yet, not after all this time. So I let it be, and I say nothing when Felicia polishes it as if it is made from the finest gold. I swallow my irritation when guests point at it curiously. I look the other way when my mother requests I get her something similar.

When I am away, Felicia tells me she spends her days keeping our household ticking over and running after Queenie. We have several people in our employment including Nosa the mayguard, a houseboy and housegirl, the driver and one of Felicia's girl cousins Eunice who also helps around the house. She loves her daughter but I know she is bored, unfulfilled. Sometimes when I ask how her day is she says what do you want me to tell you when I have nothing of substance to say? She wants to get a job, maybe working in a bank or something along those lines. I refuse to allow her to do this. Deep down I know she still wants to go to university, even now, perhaps to study law or medicine. We fight over this, arguments that shake our bedroom and leave the door shuddering. If I allow her to follow her whims people will say my wife is the master in my house, that my trousers fit her nicely. This resentment festers between us, gathering in mass till I worry one day it will push me out of our bed. I know my wife has grown to love me over the years but sometimes, unguarded, I catch a scheming expression on her face. I tell her I will give her money to run her own store selling bobas, shoes and handbags. I tell her this as if it isn't a consolation prize.

Earlier today I came into my parlour whistling to find we had a guest. He had his back to me but something about the sloppy, hunched way he sat seemed familiar. My heart raced and Felicia's laughter seemed slightly tuned out, like a bad radio frequency. She stood upon seeing me, "Peter you are finally home, how long does it take to buy ice cream for Queen? Honestly that girl has you eating out of her hands, little madam." She looked to our guest and smiled; he now turned and stood awkwardly with a cane that had been leaning against the chair, confirming my suspicions. "British gentleman, long time, you are living well my friend." Emmanuel stuck his hand out; I dropped the container of ice cream on the table. There was a wet patch of melted ice on the left side of my shirt. My fingers were cool. I shook his hand.

I had not seen Emmanuel for years; I'd heard he got discharged from the army some time back but never bothered to find him. I did not want to rake over old ground. I hugged him, the last thing I wanted to do. A chill settled inside me.

Felicia laughed, informing me that Emmanuel had been telling stories about what army boys get up to! "To think I thought I knew you all this time Peter!" My wife said. "It is nice to see an old friend of Peter's. These days, it's all army generals and rich oil contractors." This was her last comment before picking up the ice cream and walking out. I felt a buzzing in my head as Emmanuel lifted his glass of juice and swigged. Angrily, I asked him what he was doing at my house? He laid his cane down carefully. He then had the nerve to say he was disappointed I never came to see him after what we went through! That I should never have abandoned my friends like that.

"We killed a man." I spat this at him. It was the first time I had said it out loud, and somehow saying it confirmed I could never really get away from it. I could dodge and side-step but how long for? Not when the memory grows legs, not when part of it hobbles into your living room joking with your wife, holding a cane. Too close.

Emmanuel was bitter; he accused me of benefitting more than any of them. I remember his exact words. "I don't have friends in high places like you Peter. Do you know what it is to drain a man's life with your bare hands? To wait for his body to become completely still? No, of course you don't, you only watched from the sidelines yet reaped all the rewards. I've never known why the General took such a liking to you. I heard him say I like the way that Peter conducts himself, with class! You never did him any extra special favours did you?"

I was confused by this statement. When I pressed him, he laughed. "Peter you're smart but at times miss what is right in front of you. You mean you don't know about the General? You never heard about his taste for young army boys? It is a well-kept secret."

My head spun with this revelation. I swallowed the anger working its way up my throat and slowly, silently counted to ten. I managed to probe him about his leg. Apparently, armed robbers came to his house one night, held him and his girlfriend at gunpoint. Stupidly, he resisted a little. They shot him in the knee and took everything. We had come to the heart of the matter at that point so I asked him what he wanted.

"Peter, I'm in trouble, you know I wouldn't ask but... I need some money."

I gave him the money. In hindsight I shouldn't have. He will only come back for more like a leech. He may surprise me and not do so, but people rarely do. In truth, I would have done anything to get rid of him. He wobbled unsteadily out of my house, a broken man. Afterwards, I ran to the downstairs toilet and vomited, and it smelled bad to me, as though the stench had been building for years. In the kitchen I wanted to destroy whatever I could. I smashed plates, bottles, cups and glasses, scattering the place. I drowned out the noise and Felicia's wet, wild marble brown eyes rolling in their sockets. It was Queenie who stopped me, she ran into the kitchen barefoot, dripping vanilla ice cream onto clear, broken pieces of glass. Then, this evening the questions: what is wrong with you Peter? Should I not have let him in? We were inside our bedroom, where the blue wall still looked freshly painted; the double bed with its large wood headboard had matching blue and white pillowcases, sheets and a cover. The ceiling fan turned continuously; I had thrown my clothes on the floor and was reaching inside the wardrobe in my underwear. Felicia didn't look a day older than the day we met, just more polished. As bored as she was, our life so far had been good to her. She stood with her hands on her hips; the gold head wrap was unravelling itself as if my silence earlier had offended it. "No, you did the right thing, he wanted money."

"That's not all though Peter."

"I told you what happened!"

"No, you told me your version of what happened, I am your wife. Why do you still keep things from me? Since we were married, all this time, there is something. Something between us and I can't take it."

"I don't know what you're talking about; can I have some peace in my own house?"

"You want peace? Fine but I'm fed up of being stuck here while you're away playing General says! I get excited when guests come because I can talk to them, I can talk to other people more than I talk to my husband! I want to do something with my life."

"Who the hell is stopping you? You think this house; these nice things were waiting for you? I paid the price while you do nothing! The driver can take you wherever you want to go. What do you think I pay him for? I will replace the things in the kitchen."

"It was never about the bloody things in the kitchen." She screamed, slamming the door, so much harder than a woman that slight should have been able to.

I found Queenie on the wooden swing at the back of the compound; she was pulling at the rope handles and kicking her legs up half-heartedly. I walked up carrying juicy cuts of pineapple; her favourite fruit for now, it changes weekly. For a while we didn't say anything as I pushed her, containing the force of the swing with a steady hand. This I could handle.

"Daddy, why are you mad?" She broke the silence. "Have I done something?"

"No, not you Queenie. Do you know I control the weather?" I said, starting one of my tales she loved and I knew would make her laugh. Sure enough, a small smile came. "How do you make the weather daddy?"

"Well, in the morning if I am in a good mood, I rub my hands together, say a secret chant and make sunshine. Now I can't tell you what the chant is otherwise it wouldn't be mine see?"

"Ok, how do you make rain?" She asked, "Do you use the same chant or say it backwards?"

"No, I use a different chant because water gives life, it makes things grow and can erode things. It is everything. And I don't rub my hands, I call upon the clouds, I need their help and cannot do it without them."

"What if the clouds are angry with you or you have an argument with them? Can you do it without them then? What if they're sleeping and they want to be alone sometimes, like mummy?"

"I try not to anger them, I respect them because you know the elements have great power Queenie, and they can control things without us being aware of it." She scratched her newly braided hair that lay in slim, single plaits. She wriggled her mouth and face like she was trying to loosen the tightness in her scalp. I handed her a pineapple slice, watched as she took a bite.

"Daddy? Once I was mad, I ripped my doll's head off."

"Really?"

"Yes, I put it back though. Daddy, you don't really control the weather do you." She said this, as if she'd been indulging me all along, like she was the parent and I the child.

Rider Rendered Blue

When the *oyibo* men from Portugal arrived for a short visit the council wore their gleeful expressions openly and proudly. These visitors had come to the palace court as emissaries of the King of Portugal. They had heard elaborate tales of the Benin kingdom and its Empire. How it stretched beyond the whole of Idu land, into the lands of the Mahin, Ilaje, Dahomey and further still. It was Benin's imperial might and trade routes that interested them. The palace welcomed them with a warm reception and they in return wanted to give a Portuguese education to the Benin royal household. They intrigued people, with their pale skin and strange language. And they were slighter than Benin men, whose broad, sturdy shoulders were built for the demands of the land. People joked that the Portuguese would not cope in the harsh, glaring heat, but they surprised people. Even telling the council that sometimes they struggled with hot weather where they were from. They were told the Oba was too sick to personally receive visitors.

If these men noticed anything strange they kept it to themselves. After all, how could they distinguish what was the custom and what wasn't? They were in a fascinating, foreign world, everything appeared odd and interesting to them. They wanted to see it all, and the council showed them, flourishing as impressive hosts. The palace staff found themselves working constantly. Cooking and cleaning, repeatedly preening for show but they were happy to have a distraction from all that had been happening. The soldiers from the Oba's army had been instructed to cease looking for Filo. After all, she was a wife Oba Odion had never wanted and she was long gone.

In the evenings the court would entertain the visitors with music, and dancing while the councilmen drummed their fingers and nodded their heads along. They revelled in their supposedly mutually beneficial new alliance. Slapped backs and forced laughter drove conversations. But something escaped the council members: these Portuguese men were not just eyeing in admiration the Benin palace, its art, the Oba's collection, treasures and armoury. They were watching with a clever, concealed furtive hunger and disbelief, already stripping away what they could with the naked eye. They were given a ceremonious send off. For their final evening, a fat calf was cooked and the men ate till their bellies were full and they could barely move.

There was a vulnerability emanating off the palace that even the glow of that evening couldn't mask, as though if you drew a big enough breath and blew at it, it would split into large chunky fragments made up of red clay, betrayals and longings, revealing flawed walls intended to protect the inhabitants from everything. The councilmen had boasted to their foreign guests of the tribute system collected on behalf of the Oba. The reality was the opposite; they had been struggling to gather tributes from the surrounding areas for the last two seasons. People were having a terrible time feeding their families, farmers in particular because the harvest period had been and gone, yielding very little. The council couldn't have told their visitors this. Or that pile of rotten cocoa yams were more useful than their Oba who still sat locked away mumbling in solitude.

Instead, a careful picture of Benin had been presented, dressed up in tales of conquests, happy traditional songs and an outwardly thriving palace. On this front the council succeeded because the Portuguese, uncertain of what to expect had been flummoxed. Why the Benin were a civilised bunch! Such a sprawling palace, what impressive, sophisticated artefacts and cultured people and of course this was true. If you caught the chuckles darting over the holes, the high-pitched voices talking over one another in excitement and the clapping, you may have thought all was well in Benin. In the palace, they forgot about their deception and began to believe in the sweetness of the image. The Portuguese left and the council congratulated themselves for days, what a coup. But they had made a fatal mistake; they had unlocked the stranger's gate and in doing so, extended a hand to unforeseen dangers. Because more European men would come, setting in motion an unstoppable, tragically disastrous, chain of events.

Adesua, stunned by Filo's departure, continued to feel surprised for days after she found out Filo was really gone. How had she not seen it coming? Had Filo planned it? Fooling them all with that air of fragility. Filo who slipped her bracelets over the pain she had worn so openly, it had hurt to look at her sometimes. Five days after their Portuguese guests left, things were gradually returning to their normal state. Adesua sitting on the hard floor of her chamber, was thinking of the last time she had seen Filo with her sad, sombre smile that swum in her face. She never really looked at you but through you, not because you were of no interest but out of a bad habit she seemed incapable of breaking. Although Adesua admitted to herself that she felt betrayed, she knew she had no right to feel that way. But somehow a bond had formed between them that joined them together, in anticipation of a life of duty, disappointment and routine. Somehow, finding the strength nobody knew she possessed Filo had smashed it.

Adesua surprised by the anger brimming inside her stood and paced the wall on her left. There, she lifted the brass head from a dark wooden stand, thinking again of Filo's fixation with the thing. The air in the chamber seemed loaded with possibilities yet somehow she knew this was a bad sign. Terrible incidents seemed to find the palace fertile ground. Sully walked into her head, she pictured him so clearly, tales dangling from the corner of his lips, holding an audience in the palm of his hand. A rush of fear attacked her body so suddenly; she wanted to cough it out. She wondered where Filo was and if she would finally find peace. She envied Filo's newly discovered freedom. The crickets started to talk, as if alerting each other to some discovery. Adesua began to vigorously polish the brass head with her hand, as presently that action alone seemed the answer to everything.

At the opposite end of the palace, Sully was also fighting the feeling of unease. He sat several steps away from his quarters, occasionally looking up to name a glimmering star. With each attempt he hoped to trick himself into believing all was well. But the apprehension stuck and as a result he had insisted on not seeing Adesua for a few days. He was a man who paid attention to the voice within and it was telling him to leave. Benin was cursed and he knew he should go before it mercilessly stripped him too. But not yet, it wasn't enough that he was witnessing its slow destruction from the perfect position. Or that he had watched Oba Odion oversee the beginning of the palace's collapse. He just had to be patient he told himself.

Oba Odion's decline, the blood leaking through the roof, Omotole's disfigured baby; these were more signs. The palace was revealing its secrets and one day he would stumble on what he had been waiting for. He let these thoughts drift from him like smoke while near his feet a tiny glow of colour pulled his gaze down. A small ladybird crawled around aimlessly. He realised he was so deep in thought he nearly crushed it. It appeared to be in some distress. It rolled onto its back and began to twitch its tiny, curled black legs. He watched, gripped by its short, jerky movements, which became increasingly pronounced, as if it was trying to reveal something. Then it stopped, perhaps fed up with the futile attempt of sharing whatever burden it carried. It rocked back over on its front, perhaps the call of other bugs and crawly creatures luring it over. Sully watched it make its way till it disappeared out of sight. He closed his eyes tightly, wishing there were things he didn't know because knowing changed you. And once you acknowledged this you could never go back. It seemed, even the tiny creatures of the land knew this truth.

When your worst fear comes to life, a twisted, sweaty anticipation follows and hollowed out from the persistent rapping of the heart, it festers within. This Adesua and Sully discovered when they were yanked out from their reveries and thrown into a trial after the council had been informed of their affair. All they could do was stand to attention, watching as the repercussions of their actions lay within the creased folds of the council men's native wear. Waiting. The palace was agog with the news and it had spread like a disease. At the trial the councilmen were sombre, their appropriately grim expressions could have been hand drawn. There was an air of inevitability about the whole proceeding. Adesua pleaded with them, looking them in the eye when scrambling to answer some questions, then defiantly refusing to answer others and shaking fitfully as any hope she harboured dissolved in the space of breaths. She thought of Mama and Papa, how they would hang their heads in shame and what would become of them afterwards. But looming over all that was Sully, the way he stayed so still. As though he was a spectator in the whole thing, his chin poised unflinching, for all the blows. He refused to apologise, and a thin, cracked veil of shock came down as Sully, the man who could talk himself into and out of any situation, said nothing.

On that last day, there wasn't anything a soul could do to change the upside down face of their destiny. They were watched all night by a pack of sober guards in a rank, shabby out-building reserved for prisoners. When morning arrived, their hands were tied with thick, cutting rope that rubbed their skin raw as they were dragged on the journey they couldn't come back from, flanked on either side by six soldiers from Oba Odion's army. Adesua tried to not let her whimpers slip, attempting to catch them with her shocked, and flagging tongue. On their way, death wasn't in the broken, gnarled branches scattered about, or the rough, prickly frowning bush plants nipping at her legs. Or even the ground; coughing pleas disguised in red dust as the stamp of feet moved on. No, death was in the sweet, sugar-cane kisses she had shared with her lover. Sully baffled the soldiers; he was laughing to the heavens yet he would never hold a daughter in his arms, never travel with his family, to freely experience new lands the way his wandering feet loved. Never again would he watch Adesua fall asleep in his arms.

Working for the British as a scout, sent to assess the lay of the land and the conditions of the palace he had failed. He had absconded, keeping the money and in the end had fallen in love with the king's beautiful new wife. Ironically had he stuck to his end of the treacher-ous bargain, he may have been left a rich, free man. They paused when they reached a clearing deep in the dense bush, the promise of Sully and Adesua's lives not yet realised shrank back from outlines mired in sin. One soldier untied Sully's hands and handed him a long metal instrument, it's curved, menacing head shaped as in a fit of surprise. They instructed him to dig a grave big enough for two. He stooped down, arching his back, sticking the metal thing into the ground, watching as it spat piles of earth, seeing Adesua trembling without even looking at her.

At that very moment, Oba Odion finally left his chamber. He was being chased by the boy he used to be, through the palace grounds and all the charred enclaves beyond it, while the spirit of Oba Anuje looked on and the ghost of his lost son Ogiso settled into the brass head, rattling it against the floor of Adesua's quarters.

Sully kept digging, while his back ached, he couldn't feel his arms and his legs were folding. He wanted to tell Adesua he was happy they had destroyed each other together with their love, to tell her that when she laughed, he wanted to keep seeing more of her play-ful side. He wanted to tell her it was a beautiful day to die. You could see small clusters of clouds slowly, steadily floating down, as though the sky was shedding bits of itself. And the air was sweet and full of promise. And right there. There. In the far corner of himself, a headless hyena was pawing at the blood tears running down the stump of its neck, circling in on its body and him. The soldiers buried the two of them together alive, and just then, the sun God stepped out, stuffing bits of shredded, stolen moonbeam where he could. His golden rays searing through the thickened air and cutting it into slices he opened his mouth wide to swallow their cries.

Part 3

Modern London
&
Lagos 1950s

Scene

A baby with a white tongue sat in the middle of traffic. Naked, it crawled after an orange balloon fashioned into a dog. I watched the dog bounce, carried by a steady breeze, running my tongue over my dry mouth. The baby continued to edge forward as the traffic swirled. And the sky was so big and bright I had to somehow adjust my settings. I stood at the flickering traffic lights feeling jittery, anxiously waiting for somebody to scoop up the baby who so far hadn't cried. I waited for the artificial dog to bark. It didn't. A rising panic grew inside me. My left hand lay slack against my slick with sweat thigh. My right hand trembled. Everybody around seemed oblivious. A man in a Hawaiian shirt nibbled on a Mars bar, a ginger-haired woman pushing shopping bags in a pram that had seen better days laughed into her mobile phone, a lollipop lady sat crying on a bench beside the DLR station. The faulty traffic light only flashed wait. People crossed over regardless, drawing expletives from drivers who popped extra large heads out of dust covered windows before leaning back in to awkward embraces with their steering wheels.

A milk float with no driver appeared off the roundabout. It paused beside the station, empty bottles of milk jostling. The lollipop lady jumped in still crying as she drove away. The baby was closer now. I caught a glimpse of its wide smiling face as it moved determinedly towards an empty packet of Skittles lingering on the curb. A sharp pain exploded in my chest. Sweat popped on my forehead. A feeling of familiarity crept in. I opened my mouth to call out but only growly guttural barks emerged. Distressed, I scanned the scene for the orange dog. I leapt at the curb to grab the baby but it was drooling into the Skittles packet at the back of the milk float, snaking through the bottles.

On the way home, I looked up at the same big sky wondering where I'd seen the baby before. Wondering if it would change its mode of travel and attach itself to the white vapour trail of the plane overhead, taking comfort in the distance of its heavy noise. The taut pain continued to spread through my body. My hand felt sticky and a stinging sensation registered. I pulled it out of my pocket watching the blood trickle. Unwittingly, I'd cut it on the gnarly cover of a sardine can left inside it. At the front door, I fished out a stone the size of a one pence coin and swallowed it. Seventy-two hours of insomnia and counting, a no-man's land where the gutted earth harboured versions of me growing, injured. Wild eyed.

Glass Feet Stoned

It was just after 8pm when I arrived at Mervyn's office. He was just leaving. He pulled the door closed, wine-coloured briefcase in hand, and then rotated his head to the right as I approached, as if he'd picked up a warning in the air I'd be coming. Black suit, red tie, polished black shoes, looking smart, a man you could trust. He smiled a genuine smile but I could see worry behind it.

"Princess, still don't know how to return people's phone calls."

"You haven't been honest with me Mervyn."

He stood still for a moment, gathering himself. As he blew air through his lips his chest rose and fell like a balloon beginning to deflate.

"Okay, let's go to mine where we can talk."

"No."

"Come on it's me; you telling me you can't come to my house now?"

We walked to a Caribbean restaurant a couple of streets down. All the way I said nothing, waiting. He brought out his chequered handkerchief to pat his forehead.

Other than a couple at the bar area the restaurant was virtually empty and smelled of spices. It had wooden floors, dim lights and colourful paintings. Reggae music played low and soft like a lover's stroke. You could see out onto the street from where we sat.

Mervyn's gaze loitered a little too long on the outside scene. He may have sensed what was coming, maybe not the exact nature of it, but he knew I meant business. Neither of us wanted to eat. He ordered vodka, I ordered water.

Tell me what happened.

He supressed an agitated sigh.

You know what your mother was like Joy.

No, tell me.

She was vicious that evening, she said things, accused me.

Of what?

Of seeing another woman.

Were you?

No, I'm a man who flirts a lot; I can't help it I'm wired that way.

Why did you keep it from me?

Your mother thought it best you didn't know about us.

And this had been going on for?

Years.

Even while your wife was alive?

Yes.

I stayed absolutely still for a minute because I needed to.

So?

I went out, took a walk around to cool off man, I came back the base-ment door was open and there she was. It was so strange to see her dead, I swear I never touched her; I loved her. You saw the medical examiner's report.

You left her there.

I don't know where my head was at. I panicked. To find her like that, it was a shock, too much.

He looked me dead in the eye then. *I wanted to tell you.*

No, no, no, no, no. I stopped him. All at once I felt faint and sick. He was showing who he really was to me. The way he'd always been there, in the background and his boys, always there too. How could I not have seen it? I realised the night I found my mother dead I never called the ambulance. Mervyn had. After the screaming dial tone and the voice that replaced it zapped down the line and his trembling fingers hung up the receiver, he hit the ground, running away from us, my mother reduced to a dirty dead secret. I'll never ask by how much time I missed him.

I left him there at the cliff edge, to untangle the knot stretching back many years.

Then there she was, wearing the purple scarf from Mervyn's. Why in death was my mother Queen becoming real again? My glass feet broke repeatedly on the pavement. Heartbeats were gunshots fired in my chest. She was high up above, a fevered angel sleepwalking on the wings of planes.

Peter Lowon Journal Entry,
July 1964

Now that it is two years since General Akhatar has been pronounced the new minister of defence under military rule, and I am a General in my own right, my marriage has become a shell. I wanted it all, but it is never as you expect it to be. Still, I cannot bring myself to tell Felicia the one thing she wants to know. Instead, I have picked seedless fights over the years. If she cooks I tell her the eba is too hard, that her soup tastes flat. I shout her down over the dining room table on days she attempts to sit with me the way a good wife does. And wish aloud she'd cease breathing instead of asking me endless questions while she watches in horror. One night she came home late smelling of beer after running around with some of these Lagos women. I called her a prostitute and threw her out, while Queenie slept soundly. After her staying with a friend for three days, I demanded she come home, accused her of abandoning her duties as a wife and mother and of attempting to embarrass me. I have become another type of man in my own home and I don't know how to stop being him.

Felicia and I sleep in separate bedrooms. I have never experienced a lonelier feeling than the sound of her footsteps heading towards her bedroom, where the only comfort that awaits her is an empty bed. I am punishing both of us; I wonder why she stays. I kept my promise and she has a clothing boutique in Lagos where through my connections some high profile clients flock. She spends her days there, running it with her cousin's help. Felicia and I will not have any more children; I have resigned myself to it, despite always wanting more. Queenie deserves a brother and sister; she has asked me about it many times. I always give her the same answer, 'When the time is right.' Knowing that time will never come.

His name is Ben Okafor. He is a journalist with The Nigerian Trumpet, a parasite whose big shot father owns the paper amongst other ventures. I first received a call from him some weeks ago. He told me he wanted to do a lifestyle profile on generals in the military, a series that would run over a few weeks.

Initially I said no. No warning bells went off. For a while I heard nothing, and then more phone calls, he became persistent, falling just short of harassment. It was after the call from his father, a friend of the President that I agreed to see him, sweeping aside my worry. I met him on neutral ground, in an eatery with the smell of meat pies and baked bread in the air. The place had fewer people than chairs, and the walls were a pale yellow as though they had turned sickly from all the stale conversations. It was deliberately low key.

Okafor was younger than I expected, an Ibo in his mid-to-late twenties. He was a very handsome man, 6'2in tall with a practiced braggadocio and an air of wealth. I hated him on sight. He had on cream pressed linen trousers, brown sandals with his toes peeking out and a multi coloured shirt. Tucked in his shirt pocket was a pair of dark sunglasses; a cigarette dangled from his mouth. He waved me over on arrival, his lean, sculpted face breaking into a smile, pumping my hand warmly as though I was a long lost friend, his features drawn into a kind of welcome. He had a neat trick of smiling without any warmth appearing only to have moved his lips. Okafor jumped from one comment to another as though they were hot coals, touching on traffic on the way in, why I'd chosen this particular place to meet, offering me a cigarette then smiling ruefully and asking if a woman had anything to do with my decision after informing him I'd quit years ago. He had a dynamic energy, even doing simple things like patting his shirt pocket for his wallet before fishing it out from a green satchel that slumped against the leg of his chair. I tried to steady my shaky hands under the table, tried to control the heat spreading through my bloodstream. I felt naked, vulnerable. Why had I agreed to do this? This was a bad idea. I should never have folded under the pressure. I drummed my fingers on the table, nerves jangling. I must admit I embraced the small relief when Okafor stood abruptly to grab two malt drinks from the fridge at the side, before handing it to the woman at the counter who opened them with a gleaming silver opener.

For a moment, I pictured Okafor holding that opener, scraping my insides with it. He set our drinks down, folded his rangy body in the seat opposite me. The questions came quickly. What made a man like me join the army since I did not strike him as the army type? Why had I had such a quick progression up the ranks? How come everybody he spoke to about me divulged the same things? Good, fair, proud hardworking family man. Nothing to the contrary, as though I'd carefully presented the same image to everyone? I smiled when he said this. Inside I thought, don't let this parasite see you crack! Stay calm Peter, stay calm. I adjusted myself, pulled my body upright, something I find myself doing in an uncomfortable situation. Okafor had grabbed a worn, small writing pad and a broken pen that had seen better days. "Sir I'm interested in true portrayals," he said. "Fair ones, despite what assumptions you may have about me being a spoiled, rich boy. This is not play for me. I am not amusing myself till the next thing comes along."

I gave him some carefully rehearsed responses, trying to read his expressions as he scribbled away. I told him that the structure and discipline of the army had appealed to me from adolescence, the idea of a shared experience, camaraderie, protecting your country. All lies of course. I had nothing but my own self interest in mind but you cannot deliver this kernel of truth to a stranger without true context which cannot be conveyed in a mere interview to a journalist of all people! I was ambitious I said. I made the right connections, wanted to do well. After all, I had a family to provide for. Okafor tapped his pen on the pad, looking up. "You know, I like you Mr Lowon but I'm still trying not to hold it against you that you've been *so difficult regarding this interview. Do you have something to hide?" He leaned forward when he said this, holding my gaze, searching it. I took a sip from my Supermalt, welcoming the coolness of the liquid, hoping it would dampen the rising heat inside me. That sly bastard Okafor actually smiled at that point, a slow, loaded smile. I pointed out that if I'd had anything to conceal, I would never have agreed to the interview. I was a very busy man after all, a General in demand, advising on all kinds of military matters. A newspaper interview was hardly at the top of my list of priorities. Okafor continued to dig, restless in his seat, throwing a leg out, sinking back then springing forward when some small detail caught his attention, rubbing his jaw thoughtfully. Then he asked me if I had any regrets? Hah! Did this man take me for a fool? Asking me to walk into a potential land mine. I confessed I wasn't always the best son, that my father and I had had a tricky relationship, full of tenseness and misunderstanding. He hadn't been an openly affectionate father, in fact he was awkward expressing emotions. I never knew if he loved me but he was happy I joined the army, pleased about the discipline it instilled in me.*

Okafor then says he'd like to tell me a story.

"Of course" I respond, happy to take a break, to pause and gather my thoughts, to drink more Supermalt.

Some months back, Okafor was at a party, a good one as parties go. Nice looking women, plenty of people, the usual. But there was this man in bad shape with a damaged leg, most people were ignoring him but Okafor went to help. The man rambled while Okafor held his arm, taking him outside for some air. He asked what Okafor did for a living. Okafor told him. Then the man said he had unbelievable stories to tell.

Doom twisted inside me as Okafor continued with his tale. The man said he used to be in the army, his name was Emmanuel. He talked about his friends Peter Lowon, Obi and the General. He revealed things, secrets some very powerful people want to stop coming out.

I felt my top lip trembling, I hadn't heard from Emmanuel for almost a year when he suddenly stopped asking me for money. Okafor informed me that Emmanuel had died four weeks earlier, he had been in serious trouble, owed some dangerous people a lot of money. His girlfriend called the police after finding him in their apartment with a bullet wound in his head. At first I couldn't move, Okafor's voice seemed to be fading and I was busy chastising myself for my arrogance, my presumptions.

All these months Ben Okafor had been sitting, waiting on this golden egg to hatch.

"That night sir, did you know the soldier you killed had been General Akhatar's lover?"

I shook my head. The seductive Ben Okafor was scribbling almost furiously. Then, he paused and studied me. He didn't explain why he believed the ramblings of a drunken man. I felt my cheeks swelling with denials. I knew this day would come, all these years of quiet fear, of waiting, of regret. I swallowed my protests, knowing if they were released, they would die on the tips of impatient, surrounding knives.

Who

In my living room I watched Anon drown old pictures in her blue river. Images I didn't recognise, unfurling against the wet mouth of a tide; shots of a woman tying her wrapper running down a dusty road, a man cowering before a gulf in his floor, dead babies in the womb turning. Then footsteps outside caught my interest. I looked through the window, spotted Mrs Harris throwing away a large, black bin bag. The dented shapes in it spoke. The green wheelie bin squeaked as the bag landed. She looked different. Her long, lace black dress with a bulbous skirt spun as she moved, its hem whispering against her ankles. Slouchy, burgundy boots, round wire-rimmed spectacles and a black beret topped off the outfit. Her hair cascaded like a silvery waterfall down her back.

I grabbed my camera from the side table and snapped away. She stood still for a few moments, staring at something out of the frame. She sighed and my curtains trembled as though her breath had blown them. The wheelie bins were then adjusted till they were level. For a brief moment, I felt guilty watching her pale hands on the handles. She was only doing an ordinary task on an ordinary day. Mrs Harris threw her shoulders back and went inside. She emerged a few minutes later holding a long, wooden cane. Its handle curved in the shape of an umbrella's. Her back was hunched, head bent. Her walk altered by a slight limp; her face bore a pained expression.

I watched till she was out of my line of vision and Anon had eased her grip on my chest.

In the evening, a light shower of rain fell as I made my way down from the local DVD rental shop. It was after 8pm. Traffic had eased and cars drove by bearing shrunken snapshots in their side mirrors. I'd rented *The Big Lebowski*. I loved the idea of an ordinary character landing in an extraordinary situation. The rain began to fall more heavily and I counted some of its disciples. I tugged my coat hood over my head. Mrs Harris was standing at the traffic lights across the road, face illuminated by its flickering colours. Gone were the pained expression and her walking stick. She'd also changed clothes. Instead she now wore flowery red trousers, grey plimsolls and a dark, blue raincoat. Her hair was tamed in a loose bun and she clutched a white, plastic bag straining with the weight it carried. I waited for her to cross the lights and reach my side of the road. As she approached, she whistled, wet tendrils of hair stuck to the side of her face.

"My fellow water baby! How is the world according to Joy?" she enquired, smiling.

"Erm ok," I answered, resisting the urge to launch into full confessional mode. "I'm ordering takeaway and having a night of film watching. What have you been up to?"

She held her bag up as we quickened the pace. "Costume shopping!" A bus sped past splashing us.

"For a costume party? I've never been to one. What's the outfit?"

"Can't tell you, it's a surprise! You've never been to a costume party? Quite the experience my dear! You'll have to come, cancel whatever you're doing this Saturday."

"I don't have a costume though."

She fished her key out as we drew closer to our patch of houses. "Try the old vintage store on the high street, a veritable treasure trove! If you get stuck I'd be happy to lend you something."

"Thanks but-," my expression wrinkled. As if she'd guessed my response she warned, "I won't have no for an answer, have some fun for a change."

God! I thought, she must see me as a miserable human being. It dawned on me that for some strange reason, what she thought of me mattered. I had no idea how that had happened. Despite my best efforts the small bag of DVD rentals was damp. I held it tighter. "Okay but don't abandon me there. I hate it when someone invites you to a party and then ignores you for most of it."

"The worst that can happen is you'll be forced to interact with other people." She chuckled, shaking her head. "Even mad butterflies are social creatures!" She winked, hand fluttering to the side of her right leg.

"Are you ok?" I reached to steady her as she rubbed.

"It's fine, an old accident. It troubles me occasionally dear that's all."

I noticed a loose thread at the wrist of the white jumper peeking beneath her raincoat, imagined secrets clinging to frayed wrists.

"Here," I offered, "I'll take that." I grabbed her bag. We'd arrived at her doorstep and she stuck the key in the lock. "Come in and take some macaroni cheese away with you." I trailed behind her respectfully wiping my shoes on the mat with "home" printed across it. She flicked the lights on. "It's an old family recipe, you can have it for lunch tomorrow. Tell me what you think!"

In the living room I looked up at the light. A tiny Anon sat in the bulb. She pointed to the side table where a copy of the day's Evening Standard was flicked open to the property section. Doodles of forlorn looking stick men in various stages of distress sat in the margins. Drawn in red ink, they seemed to be calling to each other across the page. In the top, right corner, a smudged coffee stain was a canon ball rolling towards them. I glanced up and Anon had gone. The bulb flickered, as though she left her laughter to tangle with the light. Mrs Harris emerged, carrying a brown oven dish bearing tin foil as a makeshift cover. "Here, tuck into that tomorrow. You'll sleep like a newborn." The light continued to sputter. "I'll have to change that," she added, bending to untie the laces of her plimsolls. Heat from the bowl spread through my fingers and the smell of macaroni beneath a melted, golden cheese topping made my stomach rumble. I raised a hand by way of goodbye but back turned, Mrs Harris was already heading to her kitchen, whistling that odd, unrecognisable tune.

Later that night, I woke with vague strains of the tune running through my head. The sound of light rain hitting the windowpanes was comforting. I noticed the light in Mrs Harris's garden was on illuminating the drops of rain on my window. Looking out I watched discreetly as she dug a hole then buried a multi-coloured cloth bag. I wondered what secret had to be hidden inside damp soil. Perhaps only Buddy the Buddha knew, watching bearing mouthfuls of water. After she wandered in, I made myself a mug of hot chocolate, unsettled by my growing fascination with her. And by Anon's greed, not only invading my space but also creeping into Mrs Harris's too. Outside, the street lamps cowered as a gust of wind howled.

Faces

In the week of the costume party I photographed Mrs Harris in several guises. Anon told me to do it. She danced around the room wearing the brass head, whispering instructions, waving arms the weight of silk. Each morning, I listened for the sound of Mrs Harris's front door clicking open. Camera poised on the table, I'd lunge forward fully aware of the small window of time and take pictures. I shot the woman I knew in warm, earthy tones. I captured her face reassembling itself. I shot her dressed out of character in a dull, brown tweed skirt suit, hair restrained in a severe bun. On another occasion, she looked demure and sorrowful, swathed in an ill-fitting knee length black dress. As if she was attending a funeral. Only the hat she wore would raise eyebrows, it was a Phillip Treacy inspired, peacock-shaped number dotted with bits of gold in its netting. Another time she wore a red kilt, a short black tux jacket and sturdy, black heels. In that instance, I ran down to intercept her, pretending to be on my way to the shop.

"Hey, you look colourful today, off somewhere nice?" I enquired, slightly self conscious of still being in my pyjamas.

She bowed dramatically. "Thank you dear. I'm spending some time with my brother. He's taking me on a surprise afternoon outing."

Casually I said, "Oh, this must be the brother you mentioned briefly. I always see you as an only child for some reason."

"It depends how you define the term brother," she muttered. A leaflet distributor clutching a stash of flyers hurried past.

"Your leg seems better," I noted. "Niggling injuries are horrible."

"It comes and goes dear! Lots of people manage with terrible afflictions, things you couldn't imagine. If ever I start to pity myself, I think of the Elephant Man."

"Oh, ok." I waved her off. "Have a good time."

"See you on the other side." She said breezily, hurrying on.

On the night of the party, Mrs Harris and I got ready at my house, listening to The Smiths blaring from the radio. We smoked spliffs and I felt high on camaraderie and possibilities. Our faces were painted like skulls, with drawn-on extended crooked smiles that were sinister no matter the angle of light. We wore "his" and "hers" skeleton costumes with me in androgynous mode and Mrs Harris encased in a corseted dress. Long, black capes floated from our backs. Our heads were decorated in crowns of dead flowers, made from rose petals, geraniums and old wires.

In the streets we encountered bursts of traffic. People swelled in and out of pubs, cramped restaurants and Weatherspoons! Mrs Harris took a swig from the small bottle of Captain Morgan rum tucked inside the pocket of her cape then tugged me along. "The guy throwing this party, Otto, got most of his front teeth knocked out from a gambling debt. Try not to stare when you meet him." She advised. I nodded as we weaved our way past curious glances. We crossed a bridge that reeked of piss and alcohol, where a homeless guy holding a stick appeared like the gatekeeper and asked for my cape. We walked on. The distant, neon lights inside us threatened to become embodied.

Eventually, we reached a moody looking Victorian house with a shabby hedge. A few red bricks were stacked in the corner of the sidewalk. Music boomed and silhouettes jostled in the hazy gaze of the windows. We rang the bell. After a short wait Otto answered dressed as a pirate, sporting a patch over one eye. His exposed eye twinkling was the colour of a dark blue sapphire. "Greetings!" he announced with flourish, throwing his arms open.

We were ushered in, our coats taken and swallowed into the warmth. Mrs Harris introduced us as we weaved through the packed hallway. It was difficult not to stare at the row of missing front teeth in Otto's mouth. It made his smile look dubious. Already high, I wanted to ask how much money he'd owed and whether the heavy handlers kept the teeth. The atmosphere felt tunnel-like. Oddly shaped rooms wound off in different directions and high ceilings drew close, and then receded. Alcohol and ash permeated conversations. Bodies in costumes were mutated rats bouncing under low lights.

In the kitchen, a makeshift bar constituting several bottles stacked on the countertop beckoned. A woman sang a deep-throated blues as Mrs Harris made me a gin and tonic.

"How was the outing with your brother?" I asked, shouting over the noise.

She leaned closer, handed me a full glass. "What?"

"Your brother!"

"Oh! It was anti-climatic." Her brow furrowed in irritation. I swallowed a gulp of drink. Too much gin and not enough tonic. "How so?"

"He took me to some pretentious play in Convent Garden. The kind of thing you'd see scraping the bottom of the barrel at the Edinburgh Festival. We argued over money, my inheritance to be precise, which he still won't give me." She grabbed cubes of ice from a bucket and threw them in her glass so aggressively, whisky sloshed down the side. I leaned back into the counter. "How is that possible? Is he your blood brother?"

"No, my father remarried you see. The woman already had a child, Bryn. To make matters worse, my father legally adopted him. I wasn't the easiest of children. Anyway, when he died, he instructed my share of the inheritance to be given to me at Bryn's discretion. And of course, he hasn't, claiming I'm mad and irresponsible."

"But that's not fair!" I offered, genuinely annoyed on her behalf.

"You don't know the half of it!" she announced, shouting in my ear. "Bryn inherited the estate. After everything my father and I went through in that house, he and his mother just waltzed in and took it. It was as if my father rewarded them for being his new beginning."

The track changed. David Bowie was signalling to Major Tom.

"You know what was awful?" she continued. "When I got admitted to the mental hospital, Bryn sent me a letter with a hundred pounds enclosed. He said he was disappointed by my circumstances and here was some money to spend wisely. Spend wisely! As though I was an idiot." She sipped from her glass, shook her head frustrated. "So you see my dear, you're not the only one that has to wrestle with the burden of an inheritance. I'm not talking about just money and objects. I mean things people like you and I see clearly that others may not. Sometimes, I think I inherited a different destiny simply because my mother walked out." She gripped my arm tightly. Her eyes glowed ominously.

Later in the evening, Mrs Harris and I decided to separate and mingle. After several extra drinks for Dutch courage, I relaxed more. I'd had no intentions of launching myself sober into random conversations with strangers yet I chatted amiably with a pope smoking a spliff by the piano in the cherry-coloured living room. I danced with a Charlie Chaplin who reeked of beer. In the kitchen, I watched Mr T and Darth Vader arm wrestle. On the stairs, two bumblebees kissed passionately. I felt light and floated amongst bodies whose lines were blurring, only to emerge slumped over tables, languishing on cramped sofas and pushed up against each other in doorways. My feet began to hurt so I took my ankle length, black boots off. I dropped them amidst the pile of shoes in the hallway.

When my energy began to dwindle, I expected somebody to slot coins in my back so my eyes could shine brighter. But nobody did and the whites of my eyes continued to fill with the hand drawn movements of the night. More alcohol was shoved my way.

Hey! Have a Corona.

Want another Vodka and orange?

You're a lightweight; try some of this!

At some point, I wandered slack-jawed into the garden. Smatterings of people had gathered and I noticed Mrs Harris and Otto the Pirate by the swings. They appeared to be arguing but I wasn't close enough to hear what was being said. I felt a sharp twinge in my foot, looked down and a bit of broken glass was covered in my blood. I made my way indoors into the bathroom, where I spent some time washing a bloody, grimace from my foot.

My shoes went missing. A waifish, blonde dressed as Veronica Lake loaned me white slippers. "Cinderella you shall go home! Imagine if you could never leave the party." She mused. "Imagine if this was all there was, just this party and the characters in it, twenty four hours a day, for the rest of your life."

"Just imagine," I slurred.

After her exit, I scanned the bodies milling to and fro but couldn't see Mrs Harris. I sat against a wall in the hallway nodding off, head jerking up intermittently. Then from nowhere, through a smoky cloud I caught a glimpse of a familiar dress, a skeleton's pattern on the bodice. My eyes adjusted, took in the crown of dead flowers askew on a pile of wiry, black hair. A breath left my chest like a one winged bird. It was Anon dressed in Mrs Harris's costume, face painted skeleton white. She flew up the stairs, the traces of another life clinging to the hem of her skirt. I uncurled my body, followed her. In my inebriated state I was slower, tripping a few times. I squeezed past bodies on the carpeted stairs. By the time I reached the roof, the music had shrunk to a hum. Anon stood on the edge and was about to leap off.

"No, don't!" I urged, rushing forward. Then she vanished. Cold sweat popped on my brow. I looked down, realising I was steps away from flying to my death.

On my way back down, dice spun on the ceilings. I rummaged in the cupboard beneath the stairs, grabbed my coat and flung it on. Anon waited by a street lamp, it was after three am and the cold air nipped my skin. She picked up the pace while I trailed behind. We dashed past satellite dishes transmitting pictures of other life to sleeping TV sets. She whistled the tune Mrs Harris had been whistling the other day. That strange, melancholy song was water seeping into our movements. I kept blinking it away. It made my nerves jangle. The borrowed slippers rapped against the ground and my feet were freezing. Somewhere along the way, it dawned on me that Anon was wearing my missing boots. And somehow it made sense. She led me home. In my frosted window, Anon waited to wear limbs that ambled towards her from the four corners. I stood outside watching. I stuffed my hands in my jacket pockets, felt a folded flyer for a show called *Eat*. I fished it out, a storm was gathering in the mouth of the afro-haired woman featured, spawning creases on the shiny sheaf of paper. I tucked it back into my pocket where a broken key ring languished; I fingered the break in the key ring.

Light Spinning

I stuffed some clothes in the washing machine, including the skeleton costume. I watched its turns, the previous night calling to it, spinning too, a watery eye pressed against the glass. Later, I swept cobwebs from my head, knowing they'd reappear on Anon's open palms. That evening I rapped on Mrs Harris's door, still upset by her disappearance at the party. She opened the door puffing on a cigarette, wearing a robe bearing a flamingo print. She smelled of smoke and something sweet and exotic like jasmine.

"Ahh, Ronnie Wood," she exclaimed, peering at me as if seeing me in a new light.

I smiled uncertainly. She shut the door firmly, kicked aside a pizza leaflet that slipped from the mail flap. "You were a party animal last night, good to see you having fun."

"About that," I tucked my pyjama top in my jeans properly. "It wasn't nice for you to leave me like that. I came home on my own."

In the living room she paused, looking at me with a baffled expression. "What are you talking about? We arrived home together dearie. I walked you to your door."

"No you didn't!" I answered, in a tone sharper than I'd intended.

"I did. You were so drunk you didn't even know where you'd left your shoes. One second." She began rummaging through a green glass ornament shaped like a pearl on the mantelpiece. It sounded like whispering sweet wrappers followed by the sound of coins clashing. I wiped a perspiring hand on the back of my left buttock, feeling the thin leaf of the Iranian playing card she'd given me in hospital. I'd taken to carrying it as a good luck charm, unable to forget its burst of brightly coloured possibilities in a glum ward.

"Aha! Here it is," Mrs Harris uttered triumphantly, clutching an object that looked suspiciously familiar. A round, metallic ring poked between two fingers as she handed it over. It was my super eagle, my broken key ring with the green, white, green blocks of colour. The Nigerian flag encased in plastic. I was nauseous and gulped it down.

"You dropped it last night on the way home. I know it's just a damaged key ring but I thought you'd miss it for some reason," she explained, laughter lines crinkling at the corners of her mouth.

I fingered the break in the plastic, the same action from the night before. It was one of the handfuls of lucid moments I thought I'd had on my way back home. Now I wasn't even certain I'd had that. I didn't feel the tear until it hit my lip, until I tasted a salty sorrow with a swipe of my tongue. I wanted to tell her about how I'd begun to grow trees in silences. I couldn't bring myself to talk about it. My tongue tightened from the burden of balancing half formed things.

I smiled ruefully. "Butterflies."

"Indeed, never underestimate them. Come on, I'll show you something," she said.

The stairs creaked as we walked up. I spotted a coppery, watermark on the ceiling. It traced our movements all the way. And the exotic, sweet floral scent intensified the further we went. Mrs Harris began to hum that strange, haunting tune again.

"What is that song?" I asked, side-stepping a dustpan and brush. "You were whistling it the other day."

"It's an old Romany song about two lovers who died together promising to meet in the after life."

I felt a weird sensation in my left arm, as if the hairs were needles holding half threads in them.

"My mother used to sing it to me as a child," she continued, nudging the loft door open. "For some reason, it always stayed with me."

"Odd song to sing to a child."

"Yes it was but like I said, she was a little crazy."

In the loft we were greeted by three candles flickering on the windowsill and the coppery watermark had retreated. It was a good-sized space containing a warm, wooden floor, a slanted ceiling and orange walls. A short bookcase sat tucked away in one corner and old record sleeves of obscure artists leaned lazily against it. In the centre stood a headless dress form, flanked by slouched bin bags spilling clothes. I ran my hand over its naked, smooth body, imagining the strewn clothes were trains of thought. "Where did you get it?" Under the low lighting it was a piece of art.

"Oh many years ago now." She stood to the right studying it as if picturing that first instance. "I got it in Edinburgh from a shop that sold sewing machines. One day, they had it for sale in their display window. I'm always struck by things that are out of place, it felt right so I bought it." She took a drag from her shrinking cigarette.

"It seems…" I struggled to find the right words without sounding judgemental.

"Old fashioned?" she offered, eyes sparkling.

"Yes! Old fashioned."

"That's because it is dear." She shrugged resignedly.

I searched her features. "Do you use it often?"

"Sometimes."

"Why?" I was genuinely interested; to me it lengthened the process of getting ready.

She rolled her eyes as though I was an idiot. "Because it's fun to play dress up, no matter how old you get dear," she remarked.

In my mind's eye, I saw her working in the attic surrounded by twin dress forms, beneath a bulb lit by an orange echo, drawing her features onto heads for her army, dressing them up, sending them out into the corners of the city. And they bore mouths melted by candlelight, shrouded in the smog of God's breath.

I left Mrs Harris's with the same strange sensation in my left arm. As if the two were connected, I plucked the playing card from my back pocket. Sure enough, the spear-wielding figure had changed clothes.

At night I didn't sleep till late. I sketched pictures of Mrs Harris in her different guises. Later, I watched the drawings for changes in their expressions, revelations in the lines of their bodies. But all they did was lead me back to the same blank space.

Periodic Elements

Mercury Hg 80 = Mrs Harris
It was a ridiculous hour of the day, maybe 2 or 3am. Mrs Harris stood
amidst squares of flattened cardboard in her sitting room that would
become temporary homes for things that have no business growing
roots. She lifted them, her things, like dumbbells, as if expecting
resistance. The black rectangular radio sat listening, her sounds slipping through its speakers. She could smell the mustard from the half
eaten sandwich that rested on the arm of her sofa. A creature of the
night, she was at room temperature when she left to go next door.
She lifted the key from the potted plant underneath Joy's window;
of course it turned the lock open.

Hydrogen H1 = Joy
In sleep she followed a thought because it had something to show
her. At first, it was pure, singular. She was a grown woman with her
little girl voice, being thrown up in the air and caught. She could not
see by whom. They were brown hands and arms locking over her
middle. Each time she was thrown, glowing, meandering triangles
approached her from either side before slipping over her feet and
upwards. This happened many times until eventually she turned gold
in colour. She heated up, boiling till it became unbearable. Her head
exploded against the black backdrop revealing a red mist. The brass

head was rolling at her feet, grinning again. Then she was headless, she had no choice, she picked it up. It was a scorching helmet in her hands. She paced through the red mist feeling no sense of belonging and floated above other elements.

Carbon C6 = Queen

She was a child waking up to find her father gone. Later, her mother would make *moi moi* she'd pick at. They'd sit across from each other at the big, empty glass table and try not to tremble. In a child's way, she would blame herself and her mother for a long time.

Then:

She was clutching the brass head and a diary.

These memories became:

Padding for her coffin

Fertiliser for the soil

Clothing to wear dead

She was a nucleus curling and unfurling its distended, wet eye.

The breath on a window with nobody there, a subtle repositioning of slippers, photographs, mugs. Whispers tickling the spine of a maple tree leaning to the side. Everywhere, the dead were among the living.

Peter Lowon Journal entry July 1964

I left Okafor having confessed nothing with the mouth but everything with the body. The panic in my pupils, the sweat across my top lip, the attempt to keep my limbs still; I was dead weight in a chair. I walked away upright, down the seven steps out. I felt his eyes bore into my back.

Everything seemed worse after that. The hot air outside that smelled of sun-stroked bodies, meat pies, roasted corn. Ripe failure. The women milling about with loaded baskets on their heads and worn, heavy expressions looked at me in judgement. I stuttered and tripped over a crushed, green, soft drink can.

To avoid having any witnesses I had asked the driver not to come, so I opened the black Mercedes driver-side door. The heat hit me all at once. If a man could sit in a car and while away his life I would have done it. I sat inside for the longest time watching my hands shake at the wheel. Listening as the noises of cars, chatter, music and life were drowned out by a splintered cry that came from beyond me. I thought of calling my father, my mother, rubbing the possibility as though it was a colourless marble. They would find out soon enough, but I did not want to tell them, knowing that if I did, there would be nothing but disappointment to follow.

I spent the afternoon driving around aimlessly. Early evening, I stopped by a street vendor not too far from Festac to pick up Queenie's favourite snacks; perm dodo and suya. I got there early knowing soon queues would form.

I nodded watching the vendor's fast hands chop onions, season and salt the partially cooked strips of meat. He hummed to himself; the only dent on his perfect black skin was a pock mark between his eyes .His eyes were red, as if from worry, maybe they were always that way and I was noticing for the first time. His nose was broken and his white vest had spots of food. I felt an unexpected kindred connection. He moved his wiry, agile body effortlessly. I said "You're here every evening?"

"Three evenings a week, I do other things too sir." He answered laughing; as though being underestimated was a common mistake people made.

I asked him what kind of other things? He chuckled, telling me he was a survivor.

To my surprise, I started talking. That was how I came up with the second part of my plan, plotting with a stranger, a street vendor I had never had a proper conversation with before.

I rang General Akhatar when I got home, but he was away in Abuja and not due back till the following afternoon. Heaviness slowed me down. Sitting in my big, white house with its servant quarters I felt like a poor man. Then I was angry. Angry at myself for doing a terrible thing you cannot erase, angry at meritocracy and the way it infected your system as a young man, angry happiness eluded me. No matter what I did, it danced away because of one night. One mistake. Something else nagged, making me furious. I couldn't remember who had introduced me to the General, how we had met. In my mind's eye, I saw myself reaching back into that moment, grabbing it like a rolled up piece of paper, then tossing it away.

I knew Felicia would be due home from the shop, her car tyres whispering as she eased in through the tall, black gates.

I found Queenie on her bed, awake, looking young and wise all at once. She stood to attention, laughing in her bright pyjamas after noticing the plate of suya and dodo in my hands. She told me she had known I bought suya, that mummy would be angry if she caught us with food upstairs. We traded secretive smiles before eating. Just for an instant, I nearly folded; a father sharing dinner with his child is a beautiful, uncomplicated thing. Not on this occasion. The smell of onions in suya hung in the air; our

*hands were greased and peppered from the meat, a last supper for two
fraudulent disciples.*

*That night I could not sleep. I sat up in my double bed picking holes
through the time line of my life with a toothpick. I heard Felicia's steps
approach my room. I knew they were hers, soft, as though she was walking
through sand. They have always been that way. I knew she stood there
listening, her eardrums prickled to detect every sound, sensing something,
a feeling things would change again. She was breathing through the door
and through a war only couples fought, bruised but still human. Now we
wanted to show each other our bruises and say look what you have done.
Can you see it there? Here? There? Okay, make it go away, do magic.*

*Now I stood on the other side, my fingers splayed against the door,
listening like her. Wanting. I was a mystery to my wife; one day she had
opened her eyes and not recognised me. We stayed that way for a while,
listening to our breaths warming a wooden door, knowing each other
through body movements we couldn't see. I remembered then how she used
to burn herself by candle light, poring over old books that horded unfulfilled dreams. I wondered whether what I'd done to our marriage felt like
a massive burn chafing against her clothes when she moved. Then, the
handle turned, neither of us knowing which one had opened the door.*

She

Stood

There.

*Looking like the mother of unborn children, like the girl who deserved
so much more than some shack of a shop. I picked her up, and did something
I missed doing. I drew shapes on her body; half moons on her buttocks, in
the lined crevices of her shoulder blades, tiny snail-shaped creatures of
regret pulsing down the line of her back. A paper fan I coloured purple
with the heat from my finger over her labia. I tongued the sweat at the
base of her spine into a whirlpool, left hand prints on her thighs, and
made murals for her out of her skin. I made love to my wife, the shaking
of the bed sounded better than any music. The sweet sticky scent of her*

would be trapped in my nostrils for the entirety of my earthly life; the walls between us fell down. Her body curled around me. I swam inside her repeatedly, attempting to halve her in two: one to leave behind, one to take away.

In the morning, I reluctantly received a call from Ben Okafor.

He informed me that a source had revealed General Akhatar has been killed in a coup d'etat along with the President on their trip back from Abuja. It was lead by my old friend Obi Ekebe and did I have any comments?

My blood chilled. I replaced the receiver. Okafor would go ahead and write the expose in the Trumpet. If I stayed, I was a dead man either way. Finished. Obi and I had been friends once. We had trained together, killed together.

But by the following evening, I planned to be unrecognisable as a common street beggar, a new man with a fresh passport hidden in my inside pocket.

Intermission

An insistent knock sounded on the door. I opened it to find two uniformed policemen, one with a gut, the other trim and ginger-haired. Their expressions were unreadable. My bad news radar went off.

I said, "Yes?"

"I'm Sergeant Molden," said the shorter of the two. "This is Sergeant Murdoch." He indicated to his flame haired partner. "May we come in?"

I stepped back to make room for their entrance in my narrow hallway. Molden spoke first in a choppy fashion, each word seeming to stand alone. "Do you know the whereabouts of your neighbour, the elderly lady?"

"Mrs Harris?"

"Whatever she calls herself," Murdoch piped in. "Nobody actually knows her real name."

"I haven't seen her for days. Why? What's happened?" Fear fluttered my hand to my throat.

"She's disappeared; we need to ask her some questions."

"I don't understand. Is she in trouble?"

Molden rearranged his impatient expression and explained slowly, "It's urgent that we speak to her. If you hear anything, contact us. Have any of your things gone missing?" he asked.

Still shocked, on instinct I didn't mention the incident with the brass head.

"No." We were all standing in my living room, spare pieces of a chess game.

"And you're sure you have no idea where she is or could be?" Murdoch asked.

"No, of course not, she was my neighbour not my mother."

"We won't keep you." Molden turned to the door "We'll be talking to more people on this street at some point, it's a serious matter. If you do hear or see anything please let us know." He held a card out to me I looked at in horror before taking it as if he'd handed me rabies. From behind my curtains I watched them get into a blue Ford car and drive off.

Really! I walked back to the centre of the room as though on stilts. Mad butterflies, I thought back to our conversation at the park. A mad butterfly had told me something true after all. She was an escape artist. I couldn't help myself; I collapsed to the floor laughing. Several days later, I picked up a free City Lights newspaper from the train. There was a small feature on Mrs Harris. Wanted for benefit fraud, she had been assuming the identities of dead people for years. Stealing thousands from taxpayers, she had successfully been giving the police nationwide the slip for decades.

My theory was, fucked up people can't help being drawn to other fucked up people, sometimes unwittingly. She was duplicitous, I knew this. BUT.

Those people were already dead. What was the real harm, other than conning a system that screwed you anyway? If you could and got away with it, wouldn't you? In my warped way I was a little envious of her ruses, and her balls.

Later, I squeezed through her white unlocked kitchen window. Except for the sofa (there before she came), the fridge, the bed, the wardrobe, chests of drawers and washing machine, everything was gone. Even Buddy the Buddha, was no longer there to keep watch in the garden for only half the time. The kitchen felt barren without her collection of herbs mixing together, scenting the air with an unidentifiable perfume. They'd flown the coop with her. I ran my fingers over the black, scratched counter tops. *She was real to me.* I thought of her sitting at my hospital bed, sipping green ginger wine together on the rooftop, and eating the best breakfast I could remember for a long time. I thought of her saving my life. And my heart bloomed for her, whoever she was. Pangs of loss arrived, sudden, hard.

Days later I found her postcard in my vest drawer. It had a blue lit up question mark positioned over a man's head. It read:

Well, the jig is up butterfly, I expect the boys in blue will be round asking questions. One day, I'll tell you all about it. And… I really am Scottish. Until that time, do the right thing xxx.

She could be anywhere. "Do the right thing."

Who'd have thought?

Inside her, Houdini chuckled.

Boat

In the dream, my head smacked repeatedly against the curved underside of a boat back at those same traffic lights where the baby had wandered, illuminated by the opening of another day and the acrid smell of smoke in the air. I felt the tug of a current inside me but there was no water holding the boat, only glass everywhere and traffic lights winking. The chatter of voices filled with concern and curiosity. Cheated of water the boat didn't move, but interrupted the flow of traffic. The wound on my head stung. Blood oozed down the side of my face. Dry mouthed and nauseous, my head lolled. Through the thick, neon-coloured haze a slender, elegant figure reached out to me, grabbing my arm. Anon. She dragged me, my skin freshly stung, through ground filled with blood stained glass, glinting like jewels. Because of my position at floor level, a pigeon appeared to stumble away from the wound on my head. Undeterred, Anon dragged me to another road, only to shove me into light speed traffic. Decorated in broken glass, I fell to the ground, swallowed by engine noise, calling out freakishly in pigeon language to Anon who'd led me to the boat in the first place. I only owned half of the betrayal I tasted.

Chorus

At the medical centre, the woman in the painting of a dense forest had moved. Last time, she'd taken shelter beneath a hollow tree. This time, she was waist deep in the lake, searching for something as the painted strokes rippled. Hung on the off-yellow wall behind the reception desk, my eyes automatically went there each visit.

The receptionist named Carol, a slender auburn haired woman with overly plucked eyebrows, was talking on the phone at the back, while a photocopying machine churned out documents. She spotted me hovering, placed her hand over the receiver angling her head. "Hi Joy, you signed in for me?" I nodded, fished out a squeezed piece of paper from my back pocket. "This isn't helping." I said loudly. "I'm still not getting enough sleep." On the wall the white clock above a cluster of certificates ticked sharply. A fly in the clock skimmed the glass before landing on the nine. I paced the small reception area, hearing its wings flutter.

"Okay, take a seat. The doctor will be with you in a bit; I'll let him know you're here." Carol went back to talking into her static. The area smelt of pine, the floors gleamed and intermittently, the sliding entry glass doors delivered health care professionals bearing ID's in rectangular, blue plastic holders jangling around their necks. I sat back listening to voices filtering through from the Saratoga Room

behind me. I took a quick peek. In the centre wooden chairs were
arranged in a circle, a few people loitered. One man with earphones
rocked his head gently back and forth. Another was drawing at a
table decorated with fresh, ivory-hued gardenias where a marred
heart floated between stems. I tapped my foot absentmindedly;
watching silhouettes on the floor morph, listening to the crackle
of the voices buzzed into reception, resenting my punishment for
attempting to kill myself only once. Only once. Once. One time.

I looked up. The woman in the painting was underwater. My
breath thinned. Plastic fish made of old photo ID's swam towards
her from the bottom.

Dr Krull's room was royal blue. I wondered if that was deliberate,
to keep the likes of me calm, royal blue to smooth frayed edges. On
opposite sides but not too far away from each other were two plush
brown leather chairs. In the left corner, a silent water machine. A
wide wooden desk was filled with a stack of books and files. Almost
mockingly beside the files was a sun-drenched picture of the Dr
and his wife on a colourful street somewhere exotic. India maybe.
They were an attractive, well-adjusted couple in a removable frame.
I fidgeted in my seat while I watched Dr Krull's handsome face
wrinkle as he studied his notes. He looked Thai, perhaps Malaysian.
His angular face and glinting eyes never seemed overly ruffled but
his mouth always appeared to have more to say, twisting sardonically
or curving down. We looked at each other across the gape of space
between us, the battle line drawn using a chalky stone I could taste
on my tongue.

Dr: *How are you doing with the Sertraline tablets I prescribed?*

In my mind's eye, I saw the tablets dancing down a fat neck of
toilet water, or melting in a sink full of bleach, taking their numbness
down a plughole better equipped to manage the sluggish silhouettes,
unable to cry out quickly their tongues having been weighed down
my chemical solutions.

I nodded emphatically: *Yes, I'm still taking them but I don't know if
they're actually helping.*

Dr: *You have to give these medications time to properly take effect. Take them consistently. Tell me about your routine before leaving the house.*

I willed my legs still, stopped the knees from knocking together. A couple of doors down the circle would have more people by now. Soon, they'd be confessing to practical strangers, taking their heads off like lids on sloppy jars, waiting to see things spill.

I watched the Dr's face being kind, patient.

I check the kitchen cupboards, the wardrobe, make sure the windows are locked… About six or seven times, sometimes more if I'm feeling really anxious.

Dr: *How long does it take you to leave the house? Why the cupboards and your wardrobe? What do you think you'll find there?* He kept his expression neutral, tone pleasant, pen poised over the notes in his lap. Outside, a car tore off into the distance. Lights changed around the city, indicating when to wait, stop, go. Amber, red, green. But when should a person be green, amber and red? Which organs could I swap for lights that helped you navigate through the dark? Where would I leave my organs? On a zebra crossing, a bridge or a kerb? The fly from the reception clock had left number nine. Tentatively I said: *I, my hearing… It's changing.*

Dr: *Changing how?* A slight note of irritation had crept into his voice.

Why are you a burden Joy? A female voice declared sweetly. Don't be such a burden!

Dr Krull uncrossed legs clad in black corduroys.

My hands clasped and unclasped: *It feels… sharper. I can hear isolated sounds, details from quiet conversations, keys buried in someone's bag, that sort of thing.*

Dr patiently responded: *The human body is a wondrous gift. All kinds of amazing, unexplainable things happen. I understand it might have slightly upset your equilibrium but it doesn't sound like too much to worry about. Tell me, have you ever been deaf?*

I leaned back into my chair: *Deaf?* I repeated as if he'd just spoken to me in a foreign language. My left hand trembled on my thigh.

Dr: *Why do you check the cupboards, wardrobe and locks that amount of time? Is there something you're afraid of?*

Irritably I said: *I don't know. I thought: Shouldn't you have the answer to that? You're asking me things I already ask myself.*

The room felt warmer, claustrophobic, the space between us had shrunk. In the hallway, wheels squealed against the floor. Lunch. Ready and waiting for those in the circle; crisp salads, light Cornish pasties, thickly crusted steak pies, chickpea curry and warm, crumbly apple pies. All that sharing gave you an appetite.

I continued slowly: *I get anxious.*

Carefully, I selected my words: *I live alone and I don't want anything to have... access.*

Dr Krull: *I find it interesting that you said anything not anyone.*

I shrugged my shoulders: *Same thing. Sometimes I get this feeling of doom. This horrible, choky feeling and I can't breathe. My head hurts just thinking about it. I haven't been sleeping properly.*

Dr Krull: *Do you still swallow stones?*

Yes I answered, internally cursing my deviancy. *Sometimes.* I thought I saw a flicker of pity on the Dr's face but it was a fleeting nano second of change.

I know what you're going to say, I stated, patting myself on the back for being ahead of the curve. *Yes,* her voice said. *It's so pathetic you can predict questions about your own dysfunction.* Congratulations, *have the rest of your life to decipher your miserable existence.*

I like the taste of stones Dr. I like that you can measure their entirety with your tongue; they're definable. It pushes that choked up feeling in my throat down, right down to the bottom.

Dr Krull: *Tell me about the first time you swallowed a stone, your earliest memory.*

I don't remember.

Dr Krull: *You don't remember or you don't want to remember?*

I held his gaze steady, like one of my stones in its fragmented bottom.

I don't remember.

Dr Krull pressed pause on his tape recorder before exiting the room to get me a higher dosage of the sleeping pills he'd given me last time. I squirmed slightly beneath the gaze of his attractive wife from her compact picture frame. I set the picture face down on his desk. He'd left his blazer slung over the chair, seat still warm with his body's imprint. I glanced around the room suspiciously, checking for signs of a hidden camera and confessions becoming thumbprints on its lens. They wouldn't film without your consent, Doctor/patient confidentiality and all that. The lining of his jacket felt smooth and expensive. An image of him licking his wife's nipples with his silk-lined tongue flashed into my head. I rummaged inside the jacket, keeping my ears open. I fished out a wallet containing £50 and a folded bank statement. I took a £20 note, ripped the first page of the bank statement with his address on and stuffed both in my back pocket. Carefully, I arranged the jacket exactly as I'd met it.

Anon appeared in the Dr's chair, curled her long legs beneath her. *Take something else* she said. *Do it before he comes back.* Her voice was strong and assured. The weight of her tongue inside my head pulled me up again. Her hand slipped into his jacket, opened the wallet. Before I knew it, I'd taken a Visa credit card, a tingle hummed along my spine. My handprints fed the hungry, small gold rectangle in the corner of the card in my pocket. A ripple from the river of the painting in reception carried them away, floating on the shimmering surface. The card was still lodged in my jeans pocket.

When the Dr returned, I was getting rid of evidence. A thin line of sweat ran into my right eye, stinging a little. The dripping water fountain made small echoes in the room, now buzzing with a spark of electricity. As I struggled to breathe, Anon's face reassembled.

Dr Krull entered the room clutching a small paper bag bearing the green pharmaceutical logo. He looked concerned catching me taking deep breaths leaning forward in my seat. I didn't say any-thing except *panic attack* and continued gulping air until he took the medicines out of the bag and handed it over for me to inhale. I didn't say a word. I knew these people like neatly packaged neuroses; messy spillage meant messy consequences, the numbness of zombie land and blood in the sky. We sat that way for several minutes while he helped me steady my breathing and I tried to control sudden movements, paranoid his credit card would fall from my pocket.

Dr Krull upped the dosage of the Sertraline pills that ran into white skies and left outlines looking like small, smudged spaceships if you kept them on paper in sunlight.

I left the centre to a chorus of jangling cutlery. A stringy haired woman in reception repeatedly spun her polka dot umbrella till it clattered to the floor. Outside, the wind blew. I bought a tuna and cucumber salad sandwich from Greggs, topped up my electricity using Dr Krull's newish looking £20 note. At home, Anon the long-limbed woman was waiting on the bedroom window ledge, stroking some animal whose lines would fade by morning. I cried into my jar of slow dwindling stones, feeling my chest heave, thinking of my mother and all the lessons she would never learn from me.

Semi Circle

The heat in Rangi's bathroom felt temporary. I was bent over the tub, inhaling and exhaling almost silently, feeling his tongue moistening the dip in my back, his laughter quiet against my skin in some secret trade off. Bloody ribbons from between my legs disintegrated in lukewarm water as the speed of the fly's wings increased, circling around the small artificial sun that was the light bulb. A trickle edged down my left thigh, more bloody ribbons. I didn't have to look down to know my nipples were reacting in their familiar way, one inverted and the other distended. As if they couldn't agree on how transparent they should be about their pleasure.

Poised behind me, Rangi's muscles tensed and relaxed, his golden frame coiled. He nudged me forward so my hands were splayed on the wall in front for support. I was trying to hold on to the thoughts scurrying in my head when he bit my left bottom cheek before tracing the teeth marks with his tongue. I released a sound that was part whimper and part sigh. The small house I'd drawn on the cabinet mirror had lost its roof and no longer harboured the sounds I made. Sounds that now belonged to small creatures with sink plugholes for mouths.

Curled above our small liquid country, bathed in 60-watt light, he bent me over the tub more, holding my head under water. I opened my eyes; they stung as he slid in and out of me quickly. There was a rush of blood to my head while he moved, expanding me. In my mind's eye, his member was covered in blood, its sly slit developing a taste for it. My mouth tried to hold the bend in his long penis in mirrors without steam. He moved in and out at a frenzied pace, I knew I couldn't stay under for that much longer. Either I'd pass out or die but he held fast, slippery grip on my rubber band waist. My body went limp. My head sank further into the water, like a female flamingo mating. The 60-watt light bulb flickered.

We were gulls on a sunken bed, chasing wounds disguised as bread. Flapping our stained grey wings beneath a curved, wet ceiling, waiting for paint to fall on us; for its strong fresh scent to fill our noses while we fucked, for the sheet that hung off the bed to become white water carrying our old scenes, wet and ready to fill the doorways of their birth. I knew the gulls would go blind from the artificial light, mouths lined with tobacco when they broke their necks against the ceiling, tricked into thinking it was a sky line. Mauve paint crumbled into the whites of our eyes, a train rumbling in the distance inadvertently became a burial ground for half-formed things. Our previous wet scenes found their way into the dead gulls, waiting for the sound of the next train to warn them of their travelling funeral ground. The 60-watt bulb flickered.

We were mannequins that had abandoned the window display filling up with stones, trickling in from every angle. As the sound of roughly shaped stones rose, panic in our chests deepened. We communicated using expressions from the human versions of ourselves. We mimicked their body movements mirrored in glass. Panic in the mannequins waned. A sunken bed stained with come in the distance beckoned. Stones falling rang in their chests. Then their injuries came from climbing fences, stumbling in the dark, from wear and tear. The light flickered again. I felt my body being lifted from the tub, vaguely registering the squeaky sound the bath made as he hauled up my wet frame, hands beneath my armpits. My eyes stung from opening them in soapy water. Blood between my legs left a trail on the aqua coloured linoleum floor. He sat me up gingerly, the scent of period blood lingered in the air. He patted my cheek firmly. I blinked. His face swam.

He inched closer, voice deep and full of wry humour he said, "How was it?"

"Fucking great," I murmured, spent, as if having a near death sexual escapade was ticked of my to do list. He was striking in the light, tall and wiry. Locks grazed his shoulders; the deep, golden skin he'd inherited from his Maori father glowed. Slightly slanted dark brown eyes crinkled easily and seemed to watch you even when he wasn't looking in your direction.

We sat on the balcony in our underwear, smoking spliffs to quieten the roar inside, listening to dog howls ricocheting through the night air. I didn't ask about the wispy lock of brown hair in the bathroom cabinet that didn't belong to me, or the blue false nail studded with blinking white stones breathing beneath the bed. I didn't ask about why his tongue tasted of alcohol in the morning sometimes. He closed his bloodshot eyes, took a pull from the spliff, as if he was silently communicating with the red dog snapping in the distance, making it's way towards us. He turned towards me, New Zealand accent thick. "Do you know what happened to the gold lady's ring in my bottom drawer?" I held my hand out, he passed the spliff. I took a draw, watching smoke curling in the sudden tension. "Never seen it." My silent fury had escaped from the confines of the false nail. The red dog bearing bloodshot eyes paused to eat it. The bed sheet wrapped around me slipped beneath my inverted breast, already turning in the carnage of items on the bedroom floor.

In that weird, smoggy state between being half asleep and awake, I watched Anon from my comfortable position on the double bed. Rangi lay curled in the opposite direction, lilac sheet tangled between us and one leg half-flung over the duvet. He breathed rhythmically, chest rising and falling, making small sounds that were an odd combination of snoring and whistling. Anon stood by the stash of record sleeves, old albums of Jimi Hendrix, Marvin Gaye and The Shangri-Las and began rummaging through clothes strewn on the floor, lifting empty glasses of wine and the small atlas on the drawer to collect a torn, wrinkled piece of paper she stashed in my bag.

Rangi adjusted himself, making the mattress groan. Her hand stilled over his black smartphone, eyes daring me to make a sound. Sweat began to pop on my brow and the room became hazy. Rangi turned again, back muscles exposed. How could he sleep through this? She stood then in the light angling from the balcony, arms outstretched. I sat up, my heart beats loud, her accented voice in the space between them. Something in the air changed. Outside, two cats mating screamed. The water pipes whistled.

I stood up, hypnotised, longing for my rough stones and the reassuring swell in my throat from swallowing. Maybe she hadn't been looking for something. Maybe she'd been leaving something behind. We swapped mouths. Then she was holding the baby from the road, its yellow Skittles packet dropped to the floor silently. She began to feed it Rangi's missing ring. It smiled happily. The ribbons from the tub became bloody baby footprints on the hardwood floor. I listened for Rangi through the din threatening to swallow me. I knew the day after; he'd wear his animal mask to prowl after me in the dark. I stumbled around, longing for his sly-eyed penis to split me in two, for his semen to be a rushing river chasing oddly shaped stones.

Incision

A mouse's red head spun the day I met Rangi. Coincidentally, on my way out, the dead mouse lay just beyond my thick, brown welcome mat. It was mid movement, body arched, fearful final expression frozen. I swept it up quickly; holding my nose, already mummifying, a chalky residue coated its frame. I imagined its tiny head spinning in the afterlife, sneering at its previous attempts at living. I wondered about the versions of me doing the same thing, raising their heads above margins and shaking in disappointment, changing their expressions in slanted, translucent ceilings, watching small men made of debris limp away into the distance.

All morning I'd had a sick feeling of dread in my stomach and a bitter taste in my mouth I'd tried to wash down with two cups of peppermint tea and an out-of-date croissant. I'd padded around the flat, shutting windows against whistling that snuck in, then opening the windows again to release them. I'd have to talk to the centre about these medications they had me on that made me feel like a stranger in my own body, made me forget things.

I was sure of it. No, I wasn't sure of it, it wasn't the medications. It was me. I was the problem. Medications were there to help. Why couldn't I see that? Why couldn't I see it was for my own good? Why did I always have to ruin things with negativity?

Six o'clock that morning I'd sat up in bed listening to a scuttling in the ceiling, t-shirt damp from cold sweat, I shivered, willing myself to change. The scuttling continued. Maybe it had been the mouse trying to escape the death that awaited it in muted afternoon light. As my doppelgangers angled their bodies over a darkening skyline, the mouse's last expression reassembled in their stomachs.

Each borough had a local paper or magazine. Since my mother died, now and again, I'd scan the births, deaths and marriages sections, pen in hand jotting down names that caught my interest. Photography work was slow and it was another risky income stream. Suitably dressed in a black, knee length dress, green-eyed lizard brooch pinned to my breast, low kitten heels and twists curbed into a neat bun, netted navy hat perched on my head, I arrived at the service at St Mathew's church in Bow fifteen minutes late.

The wrought iron gates creaked loudly. Amongst the crackling, golden leaves on the short grey flight of steps, a crumpled twenty pound note jumped. A red line drawn over the queen's mouth was the inky ripple leaves curled into before shooting off in different directions. I grabbed the twenty, stuffing it inside the sleek leather bag on my shoulder. Tall, dark wooden doors were flung open and the hymn being sung was loud enough to muffle the sound of my heels clicking. A statue of Mary in the hallway stood before a painting of the last supper. Mary had no tongue. In the painting, her moist, pink tongue was on a platter, darting with the weight of things it had to say. I kissed Mary on her cold forehead, watched her hands change colour from grey to brown. Suddenly it was my mother standing before a last supper, arms outstretched, past scenes crumbling on her fingers into dust trying to communicate with no tongue.

I spotted the cloakroom at the far end of the hallway. Through the glass the jackets were neatly hung, sleeves lined up against each other as if they were an army of lockstepping men, while the bodies of the dead turned in red wine. The priest intoned in Latin. An adrenaline rush hit my limbs at high speed. I never knew what to expect in these situations. Anything could happen. The important thing was to act as naturally as possible and to get the business end taken care of quickly.

I entered the cloakroom, took my jacket off, keeping one eye on the entrance. I rummaged through the pockets of coats dangling an invitingly short distance away. The beauty of it was, people left all kinds of things in their coats; jewellery, old photos, condoms. Once, I'd found torn lace panties.

The priest spoke again, his voice a calm, soothing accompaniment to the pilfering happening in the cloakroom. Anon continued to instruct me quietly and my sweaty fingers became assured in those foreign pockets. I stuffed cash, credit cards, a watch and a red ruby stoned ring into my bag. Somebody in the service dropped a coin; I heard its slow roll on the smooth marble floor.

I buckled my bag shut, left the cloakroom closing the door gently behind me.

The service was half full, I wandered in quietly, coiled tension in my back slowly dissipating. A grey haired, middle-aged lady at the front nodded at me. I nodded back solemnly fingering the new found silence of the coin I'd scooped on my way in. The wooden pews were deep, still holding the prayers and confessions of sinners long gone. Sunlight glimmering through the scene on the stained glass window behind the pulpit gave it an ethereal glow. From the window Jesus had lost his strides in the sound of a truck pulling up on a nearby street. I heard the key turning in its stiff lock, the quiet purring of the engine cooling down.

Miss Argyle, whoever she was had friends in death. One woman in the pew to my left wiped tears from her eyes, another clutched her handbag so tightly, her knuckles strained against the skin. Somebody at the pulpit was giving an impassioned dedication. On the walls the carvings of saints leaned forward, burial soil softening in their mouths. From the bright window Jesus armed with an orange tongue would have to borrow legs from somebody he'd once forgiven.

I sensed him before I saw him. Something in the air changed, a shift I couldn't quite identify. My neck became warm. My skin tingled. The smell of an earthy-scented aftershave filled my nostrils. I adjusted in my seat as the pew behind me creaked from somebody leaning back. Curious, I turned to see a lean, exotic looking man tucking a slither of silver Rizla paper into his pocket. His locked, wavy hair was tied back. He had on black jeans and a dark tweed jacket that had seen better days but was oddly stylish. His broad nostrils flared. He placed one long finger over his lips, pointed forward, indicating for me to mind my business. Liquid light brown eyes twinkled in amusement. In that moment, he seemed changeable. As if he could inch forward and his bull's head would sprout over the subdued din or his crow hand would cover my breast and flick against its inverted nipple.

As the service rolled on, the tightness in my chest returned, an angular rip that was haemorrhaging. And suddenly I was back at my mother's funeral, amongst a cluster of mourners looking for all intents and purposes a little relieved they weren't the ones being lowered into the ground. Mervyn had wiped his tears away while people's condolences swirled in my head, sentences that broke and re emerged as small wasp-like creatures, fluttering their wings between rapid eye movement. *I'm so sorry. This is unexpected. How will you cope?*

A woman's coat flapped against slender legs encased in black tights. The white hyena in the sky bore down ready to swallow the scent whole so I gave it the wasps in my head. People looked into the rectangular chasm in the ground, as if their own eyes would mirror back the change of season. I spilled soil on the casket. It popped open. My mother sat up at the far right end of the silky ivory interior, picking the hem of her skirt, threads dangling out of the casket. I crawled towards her, stretching my hand at her face as it blurred and redefined itself. *There's no room for two here.* She said that in a dry, accented tone that flooded me with familiarity. I pressed my head against her chest, listening to the sound of taps running, of warm bath water spilling. The casket was damp; I began to feel around for a leak.

Then I patted my body down for leakage.

Then I was swept into Mervyn's arms.

Then I was silently screaming, holding onto the shuddering of his shoulders, pressing my fingers against distorted shards of light.

At the party afterwards, held in a separate room that boasted large stained glass windows and an ornate mural ceiling I watched the man hiding the sliver of silver from the corner of my eye. He moved easily, interacting with other mourners. Kids ran in and out, small mountains of food dwindled. People talked about the dead woman as if she'd never made a mistake. Maybe they did this subconsciously, affected by being in God's house. *How did you know Abbie?* The inevitable question cropped up repeatedly. I made stories up on the spot, wondering how I'd ever explain to Dr Krull the strange comfort I got from attending the funerals of others, telling myself most people wouldn't realise they'd been robbed until they'd driven off and arrived at their next destination. The fleshy bodies turning in red wine began to lose their heads. I kept my eye on the exit in case I needed to bolt. Stones rolled in my bag for comfort and as part of an escape plan.

He finally approached me carrying an empty beverage bottle. The air between us was thick with promise. When he spoke it was like being knocked over unexpectedly, a kick in the gut, a rush of warmth flooded my skin.

"I didn't know her," he murmured unapologetically. "The dead woman" he continued, smiling at the bewildered expression on my face.

I raised my shoulders to release tension. "Oh, why would you attend the funeral of somebody you don't know? It's deceitful," I said. He looked me in the eye knowingly, an unsettling tight expression on his face. "I followed you in here. You walk like a woman I once knew in Haiti. I'm sorry for your loss," he offered, just a hint of mockery in his voice.

"Thank you," I answered, surprised by the pangs of sorrow I felt.

He rummaged inside his jacket, fished out something. "You dropped this by the way." He handed me the £20 from the steps. The Queen's silent expression had subtly darkened. "Hey! I put that in my bag."

"Ah, you're not the only one with tricks. Come on, there's an interesting crypt space downstairs. I'll show you, don't make a scene."

He was so close I could smell the alcohol on his breath.

The crypt was cool but his hands were warm. He propped me up against a disused bar, slipped a finger inside me, promising to mark my underwear with cigarette burns. He pressed the bottle mouth against my back. The woman whose walk I'd inherited sat at the bottom in smoke form, curling into our breaths. Tires screeched away, stones rustled, bite marks on my shoulder formed a raging map of teeth indentations. The bodies in red wine swam after their floating, drunken privates. Sweat pooled between my breasts. I liked the metallic taste of his zipper in my mouth, the fury of his fingers sliding in and out of me frenetically, his changeable face buried in the damp, gnarly thatch of hair between my legs. His mouth sucked greedily on the arches of my feet. His hands tightened on my throat, saints on the church walls orgasmed in unison. My tongue came undone

Down

In

The

Crypt.

Chesapeake

At night the beach was pretty much deserted. Faces from the rocks slipped into the sly sea line while the waters thrashed as if a second moon would appear. Rain soaked and wind blown, I watched Rangi's lone, lean frame angling into the foamy depths. He changed with each dive and stroke, beneath the knowing gazes of underwater creatures. I leaned into the wind from my view between two rough-hewn peaks, breeze dented, scowling chip paper in one hand; greasy fat chip in the other. Shots of vinegar created sour warmth in my mouth. Above a smattering of gulls chorused loudly.

I was joyous having left behind London and the brass head beneath my bed, the fascination it held and the sick feeling it produced in my stomach. I thought of my grandfather's diary, facing the things I'd inherited breathing between the lines of a bound leather book.

The wind began to howl. My inappropriate plimsolls were soaked. Typical of me to wear the wrong footwear, *you can't even get that right*. I shivered. The salty sea air felt good, I was slowing down my demons, given them a different oxygen. The faces in the night water waited patiently for limbs. Rangi stood, water undulating around him, motioning for me to join him. "Come on!" he yelled. "Stop being an observer!" he taunted. A weird rush of intensity filled my body, even in the distance between us, the air was electric. I shook my head, scared he'd notice something we both didn't want to see rise to the surface of water. I leaned forward to get a closer view, certain his body had encountered haphazard bits of life underwater; a plane's wing, a diver's mask, the moon's silver-limbed doppelganger.

Don't be an observer. I wasn't. There I was running off with a stranger to get to know myself, convinced the limestones in my pocket had left damp stains. They glimmered in those small openings, moist and full of slow promise. If I got really anxious, I could always nibble on them. Rangi called out to me in a language I didn't recognise, water dancing with his shark mouth. I rubbed my tender neck, blinking against the tide and the memory of him trying to strangle me in his sleep the night before. I stilled my body, a statue amidst black rocks, listening to the heartbeat galloping towards my chest.

In the cosy room of the seaside B&B, the hand on my throat tightened. The earth-toned red room swam. The TV showing an old episode of The Twilight Zone flickered. I clutched at his wrist, struggling for air. My eyes watered, body wriggled, head smacked against the double bed's rustic headboard. The voice over from The Twilight Zone spoke. *You can never know what will happen during those quiet moments of night we take for granted.* I tried to speak but he was squeezing hard, face twisted unrecognizably. Greyish white television light bathed us. I kicked wildly, digging my nails into his wrist before the pressure finally eased. I flung my body sideways, grabbing the glass of cold water beside the reading lamp, throwing it in his face.

"What the fuck?" he mumbled, wiping the wetness off his face, sitting up immediately. "Are you crazy? What did you do that for?" His New Zealand accent was even thicker during moments of irritation.

"You were strangling me!" I screamed. My voice sounded paper thin despite the volume. My eyes stung. I spluttered, relieved to be able to breathe again, stumbling from the damp bed as credits rolled on the TV screen. In the bathroom, I ran the cold tap, splashed water on my face and neck, trying to ease the burning sensation in my throat. I heard him knocking about in the other room. The portable fridge door opening made a *whoosh* sound. Cold air. I sat on the toilet seat trembling, touching the marks forming on my throat, waiting for bruises to come and transform under his bloodshot gaze.

I looked up, silent as his frame filled the doorway. "I'm sorry," he said, holding a small bowl of ice. He wrapped some cubes in a white cloth, pressed them against my neck. "I didn't mean to get that way." His touch was gentle. The same broad hand and tapered fingers were capable of being both tender and destructive. He placed a hand on my shoulder. His handsome face was feral yet apologetic in the bright light. "You're alright aren't you?"

"You thought I was someone else!" I accused, still frazzled, nerves shot.

The television was now off.

"No, I didn't know it was happening," he answered, mouth a grim line. His shoulders were tight. He let out a slow breath as if releasing an internal pressure.

"Death doesn't have to be frightening; it's just a transition into another phase," he said. It was such an odd comment; I shook my head in disbelief.

"Fuck you!" I exclaimed. "And you might want to be fully awake before you start giving lessons."

He leaned closer, face inches from mine, and smiled sardonically. His golden eyes gleamed. "Watch your mouth."

"How can you be so relaxed after what happened?" I asked. "What if I hadn't been able to wake you?"

"What do you want from me?" he roared. "You want a written fucking apology? You want to hold this over my head is that it?" He walked out, flinging the door open.

I stretched my legs out on the floor, confused by his reaction, trying to ignore the roaring in my head, the clammy feeling on my neck. The pale floor glistened, I tried to stand slowly but my legs buckled. The sentence in my throat was a breathy wheeze.

I began to crawl on the floor. Fear came thick and fast. I couldn't breathe. Panic attack. I felt around the floor for something, anything to steady me. Rangi appeared in the doorway again, calmly whistling. I hated myself for my weakness, for showing vulnerability too early. I knew I was crawling into the whites of his eyes, disappearing. He watched me struggling on the floor, coolly mouthed "fuck you." Then everything went grainy black.

When I came to, it was still cold, hard floor beneath me. Rangi held a pillow and there was an intense concentration on his face as he brought it down. The burning in my throat persisted; it felt like sandpaper. The room was hazy, smudged. I couldn't make out the lines of objects surrounding me. I sat up awkwardly.

"Steady," he instructed. "It's okay; I was just going to make you more comfortable. I didn't want to move you yet."

"What happened? " I asked, vaguely aware of the weakness of my limbs. He stroked a damp twist off my forehead, pressed a kiss there. "You fainted. Has that happened before?"

"No, not that I can remember," I answered, confused by his concern and unpredictability. The sleeping blue flame inside him singed my fingers. Somehow I was grateful, it made me feel alive. He carried me out of the bathroom, took my gaze away from the ceiling. After attempting to strangle me, he fucked me gently on the damp, sunken bed.

We left in slanted, heavy rain, hurtling down tight, twisted roads in an older black Mazda I was certain wasn't even his. Kate Bush's *The Kick Inside* played on the radio. I placed my feet on the dashboard. It was hard to see through the thunderous showers but I spotted her at the top of the curve ahead, Anon, running towards us, clutching something round. My heart sank. *Did you think I wouldn't come?* she asked.

Suddenly the car swerved, as if Rangi had seen her too. "Be alert," he ordered, squeezing my shoulder. That odd intensity he had magnified. I didn't know what he meant. Was it an opening for me to confess what I saw? Or tell him what I was feeling? I turned to look behind me. Anon sat in the back seat, wet from rain, *you let me in* she said. She was holding a paperweight; a chunk had been taken out of it. An image of me broken, crawling on the bathroom floor turned slowly inside it. I realised she'd been there all along, not pushed out by different oxygen.

She'd been there, in the sneaky half smile of the woman serving at the chip shop, in the hands of the B&B owner, whose fingers lingered overly familiar on my skin as one blue iris became brown. She'd been there at the beach, rising to the surface of rough waters. My feet cramped on the dashboard. Rangi's nose began to bleed.

"That happens sometimes," he said, grabbing a tissue from the glove compartment, wiping his face, then tilting his head back, one hand on the wheel. Blood trickled from his nostrils, seeping into the paperweight scene.

By now the bruised ceiling of our room at the B&B had washed up on the shore. The gulls from the beach had followed our departure too, each sporting one blue and one brown iris. They flapped their wings violently, screaming down the sharp bends, trailing in exhaust pipe smoke.

Keyholes

It was summer when I discovered keyholes spinning in the ether, hiding figures made of dark matter that let me catch a finger in their mouths. I was seven. Nighttime in our household found me tiptoeing down red softly carpeted stairs to spy on my mother, the memory of the school day's activities sticky on my skin. I'd worn a dead blue oleander flower in my cornrows to school and the fed up expression on my class tutor Mrs Phillips face had been worth it. *For God's sake Joy, take that thing off your head! It's morbid.*

The week before that, I'd re-enacted the birth of Christ for class-mates during break time, focusing particularly on the birth scene, complete with tinfoil Jesus and ketchup blood on my thighs, huffing and puffing and crying out, the way I'd seen a woman do on TV. Mrs Phillips had been furious, barging through the circle gathered, glasses steamed up, chest rising and falling rapidly as if it would detach from her body. Her creased, knee length grey dress was fit to burst and her thin features were pinched.

What on earth? What is going on here? She zeroed in on me; lips curled back looking like she was ready to fling me into an advert for starving African children, never to see another English dawn. And my tinfoil Jesus would accompany me by a murky, half-hearted lake, counting flies hovering over our distended stomachs.

This attention seeking has got to stop! My audience of co-conspirators sniggered, scattering like marbles, they slunk off to entertain themselves in other ways, swapping their canoodling expressions for innocent ones. *Honestly, I don't know what your mother exposes you to* Mrs Phillips continued, shoving aside the small coats I'd used as straw and the paint splattered plate that acted as my moon.

You said you liked creative interpretation, I piped up defensively.

I know what I said, she spat, hauling me up. *You look absolutely ridiculous.*

I swiped a blob of ketchup from my thigh and licked it, thinking of hot dogs. The tinfoil Jesus and I were dragged into Mrs Phillips office.

Later, in afternoon art class I sucked on strawberry bonbons. Streams of sunlight fed the artificial plant life cut-outs stuck on the classroom windowsills, forming a surrounding jungle. The smell of wet paintbrushes and chalk hung in the air.

Draw pictures of your family on an adventure, anywhere you like. Mrs Phillips instructed in her typical, grim faced manner. Sadness crept into my fingers as I drew on the scratched wooden desk harbouring hangmen in its corners, that seem to be plotting to meet each other in the middle to converse in a language only unhappy children could interpret.

Everybody else's family had a roundness to them; father, mother, brothers and sisters, smiling by the Eiffel tower, eating pink candyfloss at the fair, on the carousel ride laughing. Mine seemed uneven, filled with absences I tried to measure using hands that hadn't grown wide enough to do so. Strangely loaded sentences my mother never bothered to explain lingered in my strokes. *You come from me* she'd say. *And your father has powers beyond imagination.* I considered drawing my mother sleeping in the afternoons, for hours sometimes, or the secretive, quiet conversations she had at nights to somebody at the other end of the phone. But they'd ask me why and I didn't have any answers. Lead-drawn fathers from other children's pictures surrounded me, their sympathetic expressions faint. The classmates took turns holding my dead oleander, breathing thin breaths into it in hope of a resurrection. Mrs Phillips stood over my shoulder peering at my drawing; a picture of my mother and I wearing duck heads in a rippling pond, surrounded by broken bits of bread and large footprints in the sky.

What a curious image, she commented. *Whose footprints are those? My father's*, I said.

And who is your father? She asked. *I've never met him.*

God, I answered seriously, punctuating the response with a flick of my paintbrush.

Orange paint splattered onto Mrs Phillips's frumpy, grey dress. She pursed her lips. An uncomfortable silence followed.

I stood by the slightly open door that hot summer night, peeping through the tiny crack. A man sat on our deep mauve sofa. His brown torso had a light sheen, its own exotic animal in the lowly lit room. I pictured it falling at my feet, waiting for a spell from my hands by the edge of the doorway. I couldn't see his face; I'd have to adjust my position to do that. If I leaned too far forward, they'd spot me and I'd be banished upstairs, told off for spying. I was rooted to the spot, listening to my mother's laughter. I rarely heard it sound that way. It was softer, breathy, more feminine somehow. She sat on the man's thighs, her upper body naked, a silky red camisole pooled at her waist. Her breasts jutted forward. She cooed as the man's large hand stroked her thigh before disappearing between her legs. Aware I was watching something I wasn't supposed to be seeing, I bit my lip anxiously, careful not to move and make the floorboards creak. I knew adults sometimes did those things to each other, I'd seen snippets on TV before my mother flicked the channel over.

She began to move into his hand, gyrating, head thrown back. Her mouth was slack and distorted as if would overheat and fall into the ashtray on the table, orange embers flickering in the glass. The man chuckled, a low rumbling sound. He moved down her body like some large, brown skinned python. He placed his head between her legs, obscured under the camisole. He unbuckled his leather belt.

I turned away then, weighing the secrets of the door. I slunk up the stairs carefully; head filled with this new knowledge that seemed adult and mysterious somehow. Back in my room, I peeled back the rumpled duvet, crawled into bed listening to the fan blades turning. I stayed awake for a bit, thinking of brown torsos in slim cracks waiting to be identified.

The fan blades sliced through scenes I imagined belonged to the man downstairs, who was making my mother groan like some foreign entity, exposing a side of herself mothers kept hidden from their daughters, tucked beneath their darting, moist tongues. On the dresser beside me, a paper plane I'd made from old comic book pages was half off the wooden surface, with only the sound of the blades and my breathing to propel it skywards. I pretended me and the man downstairs were co-pilots on foot. Wherever we went, the plane followed; dented by a fox's paw from a night time rummage, damp from skimming its reflection in the pond at the local park, marked by frustrated fingers trying to fly it in the trails of real planes, whose destinations we chased till they vanished from sight.

I conjured up bits of a life for this man. Maybe he got lonely sometimes and he and my mother entangled their half-naked bodies till they rediscovered themselves in each other's eyes. Maybe he was a butcher who gutted animals that dangled off ceiling hooks and pleaded for the insides they'd lost. Who couldn't get the blood off his hands no matter how many times he washed them in scalding hot water or sat in public fountains.

I saw him pushing me on my yellow BMX bike, comic book plane caught in the wheel, its tip damp from saliva and all the things he couldn't say to me yet. I rode the bike to school, ringing its silver bell to announce the arrival of something waiting in the wings, misshapen from being in the dark too long. Eventually, I waved goodbye to the bike trail disappearing on the concrete. I looked over my shoulder. The man from the dark pressed his face between the gates. In the distance of the school hall, I continued ringing the bell. I couldn't see his face but I could hear him, crying the tears I'd lent him. Prompted by the cold, the lines of the grey bicycle disappeared into the hole in my chest. The paper plane stumbled, attempting to take off from one last, large male footprint.

The next morning, a package arrived for my mother in a thick, brown envelope lined with bubble wrap. I watched her from the balcony upstairs, flanked by secrets from the previous night, knocking one foot lightly against the over-filled laundry basket. She ran her fingers over the package at first, appearing hesitant to discover it's contents. Then she tore it open slowly, a sad expression on her face. A slash of midnight blue appeared. She smiled wistfully, maybe recalling a memory, clutched it to her chest, staring at the letterbox as it noisily swung closed. The dress looked expertly cut. Held up to the light spilling from the glass on the door, it shimmered like a silken sea, whispering against her fingers.

"Mummy who got you a gift?" I bounded down the stairs a couple at a time, a habit I had whenever I got excited. "Can I see?"

"It's nothing," she said dismissively, folding the dress, her happy expression fading into the silken sea. "Just something I ordered from the catalogue. I'm going to order those dungarees you liked soon. Change that t-shirt, it has hair oil on it."

"Can I see your dress on?" I asked. "It looks nice."

"Later baby, I have to take care of a few things first. Please change that shirt!" she hollered before disappearing into the sitting room, the package tucked under her arm.

Later, I watched her try on the dress in her bedroom. It fit perfectly. We both stood inside our reflections before the finger printed mirror. Then I left her perched on the edge of the bed, unzipping. Her fingers skimmed the pulse on her neck as if contemplating throwing it to her mirror image. We didn't talk about the half naked man whose deep laughter rumbled in the cracks of our house. I didn't confide I'd told my teacher God was my father. And that he left ink footprints on creaky wooden floors and pale paper skies and could fly a model plane left-handed while the engine noise sputtered in his chest. We didn't talk about the silence at our backs rising, catching secrets in its colourless, shapeless trap. We avoided discussing the white pills she took at night sometimes. *To help make mummy sleep* she'd said. We skirted around the debris in our beds, shoes, and the most random of places and the signs of her secret life; ticket stubs to a show, lace underwear, wine corks rolling off the glass table into the echoes of something passing.

The week Mrs Phillips sent a concerned letter about me home; I bought an orange yoyo using money I'd won from a dare. It had a long white string, flashed bits of red light unexpectedly, like a torch. A quirk I liked. When I couldn't sleep, I'd sit at the top of the stairs flicking my yoyo, watching God creep into our photographs on the hallway walls, telling my mother lies, draping his arm around us lovingly, illuminated by the silent yoyo light.

Fallow

In the following weeks, the gulls from Chesapeake made random appearances. One repeatedly smacked its beak against the jar of stones on the kitchen countertop till a crack like a small scar appeared in the glass. Another having lost its head in the doorways of the flat continued scuttling headless through rooms, in search of rising ripples. One more dangled from the living room ceiling, its white convex chest swelling and sinking as the sounds of traffic spilled from its beak; tires screeching, the bleep of lights turning green, the low grumble of an engine overheating. I knew it was Anon behind it all. She was building an army, showing me she could command whatever she wanted. She was preparing them for something, laughing mockingly as panic rose inside me. I knew something dark and sinister was breathing in the flat, her hands embedded inside it, her ventriloquist doll.

Sometimes, I stuck my head out of the bedroom window to breathe another air, escape the din, or I'd turned the radio up loudly to have the false company of others, hoping to lose her in some frequency I'd attracted turning the knobs or that she'd be sucked into the static, reduced to tiny grains sparking malevolently in an electric blue kingdom somewhere. But she began to talk through the radio, interrupting heated debates and news items: *You are nothing. Nothing good will ever happen in your life. You ruin everything. Why do you even exist?* The gulls became more twisted. One sported a mangled neck. The gull from the ceiling came down, the left side of its breast gone, only darkness spun there when they gathered at my feet. They listened to her talking on the radio, growing in stature from my misery.

It was after one am. The sound of the tap dripping in the kitchen seeped into my brain. Outside, a can tumbled on the road; tires left tracks in the mouths of the odd person wandering in the cold. Green light of the 7/11 shop sign across the street coloured my vision. I lay sprawled on my bedroom floor, clutching the neck of a bottle of rum. Anon had her arms around me, her mouth orange in the light. Her lips moved but I couldn't hear what she was saying. My right eye throbbed. A small, rum sky in the bottle threatened to shatter the glass. Anon's mouth kept moving silently. My limbs were too heavy to find the words she'd left imprinted on my skin, already dissipating in the feverish sweat on my forehead. I watched her moist, pink tongue moving in the dark, wondering about all the things it had collected.

I stood in the corner of my own peripheral vision, listening to footsteps crunching on branches scattered on a trail, the demented cry of a panicked bird in the sky, what sounded like a shovel sinking into the ground. A hole expanded, the earthy smell of recently damp soil lingered, mocking laughter rose, faint, accented voices waned. There was the rustle of clothes, a man grunting and the pain in his limbs becoming mine. Anon's mouth was a burning sun. The tap's steady drip had slowed to a stutter. I shut my right eye to rest it. The left continued to flicker above small things coming over the horizon. Somebody had taken the time to dig a hole for me somewhere, a deep hole wide and big enough to store all my tattered belongings.

All you have to do is fall. Anon instructed. *Let go. It will be better for you.*

Her hand tightened on my wrist. I sat in the hole, one glazed eye watching the bottle and the drunken gulls orbiting above.

Rangi and I spent the next few weeks in our own bubble, having debauched sex and numbing our bodies to the things we couldn't talk about. We slipped into a routine of sorts. Some evenings, I'd turn up at his door with weed or skunk from a dealer I knew who sold drugs out of his ice cream van, sucking red ice-lollies during transactions. I knew the weed probably made me more paranoid but I couldn't do without it for long spells. Once, I thought I was trapped in Rangi's chest while we fucked on the staircase.

Another time, we did it on the small veranda off the bedroom. I was so high; I was convinced we'd fallen over the bars, tumbled down onto the kerb naked. Only I didn't feel the drop or landing, just my hands in the turnings of silver alloy wheels, exhaust pipe smoke spilled from my mouth as I came, head lolling between road markings. Rangi liked to drink but if he was an alcoholic he was a functional one. There were bottles stashed everywhere in his flat, as if he didn't want to have to go all the way to the kitchen if he started craving. Seductive bottles of gin, vodka, rum and wine were kept in the bottom tray of the bookshelf in the hallway, a bedroom drawer, the floor of his wardrobe. I'd sit in his minimal, faux black marble kitchen, blowing smoke into the air while he cooked. I was convinced he might have been slipping something into the meals he prepared but didn't care enough to ask him.

His fast hands fascinated me, chopping meat or delicately de-boning fish as though it were an art, fish eyes gleaming between us on the countertops. A shrunken spliff in the corner of my mouth, I felt comfortable watching him butcher things, the blade thumping loudly on the chopping board. Sometimes, he bought whole chickens, gutting their insides himself, their heads spinning in the blade. He'd dump their intestines inside jars of water, a secret smile on his face before depositing them in the fridge. He told me that once as a boy he'd gutted a pig; its last cries had haunted him through the following winter. Once or twice, he'd heard his parents repeating those cries at the dinner table and saw the pig trying to rear its head in their faces.

Now and again we ventured out. He took me to a screening of Harmony Korrine's *Mr Lonely* in a dinky little pub slash cinema in Bow called *The Hovel*. The bar was upstairs and the cinema downstairs. It was properly kitschy. The confectionary seemed to have been doused in beer, cigarettes and stale confessions. The lighting was subdued. A scrawny, pockmarked ticket attendant with grey eyes and sallow skin handed us our tickets with sweating hands. The toilet seat had collapsed and it didn't always flush. There was one small screening room with red velvet seats that snapped shut when you stood up. The din from the bar seemed contained yet uncomfortably close. As if people would fall through the ceiling and land in the aisles, mid conversation about their dog's broken leg, the stubborn child they had or how the jukebox's selection of songs was pretty limited.

Rangi and I held hands and ate sweet popcorn together. The movie, about professional impersonators who created their own world unlocked something in me. Loneliness was inescapable. Rangi liked the alcoholic priest who convinced nuns to jump out of planes. Spellbound, I watched the nuns riding bicycles in the sky, habits flapping as they spun. If only it were possible to be that free. If only I could be someone else so I wouldn't have to live inside my head. I cried silently. A man began to talk rudely on his mobile. Rangi left our row. He smacked the man on the head, took the mobile phone and smashed it beneath his boot heel. *Technology doesn't have to fry your fucking brain* he said to the startled man. When he returned, a pulse in his jaw ticked. In the shapeless dark I blinked up at him through my tears. The man, several rows behind us, muttered in disbelief but stayed seated.

Circles

Rangi and I began to hit funerals together. He'd pull up in that temperamental black Mazda with the faulty heating fan dressed in black, hands casually at the wheel. In keeping with my dysfunctional tendencies, I thought it was encouraging we had that level of honesty between us. He didn't lecture me about the dangers of what I was doing or make me feel like a bad person. He was unique in that way, most people would have been very judgemental. Instead he said, "Too many people are concerned about how others perceive them. We should all be more in tune with our desires and not care so much."

"By doing whatever we want whenever we want?" I asked, side-eyeing him curiously.

He shook his head. "When you live on the edge you experience life that much more. Elements of danger and instability make things more intense, more interesting. Too much routine and not enough freedom is what kills everybody slowly. Your unusual habits are... honest in their duplicity because at least you're making choices."

I had a feeling if I'd said I wanted to rob banks at gunpoint, he'd have let me do it, with no empathy for the distress other people would encounter. But banks were too risky and they didn't have the appeal of funerals. For one, there would be no sadness in the air, only fear. No carrying the weight of other people's losses, trying them on for size. I knew that despair, sometimes small or all encompassing. Funerals were manageable. Some days I felt inclined to steal and other days I didn't. There were times I stood on the periphery, scanning small crowds for my mother's face while Rangi sat in the car at a discreet distance, drinking under the glare of daylight.

On other occasions, he'd come into the services with me. We'd act like a couple that knew the deceased. I was astonished by his ability to blend in so quickly, his knack for making you feel both uneasy and comfortable. He imitated the physical expressions of other mourners beautifully, portraying a forlorn figure amongst the gatherings of mourners. Wielding a sad expression and slumped shoulders, he'd thread his way through pale gravestones.

People like Rangi and I, operated on a different frequency. When things got tricky, our signal was three rings to my mobile, which would vibrate silently in my handbag. I knew he enjoyed it. I wondered why he was drawn to death and whether it was for the same reasons I was. One day, we passed time in the car, a bottle of Jack Daniels between us, the engine running. He was calm hearing about my failed suicide attempt. Brushing several unruly twists away from my forehead, he said, "If more people saw death as a way of being reborn, they'd be less scared. This part of existence... it's fleeting, miniscule. Don't you feel the call of other planes inside? Don't you feel their distances shrinking?" A Sainsbury's delivery van came by; huge and white, it was purring beside us for a bit. Before I lost my courage in the jangle of its contents, I answered. "I think somebody wants something from me, to do me harm maybe. But I don't know what it is they want," I said, leaning into his bright-eyed gaze.

One evening, after another funeral raid we sat in a Rubik's cube shaped bar made of glass. We watched small shadows form over our hands and the edges of the night rising in the tumblers we drank from. I saw myself naked in the gleam of his eyes, then naked on Dr Krull's table, my medical notes spilling from my mouth onto the floor. Rangi was on form, wanting me to know all about him.

The son of an Irish mother and Maori father, Rangi had pretty much had every job you could imagine. In New Zealand, he'd worked as a trawlerman for a while, part of a crew on a twenty-one-metre twin rigger hauling tuna, snapper, salmon and all kinds of fish, hands perpetually slick with fish entrails. Sometimes working against a backdrop of forty foot swells, endless rain and gale force winds with the hazardous sea thrashing, curling and threatening to carry the men into cold, volatile currents.

"Those were rough, good times battling the elements with those men. Imagine the tough conditions, bloody fish scales, hauling heavy nets up. We made some great catches. Not everything you catch surrenders immediately." He ran a finger over the pulse on my wrist, the far away expression on his face made me certain he wasn't talking about fish.

During his early twenties, he'd travelled through South America; Mexico, Peru, Argentina, Columbia, taking odd jobs to get by. In Buenos Aires, he worked as a farmhand for a woman who prophesised about a red sky coming to kill them all and slept with a long rifle in her bed as though it were a lover.

"She was right about something coming," Rangi explained, running a hand over his jaw before knocking back a shot of whisky. "Thieves broke in one night, they shot most of the livestock, killed her with her own gun. Coincidentally, I was away from the farm that night. A woman I'd been seeing had wanted to go dancing. It was funny, while we were out, I could taste blood in my mouth but I thought it was one of my nosebleeds coming. I didn't understand until I got back to the farm the next day and saw the carnage."

In Mexico, he supplemented bar work as a nude model. One particular painter named Javier had requested him often. Sometimes they drank together afterwards, listening to old Mexican records.

"So there are nude paintings of you floating around." I smiled at this notion. "Do you think he was in love with you?"

He watched me from hooded eyes. "Why do you ask that?"

"I don't know, just a feeling. You said he painted you naked sometimes."

"Maybe he was. He was good to me." He nodded at the barman, setting his glass on the countertop for another shot. I drew my own conclusions.

In Montreal, he worked nightshifts at a factory producing mannequins. His sleep became so badly affected; he started seeing body parts of other staff coming round the conveyor belt and the mannequins walking around with bits of dawn in their eyes.

"You drift in and out of a lot of people's lives don't you?" I asked, trying to shake away the feeling of unease, the coldness in my bones.

"Maybe they drift in and out of mine," he said.

In London, he worked in a butcher's shop, coming home smelling of raw meat. Sometimes, he supplemented that income cabbing, shepherding people at all hours of the night. We looked out at the city, the traffic, the flow of people scurrying in different directions. The buildings were hazy, their lines distorted. I could see Rangi climbing into distances before leaping ahead in a change of clothes.

On the drive back home, I swallowed the stone floating in my minds eye. It sank to the bottom of my stomach, doing nothing to temper the nausea I felt. I slid down in my seat. The partially rolled down window had light spots of rain. Windscreen wipers flattened small shapes of water. The purple collar of my dress was stiff, ready to corner stray creatures of night. The streets were peppered with lights. Saviours and sinners spun in close proximity. Hands became other instruments in cold pockets.

We stopped on a bridge by the river for air. A fox was taking orders from something unseen. Rangi lit a cigarette, took a draw and began to pace the small area we'd resigned ourselves to. An empty bottle of Australian Pinot Grigio rolled nearby. My hands trembled, suddenly accosted by a memory; my mother running barefoot across a bridge, crying about inheritance being inescapable, fleeing down metallic stairs. My small frame rooted to a spot at the edge. I'm reminded of hovering above the river with metallic corners, afterwards searching for answers in my mother's expressions, before the water inherited them forever, of chasing the changes, the timeline of when it all begun.

Tracks

I woke up on the train tracks not remembering the walk up. Everything seemed to be in slow motion; the stream of night commuters, the last train announcement ringing in my ears, a crushing weight on my right arm so painful my eyes watered. Half stars blended into the mocking glints of the tracks. The train wheel against my arm was unbearable. I lay there clenching and unclenching my left fist, grunting, reducing to small parts mice would scurry over. Faces swam. Voices came from a distance. Broken, silver light danced above like shrapnel flying. I'm not sure how much time passed between coming round and finally being lifted but a slow pained breath left me and the shrapnel had begun to reassemble in my body as a siren wept.

"What's happening?" I asked the faces blending into one, my voice faint, hoarse.

"There's been an accident but you're alright now dear," a kindly, male voice said. His slim hands moved like quick sparrows. I vaguely registered his green uniform.

"I can't feel my arm anymore!" I said, desperately attempting to grab his elbow with my left hand, clutching the moments before the accident I couldn't remember. Fragments had attached themselves to the announcement sign, the boot imprint of an ambulance man, a baby tugging its mother's white collar.

I spotted Anon in the crowd holding the brass head as I was wheeled away. She looked calm. One wheel from the bed squeaked as she moved her mouth. I felt myself slipping into the dark, away from the weight of her judgement. The blurring of those lost moments before the accident became the unlikely half children of the stars.

During the ride to the hospital, the sound of tires on the road was oddly comforting. My eyes adjusted to the fluorescent lighting overhead. For a moment, I thought it was a scene from a movie maybe. That the van would flatten into a stage, the players disappearing into their corners. But the pain in my right shoulder indicated otherwise. Blood on my shirt had smudged. The lower part of my arm hung on tenuously, joined at the elbow. Light-headed, the van shook. Its ceiling became a bright, foreign sky. A drumbeat rattled the doors, faster and faster. Red earth bearing footprints with water covered the floor. Blue petals fell gently. A woman crying interrupted my thoughts, loudly at first, and then quietly, followed by the sound of a shovel in the soil and the soft murmurings of a man. I ran towards that sound, reaching the moments before the accident but I couldn't remember. I ran in slip roads going nowhere, began to scream so loudly, my throat hurt. The van screeched to a halt.

My numb arm dangled in blind spots.

I came round again in the hospital bed aware I'd lost time. I felt sick and slow, the same feelings you got following an adventure ride, knowing that the angle of flight had reassembled things inside you. Most of my right arm was gone, hacked off by surgeons. I no longer had a right hand. The right hand I stole with, masturbated with, and caught a butterfly fish from a pool with. They'd had to amputate. It must have been pinned beneath that train wheel for longer than I realised.

I knew Anon was partially responsible for the state I'd found myself in but why did I deserve this? Hadn't I suffered enough? Why had I inherited one punishment after another? I thought of calling Rangi or Mrs Harris but I'd left my mobile on the kitchen counter. I was in a world of strangers, listening through stethoscopes tapping against a God's chest. Nurses' smiles wavered as they lied to patients out of kindness. This was a country I came from. I knew the language of the damned. Through the rage, helplessness and despair, I spoke it to the ceiling.

I drifted in and out of consciousness, wrung my hand in the light bedcovering listening to an internal clock ticking. I cried when a silhouette from the ceiling leapt into black train tracks. Doctors and nurses came and went; cut-outs travelling on ripples. They hovered by my bed checking the stump. Pain medications with names I could not pronounce slipped down my throat. The withered old man in the next bay coughed out his insides, arms outstretched as if to retrieve them.

Pangs of jealousy shot through me. I'd been envying other people's movements, the fullness of them, their lack of concern that they could one day be taken away. *Even a simple action like coughing involved the arms.* I worried about the road ahead, learning to use my left hand. Who would be there when I landed awkwardly, couldn't put an item of clothing on properly or dropped things? I felt truly alone. The nurses changed my bedding, smiled patiently. "Is there anything you need? Anybody you want to call?" I looked beyond them, holding the gaze of my old body, trying to stop it from betraying me.

Once I'd seen a busker outside Angel tube station. He'd held his guitar like a lover. There was light in his eyes as he stroked the strings, voice cracking with emotion. He seemed rich with the complexities and shades of a human being collecting pennies. I'd envied his ability to connect with people so effortlessly. One day, I wanted to hold a lover the way he held his instrument, to know the notes they had within, to lose my fingers finding them. Now I grappled with the knowledge my embrace would be clumsy, unsettling and perhaps unknowable.

At night I dreamt of my missing arm. I longed for it, deep pangs that ricocheted through my body. What had the hospital done with it? What kind of instrument did they use to chop it off? I pictured Doctors wielding small axes beneath the sleeves of their white coats, trying not to drop it into their strides. Was my arm in a freezer somewhere? With limbs from other bodies, long lost to the echoes of their previous lives or buried in the soil, travelling through the undergrowth towards a fragmented new earth. Under instructions from the land, it could conjure the rest of me for a new, less troubled existence. I saw my arm in the ambulance siren, catching old scenes of me able-bodied. I saw it on empty café seats, in window displays between mannequins. I saw it on routes lined with broken signs. I felt ugly. One day I'd make love beneath a low watt bulb. This was the inheritance my mother never warned me about. My arm floated in the sea of aftermaths, between murky objects that needed to be reclaimed. I shook in the bed, my absent hand wet from touching the sea.

Dr Krull came to visit. He sat at the end of the bed looking unsure, holding a paperweight of a woman standing reaching for snow, then sitting down as the season changed.

"I know you like these," he said, placing it on the cheap looking set of drawers beside the bed. He cleared his throat unbuttoning his green suede jacket.

"I wasn't sure what to bring or whether to bring anything at all. It's difficult in a situation like this." I liked him all the more for not bringing flowers.

Funny, despite the pain and discomfort I was in, I was conscious of how I looked. No matter the circumstances, women always wanted to look their best in front of an attractive man.

"The hospital called me," he said. "They found my credit and debit card in your possessions."

"I'm sorry," I croaked pathetically. I wanted to say I didn't know what I was doing but that would have been a lie. *Can't you see I'm being punished enough?*

"It's okay," he replied. "The important thing is that you're alright. We'll have to talk about it at some point though. You're very lucky to be alive. Do you remember what happened?"

I looked up at the faint shadows on the ceiling crossing white space. "I don't remember the moments before it happened. I think I was sleepwalking."

Thoughts of Rangi's elegant butcher's hands cutting, slicing, and choking during sex, of the purple sheet slipping down his hips, the exposure of skin, the feeling of coming up for air after being choked and how my arms flailing felt familiar.

Dr Krull brought his chair closer. His hair was ruffled, giving him a more boyish look.

"Try to remember," he urged. "Don't you think it's odd that your mother's been dead for months but we haven't talked about her? It's important you remember."

I remained silent and dry mouthed, wreckage in an uncomfortable, adjustable bed.

Dr Krull continued to speak in his calm, measured way. Half of him morphed into the debris of my life.

Seeds

Mervyn came to the hospital, cut a weary and forlorn figure at my bedside. His grey, pinstriped suit was rumpled. He looked like he hadn't slept in days. His large hands trembled as he held my face, pressed a kiss on my forehead, smelling of alcohol mixed with aftershave.

"I'm so sorry this happened to you," he offered attempting to steady his succession of facial expressions: concern, pity and guilt. I looked away; I couldn't bear the pitiful looks thrown my way.

"How did this happen?" he asked.

"They didn't tell you?" I croaked, clutching the soft bedding in my sweaty palm. The skin of a day old banana on the dresser was now partially black with spots of new darkness crawling upwards. There was a beauty in the way things decayed, nature taking its course. "They said I sleepwalked right onto the train tracks." I thought for a while. "Why would I do that? What's wrong with me?"

"Oh God!" he answered, pacing back and forth. "I could throttle your mother. You've forgotten you did that as a child for a bit, right after-"

"Right after what?" I hoisted my body up slowly, sinking into the pillows.

"It's nothing, it can wait." His eyes glistened; shoulders sagged in some kind of small relief. For a while, we occupied positions at either end of a silence. Weakened from medication and the bleakness of my future, I lay there wrapped in blackening banana skin trying to hold onto a bomb.

When the nurses came to administer my afternoon meds, I willed myself to disappear under the bed, dragging my body on the floor towards the sound of wheels. Blood seeped through my bandages and into the nearest corners. The patient in the bed next to me had changed. I fell asleep to the feel of my camera in my hands. The lens whirred filling up with water, my hand caught in a flash mimicking fast moonlight. I thought about Mervyn and the anxiety he'd displayed. He was keeping something from me. I knew it. Why did it feel like everybody in my life had something to hide? Why would I have blocked out the memory of sleepwalking as a child when that was connected to losing my arm?

Then there was Anon holding the brass head from the ambulance bed. Where had she been going with it? Questions swirled in my head. The sound of stones infiltrated the lens; running water pulled the camera down. The stones rumbled in the slipstream. I tried to hold the boxy camera steady but couldn't. It flashed uncontrollably, blindingly, hiding those earlier images of the night in some grainy purgatory.

Days passed. A bright green apple replaced the black banana on my dresser. A small patch of brown, crinkly skin like a pockmark had began to spread on its otherwise pristine surface. I waited for the slow erosion to come. The routine continued. My bed sheets were newly changed: crisp and white. I listened to the daughter of a patient read her *To Kill a Mockingbird*. Her wrinkly, spotted arm trembled in delight. I was at my wit's end between the boredom and the pain. I woke up wanting to go back to sleep and went to sleep not wanting to wake up.

By the time Rangi arrived, the small TV set borrowed from another ward had begun to flicker and he looked as if he'd stepped right out of the black and white movie wearing clothes from the wrong era. There was a weight on my lids, a hovering shape I'd turned into. It was dark, past visiting hours. I didn't ask how he'd slipped in. Instead, I lifted my body up awkwardly, slowly. Still tasting sleep in my mouth. My left arm ached from lying on it for too long. I could hear the hum of the fridge tucked behind the ward reception and stray heartbeats in stethoscopes tapping against glass mouths.

I wanted to tell him I'd been waiting, that sometimes I could taste him in the small hours before dawn. Pain in my head had created a path littered with shattered reflections. My brain had landed on black tracks, then separated into frantic, blue-eyed gulls on plumped, white pillows, scraped with thin, sharp instruments. Sickness and excitement rose in my stomach as he approached. The air between us crackled with haphazard electricity. I recognised the distance in his eyes, watermarks from rain leaping off rough surfaces. I stretched my hand out to know it again, to rub my fingers in its spotted areas. My body throbbed. Then, he was beside me. How was it possible I could hear stones rolling down an echo, Anon's heartbeats between clock hands, small versions of her breathing against the hemlines of nurses' uniforms, yet Rangi's feet barely made a sound? He drew the curtains around us carefully, leaving a tiny crack. His breath on my face was warm and alcoholic. Red scratches on his right cheek were rough. I pressed my mouth on them. His hands flew to my neck, holding it tenderly. I cried into silent footsteps as he undid his zipper urgently. And those creatures of dawn, carrying gutted spaces we drank from surrounded us like quiet grenades waiting for the pull of our fingers.

He was heavy against me afterwards. He hoisted himself up, careful not to make too much noise. My nostrils were clogged with his smell of faint cologne, weed and sweat. The taste of sweat lingered longest in my mouth. He sat down gingerly, took my hand, releasing a slow breath as though tension had left his body.

"What happened to your face?" I asked. Footsteps in the hallway petered off, made me more alert.

Rangi rubbed his face, threw a worried look my way. "You don't remember this?" He pointed at the scratches, fixed me with an intense, loaded gaze.

I shook my head, closed my eyes. Tiny nuclei of colour slid beneath my lids, split then disappeared.

His eyes went to my stump. "I'm sorry Joy. That night… we argued. You weren't yourself. You were wild. I've never seen you that way. You hit me with that ornament, that brass head your mother left you."

My eyes flew open. "No, I'm sorry. Of the two of us, I think you got the better deal." A slight resentment slipped into my tone.

A throbbing in my head began to spread, till I felt like a big, pathetic ball of nerves and anxiety. "What are you saying?" I asked, my voice tiny in the dark.

He didn't answer. Instead, he rubbed a finger up and down the back of my hand slowly.

Outside, fireworks cracked and popped in the night skyline. Somehow, Rangi had slipped one into my hold. Bits of sky attached to it were gaps we could fall into. It sparkled against my fingers. And between his gestures of consolation, I wondered why he came to the hospital already smelling of sex and why this only registered with me later. I waited for the firework to go off, toppling the dangling ceiling above our heads.

The nurses became interchangeable, bearing half smiles as winter set in. They brought cups of tea, terrible, tasteless sandwiches and no hope of my life ever going back to what it was. When they washed me, I avoided looking in the mirror. I couldn't bear to see my bandaged stump, still covered to protect the skin. Sometimes I saw it uncovered, leave my body; roll around near the plughole on the grey floor. Once Anon wore it in the mirror. I spotted her through the steam in the glass crying, her moist, pink tongue heavy with some knowledge. She knew something and she wouldn't tell me. Flecks of gold spun in her dark eyes. Her crying became so loud I felt my heart stop. Rivulets on the mirror watered her stump that cruelly grew whole again before my eyes.

An image flickered in my mind's eye. Anon and I were walking on the darkened train platform, the sound of an approaching train surrounding us. Two pigeons at the far end of the platform were losing their colouring to a sky she'd already built. She pointed to a gap. I edged forward into a heat so palpable, my skin burned. The tracks became hot soil beneath my feet. I was caught in a procession of some sort. Men dressed in traditional African clothing were dragging a bound man and woman through a trail. Stray branches snapped. I tasted a metallic flavour in somebody's shortness of breath. Sweat slicked trembling hands, a rope dug into skin. Short glimpses of light between trees were blinding. Suddenly, the sound stopped. As if I'd gone temporarily deaf. I imagine pressing an ear against a surface of water must be like this; faint, traceable, individual murmurings but you cannot make sense of the whole.

The train wheel, black and heavy burst through the water onto flesh and bone, crushing it. The pain was so deep, so agonizing I would know it forever. I screamed, falling from the wheelchair onto the wet, shower floor. The nurse scrambled to her knees. I cried into the plughole, into the train tracks. Anon turned up the noise in the steamed mirror and the surfaces of water we shared.

Home

On the day of my release, I woke up to discover the man three beds down had died in his sleep. All evidence of him had been removed, only the crease in the silence indicated he was gone. I felt guilty sleeping through a death like that but he must have passed quietly, without any fanfare. It was a cold and surprisingly bright morning. Sunlight streamed through the small window. From the bed, I saw people milling about outside, facing the start of their working day. I was nauseous with dread and anticipation. The last time I'd been out in the world, my life had been different.

I sat up in bed cursing things I'd taken for granted in the past. Even the dark had been a constant companion. My body had adapted to it's modes of infiltration; it's silencing of stones in the jar on my kitchen desktop, it's power to hold my limbs hostage on those heavy days I could barely crawl out of bed. The dark treated Anon like a prodigal daughter, allowing her to spring in pockets around me, carrying bits of a puzzle that disintegrated whenever I reached for them. I missed the movements my body used to make without a careful thought but how was I to know what was to come? Now, I was an injured woman wandering through a collection of battlefields, feeling the softening skin of rotten fruit in my fingers. Frustrated, my eyes swam.

The Doctors took ages making their rounds so I didn't get discharged till after midday. I left one rotten pear and a leaking blue biro on the dresser as gifts for the next patient. A white napkin I'd fashioned into a plane was hidden under the pillow, already touching the edges of another life. The nurses had given me fresh clothes to wear; new cotton underwear, a pair of black jeans a size too big, a grey t-shirt and a snoopy sweatshirt, its long right sleeve dangling pathetically. As if it was waiting for my right arm to come back through the human traffic surrounding us.

The Doctor, a severe looking auburn haired man with a dented nose had informed me that due to my "history" they'd assign a health worker to my case to check up on me every now and again, help me adjust to living with my disability.

"Just for some support," he added diplomatically. "So you can transition back to living on your own with these changes. It can be… emotionally overwhelming at first," he said, smiling distantly, tapping his pen against the clipboard, mentally already onto the next patient. I sat there picking lint from my new jeans, blinking up at him as if he were a mirage in the wrong setting. Soon enough, one of us would shrink into a slithering of light.

"You've prescribed more sleeping pills?" I asked, weary of the constant cycle of medications.

He nodded patiently. "Yes, to help you in the meantime. Your body needs rest. If you'd been consistently taking the pills you were originally given, you may not have had that unfortunate incident I'm afraid."

"But what about finding out why I've been sleepwalking?"

He sighed audibly, rocked back on his heels. There could be all sorts of reasons. Dr Krull knows your history. He can advise you best."

I stuffed coins slick with sweat in my pocket. "What do I do if I lose time again?" Panic seeped into my voice.

"Take the pills Joy," he instructed patronizingly, as if I was a small child who couldn't quite grasp the obvious.

Dr Krull knows your history. I imagined the ink pen he held scratching one pale, blue iris out, a stethoscope strangling his neck and the struggle to breathe making him take some other form. The paper plane beneath the pillow sprouted an extra wing.

I sat in the compact, white, waiting area downstairs by the sliding doors. Tiny wax women bearing injuries hitched rides on the wheels of ambulance beds, headed towards death or reinvention. Only a handful of people were sitting down, in varying stages of illness. My left hand was jittery. I caught the tail end of a conversation a rail thin blonde was having at the phone box. She puffed on a cigarette in between gesticulating wildly. Smoke curled around the outline of a scorpion tattoo on her exposed midriff while a haggard man in a worn, black leather jacket with thinning, dark hair rushed by holding a bouquet of daffodils. I pictured the recipient, a wife or lover sitting on an uncomfortable bed eating the petals.

Then that image was replaced by one of a brown-skinned woman swimming in a river, kicking hard against a tide. The blue petal in her mouth floated like a rootless tongue. My chest tightened. My mouth became dry. The man was a fleeting thing who'd brought an unlikely passenger through the sliding doors. He jangled a set of keys nervously in his pocket. I pressed my ears against the sound, still gripped by the knowledge that unsettling things could slip into moments of weakness and holes in your day. A trickle of blue water ran down the middle of my vision, bookmarking the two worlds.

An ambulance van pulled up outside by the kerb. The doors slid open. An empty bottle of rum rolled towards heels clicking. The sharp clicking heels trapped a crinkled Trebor mint wrapper, a five pence coin with the Queen's head spinning, a torn multi-coloured woven bracelet. My mother had made a bracelet like that for me once, weaving the material between her fingers expertly, and humming.

The cracked ambulance siren was silent. Its doors smacked open and closed. Inside the ambulance were future scenes waiting to find their way into my life; trying to tie my laces one handed, cracking eggs on a shiny black desktop, watching the yolks slide down to the floor, becoming small chickens clucking erratically. I saw myself lying on the ground by the open freezer door, a cold mist on my face. I cried over the ache and loss of my arm. My body shuddered. I reached into the freezer pulling out yellow fish whose mouths kept moving after they spat out the same brass key, before melting into bright water in my hand.

The woman with the clicking heels showed her face, gaunt and knowing in the gap. A hospital ID hung from her neck. She squinted, scribbling notes in a pad. She knew she couldn't help me. I was a lost cause. She took a deep breath, released the wind from her mouth, scattering the scenes inside the ambulance. They fell into each other, changing to some unlikely animal. Yellow chickens became yolks again, I smacked a brass key repeatedly against the desktop, and fish carried untied shoelaces in their mouths. My mother's bracelet fluttered at the edge just as the siren came on, wailing in my ears.

I felt a hand on my shoulder; its broad, firm grip was familiar. "Hey, have you been waiting long?" Mervyn asked, face full of concern. He helped me up. The man in the chair opposite coughed into his chequered handkerchief. I managed a half smile that felt more like a grimace. "Thanks for coming," I answered, trying to wrestle the sinking feeling in my stomach, the panic I was feeling at the thought of being out in the world again.

"No problem. You knew I'd come. Anything for you, you know that. I'm just happy you reached out to me. We haven't seen each other much since Queenie died."

He blew a breath out slowly, as if trying to compose himself. Damp spots had spread on the collar of his crisp, blue shirt. Maybe he didn't know how to comfort me, what to say. Sometimes, people struggled in these situations. I almost told him I didn't know what I needed to hear. And Queenie? What would she say seeing me like this? It was partly her fault for inconveniently dying and leaving me alone. Anger bloomed in my chest, followed by sharp, painful pangs of longing.

"I brought you here once as a kid you know. You'd stopped breathing. Your mother was beside herself, hysterical. I'd never seen her that way." He rubbed his face, grappling with the memory. "When you finally came round, it was as if... You'd been somewhere. You were a strange child, otherworldly at times."

We crossed the stretch of gleaming, pale aisle, leaving behind groaning lift doors and the constant patter of footsteps. He'd parked his black Mercedes Kompressor right near the entrance. I slid in carefully. It smelled of mint and leather. He turned the engine and radio on; set the car into gear before expertly moving off. The bulldog on the dashboard began to nod at the panic and fear growing inside me; Anon caught the bulldog's head during two pit stops. Tears ran down my cheeks. I rolled the window down partially, leaned against it to feel the cold air on my face and the city shrinking beneath the fingers of my lost arm.

Queenie 1980's: Born

The hole came attached to the baby's ankle, just after it was born. At first it was barely the weight of a breath. Then it became dense and unknowable despite the irony of the baby who arrived into the world howling at the pale, blue ceiling, blinking frequently as though adjusting to her new setting, clenching and unclenching a demanding fist, being named Joy.

Motherhood Na wah oh! Queenie thought lying in the hospital bed, drenched in sweat and bone tired. *I don suffer for this child* she muttered, the comment barely passed her lips. The Doctor and nurse smiled at each other. After cleaning the baby up, the flaxen haired, pudgy-faced nurse handed her over wrapped in a light cotton blanket.

"Oh she's a beauty!" the nurse remarked, glancing at Queenie for a reaction. Queenie gave a wobbly smile. "Thank you. I thank God for this blessing." She felt as though she was on the edge of the moment, floating beyond the emotional connection the situation called for. What was wrong with her? Why couldn't she be over-whelmed with the depth of feeling other mothers' spoke of? Instead she was relieved. Soon she'd be able to fit into her clothes again, hold down food. Her morning sickness had been morning, afternoon and evening sickness. She'd found herself embarrassingly vomiting into a bin on the street, throwing up on a bus, darting into pubs as quickly as her unsteady legs could carry her; vomiting so much it seemed she'd lost organs in the process. They surrounded her while her head bobbed above putrid, urine stained toilet bowls. She checked they were hers by the weight of a lung in her hand, a heart circling the bowl, its ventricles flooded by flushing water as she rocked back on her knees cursing.

The baby was at her breast. Queenie felt nothing except pangs of hunger and a doom she couldn't explain. She wanted to ask the nurse why the baby's shadow was in the doorway. The small mass in her arms screamed. She knew the nurse wouldn't be able to tell her. She closed her eyes, a gauzy haze descended. Her lids flicked open. The shadow was at her breast, sucking greedily on a large brown nipple. She looked into Joy's knowing brown eyes, her irises orbited darkly. Queenie sighed, sinking into the hole. The ceiling fan spun between prior scenes of the birth.

Queenie didn't call him to see the baby those first few days. She'd refused to tell him her due date in response to feeling like an after-thought in his neat, well-organised life. *I don walka into this situation well well!* Queenie thought, chiding herself.

She missed the smell of him, that warm, earthy scent that had a hint of exoticness. She missed the feeling he gave her, the softness of her malleable body beneath his broad, steady hands. Sometimes, she pictured an atlas of their times together rising from his shoulders, that he held that world in his hands during quiet moments. It had been difficult giving birth alone, panicked and half out of her mind.

She'd been in the supermarket when her water broke, clutching a bottle of vegetable oil that fell, missing her feet by an inch. She'd called out, heart racing, mouth dry. The realization she'd be giving birth alone sank into her caving body. Somebody grabbed her arms from behind, pulling her up. She saw him then, in his other life, sitting at a wooden dining table, holding cutlery, covered in birth water.

At the nurse's station, Queenie held the black phone receiver, the dial tone a new heartbeat. Life-sized worker bees; the nurses flitted

to and fro in all directions. And the faint jangle of medical instruments, footsteps and fast instructions seemed like some unlikely
symphony a Doctor had concocted. What had she been thinking
keeping this baby? How was she going to cope? *You should have
thought of that*, she mumbled internally. Tears ran down her cheeks.
The faint ache in her grew. She took a slow breath and looked
around, trying to still her trembling body. An eggshell coloured
desk sat in the centre, stacked with notes. Next to a watch a silver
stethoscope borrowed breaths from a concave chest in the distance,
trapping an international calling card, the zip from a polka dot dress,
a brass head bearing the memory of a father's touch, the blueprint
of a baby from the blue. A swear jar with the note fu**! was perched
in the middle. Queenie resisted the urge to pick up the jar and walk
the sterile aisles rattling coins, until the delicate knot of her loose
hospital gown came undone.

Earlier, she'd torn the name band from her wrist. She looked up
at the whiteboard mounted on the wall, transfixed by the names
and hospital numbers scrawled in barely legible orange handwriting,
waiting for something to be revealed to her. She felt scared, lonely
and miserable. Part of the baby's blueprint had found its way into
her throat, scrunching into a ball. Her eyes swam. She spotted a
nurse flying towards her, face pinched. "You left your baby on the
bed! You can't do that. What if she rolled over and fell to the floor?
Oh dear, you must be very tired." The nurse remarked, searching
her face worriedly. Queenie looked through the nurse, her mouth
curving up in a half smile, half grimace.

Two days later Ella came to pick her up, dressed in a blue dungarees and tortoiseshell glasses. She hopped out of her long suffering
Peugeot and half-embraced Queenie, stroking Joy, who was cooing
in her mother's arms. The blistering wind whipped Ella's bright red
quiff, back and forth like an exotic bird.

"Get in!" she ordered, gently kissing Joy on the forehead. "Before
we catch our deaths!" She yanked the back passenger door open.
Queenie piled in, comforted by the smell of baked goods. A squashed,

empty Danish packet lay on the floor by her feet. Ella flicked the engine on. She'd parked in the small, disabled section. She stole a quick glance around, checking the parking attendant hadn't spotted her.

"She's gorgeous Queenie! Can't tell who she looks like yet though." This she threw over her shoulder, turning the radio on before reversing out of the parking lot.

Queenie adjusted the blanket around Joy as The Rolling Stone's *All Night Long* blared from the radio. The car sputtered over the roundabout and into a narrow road. At the lights, a man holding his daughter's hand bent his head, talking with a patient expression. It triggered the memory of being pushed on a swing by her father all those years ago; the scorching heat, the rhythm of the swing, how she'd nearly slid off a few times, almost falling into her shadow.

She remembered her father in his creased linen outfit, lying to her about being able to control the weather. She remembered how happy she felt because her father was Houdini, could create new weather and told her his brass head set in motion things that couldn't be revealed in the day. He was a magician who'd disappeared. You woke up one day and he was gone, leaving belongings distorting in the dark. The void left had been so big, she and her mother took turns hurtling their bodies in, filling the spare rooms in the house with all their bad landings.

Joy stretched her tiny hand, reaching for her mother's breast. Her expression was delicate; Queenie felt the weight of responsibility. What would she learn from a mother who'd already made so many mistakes?

What can I offer you but the disappointment that's found a home in me?

How can I ever look you in the eye and tell you the truth? She said silently.

The streets shrank and passed in the rear-view mirror. A purple kite above a field became a pigeon chasing its beak. A dog barking leaped into a Ferris wheel of blue sky. An old swing worked its way into the traffic, knocking against bumpers. The girl from the swing wrote something illegible on windscreens, knowing that the man who could make weather will come for her. Queenie saw her baby on the spinning rooftops of terraced houses, crawling down towards cold slip roads. She called out but the baby didn't turn around. She shuddered in her seat as car horns sounded, one hand under her sleepy-eyed child, the other clinging to an old, frayed swing rope. A wave of nausea hit her. Ella steered the car into a busy roundabout, flanked by a shopping centre and a cinema. Cars zipping by were God's toys on one of his playgrounds.

Ella changed the radio station, drummed her fingers on the dashboard before hitting the gas. "You should tell him you know. Why isn't he here?" She nudged her glasses up her nose. A gesture Queenie knew meant she was ready to argue with you.

"Where is it written that he has to know? Lots of women manage on their own." Queenie rubbed Joy's head; the car ride seemed to have settled her. She was sleeping peacefully, oblivious to the world and all its cruelties.

"Yes, I know but it's not ideal is it?" Ella asked. "And you shouldn't be one of them. You haven't worked in the shop for months. That's fine but as far as I know, you don't have a lot of savings. How are you going to live? He should be able to give you some financial support at least, no matter his circumstances. This wasn't an immaculate conception!"

"No, this was a mistake!" Queenie said, suddenly weary of it all.

"What? How can you say that?" Ella spat, a red flush crawling up her neck. "You know I can't have children. I'd give anything to have your- to be in your position. Please don't talk like that around her; babies are sensitive creatures. They can sense things."

"Spare me please," Queenie said tersely. "I'm not one of your charity cases. You have no clue so please shut up!"

The car became quiet, the atmosphere tense. The engine ran on fuel and the argument they'd just had. Ella's knuckles whitened at the wheel. The flush on her face was a half formed silent island. She flew across another set of lights, throwing a furious glance Queenie's way. God's playground and cruelties were connected. Queenie knew this for a fact. The memory of it had been clawing at her for months.

They zipped down the flyover, their silence a patchy sky spilling into the side mirrors. Queenie saw her silhouette in blind spots, clinging to tires, dragged across the streets.

She didn't know what it meant or what anything meant anymore. She sank back in the seat, rocking her baby. The smell of her own smoke slowly filled her lungs.

Queenie 1980s: Dice Eyes

Queenie sat listening in the tight hallway, trembling against a cold radiator. It was freezing but she hadn't been able to afford to heat the flat properly for weeks.

All they had was the portable electric heater whirring in the living room, melting the lids of pens and burning a small, brown cave into Joy's bib. Dice eyes in the ceiling spun. They'd followed her from sleep, grainy and constantly adjusting to the surfaces in the flat, watching the sluggishness that had taken over her limbs since the hospital. She'd tried to get rid of them, running cold water on her eyes at full blast till they stung and the tap began to hiss from the pressure, ready to uproot into her head and flood the very thing she'd been trying to submerge.

She slid down as the knocks became heavier, more insistent. Cold sweat trickled on her back. The door rattled. His large frame loomed in the bubbled glass. The silver post slot flapped. His mouth there floated in some separate ether.

"Queenie! I just want to talk. I'm worried about you," he said, the last bits of patience dwindling in his voice. He waited a few moments, then kicked the door repeatedly.

"Open this fucking door! Open it or I swear I'll break it down, you hear me?" He growled, "I'll tear this *rahtid* place apart. Let me see her. You can't stop me from seeing her!"

Queenie slid further down until she felt like nothing. Shame washed over her. She ran a nervous hand over her matted hair. *Oh God, he'll kill me*, she thought. *He'll finish me if he knows. He can't know.*

Her heartbeat tripled. Unopened mail beneath her feet grew bold, becoming flattened white tongues curling up, straining to talk.

In the kitchen, the table was stacked with empty cans of food, parts of a memory spilled from each one, cutting themselves on sharp edges.

"I'm having tea with the Queen!" she yelled, "She's expecting me at The Ritz."

He'd moved out of sight. Somehow increasing the pressure he was applying to her head. He was travelling through the bubbled glass door, watered by the angles of light she'd lost along the way. She looked into the living room. Joy crawled past the bright throw on the floor, towards the plugs. He began to kick the door again, till a small gap appeared. It rattled in the frame some more. She felt the hinges weakening beneath her sweaty fingertips. Joy began to scream, a twisted-faced angry scream that went on and on.

Queenie had found her father on a harsh blustery day. She stumbled upon him. Years later, she'd rake over each aspect, agonizingly unpicking the series of sequences. Each moment was a red brick, one shakily stacked on top of the other. Had an element been missing, the bricks would have toppled and Queenie may never have found him at all. It was a Sunday. She'd been wandering through Petticoat Lane Market, amidst the packed throngs in the centre, which splintered off into various side roads where more stalls awaited, selling everything from leather coats, knock off Singer sewing machines, board games and wigs on white mannequin heads sporting cling film mouths. The din was loud and seductive. Every couple of strides a different smell accosted you; prawns sizzling in huge black woks, hot dogs and burgers smothered in chunks of fried onions and ketchup, fried rice sprinkled with cashew nuts. Clothes for every size and shape fluttered and swayed on breakable hangers. A wind chime rang over the door of a record shop.

At exactly 2.15pm, Queenie's right shoe caught in a groove on the road. She went flying, grazing her elbow. The contents of her handbag spilled. Had the dog's head from the costume stall not landed at the feet of one of the flock of orange-robed monks ahead, had her lipstick not rolled to the feet of that same monk, had the man on the motorbike not appeared from nowhere, revving his engine and rudely cutting across the monks, causing their cluster to fracture and that particular monk to accidentally crack her lipstick beneath his sole, Queenie would never have stood abruptly and awkwardly to try to save it. She would never have knocked into the stall selling maps and atlases. She would never have noticed the heavy black boots under the stall with bits of cement and paint on them.

He sat before a building site. Construction workers trailed in and out. Sawdust and white residue covered their winter skin. Her heart began to race and her mouth ran dry. Thoughts sped up and jumbled in her head. All these years later and she'd never forgotten his face. It was him, she was sure of it. He was older of course; his handsome features more lived in, weathered. Tight curls beneath his yellow hard hat were greying at the temples. She rubbed her leg. A tingling sensation made her arms tremble. How ordinary he seemed! Smoke from the hissing wok at the next stall shrouded him, as if he would change guise by the time it curled away. How plain he looked holding a steaming cup of coffee. How ironic to find him loitering behind maps and atlases, the sly curls of smoke ready to make him disappear into an atlas. Blue plastic sheeting covering the stall flapped in his face. As though part of it would morph into a carrier pigeon reporting to the wandering God blowing silences into the city.

"Are you alright?" he asked, his voice still heavily accented.

He set the mug of hot black liquid down on the pavement.

Queenie nodded, watching the slow look of horror on his face, a flicker of recognition as his dark brown eyes darted sideways quickly. She knew she was moving forward but couldn't feel her legs. "Papa that is you? Peter? Peter Lowon? It's me, Queenie." She grabbed his arm despite herself. Thoughts in her head were bent arrows flying into other openings. Their angles of flight had caught him off guard. His left hand shook in her grasp, some small creature made of nerves and instinct. He snatched it away. "Nnno, that cannot be. I'm sorry, I don't have a daughter." He shook his head, turning away, unable to meet her gaze.

"It's me, Felicia's daughter! Your daughter, you remember. I know you remember! All these years and not one word. You remember Felicia, your wife?"

He stopped in his tracks. That look of horror appeared again. Queenie was the spitting image of her mother. "Where have you been?" she asked, her voice cracking and rising simultaneously, as if it didn't know whether to do one or the other. She halved into two, overwhelmed, she didn't feel the Singer sewing needle sinking into her tongue, stitching a blueprint of invisible threads. His shoulders stiffened. The wind puffed his orange jacket. His expression of shame contorted. Men on the site behind them leaned in and out of impossible angles, Lego people in the dangerous house. The hot liquid he set down had spilled, leaving a small trail of coffee for the motorcycle man to rev his engine through. The sounds of hammers and drills rang from the site.

Queenie looked up at the rusted bars of scaffolding she was suddenly balancing on with a drill going into her head, the churnings of her organs catching bits of air from holes in her body. Instruments of rubble winged their way into the vast, grey sky. The wandering God began to try the hard hats of men who'd disintegrated into sawdust, knocking his head repeatedly against the window. Her weatherman faced her. His body shook. And just above the din he muttered, "Forgive me."

He'd scribbled an address down for her near Liverpool Street he'd said, the road right after the petrol station that had the man without legs in the sign grinning maniacally, the faulty pump and the car wash at the back.

"Please excuse my living circumstances. I never wanted you to find me this way," he'd said.

It was strange hearing the formality in his voice before the setting of a building site. Her father, the great Peter Lowon she'd built up in her mind for years was an ordinary man after all, who seemed vulnerable and ashamed ready to collapse under the weight of it all, bits of him lost in the very rubble he'd created with his own hands.

"How have you been?" He asked, such a simple question. Standing there amongst the swirling human traffic, fingers numbing from the cold, Queenie wanted to tell him her answer was a rumbling earthquake, moss over her insides. At the back of her mind, she knew she needed to gather the contents of her bag from whatever corners they'd landed. She was shocked, angry and sad. The crumpled paper he'd handed her turned between them like a bolt. She looked at the neat, slanted handwriting for some inkling of how he'd been and who he'd become. Her mouth opened to speak but all at once the paper was burning another entry into her. And all at once, its contents of ink bomb and blood wrestled to call her body home.

The house he lived in was a shared address. When he answered the door that evening she couldn't hear a thing from the other occupants. There was only the light from a kitchen down the hallway beckoning and inside the sound of the fridge groaning. He wore a stained white vest and rocked unsteadily in the doorway, reeking of alcohol. His eyes were bloodshot. "Come up," he slurred. He saluted comically, stepped aside to let her in. Queenie brought a blast of cold air in, rubbing her hands uncertainly. "I can come back," she said, slowly becoming aware of a tension she couldn't yet identify.

"No, no, no. Not this time Felicia," he said, already stepping on the bare staircase to lead the way. A single black and white poster of Laurel and Hardy hung on the wall, curling up at the edge. It was only after passing those same heavy, black work boots caked in cement at the foot of the stairs, it dawned on her he'd called her by her mother's name. In the bedroom, the walls were unpainted, clothes were piled on a single rickety chair and the cheap looking double bed was unmade. An empty bottle of gin rolled into a corner. A dilapidated wardrobe sat miserably in the far left end.

It smelled of sweat and decay. He shut the door behind them. Queenie sat on the bed; her eyes darted around the room. He sat beside her and grabbed her arms as if the moment he had been waiting for had finally arrived. "I need to tell you something. I need you to listen to me Felicia. I killed a man, years ago in the army. I helped kill an innocent man. You don't know the things I've seen… done."

Queenie stood, unclenching her fist. "What? I don't want to hear this! I'm not Felicia. Tell me why you abandoned me all these years. Why can't you give me an answer?"

"Why can't you comfort me?" he roared. "You're my wife. Why couldn't you ever comfort me?"

Queenie never saw that first blow coming. It knocked her clean off her feet. Fist connected with bone resulting in a crunching sound. Blood spurted from her nose. Her head rang as she landed on the bed. She was vaguely aware of falling into the red mist of his eyes. Years later, she would block these details out; the feeling of being above herself watching the whole scene unfold as though it were someone else, one hand squeezing her throat, pinning her down, the other moving roughly between her legs. Rapid words like bullets. "You're my wife, shut up. Shut up." The bed creaked in a heart-crushing rhythm; hot breath marked her skin, his other face floated in the mirror and then, ultimately, the terrible weight of him, body twitching, emptying into her own.

He cried pathetically afterwards, clinging to the hemline of her skirt as she crawled out on all fours, her face throbbing and swelling,

the footsteps of her childhood self, running over some thinly shin-
gled roof, chasing a swing in a storm.

Outside her eyes stung. She walked along the street, the ache in her
head worse than a migraine. She passed the petrol station. The man
without legs from the sign was balancing on a gin bottle repeatedly
rolling into corners. For a moment, she considered stopping at the
station, sticking a nozzle in her mouth, filling her insides with petrol
before setting herself alight. Instead she walked on. Earlier scenes
became part of the edges of the night. She tried to still her trembling
body as she stumbled into the fractured face from the mirror.

Two months later, she took a pregnancy test. The line was strong.
She cried into it. And the monks from the market throng danced
around watery blue lines wearing dog heads, hiding lips smeared in
crushed red lipstick.

Session

Dr Krull had a new paperweight on his desk. This time the woman from the reception painting was inside, catching small organs amidst snow. I shook it, watching the snow swirl, smelling pine in the air. His desk was clear except for two files. He was dressed in his usual attire of corduroy pants, on this occasion, nut brown teamed with a blue pinstriped shirt. Casually, he uncrossed his legs. "I'm glad you came today Joy. I know it's been a tough period for you but it's important we continue with our sessions."

I set the paperweight down, still somewhat embarrassed that he had to see me this way, battered and somehow incomplete.

"Why do I have to keep coming here? It's…" I struggled before finding the right words, "humiliating. I'm not getting better from any of this! All you people do is medicate me and send me home." My voice raised a couple of octaves, I adjusted in my seat, noticing the photograph on the desk of him and his wife was gone. A part of me was happy at the idea of somebody as together as Dr Krull potentially having marital problems. This was wrong but I didn't care.

Coolly he said, "I get that you're angry and that's okay. You have a lot to be upset about. That's why we have this space so we can talk about things. Medication alone isn't enough. We need a combined approach to help get you better."

"You just want to keep tabs on me!" I spat. "So you can use it against me. Somebody else already watches everything I do."

He took a sip from a cup of tea on the small table between us before setting it down.

"Tell me who's watching. Is it a threatening presence, a friendly presence? You can trust me Joy."

Anon appeared on the arm of his chair, there was a hole in her stomach and the sound of water sliding down a drain. I closed my eyes, blinking the image away, sensing the bulbs of sweat on my skin.

"Why? So you can section me?"

"Nobody's going to section you. How is your arm?" he asked, adjusting his glasses, the flecks of gold in his eyes seemed more prominent.

"My stump you mean? Sometimes the ache for that arm is so bad, it becomes physical. When it does, I stick my stump in the freezer to numb it."

He digested my response quietly for several moments. "Joy I'd like to try something and I want you to trust me okay? I want you to close your eyes and relax. Can you do that for me?"

I nodded warily, sinking back into my chair. I shut my eyes, listening to the rhythm of my breathing for several minutes, allowing my limbs to loosen.

Dr Krull's voice was warm and reassuring. "I want you to take me to your earliest memory of swallowing stones. Take me to the space. Where are you?"

"I'm in a bathroom with a blue floor the colour of the sea." I murmured.

"Tell me what's in the room." His voice, seeming to be coming from some distance was an anchor.

"There's a purple towel on the rack with mud on it, a jar of pebbles on the floor. The tap's running."

"What else? What can you hear?" His tone was gentle yet firm.

"Um… uh, the television downstairs. The bathroom door is open. I can hear a New York accent. It's… Tom and Jerry I think."

"Go on," he urged. "You're doing well. What else is in that bathroom?"

"The tap is on full blast in the sink. There's an empty bottle of medication beside the tap, white pills in the sink. I can smell something strong, like… a cleaning product. Bleach! It's overpowering."

"Who's in the room with you?"

"My mother. She's-…"

"Good. What is she doing?" he asked.

My breaths were coming rapidly. The chair became a vehicle transporting me to the past, a long buried memory. My mouth went dry. "She's sitting on the toilet seat, crying and watching me in the bath, mumbling something. Sorry, sorry she's saying. She gets up, walks towards me. There's a brightly coloured woven bracelet on her left wrist. I'm-…"

"Go on. Keep showing me what's in the room. Remember, you're alright. Nothing can happen to you now," Dr Krull encouraged patiently. "Stay relaxed. Carry on. Now what's she doing?"

My body began to shake. "I'm singing in the bath. My eyes are closed. I open them. She's standing over me. She's pushing my shoulders down. She's shoving my head under water. Her hands are holding my head down. I can't breathe! I can feel the water up my nose, my arms flailing. My legs are kicking but she's strong. Oh God, I can't breathe. I can't scream. Everything's shrinking, becoming tiny, like I'm falling through static. I can't hear the water anymore. I can't hear anything. Something, somebody pulls her off me, my body is slack, I try to lift my legs but I fall from the bath. I don't feel the landing. The pebbles are scattered all over the floor, rolling into my eyes. How could I know they would follow me into the future?"

A choking feeling spreads in my throat. Dr Krull stood up. Sound was coming back slowly.

He took a few paces then said. "Why do you think your mother tried to kill you? Why do you think you buried this memory for so long?"

I opened my eyes. Tears ran down my cheeks. "I don't know. I don't know!" I roared, "Maybe she didn't love me. She was always... melancholy. Maybe that was my fault somehow."

He sat on the edge of his desk. "No. It wasn't your fault. It's never the child's fault." His mouth was a grim line. For once, his neutral expressions had vanished.

My body continued to tremble. Something had uprooted from my gut and was making its way towards the centre, causing splinters of pain like nails being hammered to my chest. I stood abruptly, knocking the paperweight. And the woman from the painting lay sideways in the snow, arms outstretched, reaching for something beyond her confinement.

In the days that followed, bits of a memory came back to me, a fog lifting from scenes I'd buried. The night I lost my arm Rangi and I had argued. I'd gone into his car to borrow a torch. The boiler had been playing up; making unhealthy chugging noises and the hot water ran cold. I remembered walking to the car, tucked behind a hearse with the words *MH and Sons* emblazoned on the side in peeling gold lettering. The cold air made me shiver. My slippers snapped against the pavement and the dewy shoots of grass sprang up randomly. I was rummaging in the glove compartment when I found them, the photographs, hidden behind a folded map of the Andes.

I spread the pictures on the driver's seat. My eyes stung. Winter chill from my lips became smog in the corners of the pictures. Straight away I knew these women were prostitutes, working girls shot in cars. I could tell from the bleakness in their gazes, secret half smiles lifting the corners of their mouths, a tiny black skirt riding upwards to meet a bought silence. These were women photographed in different cities around the world, a pair of naked pale breasts jutting, bathed in moonlight, long white beads encased in stockings, full buttocks against the wheel, bruises on an elegant neck angled defiantly away from the lens. Windscreen wipers in their mouths punctuated the language of the multi-limbed invisible thing sharing their strides, secret things that exited through the corners of frames, holding streetlight, smoke and other instruments of the night. The women were different races, dark haired, dark-eyed. I searched for the common thread. Their faces blurred, becoming one broken headlight. I carried their tears on my tongue, bits of a ceiling crumbled into their frozen movements.

I headed back inside. Cold, dead air followed. The door was on latch. Anger rushed through my veins like molten lava. I remembered screaming, flinging the brass head at him, missing by inches. Then his hands were at my throat, squeezing.

"Shut up!" he snapped. "Shut up or I'll finish you." His eyes were raging, twisted.

I don't know you, I thought. *I only know what you wanted to show me.*

I clawed at his face, scratching.

"You bitch!" he yelled, flinging me off him. And it was as if falling from a great height. The air left my body. Panic came. He began to kick me repeatedly on the stomach, grunting in the process. A carton of orange juice toppled, spilling over a slipper, which had broken during the scuffle. I'd have to get a new pair. He snarled above me, landing a backhand that knocked me sideways. I held my stomach, cowering by the table leg. The pain was agonizing, as though he'd kicked each organ in my stomach individually.

"What are you going to do about it?" he taunted. "What the fuck can you do?" He watched me struggling to move my body forward. Blood trickled into the hundred silences in my mouth. He searched my face, looking for the pig's features he thought were rearing up again, the snout winging its way into the gap. His right arm twitched at his side. A shooting pain cracked my head open. He left me struggling to breathe, footsteps fading away. The panic was overwhelming. I lay there, thinking maybe he had been the smoking gun in the farm owner's bed in Buenos Aires. Perhaps the painter in

Mexico paid for his love in currencies other than cash. Maybe the pig he'd killed as a boy continued to have human guises. I tasted its blood on my tongue. I thought of Rangi the drifter, the shaman, the night in those photographs of red light women, stealing moments from them; a ring, a lock of hair, a last rite. I imagined him leaving those items in a passenger seat, the pig's snout turning between them. I passed out. When I came to, Anon stood above me, touching my skin with cold hands, leading me outside.

I caught up with Mervyn in Harlesden at a community project he volunteered for on Wednesday evenings. A former sports centre, the faded brown building looked abandoned except for the orbs of light morphing into shapes behind the smoggy windows. It hosted pop-up comic book fairs, knitting workshops, treasure hunting days and music gigs. He was playing chess in the small sports hall when I arrived. Cross-legged, he moved a piece three squares up to the centre poker faced; he glanced at his opponent, a spotty kid stroking his chin dramatically. Reggae music played softly in the background, Peter Tosh crooning defiantly. At the far corner, a couple of kids were kicking soft a yellow ball over a damaged badminton net grazing the ground. A cluster of teenage girls wearing brightly coloured leotards was hoola hooping, throwing their bodies into the swing of the hoops. I didn't know why I'd run from the station but I felt wired. My chest was burning and my heartbeat quickened expectantly.

"I need to talk to you," I said by way of greeting. Squeals from the other end interrupted my train of thought. A bunch of other teenagers trudged in carrying chocolates from a vending machine somewhere in the building that spat out multi-flavoured delights at the jangle of coins.

Mervyn unfolded his legs, half-smiled at the boy apologetically. "Give me a moment yeah? Joy this is Delroy, our reigning chess champ and mathematical problem solver." He laughed heartily but a fleeting look of worry crossed his face. I nodded at the kid, whose retro high top fade made me think of De La Soul and sleeper summer anthems. Mervyn grabbed his Queen. "I'm superstitious about leaving her unattended," he joked, pocketing it then leading the way.

The building was a maze; hubs sprang up from every corner. In the hallway, we passed a series of spaces including a snooker room and a storage area. Unpainted walls added to the rustic feel. We followed the low lit route right to the end and out into the garden area, where misty eyed gargoyle statues wearing comic expressions dotted the green, stirring their tails in any bits of conversation that filtered through. The air between us crackled. He stood only a few feet from me but I could feel the tension in his large frame.

"Tell me the truth," I said urgently. "Are you ashamed of me?" My voice cracked a little, I berated myself internally, trying to hold back tears.

"What?" The hand rummaging in his pocket stilled. "Why would you ever think that?" Car horns sounded in the distance, leaves blew across the green. I stepped closer, watching his face for the tiniest flicker of betrayal. "Because you've been lying to me for years! You were using my mother and when you knocked her up, you continued to live your double life without any responsibility. God! I feel sick; your sons are my friends. Don't they suspect you're not who you say you are?"

The Queen was out in the open again, turning in his hand, small and pale in the moonlight. His face etched in pain, he rubbed his baldhead wearily. "It wasn't like that Joy. I loved your mother. She was a troubled, complex woman but I loved her. I knew this day would come and I've dreaded it. It's just like her to leave me to deal with this."

"Why are you trying to absolve yourself of any responsibility?" I cried, holding the sadness between us, the pangs of rejection I felt.

"I'm not your father. I wish I was, Lord knows I do but I'm not." It was said so quietly I almost missed it. This was how a ten-foot truck could hit you without sound or warning. I was close enough to see his watery eyes, the regret there. I peeled the dented truck bender off my body, raised it above our heads. "You're lying!" I accused, pointing a shaky finger. "Otherwise why stay around us all these years? It never made sense to me before but now it does. The secret phone calls, those pictures I found, gifts I wasn't meant to see. That was all you."

He threw his arms up, the red tie he wore fluttered. "I admit it, I'm not perfect. We don't always stay in love with the same people. I loved my wife. I had a responsibility to the boys. I thought about leaving her but I couldn't in the end. Your mother and I were friends at first. I- by the time we became lovers, it seemed best to keep things as they were."

"How convenient for you." I spat, walking back and forth between two gargoyles.

"Tell me who he is. I have a right to know. I know you know something."

He looked down to the ground, the sadness in his face so palpable even the gargoyles concrete expressions may have changed slightly. "Your mother was raped. Your grandfather is your father. She went to see him and... I don't think he was himself."

"That's not true!" I replied but horror was building inside me. That feeling of seeing something awful and being unable to look away. Pain shot through my stump, the taste of nausea filled my mouth. I ran to the side, vomiting into a hedge. Suddenly, certain things made sense; my mother sleeping in the afternoons, her emotional distance from me sometimes, the lies she told to save us from the truth.

Tears ran down Mervyn's cheeks. His eyes filled again as he turned the chess Queen in his hand. His chest swelled as though a river of sadness would split it open and carry us both away. I trembled watching the look of despair on his face, the pain there. I felt sick seeing Anon appear between the gargoyles, reaching into their mouths to skim her hands over the secrets they knew. Something inside me seemed to be realigning, travelling somehow. A searing pain shot through my head, then my chest. The gargoyles turned their heads, hissing into the dark.

Mervyn placed one hand on my shoulder, gently raised me up.

A part of me was dying from the shame, another crumbling from the weight of it.

I couldn't look him in the eye. I felt like nothing, a tiny speck under a shoe.

"Leave me alone," I mumbled, pulling away. I couldn't thank him for saving my life, for stopping my mother from drowning me. I stumbled through the hallway, deformed again in the light, blinded by tears. Bath water ran down the walls, its sloshing sound slipping through the plughole, filling my chest.

Outside my legs buckled in the night. I left the pale chess Queen crying in Mervyn's pocket and the gargoyles holding bits of a battered chessboard chased the small openings on me, widening in the cold air.

Echo, Belly and the Rubik's Cube

When I arrived at Murtala Muhammed airport in Lagos I couldn't bring myself to call Mervyn yet. I knew we needed to talk but I was still hurt and confused about being a hidden thing. Peter Lowon's diary sat in my handbag. Outside, the driver of a yellow taxicab between mouthfuls of pineapple slices informed me the drive to Benin was long. I thought of my mother Queen. I imagined she took Peter Lowon's diary and the brass head all the way from Africa to London, her only connections to the father whose footsteps she trailed as a little girl. I imagined she read the diary from cover to cover many times, knew it like the back of her hand; that when she passed her first school exams, she ran home to it and heaved bitter-sweet breaths of success over its pages. That she studied his scrawl and doodles, imitated them. And after she kissed the first boy who whispered chewing gum flavoured nothings in her ear and turned out to be completely useless, she weighed it in her hands and eyed it with resentment. He cursed her by leaving her that legacy. It was the curse of the broken-hearted, the way that only a father can.

Weirdly, I remembered it then: the black and white photograph from the diary. I fished it out, held it at the corner and stared at the faces, the creases. It hit me, I recognised him. Peter Lowon was the man from the café scene that trespassed regularly in my head, the one where I always struggled to hear what was said, the man who was both father and grandfather to me. He was out there, somewhere. I had met him once before. It was a memory after all, a fallen snowflake becoming a tear.

Peter Lowon Journal Entry July 1964

Dear Queenie,

I am a killer. I am a coward. I am your father.

If you find this, then you know I have gone. I was brought to this place and feared this day. The day you know what I have done. Please keep this diary, here are honest pieces of me I can offer you, hold them up to the light. I want to apologise for bringing shame on my family. I cannot make amends; I can only say that sometimes people do desperate things, terrible things. I ask for forgiveness. Queenie there are no good or bad people don't let anyone tell you this, these lines are blurred daily. The bad we often see in others, we recognise in ourselves, bouncing off our own hand made mirrors. We are all flawed people trying to make our way. Should you choose to find me one day, I am out there waiting.

Tell your mother I've always loved her and I'm sorry for being the man she suspected I was. There is no blade to cut my weakness away, no shot to numb the darkness out. Would you believe me if I told you I am a prisoner of myself? I wish so much more for you. Queenie, you are me and I am you. This is the one thing I see with so much clarity; through you I was born twice. One day you will have your own child, and you will know a joy no words can describe, no mathematical equation can depict. It is pure, purer than water, purer than air, injections of life into the blood. And you will make mistakes too! Queenie I am in pain, the kind of pain that makes you run inside to bleed on your carpet privately. I worry that one day you will forget what I look like. I worry you will see me in the faces of strangers. See the black and white picture inside this journal? I am the one on the left laughing. In case you find yourself forgetting: THE ONE ON THE LEFT. Please keep it with you.

With you I laughed. I worry about other things too: that your mother will grow old hating me, that she will count her grey hairs and hold me responsible for each one. I worry you may marry a man like me, that life will beat the importance of knowing yourself out of you. I fear your anger and emptiness within you long after you have stopped calling for me. I have cheated you and myself.

I no longer have the strength to be mad because it has been sapped by a tree sprouting roots somewhere. Wherever I am I will be running from myself. Imagine no day without night, night without the day; there is no end to this. It is an empty well running through the homes of underground creatures we never see, a tunnel through the chests of farmers toiling the land, it is the hidden void where our dreams pile up like dead bodies. It leads back to me. As for the brass head, please get rid of it. Give it to a beggar man to sell, throw it in a river or gutter. I should never have brought it into my house; if you keep it you will bear the burden of the cursed and pay in a currency not found on earth.

Today is so ordinary Queenie. You are playing by the outside tap, counting coins for your bank by the white sugar cube wall. It is the worst day of my life. It is the last time I will see you throw your arms up so trustingly to me, or hold a terrible crayon colour drawing that I will say is perfect because it is. Or attempt to measure your laugh, something that cannot be done. You cannot tell that tomorrow your world will be different. Right now the mayguard is lazily swatting flies from his face, no longer pretending to do his job. The house girl is peeling yams in the kitchen. Aunty Eunice is hanging clothes on the washing line, a yellow vein shot through the sky, which is throbbing, swelling with lost years to come. Your mother is standing at my shoulder. Life carries on, Queenie. When you have ceased asking questions and my name has turned to dust in your mouth know that:

I am the father whose feet you danced on, I am a million broken stars at your fingertips, I am the night sky's discarded brother, I am a blanket made of rain. I am the conscience searching for your footsteps; I am the Harmattan wind whispering secrets that will fall into the foamy hem of the sea and wash up on the beaches of other countries as rough pebbles and hollow seashells.

I am beating.

I am

I-

Benin

My guide Nosa didn't talk much but when he did, he made it count. He seemed to be casually efficient with everything; expressions, explanations, even arguments. Illustrated by his curt dismissal of a driver he'd cut across earlier in traffic, swatting the irate man away like a mosquito. It was sweltering; the heat made my skin clammy and my white, cotton blouse clung to me. Anon and I sat side by side in the back seat, restless from the hot material, woozy due to the occasional jostling and headiness of being in Africa. Our palms grazed ancestor's heartbeats.

Dust swirled into the scenes around us; the long stretch of granite strip twisting like a concrete snake in the heat, its offshoots holding items of luggage for passengers yet to collect them. Bike riders swerved in between vehicles, car horns blared loudly as the traffic continued to build. Buses and vans blocked each other off in the rising din. In the car side mirrors, barefoot children sporting adult mouths sold bottled water, groundnuts, plantain crisps, and bread. Mothers carrying babies tied to their backs listened to their adult tongues pressed against the hollows of their spines. We passed the odd huge billboard now and again.

The brass head was stashed on the floor between my legs, at the bottom of a black bag, the rustling of a British Airways tag its only companion. I watched Nosa's hands on the wheel, the lines of scarring across his knuckles and chest. A young girl chasing our car tried to sell me stones I'd already swallowed, rough and warm, they turned in her hand. When she shoved them in her pocket, they became new beginnings falling against humps in the road.

Nosa adjusted the rear-view mirror, throwing a quick glance my way. "Are you alright? We can stop if you need to be sick."

"No, let's keep going. It doesn't matter how long it takes, even if we get there by evening. Carry on," I instructed. Anon sat quietly, scrawling the name Adesua in the dust on the window. The flying plastic man Nosa had tied to the rear-view mirror spoke to us in our mother tongue.

Nosa's long, elegant fingers gripped the wheel as if it was an instrument. His dimples deepened as he waved over a heavy set, big bosomed woman he knew. He bought a calling card from her. She thanked him, popping her gum, flirting and calling him a gentleman. We stopped for gas. I watched him from sly lids filling up our black Vauxhall Cavalier that had seen better days; his lean, handsome face broke into the contained expressions I was getting used to. He mopped his forehead with a white handkerchief, tucked it into his pocket, whistling as he angled the pump deep into the petrol slot.

"Do you think we could stop by a 7-Eleven at some point?" I asked, blocking the light hitting me with a hand over my eyes, acutely aware my English accent sounded even stronger in these surroundings. He laughed, features transformed in amusement.

"This isn't London. We don't have 7-Elevens and shops every twenty minutes. Why can't you get what you need here?"

"They don't have what I need here," I replied, fidgeting in my seat, refusing to confide that the warning pains of my period had hit my stomach that I was worried I'd bleed on his seats.

Instead, I asked, "How did you get those scars on your chest?"

"Oh that," he said nonchalantly. "Armed robbers cut me there and in my stomach on this route one night, left me for dead."

I wanted to ask what an Economics major was doing hauling passengers back and forth over a route that had nearly killed him but I didn't. Instead, I watched the map Anon drew on the window fading a little, as the day got darker.

Clay

It was her dead babies that led Filo out of the palace. She'd been feeding the chickens on the grounds when she stopped midway, yellow grains spilling from her palms into the mouths of her children, who'd gathered around her in a semi circle. The chickens went silent. Her babies began to cluck. Filo understood their new language. This was what Kalu the medicine man had promised her. *Watch for your children, they will come back to you. They will lead you to your future*, he professed, laughing in the rainwater that fell over their naked bodies.

Kalu had been her secret companion since the day she'd found him in that clearing in the forest, half-starved and clutching a handful of white bones to his chest. After she nursed him back to full health, they continued to meet away from the watchful eyes of the palace and planned the unravelling of the Oba, the king who had cheated them both. It was Kalu that helped her call the spirits of the previous kings. And it was Kalu who told her what was deemed to be her weakness was actually her greatest strength. Nobody would suspect the mad wife of setting the wheels in motion, of turning them with a sure finger. Filo sent her babies to cause the very thing her Oba had mocked her for.

At night she slept in her quarters rubbing her stomach, watching it grow, pregnant with the silent silhouettes of her children. She called to them, clucking her tongue and chasing their lost features in the night air. She and Kalu built their likenesses from clay, painting their mouths blood red, giving them white bones to hold as they were dispatched all over the palace, a quiet, invisible army dogging the Oba's footsteps, toying with his perception, shattering in his vision.

That bright day at the palace, her babies came back to her, glorious in the light, speaking the tongue she'd taught them. They ate from her hands, led her past the swirling activities, past the guards they'd left temporarily blind and into the waiting arms of the day, touching the promises of the future.

And so the small procession of dead babies continued to cluck on the long, dusty trails they followed, telling Filo about the parts they'd played in the fall of a kingdom, changing into their chicken guises when Kalu's whistles became warning winds.

Benin

"How far are we now?" I asked, pushing snapping branches away from my face.

My armpits were damp and the ache in my stomach had only intensified over the lengthy walk we'd had across seemingly acres of, rough, sprawling terrain. Two jagged people the Gods had carved in a hurry, crossing dense, wild forests that threatened to swallow us. We'd left the car parked on a thirsty, empty stretch of road. The small plastic man Nosa jokingly named Baba dangled from the rear-view mirror knocking against his reflection after I'd spun him one last time. A faulty water pump by our parking spot had given me nothing but hot air.

"Nearly there." Nosa answered, talking through a stick of sugar cane. His long strides ate up the ground. He carried a shovel in his left hand as if it weighed nothing. The *thwack thwack* of the cutlass in his right hand cut a path for us. "The ground's changing, this is royal land," he said, slowing down a little for me to catch up.

The black bag slung over my shoulder bobbed against my side. Since the accident, most people either acted awkwardly or didn't

quite know where to look. Not Nosa though. "What happened to
you, lion fighting?" he'd commented that first time I'd met him playing cards outside the Western Union stand by the bus depot. And
somehow his lack of concern at offending me was refreshing.

Nightfall arrived. A flock of birds shaped like a plane's wing flew
ahead, calling out to their two-legged relatives. I knew when we
got there because the air changed. It was thicker somehow. Dead
kings had drained all the water pumps, which hissed in the heat.
Nosa fished a torch from his pocket. Anon began to lead the way.
She guided us to the gutted terracotta palace, glimmering in the
night. The hairs on my neck stood to attention. We passed through
old ghosts wandering the grounds, touching walls that resurrected
under our curious fingers. Anon took us past the palace walls, past its
chattering rooftops, waiting to tumble into the vast sky. We trudged
deep into the dark, into a clearing in a hidden forest. Anon began to
dance and cry over the land, her feet softening the soil. I knew then
that she was dancing over her grave.

I fell to my knees, digging beneath her footsteps. Nosa had lost his
sugarcane stick to a lonely ghost who was using it as an instrument,
playing a melancholy tune into the lost kingdom. He followed suit,
sinking the shovel into the ground. My hand grew bolder in the soil.
We dug until my fingers ached and the past scenes from the palace
became tiny broken objects in my peripheral vision. We buried the
brass head deep in the ground. When we came up for air, Anon had
stopped crying and was offering her limbs to the torchlight.

For the first few weeks, I slept like a baby. I felt human again. I'd
gotten a one-way ticket so took my time rambling about. Sometimes
in the early afternoon, I'd walk up to the local bus depot; weave
my way between the vans and street vendors brandishing magician's
tongues, darting around in every direction, unwittingly chasing the
journeys of hands at the wheel. I'd catch a bus to one of several
bustling markets. There, I'd barter with sellers to buy material and

small wooden figurines I didn't need. I'd stand at the edges listening to the din, pidgin in the punishing heat, sandals covered in dust, waiting for my mother's tongue to migrate into the noise, bending in the light; moist with all the half-truths she'd told me.

I learned how to make goat pepper soup from Mama Carol who ran the boarding house I was staying at, a ramshackle white building where clusters of mosquitoes shaped like small countries sang on the netted, peeling green door before dying mid-conversation. I attempted to make the soup one day, but the goat's head pressed its mouth into the gap, telling me the stones in Africa tasted different. Sometimes, on his way back from a run, Nosa would stop by. We'd sit out in the breeze drinking palm wine, discussing the house he wanted to build and how he found himself visiting the scene of his near-death, collecting his organs again and again as if they were passengers. We'd watch the scrawny local dog chasing its tail in front of other houses, before dragging random things to the side of the road.

I accidentally got a job helping the local tailor. It started when I sought advice about making items from the materials I'd bought. She let me use her back room. I began making curious things; small market scenes, interactions of people I'd spotted in the day, headless creatures stumbling towards a sun. It became a kind of therapy, producing objects in the hot back room with the fan blowing on my skin. And the yellow and black butterfly fish swam in the window as though it would survive in any surface. News spread. In town, people started to call me the one armed wonder.

London seemed a world away.

On the last day of my first month, I phoned Mervyn from a call centre. I told him that sometimes, when the electricity stopped, I traced the things I'd built to the sound of the generator, that those small figures with unfinished stories carried them into the dust. He didn't laugh. Instead he said *I'm glad you called, you're like a daughter to me. I'm happy you're okay. Call again sometime. Let me know when you're ready to come home.*

In the evening, I tucked a leather bound book under my arm, dragged a small stool out to the front of the boarding house. I got comfortable cutting old newspaper clippings; drinking cold bitter lemon and watching car headlights become spotlights for things in the dark.

At first I thought it was a trick of the light when I spotted it but the scrawny street dog stood on its hind legs barking, and then retreated back in alarm. It appeared in a trail of exhaust pipe smoke from a black jeep groaning past. A clay baby stumbled in the middle of the road, clucking then mumbling about the kingdom, clucking then spilling yellow grains out of its mouth, holding the blue flame from my kerosene lantern.

Its gaze was fixed in the distance, at the sprawling, dense lands beyond, where the terracotta kingdom once glimmered. It's small chest rose and fell as we shared the night's heartbeat. Transfixed, my eyes followed it all the way down to the end of the street, till it disappeared from my vision, shattering in the white. I waited for it's clucking once again but the small chasm in the air closed and the crickets wanted to be heard.

I rocked back on my heels, listening for the dog on the tin roof next door to make it's way back to the blue flame. I thought of Anon losing her limbs, her mouth now silent in my hand. On the plot of land tucked behind the boarding house, right arms grew in soft soil, rising amidst yams, cassava, bitter leaf, waiting to bend in the afternoon light, catching fragments of their various lives. I listened for the ripple a butterfly fish made in glass. I held my father's diary, stroked the warm leather. Grappling with his legacy, I opened the pages and sat under water, waiting to begin again.

THE END

Acknowledgements

My gratitude and thanks to the extraordinary Alex Wheatle; top corner stone, literary co-conspirator and friend, thanks for believing in me during hard times and offering invaluable support. To my lovely agent, the inimitable Elise Dillsworth, thank you so much for being passionate about the work, steering me wisely, all the things an agent does quietly, cups of tea and phonecalls! Big thanks to the dedicated Jacaranda team, Valerie and Jazzmine for taking a risk on a plucky outsider and all your hard work. To my editors Rukhsana Yasmin and Valerie Brandes for sharp eyes and brilliant guidance. Julian Brown for the years and encouragement. Maggie Gee for reading that second draft. The wonderful Yvvette Edwards for support, advice and lots of laughter. Malaika Adero for championing me states side. PR extraordinaire Sue Amaradivakara for excitement and belief in the project. My first and unforgettable mentor Donna Daley-Clarke for wit, patience and understanding. Spread The Word for the Flight programme and their continued support, Words of Colour and Black Book Swap for providing platforms for writers. And Jenneba Sie-Jalloh for seeing something in my writing years ago, thank you, I'll never forget.

About the Author

Irenosen Okojie is a writer, curator and Arts Project Manager. She has worked with the Royal Shakespeare Company, the Southbank Centre, and the Caine Prize. Her short stories have been published internationally, including the *Kwani 07* and *Phatitude*. She was a selected writer by Theatre Royal Stratford East and Writer in Residence for TEDx East End. In 2014, she was the Prize Advocate for the SI Leeds Literary Prize. She is a mentor for the Pen to Print project supported by publisher Constable & Robinson. She lives in east London. *Butterfly Fish* is her first novel.